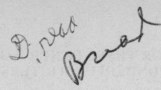

She shook her head, flexed her bruised and battered muscles and began to rise.

With her head still spinning, she wondered vaguely how she'd managed to get back out of the mine. Then she caught sight of what had stopped her tumble, and she froze.

Old scuffed boots, hand-tooled with intricately carved tips, topped by soft suede pants. Long, hard male legs. Sexy, sinuous legs. Muscular thighs, slim hips. A gun holstered low around those hips and tied around one of those thighs.

Sedona gulped, her gaze sweeping upward. He filled out his old shirt, too. Big shoulders—wide, hard. Nice chin. Better mouth—agape for one second, then slammed shut in a fierce scowl. She ignored that and took in his chiseled cheekbones, slight shadow of a beard, hooded eyes. Brown? No, black, like his hair and the low-riding hat. She searched the shadows near his eyes and could have sworn she saw sparks flickering there.

She didn't know who he was, but she did know that this was nobody's angel.

—from *Nobody's Angel*
by Barbara Cummings

PLEASE LOOK FOR THESE OTHER WORKS BY THESE WONDERFUL WRITERS

LINDA LAEL MILLER

Two Brothers, Pocket Books, November, 1998. A Western romance about identical twins, presented in a unique way.

SUSAN WIGGS

The Charm School, Mira Books, March, 1999. Swept into an adventure by the boldest captain on the high seas, a plain and awkward Boston spinster is transformed into a beguiling adventuress.

RUTH GLICK, A.K.A. REBECCA YORK

Shattered Lullaby, Harlequin Intrigue, January, 1999. When Jessie Douglas saves Miguel Diego's life, she must convince him that the only way to save their lives is to join forces.

MARY JO PUTNEY

The Rake, Topaz, April, 1998. A new edition of the classic RITA-winning historical romance.

PATRICIA POTTER

Star Finder, Bantam, November, 1998. Clan leader Ian Sutherland must decide between two loyalties: an endangered young widow and her two children—or his seven-year-old sister, lost in the turmoil after the battle of Culloden.

PATRICIA GARDNER EVANS

Watch for *Tyree,* sequel to RITA award-winner *Silver Noose,* and the return of Eisley in the romantic thriller *Quinn Eisley's Wife,* coming soon in 1999.

In Our Dreams

Linda Lael Miller
Susan Wiggs
Courtney Henke
Patricia Potter
Ruth Glick (aka Rebecca York)
Corey McFadden
Mary Kirk
Patricia Gardner Evans
Barbara Cummings
Mary Jo Putney

Introduction by Tami Hoag

Zebra Books
Kensington Publishing Corp.
http://www.zebrabooks.com

ZEBRA BOOKS are published by

Kensington Publishing Corp.
850 Third Avenue
New York, NY 10022

First Printing: October, 1998
10 9 8 7 6 5 4 3 2 1

Printed in the United States of America

To Melinda Helfer, the truest of friends

ACKNOWLEDGMENTS

Many people's efforts, as well as countless good wishes, went into producing this anthology, and we thank everyone who participated in any way most sincerely. Special appreciations go to Linda Hayes, Kathryn Falk, and Leslie Kazanjian, for their thoughtful advice and support. To Melinda Helfer, Damaris Rowland, and Elaine English, for their large roles in helping us turn a dream into reality, we owe a debt of gratitude that can never be repaid.

All royalties from the sale of this book will be donated to the Amiga Foundation Trust.

Table of Contents

Dear Reader,

Imagine that you're traveling abroad when war breaks out and traps you on the wrong side of the ocean. Who better to rescue you and see you safely home than that hero of the big screen, Jack Ryan, played by Harrison Ford?

Imagine that you're a Grecian maiden, cursed by the gods. Who better to free you than Hercules—with the charming smile and sexy body of Kevin Sorbo?

Imagine that you go to see the new doctor in town only to discover that he looks remarkably like George Clooney, *ER*'s Dr. Doug Ross.

Imagine that you're in Camelot and that King Arthur is alive and well in the form of Sean Connery. . . .

What woman hasn't dreamed these dreams at least once in her life? What woman's senses haven't been stirred at one time or another by a hero she's seen either in a movie or on television? Maybe it's *NYPD Blue*'s Bobby Simone, played by Jimmy Smits, who sends your senses reeling. Or maybe it's Adrian Paul as Duncan McLeod, *The Highlander,* who has won your heart. Or maybe—just maybe—you harbor a secret wish to be lost in space with a Klingon named Worf (Michael Dorn).

Well, you aren't alone. The award-winning, best-selling authors of the stories in this collection are women just like you, whose hearts beat a little faster when they see a hero come to life on a screen.

If you've ever wondered where writers get their inspiration, this is your chance to find out. By telling you in their own words how these icons of romantic heroism inspired them, the women who wrote these stories are inviting you to share *their* fantasies.

So find a sun-drenched garden or a lonely stretch of beach. Find your own special place, and let your imagination roam free. Let some of your favorite authors take you places you never dreamed existed.

In the contemporary world, travel from Paris to America's heartland with Linda Lael Miller, Susan Wiggs, and Patricia Gardner Evans. Take a trip to the Old West with Patricia Potter or Barbara Cummings. Spend a few days in Regency England with Corey McFadden. Let Mary Jo Putney transport you to Camelot. Allow Mary Kirk to sweep you further back in time to a magic Celtic land. Go to ancient Greece with Courtney Henke. And, if you're really adventurous, leap into the future, to the distant planet Jalar, with Ruth Glick (aka Rebecca York).

No matter where you go with these talented authors, I guarantee you'll meet a hero you'll never forget.

Have a wonderful adventure!

Warmest wishes and happy reading,

Tami Hoag

Never Been to Anphar

by

Linda Lael Miller

Author's Note

You will notice, as you read, that I have barely described Maggie, my heroine, at all. That's because I want you to imagine yourself in her place—a little younger, maybe. A little thinner.

As for the hero, well, he bears a striking resemblance to Harrison Ford in his role as Tom Clancy's Jack Ryan. A little younger, maybe. A little thinner.

Maggie Ellington's first thought, when the gunmen burst into the ambassador's quietly elegant second-story dining room, was that she might never see her children again. Her second was that this could not possibly be happening.

Not now. Not to her.

Then, in the space of a split second, such a sickening combination of horror, fury and grief seized her that she might have forgotten to duck if the man seated next to her hadn't clasped her by one hand and wrenched her under the table. No more than an instant later, the intruders opened fire from all sides, using high-powered assault weapons, and bullets spattered the length and breadth of the room.

There were screams, audible even over the terrible staccato cadence of the shots, and after the first tremulous moments of silence, the chandeliers came down in tinkling shards, a crystalline rain.

Maggie's impulse was to scramble out from under the table and bolt screaming from the room, but once again her dinner companion interceded, wrapping one arm around her waist and closing the other hand tightly over her mouth.

Another explosion of gunfire erupted overhead, but this time there were no cries afterward. Maggie closed her eyes, breathing hard through her nose, her rescuer's palm fairly crushing her lips into her teeth.

This new and tenuous calm was, in some ways, more terrifying than the shooting spree had been. It smelled of smoke and blood and pulsed with unspeakable possibilities and portents.

"Listen to me," the man said, barely breathing the words against her ear. He'd told her over the soup course, she recalled now, with incomprehensible clarity, that his name was Judd Killgoran. "They're going to look under here at any second. Lie down and play dead, as in *don't move*. Don't make a sound. If you do, they'll take us out. Do you understand?"

Maggie nodded, although she wasn't sure she could trust herself not to shriek hysterically the moment Killgoran took his hand away.

He eased her down onto the ambassador's Persian rug, and they sprawled there together, in the tangle of bodies. The coppery scent of blood was so pervasive that Maggie could taste it, see the crimson glow of it even through her eyelids. There were other smells, too—ones she couldn't afford to identify, because if she dared to sort them out, nothing would keep her quiet.

She felt the stuff of life seeping through her white silk dress. Felt it warm and sticky against her bare skin. Close by, surely within arm's reach, someone, a woman, made a soft, mewling sound.

Killgoran, lying across Maggie like an exhausted lover, stiffened momentarily, but the warning was clear nonetheless, and urgent. Maggie thought of her babies, far away, safe—*waiting*—and lay utterly still.

The sleek outline of a pistol impressed itself onto her breasts, as distinctive as a tattoo; Killgoran was armed. She found the realization both reassuring and frightening.

The tablecloth was flung upward, and the woman whimpered again, a burbling, insensate sound. *Oh, God,* Maggie prayed, *let her be unconscious.*

The assailants spoke a quick, guttural language, and Maggie actually felt the sweep of someone's gaze moving over her, raising the tiny hairs on her nape and the backs of her arms like an ill wind. She did not breathe, did not even dream of breathing.

All her thoughts were of the injured woman.

Where there had been an awful tranquility, in the ringing aftermath of the machine guns, now there was noise, light. The blood seemed to deepen around Maggie, to seep into her very pores. She had gone cold, unable to perspire.

She felt a tearing away, a sensation of the mind and spirit

rather than the body, as the woman was dragged from beneath the table. It was as though the two of them had been joined somehow, by virtue of their gender, their humanity.

The report of a single shot pulsed in the air.

That time, Maggie did flinch, but Killgoran absorbed the motion; nearly imperceptible though it must have been, she felt it reverberate through his muscular frame.

There was more talk between the gunmen, crouched on the floor, close enough to touch. They smelled of sweat and fear, these men, and seemed to exude an odd, spicy heat, like mummies who had flung off their grave clothes. Precisely when Maggie thought she would come apart in pieces, that the sobs clamoring inside her would break free and turn to screams, the tablecloth fell back into place.

Maggie was exultant with relief, and then ashamed.

After a time, she lapsed into a sort of dream state; it was as if she were separated from herself, floating a few inches above her own still, blood-stained body. The sensation was so overwhelming that she began to think she'd been shot after all. That she might already be dying.

She drifted, almost placidly now, like some waterborne plant, riding the wind-ripples of a pond. Sound receded to a faint, distant murmur, and the weight of Killgoran's body, once crushing, became a matter of indifference.

Nothing seemed real except for the slow, pounding beat of her heart. Or was it his? Maggie didn't know, didn't care. She held on to the sound with her mind, followed it through the darkness like the beckoning voice of a guardian spirit.

She had no idea how much time had passed when her protector began to stir; it was as if the power of motion had returned to him muscle by muscle, first a mere tremor far beneath the skin, then the rise and fall of his chest as he breathed deeply. At last, he raised himself a little, laying one index finger to Maggie's lips lest she speak. Listening.

Her senses, dormant mere moments before, were suddenly heightened to such a pitch that she felt that, too—his listening—

an active thing, a buzzing stir in the heavy air, as though he heard through his skin, his hair, his fingernails, as well as his ears.

Maggie watched, still dazed, as Killgoran raised the tablecloth a little way and peered out.

The silence was all-encompassing, a strange and separate atmosphere; they could have been alone in the vacuum of space, adrift on some asteroid, instead of hiding beneath a long, once-gracious table in an embassy dining room.

"Stay here," Killgoran said, so quietly that he might have sent the words to her by telepathy, rather than common speech.

Maggie clutched at his dinner jacket for a moment, not wanting him to leave her alone, and then, shamed by her own cowardice, released her hold. All around them, the dead slept, and she wondered if their ghosts kept distracted vigil, uncertain and new, still startled by the sudden, horrible parting of flesh and spirit.

Maggie closed her eyes, and tears trickled down over her temples, into her hair. She began to review facts, making her way from one to the next, as though each were a station on a strand of prayer beads.

She'd come to Anphar, a small island nation off the northern coast of Africa, the day before, with Frank Gedge, who had been sent over to serve as a special assistant and advisor to the newly established American ambassador. She was a mere courier, recruited on short notice from the research staff at headquarters. Because Frank had fallen ill at the last minute, Maggie had attended the dinner in his place.

Judd Killgoran, who had technically saved Maggie's life, had said little during the meal—a last supper for most, probably all, of the other guests—except that he was a journalist. His usual beat was not the diplomatic scene, he'd claimed. He generally wrote about computers, the Internet, virtual reality, high tech stuff.

Maggie's impression of him had hardly been a heroic one. He was of medium height and build, nondescript, really, with brown hair, somewhat mussed, and brown eyes. He'd worn glasses, she remembered, and a rather rumpled sports jacket, and his features were craggy—unappealing, taken separately, but intriguing as a whole.

She allowed herself a deep breath, however tainted, and continued the mental litany, because Killgoran was still gone and she was lying amongst dead people, and the only way to hold that thought in abeyance was to think of other things.

Her children.

Susan and Mary Catherine, fraternal twins, were six years old. They were with her mom and dad, in Arlington, literally counting the hours until she returned. There was a special calendar in Nana and Poppy's kitchen, and every night, before going to bed, each child would affix a colorful sticker to the appropriate day, officially consigning it to the past. She could see them so clearly, could almost touch them. They were far more real, in that moment, than the carnage that surrounded her.

For other children, a parent's brief absence wouldn't have been such a big deal, but Susan and Mary Catherine had lost their daddy two years before, in an airline disaster. They needed rituals and talismans just to let their mother out of their sight.

And here she was, awash in innocent blood, by no means certain that she would live to see the morning.

Briefly, she entertained the idea of death. David would surely be waiting for her, if she passed over. Dear, funny, smart David, whom she had loved so completely that for a year after Flight 2270's still unexplained mid-air explosion, she had expected him to appear at the back door one night, swinging his briefcase in his hand and saying it had all been a mistake. He hadn't been on that plane bound for Toronto, after all. He'd merely been away on secret business for his law firm. . . .

But it was no mistake.

David's body had been one of the first to be identified, and eventually, painfully, Maggie had come to accept that he was really, truly gone.

Her thoughts returned to her daughters, as though wrenched there by the tug of some cord fastened to a wall in her heart. Dying was not an option, no matter what she had to do to prevent it. She had promised the twins, scout's honor, that she would return. Despite their great, warm, tangled network of grandparents, aunts, uncles and cousins, they needed *her,* Maggie. Their mother.

I'll come home, she promised them silently. Only it might mean a few more stickers on a few more calendar spaces than she had planned.

Killgoran returned at about the time Maggie had decided that he'd either deserted her to save his own skin, or been captured by whatever fanatical political faction had taken over the embassy.

"They're all over the place," he said, scrambling back under the table. While he spoke, he moved among the scattered bodies, checking in vain for pulses. "Are you hurt?"

She'd had plenty of time to take inventory. "I don't think so," she replied, instinctively keeping her voice to a whisper.

"Good." He came back to her side, and for the first time it struck her that he was uncommonly brave, for an ordinary citizen. Furthermore, he seemed to know something about scoping out besieged embassies.

She sat up on her own, careful not to knock her head on the bottom of the table. "What do we do now?" she asked. Surely he had a plan—he was so obviously a person of action. What remained to be seen was whether it was one she could live with, literally and figuratively.

"We wait," he said. "There's a guy stationed in the ambassador's personal office, tuned in to CNN. My guess is, the minute there's any sign of media coverage, they'll all be in there, crowded around the tube. That will be our best chance to get past them."

Maggie felt tendrils of her hair sticking to her cheek and raised a hand to brush them free. Bile rushed into the back of her throat as she remembered the blood, and she began to retch, softly but compulsively.

"Don't," Killgoran said, just as quietly. As if you could stop something like that by mere willpower.

Miraculously, she stopped. "Who are they?" Maggie managed to gasp, when she'd caught her breath. "What do they want?"

"They're just another weird political-religious faction. And they want to overthrow the government of Anphar, such as it is. My guess is, they've succeeded."

Maggie's mind, like her heart, was filled with sweet, poignant visions of her daughters. Her parents. Her friends. Even her dog, Snidely.

"Then what makes you think we're going to get out of here?"

"One of the few choices I have left, at the moment, is what to think," Killgoran answered flatly. "Therefore, I choose the happy ending."

"Me, too."

He smiled, albeit ruefully, and cupped her cheek with one hand. The motion gave a glimpse of the shoulder holster under his sports coat, and she remembered the gun.

"Since when do journalists carry weapons?"

Killgoran didn't answer. In fact, he left the question hanging with such deftness that Maggie wondered if she'd spoken aloud at all.

"Sit tight," he said, "and keep an eye on the door. When I signal, we're out of here, so keep up. Got it?"

Maggie had rallied enough to be irritated by his officious manner, but since she didn't have a better idea, she kept her opinions to herself. Once she was out of the embassy, out of Anphar, she would probably never see Killgoran again anyway.

She nodded. "I'll need therapy to get over this," she said, more to herself than Killgoran, who was arranging the edge of the tablecloth so that she could see without being seen.

"A small price to pay," he answered, and was gone.

A raucous cheer went up, far down the hall, and Maggie hoped it meant the revolutionaries were seeing themselves on TV. She imagined them waving their machine guns and shouting things like, "Hi, Ma," and then ascribed her whole train of thought to shock.

Killgoran was back long before she expected him, a shadow in the great double doorway, gesturing.

As grateful as she was terrified, Maggie scrabbled out of her hiding place and dashed toward him with such exuberance that she collided with him. He was making no effort to hide the pistol now; it was out, and in his hand, sleek and dangerous-looking.

"You are not a journalist," she accused.

"Another reason to think positively," he replied. "Come on. If we can get to the wine cellar before their fifteen minutes of fame are over, we might have a chance. There's an outside door there, leading to a garage area—I think we can steal a jeep."

Maggie didn't let herself consider the logistics of that. She had lost her shoes somewhere, and so ran barefoot behind Killgoran, forced to keep up because he was holding her by one wrist.

They dashed through a warren of shadowy hallways, passing more than one body along the way.

Maggie, probably the least adventurous person in the world, was contemplating career options. When she got home, she decided breathlessly as she ran along in Killgoran's wake, she would sell the small house in Washington, move to rural Maine or Vermont or Maryland, and open a shop, selling either books or health foods, or both. The twins could attend a country school, have a pony perhaps, and a big yard to play in.

The voices registered, just ahead and rapid, in a language Maggie did not recognize, and again it did not occur to her to take shelter. It was Killgoran who jerked her into a dark room five seconds before the men passed along the corridor. Obviously, everybody involved in the coup wasn't interested in getting CNN's take on the situation.

Maggie held not only her breath but, it seemed, the very beat of her heart, until the sounds of talking and footsteps were long gone. And only then did she realize that she had sagged against Killgoran like some giant doll with nothing but beans for stuffing.

She started to jerk away from him, but he held her still. His eyes glittered in the half-light.

"We're not out of the woods yet, lady," he said, close to her ear. "Don't make any impulsive moves."

She dragged in a breath, and tears smarted, unshed, behind her eyes. She managed a nod, and he loosened the tight hold he'd taken on her forearm.

He checked out the corridor with all the caution of a heavy player in an action movie, the pistol ready, and then pulled her after him, out of the room where they had taken refuge. They moved slowly, ever so slowly, through more hallways and passages, and finally the kitchen was before them, a dazzle of light and gleaming steel equipment.

The chef, his helpers, and the uniformed staff were all dead, lying or sitting in pools of blood, their features reflecting eternal bafflement. No one else was visible, but the sound of a newscaster speaking fast, earnest English was audible from some nearby room—probably a small office or butler's pantry.

Killgoran assessed the situation, drew a metal tube from his jacket pocket, and fitted it to the barrel of his pistol. Signaling Maggie to remain where she was, he followed the sound, turned from prey to predator now.

He disappeared from view, and Maggie heard a soft, pumping noise. Then nothing.

She thought she'd be sick, but after a moment or two of deep breathing, the sensation subsided a little.

Killgoran came back, waved her toward an inner door, probably leading to the wine cellar. When he didn't follow immediately, she turned back and saw that he'd opened the great steel refrigerator, pushing aside a dead man in a chef's hat in the process. The cook's body had left a large, gruesome red streak down the length of the door as he fell.

How could Killgoran think of food at a time like this?

He filled his pockets with packets of lunch meat and a small wheel of cheese, tested an egg against the framework of the fridge to make sure it was hard-boiled, then appropriated a few of those, too.

It was not in response to her glare that he finally came away, she knew, but she let herself believe it was because it gave her a modicum of comfort to pretend she wasn't completely powerless.

In the cellar, Killgoran climbed onto a crate and peered out through a barred window. He didn't confide what he saw, but simply peeled one of the eggs with an expert motion of his nongun hand and popped the white globe into his mouth whole.

"Protein," he said. "It's a low blood sugar thing."

Maggie did not pursue the statement. "So, are we going to steal that jeep or not?" She wanted to get it over with, the escape, its aftermath, the whole thing. The sooner it was all just a bad memory, the better.

"Yup," Killgoran replied, unlocking the outside cellar door, turning the lock with such delicacy that Maggie heard only the faintest click. It was then that she realized they were still whispering, had been all along.

"Gotta wait for the old blood sugar to rise," Killgoran said.

Now that freedom was a threshold away, Maggie wanted to bolt. "We just had dinner," she pointed out, striving for patience.

"I was only pretending to eat."

Maggie, who had been pacing, stopped. "Why?" she demanded, though she already knew. Damn it, she knew. "You *expected* that attack."

He sighed, thrust a hand through his hair. He was as bloodstained as Maggie; his clothes clung to his body the way her dress did. The two of them, she reflected distractedly, looked as though they had walked away from a fifty-car pileup.

"Our Intelligence indicated that there might be a problem, yes."

"Your 'Intelligence'? Exactly who are you?"

"Do you care?" Killgoran countered. He studied her thoughtfully. "Okay, you've got to have an answer; I can see that. So here it is: I'm your only hope of getting out of here alive."

Maggie had never felt so betrayed, not only by her boss, but by Killgoran, by her own government. The travesty was as terrible, in its way, as the wholesale slaughter that had taken place in the ambassador's dining room that very evening.

Only immediate circumstances kept her from spitting in Killgoran's face and walking away. He'd been right, after all—he was her one chance of staying alive.

"How could you?" she asked, in horror as well as fury. "How could you sit quietly at dinner, knowing something like that was going to happen?"

Killgoran met her gaze squarely. "I knew there would be an attempt to overthrow the government," he said. "There was reason to believe it might go down today, this being one of their holy days. I didn't begin to suspect it would happen here, unfortunately, until it was too late."

Maggie pried the sticky skirt of her once-white cocktail dress away from her right thigh. Swallowed yet another fit of panic. "Then why were you here? Armed, no less?" she persisted. "Pretending to eat?"

"I was assigned to protect the ambassador."

"You did a hell of a job."

"Thanks. I guess this year's merit raise is out."

"Has your damn blood sugar come up, yet? I'd like to get out of here, if you're quite ready."

He laid one hand to his flat stomach, fingers splayed, and frowned meditatively, apparently tuning in to some internal signal. "Yeah," he said. "I think I'm okay."

Killgoran eased the cellar door open; waited a second. Maggie braced herself; she hadn't considered the possibility of an alarm until then. There were a lot of things, she thought grimly, that she hadn't considered.

No sirens sounded.

The revolutionaries had surely had help from the inside; they would have taken care of such details before breaking in.

"The guards—" she whispered, as they slipped through heavy shadows toward the predicted jeep. She remembered the handsome young men, sweltering in their dress uniforms, posted at the embassy's front entrance. One of them had checked off names on a clipboard as the guests entered.

"Don't ask," Killgoran replied bleakly.

Maggie bit her lower lip.

"You talk a lot," her companion observed. "Are you always like this?"

She was grateful for the stinging fury his words roused in her; it gave her a few moments' distraction from the fear that quivered in the pit of her stomach and wobbled in her knees. "Bloody massacres generally affect me this way, yes," she snapped back.

They had reached the jeep, and Killgoran hoisted Maggie up into the passenger seat, moved in a quick crouch to the other side, got behind the wheel. "Didn't they tell you things like this could happen when you signed on? Do you read newspapers, watch television?"

"Smart ass," Maggie muttered, and though it was an inane thing to say, it still made her feel a little better. At Killgoran's motion, she slipped down onto the floor of the vehicle. Later she might think about how convenient it was, that jeep being where it was, with the keys in the ignition, but at the moment nothing mattered except getting away. Going home to her children, her friends, her family.

The sound of the engine starting up seemed perilously loud, even though there were explosions all over the city.

"I'm just a courier, that's all," Maggie said. "I shouldn't have been at that dinner at all."

"You've got that right," Killgoran answered, shifted into first gear, and hit the gas pedal.

The embassy, being relatively small and heretofore unimportant, lacked the usual outer walls, a fact for which Maggie was wildly grateful as she and Killgoran crashed down the ten-foot cyclone fence and sped over it, scallops of barbed wire and all.

Behind them, gruff shouts rose, and bullets made a *ping-ping* sound as they struck the fenders, the bumper, even the windshield.

"Stay down," Killgoran yelled, quite unnecessarily.

Maggie, already kneeling, the bouncing jeep seat like an altar before her, prayed in earnest—that they hadn't punctured a tire going over the barbed wire, or lost one to gunfire. That they would make it to wherever they were going. That there were American troops somewhere close by, to defend them.

The jeep careened through streets smoking with rubble, and even though the gunfire had fallen away, it would have been ludicrously optimistic to think they were even remotely safe.

"Where are we going?" Maggie cried, holding on for dear life as the jeep swerved around corners and jolted over piles of debris littering the roads. She gave a fleeting thought to her passport and government ID, her suitcase, laptop computer, and handbag, all of which were still at the hotel. She'd carried an evening bag to the embassy, and abandoned it on the floor beneath her chair when she and Killgoran had made a run for their lives.

"The waterfront," Killgoran shouted back. "There's a Glock under the seat—get it out, just in case."

Maggie's stomach rolled. She wouldn't have known what a Glock was if it hadn't been for all the mystery and suspense novels she read. She'd never held a real gun, let alone fired one.

Nonetheless, she groped along the floorboard, found the semiautomatic pistol, and drew it out.

"Careful," Killgoran said, as they hurtled around another corner. Maggie might have gone flying out the side of the jeep if he hadn't grabbed her hard by the shoulder. "She's got a hair trigger."

Maggie eyed the pistol with mounting horror and laid it carefully on the jeep seat, barrel pointing away from both Killgoran and herself. "I don't know how to shoot," she felt compelled to say.

"You might have to learn," Killgoran replied. "Cover your head and hold on. There's a roadblock just ahead."

Before Maggie had time to be properly terrified, they smashed through another barrier. Gunshots and shouts followed in their wake, but Killgoran kept the gas pedal flush with the floor. She didn't realize he'd been hit until the jeep nosed into the surf, sending fifteen-foot sprays of saltwater up on either side.

He slumped forward, his forehead resting against the wheel, a circle of fresh crimson staining his ruined coat at the right shoulder, and precisely when Maggie allowed herself to consider the possibility that he was dead, he turned his head and grinned at her.

"These guys coming toward us?" he said. "Don't shoot any of them, okay? They're U.S. Marines, and they're gonna take us home."

Maggie began to sob then, with such depth and violence that the young soldier who hoisted her out of the jeep nearly lost his balance and fell into the surf. They were put aboard a launch, she and Killgoran, and taken to a larger ship waiting well off shore.

Maggie was treated for shock and sedated. When she awakened, she was lying in a hospital bed, in a private room, and there was no sign of Killgoran. She was covered in bruises and abrasions, and every bone and muscle ached, but someone had washed away the blood; she no longer felt the need to shrink away from her own skin. Thank God.

Presently, when Maggie had acclimated herself to these new surroundings, a handsome, middle-aged man with a military haircut entered the room, smiling with bureaucratic benevolence. Brass gleamed all over his uniform.

"How are you feeling, Mrs. Ellington?"

Maggie's head was splitting, and she was nauseous, but she smiled thinly and lied. "I'm fine. Where, exactly, am I?"

"Rome," said the visitor. "No need to worry, Mrs. Ellington. You are quite safe. My name is Benjamin Abbot—Major Benjamin Abbot—and I'm here to debrief you."

She made a slight, wait-a-minute gesture with one hand "Judd Killgoran—the man who was with me in Anphar—how is he?"

There was a pause, and the major put on a doleful expression, donning it like a mask. "I'm sorry. He did not survive."

He was lying, Maggie concluded—or was that only wishful thinking on her part? She blinked rapidly to hold back tears. She knew little or nothing about Killgoran, and yet an important bond had formed between them, during their ordeal. The thought that she would never see him again was devastating.

"I see," she said, holding her head high. She had some experience with grief, after all. With putting up a brave front.

Abbot began then to "debrief" Maggie, specifically about the events of the past thirty-six hours. What it all boiled down to was that she had not been present at the embassy massacre, had not even been in Anphar. No, indeed, the major informed her, she had suffered a stomach complaint en route and been hospitalized in Rome. She had never heard of, let alone met, a man named Judd Killgoran.

Maggie listened quietly until the speech was over. She had called home from her hotel soon after arriving, which meant that her parents, at least, knew she *had* been in Anphar, but she didn't mention the fact. "I'm just supposed to forget that I was in the middle of a revolution?" she mused aloud. "That I saw people killed?"

Major Abbot pressed his lips together in a hard line, then replied, "There is nothing to forget, Mrs. Ellington. Tragically, no one survived the attack on the embassy. Therefore, obviously, you were not present."

"Why all the secrecy?"

He smiled. "Why, there is no secrecy," he said expansively. "None at all." He laid a packet in her lap, and when she opened it, she saw an airline ticket, first class, a new passport, and an adequate supply of both Italian and U.S. currencies. "Have a good trip, Mrs. Ellington," he added, on the way to the door. "You'll be contacted soon, about a little—er—settlement from the hotel, here in Rome, where you got the tainted food. I'd suggest that you accept it."

Maggie watched the major until he'd gone, eyes wide in her aching head. With every passing moment, the horror in Anphar seemed less and less real, as though it were actually being removed from her mind through some sort of chemical thread pulling. She had no reason to cling to it—except for Killgoran, the man who had saved her life.

Was he truly dead?

She lay back against her pillows and closed her eyes. Pain pervaded every part of her now, and when a nurse same in, moments later, to administer some sort of injection, Maggie submitted without protest.

In the misty depths of the night, she thought she saw him, Killgoran, standing beside her bed. His arm was in a sling, and he wore hospital garb not unlike her own.

"How you doing, Maggie?" he asked, in a raspy whisper.

She smiled. "I knew you weren't dead."

Killgoran did a very unKillgoran-like thing then. He bent and kissed her forehead. "You're dreaming," he said, and started to move away.

Maggie grasped at him, felt the IV needle and tape on his hand. "Thank you," she said. "For getting me out of there."

He grinned, but even in the shadows, dream or no dream, she saw sadness in his face. "No problem. Take care, okay?"

Maggie wanted to cry, but she'd done too much of that lately, so she didn't indulge. "Okay," she promised. She closed her eyes, because they burned so, and when she opened them, he was gone. Forever, like David.

Four days later, still shaky and three-quarters of the way convinced that she had imagined the whole Anphar experience, Maggie was driven to Rome's Fumacino Airport in a limo with tinted windows, VIP style. Her seat on the airplane seemed curiously isolated; the nearest passenger was at the back of the cabin, behind a newspaper.

She entertained a brief fantasy that it was Killgoran, but when the mimosas were served, the man lowered his copy of *USA Today* and revealed himself to be a portly Italian businessman.

Maggie, feeling more like a convalescent than ever, huddled inside a blanket and stared blindly out the window. Soon, she consoled herself, she would be home, with her daughters, her family. Back in the comfortable flow of her life.

She could hardly wait to gather her children close and hold them, but the experience in Anphar had changed her in a very fundamental way. Touched her on a level that even David's tragic death had not.

She had seen, firsthand, how precious life was, but it was more than that. For all the terror, for all the danger, she had never felt more alive than she had in those hours with Killgoran, escaping from Anphar.

The question: was it the inevitable flow of adrenaline that had awakened some heretofore hidden part of her nature, made her somehow more complete as a person? Or was it Killgoran?

Back in Washington, safe at home after a joyously frenzied reunion with her daughters, Maggie stood alone in her moon-washed bedroom, holding a framed photograph in both hands. Herself and David, smiling, in wedding finery. Without the faintest glimmer of the tragedy that awaited them only a few years ahead.

She pressed the photograph to her chest and closed her eyes. She'd been frantic to look at David's face again, to grasp at precious memories that seemed more ethereal with every passing hour. Maybe it was the shock of what supposedly hadn't happened in Anphar, but up until that moment her late husband's image had eluded her.

Despite the government's careful instructions, she remembered Killgoran clearly. Could not, in fact, get him out of her mind. It was insane, given that she hadn't even known the man.

Still, for all Maggie's joy and relief at being home, and safe, there was an empty place in her heart, a place where Killgoran would fit nicely.

Six months later, in Maine. . . .

Maggie, seated before a card table in a corner of her huge old-fashioned kitchen, peered at the computer screen. Since the move to the small town of Blueberry Cove, where she'd opened a combination health-food and book store, she had been happier than she'd thought possible.

The twins loved their country school, and Snidely, their black and white Australian sheepdog, was in heaven. He took every opportunity to dash along the beach, in the cheerful, hopeless pursuit of sea gulls, no matter what the weather, while Maggie and the kids bounded after him.

Maggie had made a few tentative strides toward lasting friendships—down-easters being notoriously wary of outsiders—and even though the store was still in the red, money wasn't a problem. David had left her well provided for, even without the enormous compensation check (as if any amount could compensate) she had received from the airline after the disaster. Then there had been that "settlement," enough to see both Susan and Mary Catherine through Ivy League schools if that was what they wanted, from the restaurant in Rome that had allegedly given her food poisoning. An establishment she had never visited.

Maggie's new life was satisfying in general, but when the house was quiet and the kids were asleep, she often grew restless. Occasionally, late at night, she liked to switch on the computer and surf the Internet, communicating anonymously with other lonely people all over the world.

Scanning her e-mail, she came upon an address she didn't recognize. When the words of the message appeared on her screen, she blinked, startled.

WHAT IF YOU WEREN'T DREAMING? THAT NIGHT IN ROME, I MEAN?

She fired back an answer. WHO ARE YOU?

To her amazement, the reply was back almost instantaneously. Whoever had sent her that message must have been online, waiting. Watching.

NAME'S JACK KERRIGAN. COMPUTER GUY. NEVER BEEN TO ANPHAR.

Maggie's heart raced. ME EITHER, she wrote. HOW'S THE BLOOD SUGAR? She put the cursor on the "Send Mail" icon and clicked twice.

GETS LOW, came the reply. GOT TO HAVE PROTEIN.

Maggie braced her elbows on the table and thrust her fingers into her hair, struggling to maintain her composure.

WHERE ARE YOU? Kerrigan's message continued.

She replied with her telephone number, then waited on the

edge of her last nerve for the ringing to start. Instead, another message came over the Internet service.

BE MORE CAREFUL, MAGGIE. FOR ALL YOU KNOW, I COULD BE A NUT CASE.

ARE YOU? she immediately countered.

DEPENDS ON WHO YOU ASK, he replied.

She laughed, alone in her kitchen.

And so began the computer correspondence between two people who had never been to Anphar. It went on for a full six weeks—weeks during which Maggie poured out her soul, and received equal portions of Jack Kerrigan's in return.

Then, one windy spring day, when she was walking Snidely on the beach, he was there. An ordinary figure, really, clad in jeans, sneakers, a T-shirt and windbreaker. The wind rumpled his hair, and his expression was serious.

"Hello, Maggie," he said.

She suppressed an urge to fling herself into his arms. "Hi," she replied, feeling ridiculously shy.

"We have to start from the beginning, you and I," he said quietly.

Maggie nodded. "But we can tell each other the truth, can't we?"

He studied the sky for a few moments, considering. "We both know the truth," he said. "It's better to leave it at that."

"Why is it all such a secret?"

"Political stuff. Trust me, Maggie—it's better to leave it alone. I'm a guy you met on the Internet. We struck up a friendship. We'll see what comes of that."

She let go of Snidely's leash, and the dog ran in circles around them, barking exuberantly. Maggie held her breath, then put the question she had not dared to raise before, during their e-mail conversations. "You're not doing that same kind of work anymore?"

He shook his head. "I do computer consulting. Pretty dull guy, all things considered."

Maggie laughed. "A pretty dull guy who uses an alias."

He sighed. "Actually, Jack Kerrigan is my real name. Judd Killgoran was the alias. Could I kiss you?"

"I think I'd like that," Maggie said.

And she was right. She did like it.

Bridge Of Dreams

by

Susan Wiggs

Author's Note

Daniel Day-Lewis brings a command and an intensity to the characters he plays—a warrior/lover in *Last of the Mohicans,* an anguished Irish son in *In the Name of the Father*—and I've always imagined he'd play a marvelous musician. If the soul of an artist could ever be captured, I'm convinced that it would happen in Paris.

I feel ridiculous standing here, but I've come to keep a promise made a decade ago. I'm pretty sure he won't come. Frankly, if there was the faintest possibility that he would, I might not dare be here at all. It would be too awkward, too humiliating.

Ten years as a high school teacher have made me more or less immune to being humiliated. Still, you can't really pretend you just happen to be waiting on Pont-Neuf smack in the middle of Paris for no particular reason. Luckily, there's a park here—the famous Vert-Galant where the bridge meets the tip of the Île de la Cité—so I feel somewhat less conspicuous as I loiter. As I wait.

Wait for what? After all, it's been ten years since we made our promise. I don't expect him to remember.

I've arrived too early—a habit of mine—because I didn't want to feel rushed. Because I wanted to be sure to have time to duck into the public rest room—it's still here, adjacent to the stairs leading to the Metro—check hair, makeup, outfit, breath.

Just in case.

On my arrival in the city yesterday the first thing I did was go shopping. You really can't enjoy Paris wearing high school teacher clothes. Ignoring price tags, I wandered the boutiques of the Placé de Vendôme and picked out things that said "Paris"— but not too loudly. Almond-colored linen, a bright Hérmès scarf, shoes, and a bag. So if nothing else happens this entire week, at least I got a great outfit out of the deal.

I bite down on the Tic Tac I've been rolling around in my mouth. Will he kiss me?

Listen to me. Somewhere in the back of my mind, do I actually think—hope, pray—he'll show up? Do I think he'll come walk-

ing around the corner of this pigeon-infested equestrian statue
and sweep me off my feet?

That's what this city is about, I remind myself. Here particularly, in this little garden where the two sides of the bridge meet
like blood vessels joining at the heart. It's one of the smallest
parks in Paris: green lawns, gravel walkways, pink blossoms
opening on the trees. Paradise in miniature, right in the middle
of the city of lovers.

They're everywhere, as I'd known they would be. A couple on
the steps leading down to the Seine leaning dreamily into each
other's shoulders. . . . Two older people strolling along, his beret
still jaunty even though he relies heavily on his cane; her stock-
ings thick but her smile genuine. . . . A pair of students reclining
on the lawn, each propped on an elbow and gazing with heart-
breaking earnestness into the other's eyes.

I try to regard all this with self-protective cynicism, but it's
not working. Today is the first of May, the weather is perfect, the
bird and flower sellers create an explosion of color along the
edge of the Île, and it would take a harder heart than mine to find
fault with people who are in love and showing it.

Besides, I was one of them once. Half of a glorious pair. Only
for a blink of time—a night, a dazzling dawn, a sunny morning—but I can still see something of myself in the girl who tucks
her head into the lee of her boyfriend's shoulder, in the woman
leaning across her shopping parcels to kiss the man walking with
her.

I suppose I've come back to recapture those feelings in some
small way. And because I promised.

It was pretty simple to ascertain that he wouldn't be here. His
schedule, after all, is more or less a matter of public record. That's
one of the advantages I've had for the past ten years. He became
world famous, while I became a French teacher.

Then why am I so nervous? Jumpy, pacing the curved stone
perimeter of the Vert-Galant, my gaze focusing on every lone
male I pass. I even give a second glance to the *clochard* slumped
over, muttering to himself on a bench in the shade. I keep think-

ing: What if . . . ? What if he does show up? What then? What would we possibly have to say to each other?

And then the morbid thoughts come. Good God, what if something horrible happens—that ghastly *Affair to Remember* scenario and he's hurrying across the street to reach me and I don't see him get run over by a truck?

I should have written to him. Found his fan club on the Internet and sent him an e-mail. A simple note: *Will you be there or not?*

The trouble is, he's become so renowned that he probably has a staff to read his mail. They'd have dismissed me as a groupie, a crackpot, maybe even a stalker.

Best to keep it quiet. No one loses face. No one has to think up an excuse. I take a week off school, I visit Paris and spend so much money it feels like passing a kidney stone, and I go home knowing I held up my end of the bargain.

Some coldly practical part of me concedes that there is no reason on earth he'd remember the promise we made to each other so long ago. Lord knows, I barely remembered it myself. Even the most intense of life's pleasures can be dulled by years of daily routine. But at school one day in April, as I sat at my desk, I flipped the calendar open to a day I was supposed to hold sacred in my heart—The First of May, 1998.

We had agreed—conditionally—to meet here on this bridge, on this date, at high noon. It seemed simple. Romantic. Playful, even. And quite easy to agree to, since neither of us had any expectation of keeping the promise.

So this way is best—no letter, e-mail, nothing like that. I always wanted to come back to Paris, love affair or not, and now is as good a time as any.

For no particular reason, I sit down and double check the arts section of the *International Herald Tribune* I bought at a bookstall on the quay this morning. The Ensemble Echappe is performing tonight in Brussels at the Theatre de la Monnaie. The performance has been sold out for six weeks.

So I really don't have to be nervous. I calm myself by standing here in this place where I watched the sun come up over the back of Notre Dame ten years ago. And I can see him again, putting his hands on me just so as the lights on the bridge winked out, all at the same time, to make way for the dawn. And when he kissed me, I remember thinking: The world begins and ends with this kiss.

I should have listened to myself. At twenty-two, I was both wiser and more naive than I gave myself credit for. I was still a work-in-progress, emotionally newborn and given to clueless profundities that sometimes took people by surprise. Something happened that night, something my heart knew but my mind dismissed. It was the first time I had kissed someone and actually felt the magic. The shock of recognition that something more than hormones might be at work.

Even now, I try to rationalize. It was ten years ago and it was Paris and it was every kind of cliche you can imagine. Moonlight, red table wine, fog hovering over the Seine. And him.

We shouldn't have met. Under ordinary circumstances we wouldn't have met. We would have been like two stars in parallel universes, each oblivious of the other, each a complete entity unto itself.

Until we met. I remember, then, wondering how in God's name I hadn't known I needed him. That he would complete me. And it was the same for him because he said so. He said it first, in fact.

There was an extraordinary moment of connection between us. Even more extraordinary because neither of us expected it. Yet we both needed it. Wanted it.

I was a wide-eyed student from the heartland, where Americans are at their most American. For my last night in Paris I'd lucked into the hottest ticket in town—the gala opening of an avant-garde ensemble everyone in the music world was talking about. At a small art gallery, I'd made the acquaintance of the music critic of a prestigious magazine called *Matière*. For no reason I could fathom, he took a liking to me. At that time in my life, I suppose I had a certain befuddled charm. The critic would be out of town on this particular day, so he gave me his pass. "And don't skip the reception afterward," he admonished. "It's catered by Bonterre et Fils."

I recall clearly what I was wearing that night—a black silk sheath with a Dior belt and big jewelry. Thank God for Marie-Noel in whose home I had been staying. Marie-Noel was the epitome of Paris chic: stark yet sensual, severe, but only intimidating when she wanted to be. She did my hair that night (*"Tiens, if you are going to the Theatre Sanctuaire, then you must look as if you belong there"*), and she fixed my makeup and gave me something to wear. I was terrified that I might look like me only ridiculous; that's what usually happens when I dress up. Instead I looked exactly right. I didn't look French or even like someone pretending to be French; I resembled an elegant visitor who is quite comfortable in her surroundings.

He later told me he could tell the difference.

But I felt wonderfully chic as I emerged from the Metro station at St. Germain and walked down the boulevard to the Sanctuaire. Stepping past an ancient wrought-iron gate, I entered a tiny walled garden of espaliered yew trees and roses where the caterer was setting up for the reception afterward. The converted church is known for its perfect acoustics, created by medieval masonry of unparalleled precision. Inside, the sanctuary had been set up for the recital with the kneelers turned frontwise and multilevel platforms for the musicians. I had no idea what to expect as a hush came down along with the lights, and the stained-glass windows shone like jewels, adding mysterious color to the artful set.

The musicians arrived, greeted by polite applause that crescendoed as they took their positions. Right away, I fixed on him. He stood taller than the others, an ordinary-looking violin in hand, a half smile on his face, his hair too long but somehow appropriate. Even from a distance, I detected an intriguing look in his eyes. A look that said, *Come listen. I want to take you somewhere.*

The applause gave way to a few moments of breath-held silence, and then the music started. The first note was a long, subtle strain from the very heart of his violin, which was then joined, with exquisite delicacy, by the flute. I found myself on the edge of my seat, heart and throat full with the power of the music. He played with his eyes closed and a distant look on his face, the notes pouring from his hands like droplets from a waterfall. The program consisted of Dvorak and Vaughan Williams enchantingly juxtaposed with ancient and traditional folk music that felt bred into the bone of every listener, even as it stirred our blood. The ensemble finished—stunningly—with a Debussy as I'd never heard it played before or since.

Each musician was gifted beyond measure, but his performance on the violin was peculiarly affecting, a mingling of religious ecstasy with the earthy, profound tones of the blatantly secular. In the shadowy staging he stood out, a thin, brilliant flame against black velvet, the sight of him too intense to bear and yet, at the same time, so captivating I couldn't look away. Even before I knew his name, he held me in his thrall; I couldn't wait for the house lights to go up so I could check the program, read the name. . . .

I sat blinking in the sudden light while other people—all of them dressed to kill, most of them craving a Campari and a Gaulois—filed out to the garden for the gourmet reception.

He wasn't French? But he'd been so perfect while playing the Debussy. So *French*. In fact, all during the second movement I had rehearsed my compliments. I'd tell him in my most fluent French how much I'd enjoyed his performance. I murmured the praise over and over in my head until I could taste the words, until they became part of me. But of course, when he appeared—face scrubbed, collar unbuttoned, hair damp—I could say nothing.

And so he did the talking. "Champagne?" he asked in English. "You look as if you could use a glass." He pried open my fingers and placed the chilly crystal flute in my hand.

"How did you know I'm not French?" I asked, then bit my lip, mortified by my own lack of poise.

"Why didn't you realize I'm not?" he countered, flashing the grin that within a few years would grace concert halls and CD dust jackets around the globe.

But we didn't know that then.

"You're Irish," I said, scintillating in my brevity.

"From County Kerry. You're American."

"From Terre Haute, Indiana."

Something happened after that initial, awkward exchange. There was a looseness, an ease. Speaking English in a sea of Parisian elite, we drifted like two shipwreck victims in a lifeboat. We talked endlessly, and I'll never be sure how we managed, because people kept stopping by to congratulate him on his performance. He possessed that trademark magnetism, that presence, even then. He drew people, not by doing anything overt but just by grace of being there.

And already I felt it. The future of anyone foolish enough to brave being with him. You become a satellite. Your orbit is unstable. No one notices you.

Over the course of the evening, I learned the essentials. His mother was a poet who raised him alone in the brutal splendor and poverty of Western Ireland. He sang in church, his uncles taught him to dance, and one night when he was very young his mother took him to hear a Ceili band. He begged the use of a violin, and someone in the band gave him an old one to take home. Every day he practiced, using his own ear as a guide, playing melodies he knew from his mother's singing and from church and the local radio stations. In the summer when the sun set late, he'd walk the high rocky meadows overlooking the Atlantic and play tunes entirely of his own invention.

A year later the band returned, and he performed for them— very badly, his technique clumsy and primitive. But the fiddler in the group heard something. Or perhaps saw something. The magic or the gift or just a hunch; he was never quite certain. He was sent to Galway for lessons, outgrowing his teacher within a few years.

Eventually he won a spot with a London quintet that was hailed as brilliant, then sank into a morass of political and financial difficulties. The only element that emerged intact was him—a tall young man with the sort of magnetic beauty you see in Rossetti paintings and a gift that had the power to mesmerize.

He'd come to Paris at the beginning of spring to play with the most avant-garde ensemble in Europe. None of this surprised me. Not the rich abundance of his talent, not my own certainty that he would succeed beyond his wildest dreams. Did I have some prescience to predict accurately that here was a man destined to be a gift to the world? Or was it simply obvious?

In the years following our May night, I observed his career from a distance, tracking his trajectory like an astronomer—unsurprised, yet still amazed. His combination of physical beauty, soulful talent, and personal magnetism made him the obsession even of aficionados who were supposed to be above such slavish admiration. He took risks in his art, choosing pieces and ensembles that would have killed the career of a lesser talent.

And then, of course, came the tabloid-style gossip and paparazzi harassment. Invasive telescopic lenses captured him standing atop a windswept bluff, his head bent as he and a priest in a cassock stood over his mother's grave. Or—far less flattering—moist-lipped and bleary-eyed from a night of partying at Clio's New York, his arm draped around a woman with too much cleavage showing. Or fleeing a London solicitor's office in dark glasses, pursued by someone who claimed to have given birth to his triplets. The scandal sheets linked him to an anorexic flautist, a Kenyan princess, a Gap model, and an Olympic swimmer. He became public property, handling the fame, the accolades, the awards with outward grace.

But sometimes I'd think back on the night we met and wonder. Did the constant attention satisfy, or did it separate him from the world? Was he happy, or was that just something he said in his press releases?

Did his heart love as easily now as it had ten years ago?

I always buy his CDs and pore over the liner notes, searching the phrases for some inkling of who he has become. A world-class musician, yes. An artist. A star.

But only when I listen to the music do I get a glimpse into his heart. I hear passion and grief and ecstasy in his playing. Joy and pain, comets and shooting stars.

The launch party was winding down, but he exuded a manic, pumped-up energy, high on his own riveting performance. In charmingly broken French, he thanked the *mise en scène* crew and the underwriters and sponsors, all of whom eyed him with equal measures of fondness, awe, and ownership.

Without asking me—he must have known exactly what I was thinking—he took my hand and we left the sanctuary together. Outside, a light shower had washed the streets clean, leaving behind the warm aroma of damp asphalt. A freshening wind blew along the boulevard and we walked, stopping at a zinc bar for a drink of Ricard with an angular bottle of cold water.

He sat across from me at an impossibly tiny table, the enameled surface stamped with the Campari logo. He touched me with one finger, running it up along the inside of my arm.

"Now you," he said with that quiet, bemused solemnity. "Tell me."

I really didn't want to explain my circumstances. I wished my powers of invention were better so I wouldn't sound so dull. What did it matter who I was, where I came from? Especially after hearing his story. Nothing so romantic or even interesting. My motivations were painfully simple: an early fascination with an old Gerard Depardieu film, *The Return of Martin Guerre*. A feeling that in my small family, in my small town, I never really quite belonged. A fortunate school program in which students were exposed very young to foreign languages. In college I chose to major in French. I wanted to be a French teacher and read Colette and Balzac and Marcel Ayme in the original.

Does he remember any of this? I wonder, checking my watch for the hundredth time, reminding myself he's performing in Brussels tonight. Does he remember that we drank Ricard, that the air smelled of rain and flowers and exhaust, that he touched my arm?

Apologetically, I told him everything, the recitation taking all of five minutes, right up to the great climactic confession that I wanted to teach French in a private school, live in a small wooden house with shade trees, and own a cat and too many books.

And now I do. All of the above. The school is a Sacred Heart academy—all girls—with huge trees lining the main avenue leading to the campus. A gauntlet of ancient oaks forms a green tunnel leading to a safe place like a fallout shelter during the war. Going there is like traveling backward in time, back to girls in plaid uniforms and matching hairbands, pale and earnest and naively wealthy. They love to talk, and I make them do it in French.

They call me *Mademoiselle*.

Oh, God. I'm glad he won't be coming. Aren't I? Suddenly I wish I'd done something extraordinary—become a foreign diplomat or published a book of poetry or climbed a mountain in Katmandu.

On that first—that only—magical night, we didn't know what the future would bring; we only knew what our dreams were. We didn't know anything except that we were wildly attracted to each other. The hours flew by; we talked of everything and drank wine together at a cafe filled with cigarette smoke and mediocre live jazz.

Hand in hand, we took the Pont-Neuf up over the river, stopping in the middle to look back at the jumbled rooftops of the Latin Quarter. In the predawn, under a sky of nacre, the Left Bank was still a hive of activity, suiting our mood, for we were both flushed and restless with mutual fascination.

My dreams seemed so small compared to his, but he made them important. He was the first person to whom my dreams actually mattered. At the time, I had no idea he'd be the last. In the years that followed, I met a lot of people. I dated, took vacations, went out with friends. But my dreams always went back to that bridge, that night, all soft and misty after the rain.

"There's no reason you should believe this," he told me, "but I've never felt this way before." He touched me under the chin to make certain I was looking up at him. "Are you sure you have to leave?"

"I have an afternoon flight to New York."

"So cancel it."

"I can't. I'm flat broke, and—" I simply quit. There was no point in rattling off excuses. "The fact is," I said, "you've got to perform and travel, and I have to go back to the States. But—just for fun—what would you do if I stayed?"

"Do you have to ask?" He took my face between his hands.

"I'd fall utterly in love with you. And it wouldn't take long." He bent slowly, each heartbeat an agony of anticipation, and just before he kissed me, he said, "It's already starting to happen."

And that was it. The kiss that changed the color of my world, made me believe I could fall in love so hard and so fast that I'd forget who I was and become someone else entirely. The notion scared and exhilarated me. It was as if life itself sped up, the clouds racing and flowers blossoming with the surreal velocity of time-lapse photography.

The sun rose far too soon; I looked in the direction of Montmartre and saw the domed alabaster mass of the Sacre-Coeur Basilica beginning to glow, a sentinel to the dawn.

Our kiss was both hello and goodbye, and we both knew it, both resisted it.

"Meet me," he said. "Come back here and meet me."

"I can't. Really—"

"When can you come back?"

"When can you?" I countered.

And we stared at each other, filled up with the enchantment of attraction, lust, and the shining promise of a love that could happen between us if only circumstances would permit it.

But after that exchange, we stood at the impasse. We understood the impossibility. I had to return to the States to live in the most modest of circumstances as a first-year teacher. He had to travel and perform, and though we were young we understood the demands his art would place on him. Hundreds of performances a year. Cities across the globe. Endless rounds of parties for promotion.

How could either of us believe falling in love would be possible?

Simple. Because the young always believe love is possible, that even the busiest life has room for it.

And they're almost always wrong.

We never spoke of it, but I think we started justifying our parting even before it happened. This was all just animal lust. Instant chemistry because we were both young and healthy and alone in the world's most beautiful city.

Neither of us knew—nor would dare to suggest—that this was the once-in-a-lifetime meeting. Yet both of us felt, at that moment, like people who might come to love one another with a passion that could sustain them for the rest of their lives.

"We can't promise each other anything," I said.

"We'll write, phone—"

"No, not that. Too awkward. And when one of us quits calling it'll hurt."

"Are you always this cold-blooded and practical?"

"Yes. Are you always this impetuous and romantic?"

"No. Only with you."

I remember staring at him, speechless with a sudden shock of recognition. I finally figured out what my heart had known the moment I laid eyes on him. I could love this man until the stars fell down.

I had to move away from him then, touching the stone rail of the bridge. The lights blinked out all at once, giving way to the rising sun. A veil of mist shrouded the Seine as the city began to bestir itself for a new day. We could hear bargemen bidding on cargoes at the *criée* in front of the Maison des Mariniers. Their wives, in cotton aprons with huge pockets, were already pegging out the laundry up over the decks of the barges.

Life was rumbling on. Life would not stop for us.

"Come on, I'm desperate here," he said, more persistent than I. "Give me something. Tell me I can call you on New Year's Eve or—"

"Let's meet back here," I said.

"All right. When?"

After a long discussion, we settled on a decade. A year was too short—I'd still be broke and he'd be on the road. Five years? Too dangerous. Too likely to happen, and we might be too vulnerable then. Or involved in a relationship that wouldn't withstand this sort of thing. So ten years. A perfectly round number, a date far enough in the future to defy practicality. There would be no dishonor in not showing up, we agreed. If one of us didn't show, the other would not ask for an explanation, nor be entitled to one.

So those are the rules. I like rules; I am comfortable with them. I'm holding up my end of the bargain by coming here. He's holding up his end by staying away. It seems right. It fits.

I won't let myself be disappointed because I haven't let myself expect anything. Even though hours have passed—the *gendarme* patrolling the Vert-Galant keeps sending inquisitive glances in my direction—I linger. I have no idea why I hesitate; probably because this is Paris and it's the first day of May and the weather is so insanely glorious I can't bring myself to move.

I keep waiting, watching. *Clochards,* sandwich men, handbill distributors, and sidewalk artists come and go throughout the afternoon. Freshly washed laundry still hangs like ensigns over the barges, just as it did ten years ago.

I start to nudge myself toward a final acceptance. I should be feeling some sort of closure by now. The encounter that has haunted me for years should finally fade into oblivion.

There's a sandwich shop on the Left Bank that makes a gorgeous *croque-monsieur* dripping and bubbling with broiled Emmenthaler cheese. I should go and have one and finish reading the paper. Yet, still, I wait because, in spite of everything, I keep thinking, *What if . . . ?*

The sun touches the treetops in the west; the day is almost over. Men carrying briefcases are leaving the Prefecture de Police, and the bird and flower sellers are folding up their stalls for the night. I have no right to feel this lump in my throat, but it's there as I walk down the center path of the Vert-Galant and cross to the Île de la Cité. A flower seller, her back bent and a blue printed scarf covering her head, nods at me as I pass. On impulse I buy a bouquet of roses from her, pink ones, the color of spring, the color of hope.

It would be way too depressing to take the flowers back to my little *pension,* so instead I return to the bench where we once sat and talked and held hands to greet the dawn. Ten years later, the wrought iron bears a new coat of shiny green paint. The plane trees surrounding it nod in a light breeze off the river. Almost furtive, almost fearful of being caught, I lay down the bouquet, unembarrassed by the maudlin symbolism of the gesture.

And then I turn and walk away.

I'm already forcing my mind ahead, already thinking I'll stop at a sidewalk cafe for an aperitif, then return to the *pension* for a bath and have a late dinner out somewhere. A busy restaurant where I can people-watch and eavesdrop on their conversations.

But no matter how hard I try, part of me still waits stubbornly on that bench, not wanting to close that door, never wanting to, even though I know I must.

I hurry, longing to be away from there, trying to flee the hurt I shouldn't feel but do anyway. I keep thinking that if I can make it to the end of the bridge without shattering, I'll be all right.

A *camion* rumbles past, and the traffic sounds rise as the light changes at the boulevard on the Left Bank. And for some reason, out of all the noise and bustle of the city, I hear a car door slam.

It's something my heart knows. *Turn around. Take a look back. Make sure you're not missing anything.*

He emerges from a black Citroen limo, and I know him instantly, the energetic movements, the sunlight striking a bright shock of hair. He is larger, more imposing than I'd anticipated. And he's holding the bouquet that I left on the bench.

The bouquet drops, forgotten, to the ground between us as he joins me on the sidewalk of the bridge.

"Ten years ago you stole something from me," he says. The intensity in his eyes shocks and frightens me.

"Stole what?" I ask, my voice betraying me, breaking hoarsely over the words.

He takes both my hands and stands facing me while the traffic rushes past. A double-decker tour bus, crammed with Japanese tourists and their cameras, gets caught at the light.

Sad, solemn, determined, he says, "My heart. You stole my heart."

I can't help myself. The tears spill over. I want to tell him that he's missing his performance, that he shouldn't be here, but all I can say is, "I didn't know, all those years ago, that I'd never feel this way again."

"I didn't know either," he admits. "That's why I had to come. And to think I almost missed you—"

"But you didn't. I waited."

And for the second time he kisses me, and it must look to the tourists like a classic Paris kiss, because their bus driver honks the horn as it lumbers past. A dozen cameras point in our direction. In spite of the tears, I'm laughing as I pull away and put my hand in his.

We walk together to the tip of the Vert-Galant where the masonry slopes down into the slow-moving river. The whine of traffic and the calls of the boatmen fade into the background as a church bell starts to toll. I don't know where this will lead, but when I look up at him, he is smiling. And the sun is shining.

Moon over Miranda

by

Courtney Henke

Author's Note

My inspiration for this story was the gorgeous Kevin Sorbo in his wonderful role as Hercules, in the TV series *Hercules: The Legendary Journeys*. Mythic creatures, epic adventure, a stunning, buff hero—what woman *wouldn't* be inspired? When you add a hearty dose of laughter to the mix, as the show does, you have a perfect breeding ground for my favorite kind of romance.

Halfway up the face of the towering cliff, Ro ran into trouble. That was when the winds, who had been pestering him all evening, managed to blow him off.

With supernatural speed and agility, he caught a sturdy shrub that grew from a crack in the rock face, nearly tearing his arm from its socket.

"I hate it when that happens," he muttered. He was dangling like a minnow on a hook in the light of the full moon. His shoulder was probably dislocated. He had no hope that the winds were going to leave him alone. And he had an innocent to rescue.

Just another typical evening.

Hand over fist, grimacing as his shoulder slipped back into place and immediately began to heal, he began his ascent again.

It seemed to him that a son of Zeus ought to have better choices. But in reality he was caught in the crossfire between his father and his father's wife, Hera, who hated every by-blow her husband had spawned. Being among the many such unfortunates, he had lived from birth with one of Hera's infamous curses. A curse that dictated his entire life.

The good news was, he'd learned to make use of it. When the moon reached its zenith, he would shape-change into a wolf. But before then, for those few hours that the moon was rising and the transformation was churning inside of him, the forces of Olympus would combine with the senses of the Beast to make him the most powerful mortal on earth. The fuller the moon, the more powerful he was. As always, he would use his power to fight injustice.

Tonight, the night of the full moon, the Winds seemed determined to stop him.

A fist of damp air punched Ro's right cheek, snapping his head to the left and into the cliff's face.

"Back off, Zeus-spawn!" hissed Notus, the South Wind, the mother of all storms. "Go back to Athens!"

Ro slid to his left and encountered an icy blast of sleet—Boreas, the North Wind—which sent him skidding back to his right.

He worked his jaw, flexed his hands, and renewed his climb toward the tower that rose from the top of the cliff. He didn't have time for this game. Something deep was afoot, and he suspected the letter from his brother that had prompted this rescue was sadly understated. "There might be trouble," the letter had said.

"No mention of Hera's two favorite pests, of course," Ro muttered. "Ah, damn!"

Two blows, cold on his left and wet on his right, joggled him dangerously. *"Go Back,"* he heard whistling through the sand and stones. *"Get Down,"* shuddered through his bones.

The two voices—with occasional glimpses of the speakers—had followed him up Aegean Cliff, which stood as a buffer between land and sea, a gift from Athena to a grateful king. For two leagues, he'd swiped at Notus' and Boreas' shadows, hitting him from the dark. When a third voice joined the chorus with a whispered, *"Turn Away,"* he groaned.

"Hera's *three* favorite pests," he murmured. But this one, he could intimidate—usually. Narrowing his blue eyes on the pile of rubble before him, he hugged the cliff face, waiting for that whisper again.

A tickle on his ear signaled the moment to strike. With lightning speed he snatched the air at his shoulder and drew it around to his field of vision. "What do you think you're doing?"

The wispy form of a young man, garbed in flowing pansy blue, grappled at the huge hand that circled his throat. Zephyr, the West Wind. "You're hurting me," he whined.

"It's nothing to what I will do to you." It was an empty threat, but Zephyr didn't have to know that.

The little demon squirmed. "I—I'll—I'll push you off!" He

twisted in a pathetic attempt at a cyclone. "Leave me alone!" he huffed, when it was apparent that Ro was still firmly entrenched.

"Not until you tell me what you're doing here." Ro shifted his grip. "Did Hera put you up to this?"

"I'm not telling, you stupid mortal."

From the corner of his eye, Ro saw the icy shape of a brawny man with fists raised. Boreas. On the right, he heard the howl of Notus, the she-storm, heading toward him again. Doubtless, they didn't like the way he was manhandling their weaker brother. He could see they planned to strike together this time, which would clap him between them and squash him like a mosquito.

Ro scanned the surrounding cliff, took note of a good-size outcropping a couple of arm length's below and to the right, and rapidly formulated a plan. He'd have only one chance. As Boreas reared back to strike and Notus whipped her hair into a blow of iron, he tensed. One . . . more . . . moment. . . .

"You're dead, freak," Zephyr sneered.

Ro dropped like a stone, releasing Zephyr an instant before he grabbed the trailing edges of Boreas' and Notus' garments, sweeping them together. With a thunderous clap of sound and brilliant light, the elements clashed—at the same instant, Ro landed on the outcropping. He dug his feet into a crevice, slammed against the rock face, and held on.

Ice chunks the size of goose eggs pelted down all around him, and gravel, loosened by the force of the collision, stung his shoulders.

"What did you do to them, you meanie? You hurt them!"

With a sneeze and an angry growl, Ro gritted his teeth and hauled himself up. Ignoring the ineffective Zephyr, he grinned at the sight of snow pouring out of the sky in midsummer—the result of the meeting of the two polar Winds. They were out of commission until their rebirth at dawn, but who could predict what Hera would send next? That it *was* Hera dogging his heels, he didn't doubt.

Resuming his climb toward the tower window, Ro picked up his pace. Blood oozed from a gash on his forehead, and it smarted as it healed with preternatural speed.

Zephyr pounded ineffectually between his shoulder blades. "You brute!" he cried. "I hate you!"

Few mortals could hear the words the Winds spoke. As far as Ro knew, he was the only mortal who could actually see them. Lucky him.

He reached the end of his patience at the same time he reached his goal. Vaulting to the wide window ledge, he launched himself inside with a yell. The force of his action sent him rolling full-length into the round-walled room. He landed in a half crouch against the opposite side, beside a massive wooden door, his hands held at the ready for whatever awaited him. His curse-sharpened senses instantly registered the opulence and the candle smoke—and the shriek of a missile in flight.

Ro leaped for the shelter of a paper screen as a vase crashed into the wall beside him. Peeking around the screen, he searched the smoky darkness and saw a tall brunette woman dressed in ethereal white silk. As she reached for another pot to throw, she glanced at him, and blue clashed with green as his gaze met hers.

"Not another one," she groaned—and raised her arm.

Ro tensed, then realized she wasn't aiming at him. He didn't actually have to look, though, to find the target. All he had to do was sniff the air. Not far from where he crouched, a squat man stood beside the wall, smiling a happy, toothless grin. He was quite naked. And he stunk.

The pot landed squarely on the little man's temple. He went down like a ninepin, still grinning, landing in a pile of what had to be his own battered armor.

The woman dusted off her hands and smoothed her hair. Ro couldn't imagine why. There wasn't a curl out of place or a smudge of dirt anywhere on her.

"Still here?" she asked, giving Ro a negligent glance as he emerged cautiously from behind the screen. "You heroes are a persistent lot, aren't you?" She tilted her head. "Unless you're . . . not a hero?"

For a moment, he thought he saw uncertainty in her hard green eyes. "I won't hurt you," he said softly. "I'm here to take you home."

"Of course you are." A smile crossed her lips. "But you have a proposal for me first, right?"

"Actually—"

"Don't bother. I know the routine." She spun away and reached for a piece of the man's armor, tugging it ungently from beneath his inert form. "First you say, 'My beautiful Miranda, I want to take you away from all of this.' Then it's, 'I want to give you the world, Miranda, make you happy, Miranda, fill your life with love,' yada yada ya." Her hand swept the air to encompass the room. "You want to make me happy? Clean up this mess." She flung the breastplate out of the east window.

"You don't want to be rescued?"

"Why should I? A cage is a cage." She spoke the words so lightly he thought he imagined the underlying hint of bitterness.

"I'm here to take you *out* of the cage."

She tossed her head. "And into another. Look, it's okay. You can't help yourself. Obviously, you're not one of the intelligent ones."

He bristled.

"Mogg, here"—she poked the lout with the toe of her delicate slipper—"he's not too well endowed on that score, either. You know how I can tell? Stupid ones always think it's about sex. And brawn. And rescues. Puffed-up shows of masculinity and power."

"Hey, hold on, dead-eye—"

"For what? What are you going to do? Force me? Wrestle me? *Touch me?*"

The hope in her green eyes wasn't real, he was sure, but his task didn't involve judging this Miranda character, just getting her out. The fact that it would be a kidnapping, not a rescue, bothered him, but not much. She *was* a prisoner of some sort, or she wouldn't talk about cages.

Still, he took offense that she seemed to think him some kind of half-wit—he, the darling of the Athenian Logic Society. He wouldn't turn into a mindless beast for several hours yet.

"We need to get you out of here," he said.

She sighed and flung herself onto a silk-covered divan, sending her silver earrings dancing. "Look, sweetheart, I know you think you're helping me, but you're not. I have everything I could want here." She plucked a fat grape from a bowl on the small table beside her. "I have hot water three times a day for bathing, stuffed partridges and spiced dates to eat, and scrolls to read from every bard who's ever made Athena's top ten list. If I go with you, what'll I have?"

"You'll have more important things than luxury."

"Nothing's more important than luxury."

"What about freedom? Love?"

She gave a bark of laughter, choking on her grape. "By the gods, not just a hero! An idealist! Fine. Love is good. But you'll have to prove your so-called love if you want me to go with you." Rising, she sauntered back over to where Mogg still slumbered happily.

Surely Ro must have imagined that flash of yearning earlier, just as he was imagining the misty regret now. This woman didn't have enough soul for such feelings.

Then again, he wondered what she'd look like mussed and dewy from lovemaking.

The instant the thought flashed through his mind, he was appalled by it. What in Tartarus was wrong with him? He didn't even like her!

He had to hurry, get them both out of this mess. But how? What was he going to do with a princess who didn't want to be rescued?

"So." She shoved the rest of the noisome leather pile through the window and turned to assess him. "Okay, I've decided what you can do to prove your love. I want you to run around the room on your knuckles."

Ro's ears pricked. Distantly—at the bottom of the stairs, perhaps—he heard the thud of a booted foot. "Princess—"

"I forgot. You've probably never seen a menagerie, so you can't have seen a monkey. Can you juggle?"

More feet. Guards from below, coming to see why armor was raining on their heads. "Princess—"

"Too bad. Then jump up and down and cluck like a chicken."

They were about to be invaded, and she was talking about chickens? "No," he growled.

The word seemed to echo around the room, hanging like fog, thick with an import he didn't understand.

Her taunting smile slipped. "What did you say?"

"I said no." He circled the room, grabbed a soft blanket that would do as a cloak, and flung it around her. "We're leaving." When she didn't move to help, he grabbed her arms and gazed down into her pale, upturned face: "I won't take you by force, Princess, but if you're going with me, we must leave now. Before the moon gets any higher."

She was staring at his hand on her right arm. Then, slowly, she raised her gaze to stare at his face—stupidly, as if she were dazed.

He gave her a shake. "Sometime this epoch, Princess."

"What happens when the moon gets higher?" she whispered.

"You don't want to know."

The troops in the stairwell sounded like rocks on a bass drum to him. With an impatient snarl, Ro released the unmoving Miranda and whirled to meet the threat.

The door burst inward and crashed against the wall. Two female warriors leaped into the room, with two more behind them. It crossed his mind to wonder why Amazons, who weren't known to be mercenaries, were guarding this princess, but he brushed off the thought. Amazons or not, he knew by sound and scent that at least ten crack fighters were nearby.

No problem.

The four inside brandished their swords. He grinned, baring his teeth and long-fingered hands. The Beast he would become surged through him, joyful at the promise of blood.

Something of this must have shown on his face, because the leader's stance tightened. "Circle him."

Like a troupe of acrobats, they began to slide around him. Then, with an ululating battle song, they attacked.

Ro ducked beneath the sweep of steel and kicked out, knocking the legs from beneath one warrior. Sensing another's thrust, he rolled to his right, leaving the second guard to slice stone instead of flesh. With a cry, she dropped her sword from the "sting" and cradled her hand.

He turned to find the third guard in mid-swing, with a thrust calculated to cut him off at the knees. He jumped high, leaping over her with a roar, and came down in the face of the fourth. She went down, her head hitting the heavy portal beside her with an ugly thud, knocking her unconscious. Quickly, he shoved a fifth guard back through the doorway, growling in pleasure as she began a tumble down the stairs, and slammed the door to prevent reinforcements. With no key for the lock, he snatched his unconscious enemy's sword, shoved it deep into the hinges and, in the same fluid motion, whirled to face the other three guards.

They had backed away to opposite ends of the room, stepping lightly, their swords drawing circles in the air as they reassessed the threat he posed.

Miranda appeared suddenly at his elbow, struggling to fasten the blanket with a silver brooch. "I want to go with you."

One, as he'd mentally dubbed the leader, danced forward to thrust at his head, forcing him to dodge; then she flipped herself back out of reach.

"Get behind me," Ro said, without looking at Miranda. He scanned the area for a rug, a loose hanging, anything to throw over the Amazons, but found nothing within reach.

"Didn't you hear me? I said I want to go with you."

"I heard you," Ro replied, watching Two abandon her chipped sword and pull a heavy chain from her belt. "But I'm a little busy. Duck!"

He shoved Miranda down as Three lunged. He grabbed the oncoming wrist and flung its owner overhand. She flew through the air to bash into Two, still swinging her chain, throwing them both backward, into the south wall.

A steady thump told him the reinforcements had begun their assault on the door.

"Great rescue," Miranda muttered, and shoved him toward the window.

Her unexpected action sent Ro stumbling into the middle of

the room. He swore, feeling exposed, but before he could lunge for cover, she pushed him again. "Are you insane?" he cried.

"Trust me," she said.

Trust her? A woman who had ordered him to cluck like a chicken? Yeah, right.

Then again, the guards *were* about to break through the door.

Ro leaped for the windowsill, with Miranda close behind. At the same time, Two pulled out her crossbow, took aim, and fired. Miranda cried out and flinched to the side.

Ro watched in astonishment as the bolt, which *should* have hit Miranda, bounced off *nothing,* then ricocheted upward, straight into his shoulder.

He roared as surprise and pain lanced through him. He yanked the bolt from his flesh as Miranda jumped up to stand on the sill, beside him.

"I hate it when that happens," she said. Then, as the door splintered and troops poured into the room, she threw herself at him. "No time to climb!"

Ro lost his balance and, with Miranda clinging to him like a limpet, tumbled into the dark void. He had fallen off chairs before, fallen off a fortress wall once, even fallen off a barn roof, playing eagles with his brother. He knew what falling felt like—the rush of blood, the sensation that you had somehow left your heart and stomach at the top level—and this wasn't it.

There was no rush, no sensation of leaving his insides behind, because they weren't falling. Instead, they were drifting like goose down. A man-length away from the tower, they floated downward through leagues of empty, black night.

His breath caught. "By Selene's silver glow, what's happening?"

"I told you to trust me," Miranda said.

Her voice sounded strained, and her grip on his chest and mid-section was almost suffocating.

"You're holding us up," he murmured in awe.

"No. I'm holding *you* up. I don't know what's holding me."

But she had known this would happen, he thought. He encircled her with his arms, hugging her beneath her buttocks as he tilted them more upright.

It had stopped snowing, but the collision of Boreas and Notus had covered the moon with clouds. Overhead, the light of a torch appeared in the tower window; Ro doubted, though, that Miranda and he were visible. In any case, no random arrows pierced the night, and after a few moments, the torch light disappeared. No doubt, the Amazons were in pursuit. But the path from the fortress down to the beach would take them forever. He'd checked. He and Miranda were safe.

Miranda shifted her grip slightly. He tightened his. His heart suddenly tripped over itself at the feel of her warm, lithe body snuggled against his. How long had it been since he'd held a woman this close?

Far too long.

While the world called him Hero, women called him Beast, good enough to save their village, not good enough to love, or even to touch. If Miranda knew who—or what—he was, she would drop him to the beach far below, wipe her perfect hands on her perfect gown, and go live a perfect life with a perfect prince.

"Why did you decide to come with me?" he asked.

Her answer was immediate. "Because you touched me and it didn't make you a demented lunatic."

Startled, Ro drew back his head to gaze into her deep green eyes.

"And because chickens don't growl," she added. "And because your teeth are sharper than they were. And because you came in with a gash on your forehead that disappeared during your battle. But mostly," she finished softly, "because you said no."

She knew what he was, and she didn't care. No fear tainted her face, no sick curiosity. Only acceptance.

What was happening here?

Her breath smelled like warm honey. Beneath the blanket-cloak, her skin was apricot-soft against his arms. It wasn't the perfect, exterior package that cried out to him, though. It was the way she felt snuggled into the curve of his body, the way her voice caressed his ears, the way her firm, rounded flesh felt in his hands. Everything about her called to his curse-sharpened senses, and the animal beneath. Yet it was even more than that.

"You really didn't need a rescue, did you?"

She shook her head.

"Then why were you in that cage—or any other cage?"

She gazed deeply into his eyes. "Because I'm cursed, too."

He felt his heart leap. A kindred spirit. She'd recognized his curse because *she* was cursed. How? And by whom?

Before he could pursue the answers, Ro heard a groaning sigh, one that hadn't come from either of them. When they dipped in the air, he knew something was wrong.

He tore himself free of Miranda's gaze to search the darkness around them. The beach glowed far below. The clouds overhead had begun to roil, shifting away from the full moon, and, in the silver light, he saw the shadowy figure dressed in pansy blue. Zephyr—and he was turning purple with strain.

"You really don't know what holds you up, do you?" Ro asked.

"No," she answered, frowning. "But I figured, if I held on to you, we'd both be okay, because whatever it is, it never lets me fall."

"It," Ro realized, was actually "they." Except that "they" were down from three to one because he'd incapacitated two of them. Zephyr was it, and Zephyr wasn't much.

"I don't want to save you," Zephyr hissed from below.

No kidding, Ro thought. But he also understood that for some reason, Zephyr was compelled to try to save Miranda.

The warm wind shifted suddenly. Ro saw Zephyr make a frantic grab, but without the support of his stronger brother and sister, he was as useful as smoke. A fact soon proven when his arms vanished.

Ro and Miranda hung suspended for an instant, then dropped like stones. Miranda gasped but didn't scream. Ro felt the familiar rush of organs, and could think of only one thing to do. Fighting through the wildly flapping blanket, he grabbed Miranda's arms and pulled.

She convulsively locked her fingers and ankles behind him. "What do you think you're doing?"

"Zephyr can hold one! You'll be safe! Let go!"

"No!"

The blanket, along with her stubborn strength, worked against him. He couldn't break loose. "Damn it, woman! I've fallen before and lived to tell the tale!"

"I'm not letting go!"

The white beach rushed toward them with sickening speed. It was pure instinct—or maybe the memory of playing eagles—that made Ro flatten in the air and grab for the blanket. He slid it through his hands until he had the corners tight in his fists. The blanket flared, bowing over them like a tent, and they immediately jerked to a slower rate of descent.

Not slow enough, he thought. The bird act wouldn't soften their landing sufficiently to save a normal human, but as long as Miranda's silver brooch held the blanket to her gown, as long as he hit the ground first, they would have a chance.

"We're moving away from the shore!"

"Good!" he cried. "We'll land in the water."

"Not good when it's full of rocks!"

By Zeus. He remembered. Not rocks. Monstrous, jagged *boulders*.

He had heard that when a person was about to die, his whole life flashed before him. Which maybe meant they wouldn't die, because all that flashed before his eyes was everything he *hadn't* done: he'd never told his brother how much his common sense had meant to him over the years; never given his niece the doll he'd carved for her; never traveled to places the bards sang about.

Never loved a good woman.

He pulled back to gaze at Miranda's full lips, look into her frightened green eyes. Worlds were in there, worlds he'd never known.

"I'm out of ideas, hero," she whispered.

"I'm not," he said. Before he could change his mind, he brought his mouth together with hers.

The touch of their lips was like the crashing thunder of the winds. Suddenly, bodies pressed, with pulses racing and tongues meshing. Ro felt Miranda's kiss in every fiber of his being. Passion ripped through his veins like wildfire, and yearning plucked at his heart. This wasn't mere physical desire. This was *completeness,* and he'd never known it before.

And if they dashed against the rocks, it would end before it had a chance to begin.

Ro tore himself away from paradise and pushed Miranda from him. With a cry of distress, she fought to grab on to him again. In the brief struggle, her blanket flapped loose, and the silver brooch popped, scoring him on the neck. Ro evaded her clinging hands, folding his arms by his sides to arrow down and away.

The rocks loomed closer. He could taste salt spray. And Zephyr was nowhere to be seen. Had he saved her? Or had he killed them both?

A howl of frustration built to a roar that burst from deep in his chest. Why had he been shown the possibility of happiness only to have it snatched away? The sound of his rage filled his head and throbbed in his ears; it was so loud that it covered the sudden *whoosh* of air around him.

He slammed to a halt, less than a hands-breadth from the jagged rocks. For less than a heartbeat—long enough to see a limp Miranda hovering above him—he was held there on a hot, dry bed of air. Then, the bed inched out from beneath him, and he was dumped into the icy water.

He came up spluttering, knee-deep in the sea. He crouched, ready to catch Miranda if need be, but she floated to shore, cradled in the wake of Eurus, the East Wind.

"My timing, as always, is right on," said Eurus. Her spiky red hair and black leather vest and breeches stood out sharply against the white sand—as did the tattoo on her shoulder, an image of the rising sun draped in a banner that read "Mother." "Betcha thought I was gonna let her splat, huh?"

"I am *not* in the mood for this," Ro muttered, wading ashore. His gaze was on Miranda's inert form, still hovering above the sand. "What did you do to her?"

"Nothing! I couldn't even if I wanted to! But I was in a hurry, so I sucked all the air from around her. I did it to *save* her."

With a bestial roar, Ro lunged at Eurus, latching on to her studded collar. "If you're supposed to protect her, why did your whole family attack me when I was trying to rescue her?"

Eurus choked and wrapped a small whirlwind around them, lifting him off of his feet. "I don't know! Zephyr hates you, and maybe the others came to help him fight you. Let me go!"

Ro's Olympic grip remained unshakable. "Tell me the truth."

"I am! I've been gone! I don't know why they attacked!"

"And Miranda?"

"She'll come to!" Eurus rasped out. "I swear by Eos!"

Ro believed her. He let her break loose—and he immediately dropped to his feet on the sand.

Eurus' kohl-lined eyes narrowed on him as she rubbed her throat. "Oh, *thank* you, Eurus," she coughed. "Thank you for saving me from those big freaking boulders. I know even *my* healing powers wouldn't have gotten me over the damage they'd have done!"

Ro forced his head clear, logic over the animal. In his run-ins with the four Winds, Eurus had always proven the bluntest of the siblings. She was quick to temper, deadly in her job, a dirty, cyclonic fighter. But she had an unbreakable code of honor: she never lied. Which led to the conclusion that he was being an ass, which he hated only marginally less than being a wolf.

"Thank you," he said, and meant it.

She shrugged with a grin. "Forget it. You're not exactly yourself—or you won't be soon—and I *was* a little dramatic with the entrance. But when I felt her drop, I had to kick ass all the way from Egypt. See, Zeus cut a co-op deal with Osiris, and sent me and Sirocco to go stir up a few sandstorms. Personally, I'd rather blow somewhere nice and tropical, but, no, I always get the freaking desert.

"Anyway—" She set Miranda gently on the sand, gazing at her with what almost looked like affection. "I don't mind this gig, y'know? She's a good kid. Nicer than I'd be, that's for sure. Hera's given her the royal shaft with that curse of hers."

"What's the deal?" he asked, glad that with Eurus he didn't have to worry about being subtle.

Eurus looked at him, startled. "You don't know?" A grin spread over her black mouth. "Will wonders never cease? You, going into a mission underinformed. I'm telling Athena."

"Can it, Eurus. Tell the story."

"It's kind of funny, really . . ." Taking note of his narrowed, lupine eyes, she cleared her throat. "In a horrible, nasty way, of course. It really started with Aphrodite. Miranda's fiancé compared her beauty to the love goddess'. Since Miranda was plain as a mud fence, Aphrodite wasn't amused. She wanted to put the zap on her, change Miranda into a cow. But Hera, who loves to piss on Aphrodite's sandals—besides feeling like she's owned the cow concession ever since the Europa incident—heard about the deal just in time to change it midway. Hence, the curse."

"What did she change it to?"

"Beauty. Flawless beauty." Eurus shrugged. "Perfection Hera wanted and perfection she got, to the point of driving men mad with wanting to possess it. I remember one guy. Warlord. Came to do a little raiding on her fishing village, took one look at her face, and wasted the place. Killed her family, her fiancé—who, by the way, had put bars on a cave in the hills and kept her there for six months, just staring at her. The only good news— if you can call it good—is that none of these morons actually touch her. Like, it would spoil her or something. They just want to *own* her. And they'll do anything to take her away from whoever's got her at the time."

Eurus let out a sad sigh. "In the eight years I've been watching her, this poor kid's been locked up, stolen, totally cut off from humanity. Kings, lately, showering her with every luxury imaginable, which, I guess, sounds great until you get it. Like this last bozo—putting her up there like a rare vase or something." She cocked her head. "But you didn't fall for that face, didja babe?"

Ro noticed Eurus' knowing smile—she'd obviously seen the kiss—but he didn't comment on it. He could only think of Miranda. Eight years. She'd been imprisoned and decorated, but never loved, by greedy men for eight years. No wonder she had such a jaded cynic's heart. It was a miracle she hadn't gone mad. "Guess all that Zeus-blood finally did me some good," he said. "Protected me."

"If that's what did it. Could be the animal, though. Won't know unless you try it," she said slyly.

"I can't. And you know it." Ro shuddered at the reminder of what had happened the only time he'd ever given in to passion during a moonrise, back before women started calling him Monster. He'd been young—a randy youth—and hadn't considered how the Beast might demonstrate his passion. The girl was still living with the scars from his teeth and claws. And he was still living with the guilt.

"Guess it might be a bit risky," Eurus sighed. Then, shooting him a grin, she whistled for her chariot. "Well, it's been real, but I gotta go bury me a city." She rose, spinning into the night. "I'll bet your changing-into-a-beast thing doesn't seem so bad up against Miranda's reverse-Medusa thing, huh?"

He glanced at the full moon, visible faintly behind the clouds, coming closer to its peak. He could feel the "thing" roiling inside of him, heating his blood and his emotions, making clear thought harder to achieve. But his fear and isolation was nothing compared to the loneliness Miranda must have felt all these years. He had his brother's family, and half brothers and sisters galore. And he had the daylight hours when he was free of the curse. Miranda had no one, and no time, that she lived free.

"No," Ro answered softly. "Not so bad."

Harley, Eurus' fleet chariot, thrummed into view, sliding smoothly beneath her. Eurus grabbed the handles and leaned back in the seat. "Hey, Ro, one more thing. Next time you see Zeph, go easy on him, okay? He's a wuss, but he's my brother." She began to draw a cloak of whirling sand around her. "You know how it is."

"Wait! Don't you have to watch over Miranda?"

"I only do the big stuff, the dust devils take care of the rest. Unless you plan on climbing more cliffs, she's okay. Besides, I figure you two need to be alone. What's the world coming to when *Zeus'* son doesn't want to jump a woman's bones?" Eurus shook her head in disgust and roared up and away. "Must be love!" she called out, voice fading into the night.

It took several counts for silence to descend, the only sound marring it the lapping of the sea's gentle waves on the sand.

Miranda whimpered and raised a hand to her forehead. He resisted the urge to run to her. By the gods, he *wanted* to jump her bones. The tightly leashed Beast inside of him, which was gaining power steadily, wanted it as well. But he would not take her like that, not with the wolf upon him.

As for Eurus' comment about love . . . he couldn't think about it now.

Ro kneeled by Miranda's side. Not a hair was out of place, not a grain of sand stuck to her flawless skin. He narrowed his eyes, searching, and finally caught a glimpse of red, then another. It was as Eurus had said: hundreds of dust devils, creatures no bigger than ants, swarmed around Miranda, their pitchforks constantly grooming, their pointed tails and horns creating the breeze that kept everyday dirt off. They swirled over her face and eddied around her ears, a river of tiny workers.

He tentatively put a finger into their path, and they eddied around that, too. He remembered the way the crossbow bolt had bounced off of her, and his anger rose hot at Hera's injustice. Perfection all right, sealed like a cask of fine mead, enforced by the Winds' capricious little cousins.

Well, they couldn't keep him away. Although, as he felt another surge of the beast, he was afraid it might be better if they could.

"Miranda," he called gently. "Wake up, Miranda. Show me your beautiful eyes."

Slowly, she focused on him. For an unguarded moment, a smile lit those eyes, illuminating what Ro wanted to believe was there. But the nameless emotion vanished in concern as she gazed at his shoulder and neck. "You're hurt."

"It's healing." The crossbow wound was already closed, he saw as he shifted his tunic aside. But his neck was still bleeding. "I think your brooch got me."

"Won't it heal, too?"

"Not for a while. Like the rest of your jewelry, your brooch was silver. Silver does weird things to me."

She touched her earrings where they dangled from holes in her lobes. "Should I take them off?"

He shook his head. "They suit you."

Their gazes locked. Soft, warm, infinitely precious, he wanted this woman for more than just primal urges. And he wanted no secrets between them.

"Eurus told me about your curse," he said.

She blinked and lowered her lids to stare at the laces on his chest, shuttering any fleeting emotion. Great move, he thought. His brother had always said he had the finesse of an ox. "I'm sorry about your family."

Slowly she raised her gaze, her expression unreadable. "Everyone dies, hero. More around me than others."

"I understand. I really do."

She studied him for another moment, then shook her head and looked away. "The East Wind is called Eurus," she said. "Is that who catches me?"

"This time." He reached down to pull her up to stand beside him. The movement brought her face close to his.

She met his gaze. "You didn't have to do that, you know."

"What? Sacrifice myself to save you? Help you to your feet?" He lowered his head. "Kiss you until your toes curled?"

Her gaze flickered to his mouth. "Either. All. I don't know."

"I think I'd be a poor hero if I didn't at least help a lady to her feet, don't you?"

A ghost of a smile flitted across her lips. Then she lowered her gaze to his chest again. She opened her mouth to speak, closed it, stepped away quickly, and searched both ends of the beach. With a brief glance at him, she started north.

Ro watched her, bemused. Not a speck of sand clung to that perfect form; not a single, shiny hair was out of place. But he had the distinct impression that she was completely mussed.

Picking up the blanket, Ro trotted to catch up with her. As he fell into step beside her, her arm brushed his, then again, as if she couldn't help but touch him. Feeling awkward but lighter in spirit than he had in years, Ro took her hand. She glanced up, startled, but left it there.

He focused on their path. Ahead, the beach spread silver in the moonlight for leagues, the cliffs beside them snaking inland and shrinking to the horizon. Poseidon had retreated from a centuries-old battle with the land here, leaving the wide, white sands isolated from the easy trail. The road the Amazons must take was to the tower's south, so they were safe on that score. Or they should be.

Shaking off the nagging feeling that this whole business felt odd or wrong in some way, he gathered his wits to focus on his task. He remembered a fishing boat lying on the beach halfway from his last camp to Miranda's tower, probably washed ashore during a storm. It had seemed seaworthy, although he hadn't checked as he'd passed. If it was, he might have a plan.

The thought pleased him.

Miranda glanced up, and ducked her head when she saw him smiling at her. "This is awful," she said. "I'm blushing. Must be the sea air."

"I don't think so."

She slanted him a sad look. "It has to be. After eight years of . . . well, I—I don't think I have any shame left."

A chill tickled his neck. Not knowing what had alerted him, he stiffened, glanced left, right, above. A glint of light on the cliffside caught his eye, but it was gone in a blink.

He sniffed the air. Salt, dead fish, sea smells only. He was on edge, he knew, because of unanswered questions—like the Amazon presence when he'd never heard of them turning mercenary. A warm breeze, a thread of Zephyr's former self, blew over their skin, sending her subtle fragrance to his sensitive nose, and he decided his Beast instincts must be working overtime. By the gods, she smelled like the Elysian Fields!

"I have a favor to ask," she said.

"Anything," he replied.

She hesitated. "There's something I've wanted to do for years, but I couldn't because . . . well, there wasn't anybody . . .

I mean, with men being the way they are around me. I'd like to do it now. If it's okay, I mean."

Amazing how fast he could go from being alert to danger to horny as Zeus. He shifted in discomfort. "All right."

"Really? Are you sure?"

He nodded—though he wasn't sure at all.

She gave him a shy smile. Then, eager as a child, she went on with a skip. "Okay, I hope I get this right."

Ro waited impatiently.

Miranda drew a deep breath, her breasts straining against her filmy gown.

He swallowed hard.

She cleared her throat. "Ready?"

He nodded again.

"Okay, here goes. A priest, a merchant, and a duck walk into a tavern. And the duck says to the owner . . ."

A long time later, Ro wiped the tears of laughter from his eyes.

"Wait! I have another one!"

"No more! I can't take it!" He coughed, chuckling, and shook his head. "I haven't laughed this hard in years. My ribs actually hurt."

"Then you tell one."

For several leagues, they had exchanged joke after joke. Some she'd told were so old he'd heard them in Phoenicia, some he'd never heard before, all she'd collected from eavesdropping on guards. Who'd have thought that the thing she'd missed second most was laughter? And who'd have thought it was something he'd missed, too?

"I don't know any more," he said finally.

"Me, either."

"Thank the gods."

That set them both off again, but their whoops slowed eventually, and she took his elbow. Between bouts of laughter—maybe to lessen the poignancy—they'd talked of their childhoods, of the curse that made him a wolf between moon's zenith and the first rays of the sun's light, and of hers that had made her so many men's prisoner.

He told her of his mother, whose only mistake had been to catch Zeus' roving eye, and how Hera's jealousy turned her into a wolf just before giving birth to his brother and him.

"I lost my mother, too, just after I was born," she told him. "And then my father and sisters . . ."

"I know." Ro squeezed her hand.

Their steps drifted closer. Hesitant, she touched his ribs. "Still hurt?"

"No, I told you I'm a fast healer."

She touched the brooch score on his neck, still sticky, then stole her arm around him. "Most of the time."

He lifted his arm, and as she snuggled beneath it, he smiled. He could almost believe they were two normal lovers walking on a moonlit beach. He wanted them to be. More than he'd ever thought possible, he wanted them to be normal. And lovers.

He stopped and turned her in his arms, searching her shining face. He didn't want this to end. Ever. "Miranda, I—I want you to know—"

"Shut up," she murmured. "Just kiss me."

She lifted her mouth to his, and he lost himself completely. Warmth, honey sweetness, a yearning that matched his own combined with a regret he didn't understand. Passion tempered with need and loneliness and the knowledge that it could somehow never be real fused them into one, joining their bodies, their souls, freezing time into a single, silver moment that would have to last them the rest of their lives.

"I have to tell you something," Miranda said against his mouth. She wasn't laughing anymore.

"Later," he said, and tried to deepen the kiss.

"No, it's important, and I . . . well . . . okay. In a minute." She sucked his lip into her mouth and swirled it with her tongue, stroking his leg with hers.

He wouldn't let it go too far.

He wouldn't let it.

He wouldn't.

The animal inside of him raged in response to urges as old as mankind. Her breasts pressed to him; he could feel her hardened nipples on his chest. Her slender body molded itself to him, moving with ease in his arms, as if she were a forgotten piece of him. She offered everything, and he wanted it.

No matter how he got it.

Ro broke away, breathing harshly into her hair, fighting for control. In the space between one thought and the next, he'd nearly lost himself to the Beast. He would not—would *not*—do this.

"What's wrong?" she asked from his shoulder.

"Nothing. Everything." He pulled away, pacing down the beach, trying to shake it off.

"Wait! What's the matter?"

He could hear her feet crunch against every grain of sand behind him, smell each element of her fragrance. His bones ached with wanting her, and with the metamorphosis that he was undergoing. Even as he thought it, he realized he couldn't even articulate his frustration because his animal-self had fogged over too much of his mind. He halted, clenching and unclenching his fists, reciting mathematics his friend Pythagoras had shown him, until he had blown some of the fog out of the way.

Miranda was smart enough to keep her distance, he saw as his mind cleared. With difficulty, he gave her a crooked smile. "What's the matter, you ask? You want it alphabetically, or in order of urgency?"

"I'm so sorry."

"It's not your fault. You didn't cause it—and you wouldn't be able to do a thing about it if I tried to make love to you and ended up disemboweling you." He uttered a harsh sound of frustration. "Once. Just once, I want to know what it's like to be a normal man."

A moment of silence passed, then Miranda said, "If you were a normal man, you wouldn't be able to touch me, much less make love to me, would you?"

They stared at each other. He'd known the reality of their

situation, but until now he hadn't truly felt its hopelessness. Only an arm's length separated them, but the distance yawned like a chasm.

Shutting down the heart he'd finally found, Ro shook himself like the wolf he was becoming and took his bearings. The moon was nearly to its zenith, the transformation a fiery ball curled inside of him, waiting to explode in its final, dramatic moments. They would have to hurry. "Come on," he said. "Over that promontory."

Ahead, a spit of piled rock jutted out from the cliff into the breakers. He took her hand and helped her scramble over the headland. Once there, he scanned the sand.

The small boat he'd remembered lay halfway up the beach, partially buried, surrounded by driftwood. "There," he said, pointing.

Miranda gave him a questioning look but said nothing, and they made their way to the boat. Ro took hold of the prow and pulled it from its internment to study the bottom. Wood seemed to be sound. He strained to push it into the water, then held it steady. It bobbed like a milkweed pod.

"It's a boat," said Miranda stupidly. She'd followed him into the water. It swirled around her without dampening an inch of skin or a stitch of gown. "Wh-where are we going?"

Ro saw wariness chase across her face, and maybe a bit of hope. She couldn't decide if he was as immune to her as she'd thought, or if he was up to something nefarious.

" 'We' aren't going anywhere." He dragged the boat back onto the beach and turned, meeting her gaze. "You are."

She stared at him in confusion. "I'm lost."

"You're going to get into this boat and sail away."

"Alone? Me?"

"You." Ro caressed her cheek. "I know how it feels, remember? I know how badly you want to be normal, how you want a real life, because I feel that way, too, every single day."

"You can have it," she whispered. *"We* can have it."

"Can we? What if it's not Zeus' blood that makes me immune? What if, when I'm not mid-change, I fall for your beautiful perfection like all the others?"

She hadn't thought of that. He could see it in her eyes; she suddenly equated him with Mogg, and she didn't like it.

Ro turned her to face the open sea, and west. "Look out there," he said. "Smell it."

A stray breeze blew inland, carrying the odor of far-off lands, making the fire inside him burn brighter, but differently. He forcibly calmed the Beast, the jittery emotions that swamped him, and felt Miranda relax beneath his hands.

"When I was a boy," he told her, "my uncle, who raised my brother and me, used to tell us wonderful stories of his travels. Out there, straight across the ocean, is a land so fertile and green it'll take your breath away—a place in a valley surrounded by seven hills. In that valley, far from these shores, the arm of Olympus is weak." He closed his eyes and breathed deeply of her scent, memorizing her. "You can be normal there."

"Don't you want me here, with you?" she asked.

His harsh laugh lacked any hint of amusement. "I want you more than the stars want the heavens, Miranda. But I want . . . no, I *need* to give you something you haven't had in eight years— a choice."

She made a sound and trembled beneath his hands. "What about you?"

"If, after you taste your freedom, you still want me, send word to my brother. I'll come. With your curse out of commission, it won't matter if it's my curse or Zeus' blood that's making me immune now. And at least we'll have the daylight hours, and the one night a month when there's no moon, that we can be together without worrying that I'll do you harm."

She frowned. "But won't your curse disappear, too, if you go to this valley of seven hills?"

He hesitated, but he couldn't lie to her. "No. I'm bound by blood forever. But you're bound only by Hera's will. You can escape."

She was silent for a long moment, lost in some secret place. "You would do that for me," she said.

"Of course."

She blinked back a spill of tears. "It wasn't supposed to happen this way," she whispered. "He said— The voice said—"

His senses came alert in a flash. "What are you talking about, Miranda?"

"He said you were a monster. He said—"

"Who said?" He grabbed her shoulders.

She gasped and slipped away, pushing him toward the boat. "Oh, gods! How long have we— You have to get out of here!"

Ro fought her as he tried to find the danger. But it was too late.

A crossbow bolt thudded into the boat, a hair's breadth from his thigh. The bolt's unusually long shaft, the fact that it had gone clean through the heavy wood, and the black iron tip told him who had fired the shot.

Miranda's eyes went wide, her expression wild.

He shoved the thought that she had known this would happen deep inside and pivoted to meet the threat.

"Well, well, if it isn't the Amazon contingent," he said with a feral smile. He surveyed eight well-armed women who were slowly fanning across the beach, four of them last seen at Miranda's tower. He edged between their phalanx and Miranda, his brain plotting an escape route even as the animal inside him snarled to be released. He didn't want to think of Miranda's possible part in this. He couldn't.

"Surrender peacefully," said the tallest, the warrior he had dubbed One, "and we might let you live, Beast."

Ro felt a growl build in his throat and swallowed it. "You can't hurt me, woman. Go back the way you came, and I might let *you* live."

"Ah, how the mighty set themselves up for a fall," she said, and with great show, pulled out a bolt that gleamed dully in the light of the high moon. "I think this levels the playing field, don't you?"

The bolt was sheathed in pure silver.

"Clever," Ro rumbled, but he knew now what was going on—or thought he did. It was all connected: the Winds' attack, the Amazons, the letter from his brother begging for Miranda's rescue, even Miranda's betrayal. But how to escape the grand plan he suspected was in motion—that was another story. "Miranda, get into the boat."

"They'll kill you," she hissed. "They can't hurt *me*."

"Maybe, maybe not. Silver affects both of us, I think. But they don't really want to hurt you." He met her gaze squarely. "Do they, Miranda?"

She gaped, but said nothing.

Ro shoved her into the boat as the attack began.

Three fighters had gotten close enough for Ro to smell their scent over the sea bracken they had worn to mask it, one swinging a grappling hook, another a net. Ro bared his long teeth and swung to his left, away from them. As he'd thought, the three were diversions. He dodged an arrow that hit the sand, dropped to all fours to roll the legs out from under an attacker, then pounced on a shorter, mace-wielding woman, knocking her unconscious with a single blow.

A warrior headed toward him, and he leaped into the air, landing on her with both knees, shoving her into the sand. He growled a warning to the others as he backed toward the boat, holding them off as he kept a wary eye on One's silver bolt. He could feel the blood lust, but he had it in hand. Even this close to change, he could control it.

They regrouped. Six Amazons still stood, watching, waiting. They massed for a second assault. He tensed.

"Stop!"

The command startled them all. Before he could halt her, Miranda broke cover, running toward the women.

His distraction was all the Amazons needed. A pair of nets settled over him like a double shroud.

"No one was supposed to get hurt!" Miranda shouted. "Damn it, stop! Hey! What are you doing?"

Ro didn't battle the heavy rope, or the weights that held it to him, except to shift his head to look through it. The change had paused, like the calm inside one of Notus' hurricanes, but the pause wouldn't last long. For everyone's sake, he had to play this very carefully.

"Let her go," he said, his voice the Beast's rough silk. "She's done nothing to you, Amazon, but bring me here."

The curtain of bodies around him parted, revealing One next to a circle of spears surrounding Miranda.

A cage! They had put her in another cage!

Gritting his teeth, he fought his fury. "I said, let her go. She wasn't part of your deal. . . . Or was she?"

Miranda turned, startled, and One gave him a shaky smile. "Deal?" she said. "What makes you think there was a deal?"

"A silver weapon that you didn't use in the tower." He nodded toward one of the fallen. "And grappling hooks for the descent on the cliff. You had this planned a long time ago. I'm actually impressed. No one's ever managed to defeat me so handily." He smiled inwardly as One's smile changed to a smirk. "Does my brother even know she exists?"

One shook her head and swaggered toward him, her crossbow lowered. "Your brother is, by his last letter, knee-deep in a new kind of wheat. Boring stuff."

"Not to a starving kingdom." He had to keep One talking, and his brother's agricultural achievements wouldn't do it. As he spoke, he used a new-grown claw to slice through the bonds at his feet. "Did you plant the boat, too, as an ambush point?"

"No. That was . . . the Fates, perhaps. It doesn't matter. You were moving so slowly, a snail could have caught you."

Ro rumbled a growl, but restrained himself. "So," he went on as he switched to the rope by his ankle, "I hadn't heard that any of your other sisters had made alliances with Hera's minions. What finally pushed you over?"

One paused. "I don't know what you're talking about."

The women around her glanced at each other, uneasy, and Ro smiled to himself. "Sure you do." He felt a pop of hemp and moved his claw up to the next section of rope. "Let's see. I'll bet it went something like this—'You take care of him for me, and you get to keep Miranda.' And what self-respecting Amazon wouldn't want a weapon that would turn men into drooling idiots? Besides"—another strand gave way—"who could resist that little voice whispering in your ear night after night."

One's expression went completely blank. She hadn't really believed he knew it all, until then. And until the air beside One began to coalesce, to form into a familiar shape, Ro hadn't been sure, either.

"You think you're so smart," sneered Zephyr as he formed. "But you aren't. As soon as the moon hits the top of its arc, I'm going to kill you."

"Don't you mean *she'll* kill me? Face it. You couldn't kill me if your existence depended upon it."

Zephyr snarled and wrapped his pansy blue body with mist. "I can't tell you what I went through, who I had to bribe, to find out what it takes to kill you, wolf-boy. But it'll be worth the trouble. On the night of the full moon, at the moment of transformation, somebody puts a silver bolt through your heart, and you're history."

"And all because of one teensy defeat at Thrace?" Ro frowned in mock confusion. "Or was it the other sixteen defeats before that one?"

"Don't push me, freak."

"Or what? You'll call big sister Notus to save your sorry ass?" Ro gave an exaggerated gasp. "Oops, that's right. She's a giant snowball."

Zephyr burned purple with fury. "I'll make it hurt. I'll tell her to start cutting on you now. A few preliminary jabs ought to take you down a few pegs."

Ro heard Miranda cry out, and he squashed the instinct to look at her. Fought hard against the need to go to her, to comfort and protect her. He needed his wits, as well as strength, to get them out of this. And as the moon came to within a notch of its zenith, those wits were going fast. He needed to push Zephyr to action, to escape the net, and get to One before she shot him. *And* he needed to keep Miranda out of the line of fire.

"What's the matter, monster?" Zephyr asked. "No last words for your lady-love?"

"Who? *Her?* You must be joking." Ro laughed, ignoring Miranda's audible whimper, hoping for her forgiveness. "What, you thought because I kissed her . . . ?" He narrowed his gaze on Zephyr's angry shape. Two man-lengths separated them, maybe less. "You were using her, weren't you, and not only to lead me here. You thought I'd fall in love and it would give me an added measure of pain to think she'd betrayed me."

Ro sighed, at the same time he sawed through the final bond. "Sorry to disappoint you, Zephyr. But I don't care. Miranda is nothing but a selfish, vain female who wouldn't know love if it bit her in the face. I mean, she's a great kisser and everything, but what would I want with someone like her?" He tsked, shaking his head.

"You love her," Zephyr ground out. "I saw it. I know it. I *planned* it."

"As usual, Zephyr, you should've run to Boreas to do your thinking for you. Don't you see?" Ro poised, gathering his considerable strength, spacing his words deliberately. "Even if you kill me, I've . . . won . . . *again.*"

With a roar that equaled his sister's, Zephyr lunged. Ro leaped to his feet with the net in his arms and charged forward, prepared to meet Zephyr head-on, then dive straight for One—and the silver bolt.

But he'd underestimated Zephyr's hatred. Instead of simple resistance, he met a solid wall of wind and sand that stopped him cold, then tossed him into the spears and on, up the beach. He lost hold of the net as his body plowed a furrow in the sand.

He'd hurt his opponent, he was certain. But when he heard Zephyr's evil laugh high above, and felt the horrible heat of transformation blossom in his gut, he knew that he had only heartbeats before Miranda and he would both be lost. He had to get the bolt.

With a howling battle cry, Ro sprang up and started running. Zephyr whirled toward him. One lifted her crossbow, and Ro tensed his powerful muscles for a leap to cover the distance between them. Zephyr dropped to the center. One narrowed her sight and took aim.

And Miranda came out of nowhere.

Ro saw her leap between him and the bolt, saw Zephyr veer to try to avoid her, heard the *thwack* of the crossbow string—and the angry hiss as hot Zephyr hit the cold ocean and died. And as Miranda flung herself into his arms—aided apparently by an accidental, and powerful, shove from Zephyr—he believed for an instant that, somehow, the Fates had spared her.

But when his arms came around her, he knew the truth. It hadn't been Zephyr propelling her into his embrace. The short piece of the long Amazon bolt sticking out of her back told the story quite well.

"I hate it . . . when that happens," she said with a wheezing laugh.

Ro said nothing. He couldn't. Pain seared through his body from the point where the bolt had pierced his chest, joining them—together in death as they had wanted to be in life. He had failed.

His knees buckled, and he sank to the sand, hugging her precious body against him, cradling her head to his throat. She folded her legs, too, moaning at the movement, but she held him as tightly as he held her. The heavens seemed to whirl about them, crackling with fire, but he couldn't see it through the tears that clawed at his lids and fell down his cheeks.

She drew her head back, enough to see them. "Don't," she said weakly, as moisture pooled in her glorious green eyes. "Please don't."

"Why did you do it?" he asked, his voice harsh.

"To prove you right about silver?"

"Oh, Miranda," he groaned. "You were trying to save me. And after all the things I said— I didn't mean them."

"You should have," she whispered. "They were true. Yes," she went on when he shook his head, "I'm selfish and vain. He promised me . . . But I knew, don't you see? Or at least, I should have. I . . . I should have known he wouldn't end my curse. I should . . . have known . . . I'm . . . the real Beast . . . not you . . . never you."

She moved her hands convulsively on his back, as if she feared falling. Ro sucked in a pained breath. She gave a cry of horror as her fingers found the point of the long shaft and she realized that it connected them like fish on a spit. The silver had done its worst. To both of them.

She rolled her head from side to side, tears spilling down her cheeks. "I'm sorry," she moaned. "I'm so sorry."

"I'm not," he told her, wishing he had the strength to say all that was in his heart—how the brief time they had spent together had been everything to him, how the emotions he'd tamped down for so long had burst from him in her presence, not from the Beast's heart, but from his own soul. But he couldn't say the words through the pain or the change or the hot, dry wind that was suddenly howling around them.

Her mouth worked. "I love you," she said quite clearly. Then, suddenly, she slumped in his arms and closed her eyes.

And Ro, knowing that he'd succeeded in at least one thing, screamed his grief and fury to the night sky.

Because the moon had just now hit its zenith. The Amazon had fired early. And only one of them would die.

Ro awoke to the chill and gray light of Eos, the dawn. Curled on his side, he lay disoriented for the space of a heartbeat; then, it all came rushing back. He sprang to his knees, grabbed first at the sand, then at his chest, but he found no Miranda, no bolt, and no wound.

Throwing his head back, he let out a very human howl. "I didn't get to tell her that I loved her!" he shouted to Zeus. "You couldn't even give me that, damn you!"

His voice echoed off the cliffs, washing away in the soft sound of the sea.

"Boy, did you wake up on the wrong side of the beach."

The sound of a woman's voice brought him whirling on the sand, hands ready to tear apart an Amazon. Any Amazon. At least one of them was going to pay for Miranda's death.

But the woman who stood watching him was not an Amazon. Brunette and tall, she stood facing him, her hair tangled and dripping sea water, her features smudged and blotchy from the sand and salt. Her eyes, however, were a clear, sparkling green.

"Is this grouchy morning routine something I should plan for in the future?" she asked. "Or is it a one-time-only deal?"

Ro just stared.

She huffed. "Men. You die, you spend the night on the beach, rig a sail or two, and they forget you." Despite the mock indignation, uncertainty flickered in her eyes.

"Miranda?" Ro whispered, and when she smiled, it was like the sun had bloomed inside his chest.

He scrambled to his feet and swept her into his arms. "I love you," he said over and over. "I love you."

"I love you, too." She kissed him enthusiastically for a few bright moments. "I really do."

Ro pulled back and searched her frantically for a wound.

"Nothing there," she said. "Or on you. I checked."

"I don't understand. We— You—"

"Look, hero, everybody from last night is gone. You and I are whole, and, more importantly, not dead. I even seem to have gotten rid of a nasty curse. So," she continued with a hot sigh in his ear, "since we're in this rather remarkable position, does it really matter if we understand it?"

He shook his head and held her again, burying his face in her salty hair, drinking in the scent of her, the feel and taste of her. She was right. For now, this was enough. "You're a mess," he whispered into her hair.

"I know. Isn't it wonderful?"

"By the gods, it's the most wonderful thing I've ever seen."

He drew back to kiss her again, but he hesitated as the first fiery rays of light burst over the cliff behind them, coloring the boat red and orange and glittering over the ocean.

As realization struck, Ro felt himself go weak. "Is it dawn?" he asked quietly. "Just now?"

"Yes."

"When did you awaken?"

"I don't know. A while ago."

"And was I a wolf?"

Miranda started to answer, then raised startled eyes to his. "You were a man," she whispered. "Didn't you tell me you would stay a wolf until dawn's first light?"

He nodded, glancing around as the wind blew warm from the sea. From the west.

A weapon. He needed a weapon.

"But that means your curse is broken, too!" she cried.

"It also means that we're in trouble." He grabbed a piece of driftwood and turned to find her frowning. "Wind is reborn every day at dawn, ar.d if Zephyr's still insane, and I don't have the power of the Beast—"

"Oh, no," she said, and turned her frightened face into the wind—the West Wind—as it gathered force and swept into shore in a pansy blue swirl of mist.

Ro raised his club. The form spun, amorphous. Ro stared at it; then, as it took shape, he dropped his arm. His jaw quickly followed.

"Well? What are you staring at?" asked Eurus, her chin high. "Haven't you ever seen a dress before?"

Ro blinked, then blinked again. Eurus stood before him, sheathed in a glowing gown of pale blue flower petals, with hair the color of the rising sun pinned neatly in place by white rose buds. Gone was the leather and the kohl eyes. In their place was a vision. "You look . . . beautiful."

Eurus smiled self-consciously, and twitched at her dress. "Yeah? It's not too much?"

"I'd say it was perfect," said Miranda. "And I should know."

"You can see her?" Ro asked in surprise.

"Sure she can," said Eurus. "It was really quite a piece of chemistry, that episode last night. See, Hera's curses can't occupy the same space, so when the silver joined your hearts—" She stopped and pointed at the driftwood that Ro still held at the ready. "You're not going to use that, are you? You know that I didn't have anything to do with Zephyr's stupid scheme. Don't you?"

Ro looked at the forgotten club, then tossed it back onto the beach. "I do know. I heard you, there at the end, didn't I? You routed the Amazons."

She grinned. "Didn't have to. They turned on that bitch leader when they found out about the deal she made with Zephyr, which, to them, was just as bad as if she'd been in cohoots with Hera herself. You know how Amazons are about Hera. I just took 'em home. And now Zephyr's imprisoned for about a thousand years, and Zeus was so impressed with my Egyptian campaign, I get Zeph's old job. Cool, huh? The tropics."

"The bolt didn't connect our hearts," said Miranda suddenly.

"Oh, but it did," said Eurus. "Inside, where it really counts." When they seemed confused, she rolled her eyes. "Look, I'll pulverize the first one who laughs, but it's very simple. You two have something my brother will never understand in a million years, something that even Hera's twisted power can't squash, something that lets you into each other's souls and allows you to see the Wind. Something sacred. You have love. *True* love. Get it?"

Ro got it.

He and Miranda exchanged warm glances. "I don't feel like laughing," he said. "Do you?"

"No." She positively glowed. "But I do feel like going for a sail."

"Oh? To where?"

"How about those seven hills you talked about? The thought of no gods is appealing, even without a curse to escape."

Ro smiled. "We'll build an empire."

"I'd settle for a farm. With you."

"And my brother and his family. I wouldn't feel right without him around."

They climbed into the boat and settled onto the only seat, side by side. Ro held Miranda close, noticing the way the sunlight sparkled in her eyes. But it was of moonlight he was thinking. He would see the moon rise over her, as it had last night, but he would never again have to fear his response to the alluring vision of her bathed in the ethereal glow. For the first time in his life, he looked forward to the night.

He smiled at the thought as Eurus filled the boat's sail with a steady, gentle push.

"Seven hills," Miranda said, snuggling into the crook of his arm. "Does this fabulous place have a name?"

"My uncle named it after me," he replied, his heart bursting.

She looked puzzled. "Ro?"

He shook his head. "Romulus."

Miranda sighed happily. "Then, Romulus, show me your paradise."

"With pleasure, my love."

"By the way, this brother of yours. What did you say his name is . . . ?"

Showdown

by

Patricia Potter

Author's Note

Among heroes, my favorites have never been the men who always do the right thing. I'm fascinated instead by the man who rises reluctantly to meet a challenge. In his role as Paden in *Silverado,* Kevin Kline epitomizes that reluctant hero. I suspect that is why I love westerns as I do: so many people—ordinary people—became reluctant heroes just to survive.

Texas, 1875
4 P.M., Thursday Afternoon

Jared Walker's shadow lengthened on the dusty Texas street. The fingers of his right hand tingled. They seemed to have a will of their own, those fingers, and they itched to move toward the Colt.

Live or die. Kill or be killed. Which was it going to be?

He stood motionless in the main street of New Hope, waiting for the man some sixty feet away to reach for his gun. God knew, there had been enough like him.

How many times had he stood like this, waiting for another man to make the first move? How many bodies had he left for the undertaker? He had tried to forget the faces, each one contorted in pain or surprise as his bullet found its mark, but the gallery that he carried in his head never closed—not even in his sleep.

The face of his present challenger was young. He looked little more than a boy, but Jared had learned long ago that men like him, men with boyish faces and a longing for immortality, were far more dangerous than older, wiser men. And this man, Billy Joe Carter, had more reason than most to want to kill him.

He hadn't wanted to kill again, ever, and if it were only his own life he was risking, he wouldn't. But other lives were at stake. The lives of people he had called friends and neighbors for the past two years. He wouldn't abandon those people now, despite that they had all abandoned him.

Even Mary Beth.

Was she watching? He tried not to look at the stores lining the street, tried not to hunt for that special face he knew he wouldn't see. In the past forty-eight hours, their love had been tested—and found wanting. No, he might look for Mary Beth, but he wouldn't find her. And in the time it took him to accomplish his futile search, Billy Joe Carter would kill him. Not that it seemed to matter.

Jared shifted on his feet and tried to concentrate. The silence surrounding him was overwhelming. It was late afternoon, yet stores were closed, windows shuttered. Horses had been removed from the street where they might wind up in the line of fire. It was as if the world had stopped, and he and young Carter were the only two survivors.

Jared knew, though, that another man waited in the shadows, ready to take Carter's place. If he wanted to survive this challenge, two men had to die. He wasn't being given a choice. But then, he'd never been given one.

Carter rocked on the balls of his feet, and Jared felt his fingers flex again. Damn those fingers, so ready to kill. He'd spent ten years honing that killer's instinct, and two years of raising cattle didn't seem to have dulled his edge.

He should have known better. He should have known he could never escape the stench of death. He should have known he could never escape Tom Garrett, the man he'd been.

There is always a choice, Mary Beth had said as tears glinted in her blue eyes. He didn't believe it, though. The only time he'd been given any real choice was twelve years ago; the path he'd chosen then had determined all roads he'd taken since. And it seemed that all roads were going to end here, in New Hope, with Billy Joe Carter facing him from the opposite end of the dusty street.

He had heard that your life flashed across your mind when you knew you were about to die. It had never happened to him, not in any of the many times he had exchanged gunfire with strangers. Yet as he stood there, the hot Texas sun blasting his back, soaking his shirt, waiting for Carter to make his move, in his mind's eye Jared saw every one of the past twelve years in slow, excruciating detail. . . .

* * *

He was eighteen. A Kansas farm kid who could shoot a rabbit from a thousand yards away. His pa was proud of his skill. He'd won every turkey shoot in west Kansas. At the last one, they had given him a new and rare Henry repeating rifle. He had won a pistol, too, in a private contest that his pa didn't know about. A rifle for killing game was one thing; a pistol, good mostly for killing men, was another.

His pa was a Quaker, a pacifist caught in a war that had neither use nor sympathy for those who refused to take sides. Quakers didn't believe in killing—ever. But Tom Garrett knew he was good with a gun, any kind of gun, and he secretly admired the legendary bad men. He'd been practicing his quick draw on the prairie, far away from his pa's gentle eyes. He figured he could draw as fast as anyone alive.

He wanted to test his skills. He wanted to join the army and fight the Rebs. But his mother was sick, and his sister was only ten, and his pa couldn't handle the farm alone. So here he was—grudgingly—feeding chickens and milking cows, with rebellion frothing inside him.

In fact, he was driving in some milk cows when the gunshots rang out, blasting loudly across the open prairie. He spurred his horse toward the farmhouse and spied four riders milling about, tearing down fences, driving out his father's gelding and the old mare. Tom looked for his father, his mother, but didn't see them.

He did see one of the raiders fling a torch at his family's neat little house.

Without hesitation, he took his treasured rifle from its scabbard. His father thought he carried it for hunting, and he did. But knowing that "Bloody Kansas" had come by its name honestly, he also carried it as protection against human dangers. It seemed every thief and killer was using the war as an excuse to rob and loot and kill: the Jayhawkers and Red Legs, different sides of the same coin.

He didn't care who the men were as he rode hard toward the house. None of the raiders saw him approach. They were far too busy destroying what his father had spent fifteen years building. When they turned, it was too late. Too late for them. His fingers closed around the trigger again and again, not stopping until three of the four lay on the ground, and the fourth—a sorry excuse for a lookout who couldn't be more than fourteen or fifteen—was hightailing it across the fields.

Tom started to aim, then stopped and lowered the rifle. He couldn't shoot a child. Besides, he had to see to his family. Though, in his heart, he knew in what state he would find them . . .

4:02 P.M.

Little had he known, Jared thought, when he lowered the rifle and allowed that fourth raider to escape, that he'd made a choice that would dog his heels all of his adult life and, finally, bring him to this: a showdown with the kid he'd let ride away.

Was it his imagination or was his shadow lengthening? Only a minute or two had passed since he had walked into the street, yet the shadow loomed so large. Or was he seeing the shadow of the man he'd once been, the man he had tried to bury, along with his reputation? The man whose fingers inched toward the Colt in its holster.

Jared's gaze held steady on the man opposite him. He hadn't always known the names of the men who had tried to best him. He knew this one, though. Billy Joe Carter, youngest brother of the men who had murdered his family. The men who he, in turn, had killed. Carter still didn't look old enough to be living for revenge. He should be courting a girl, building a future, not throwing his future away for the chance to avenge his brothers.

Jared studied him closely, saw the determination, fueled by hatred, radiating from him. He'd been determined enough to force this showdown that he'd threatened to burn the town if his quarry wouldn't face him. Jared didn't doubt that Carter and the cousins he'd brought with him could do it, yet he might have called the man's bluff—except that Carter had also threatened Mary Beth. That was a risk he wasn't about to take.

Maybe Carter was bluffing. Then again, maybe he wasn't. Either way, the message was clear: Carter wouldn't accept his refusal to fight. He wanted revenge. He wanted to be the man who killed Tom Garrett. And he'd wanted a town full of people to see it. Nor was there any law to stop him; New Hope was too isolated, too peaceful, to need a sheriff.

And so here he stood, Jared thought, left once more with no choice but to kill or be killed. That's the way it had always been, and that's the way it was—no matter what Mary Beth thought.

This time was different, though, he admitted. This time, he was going to lose his life, no matter the outcome of the gun fight. Either Carter would kill him in fact, or he would kill Carter, and at the moment he did, he'd lose his home, his friends, and the woman he loved; if Billy Joe Carter dropped to the street, dead, Jared Walker would die, too—and Tom Garrett, gunslinger, would be resurrected.

Carter moved a couple of steps to the right in a clear effort to gain a better position, one that did not make him face straight into the sun. Jared knew the problem Carter was having. He always made sure that his opponent would have to squint into the sun. That's what it was all about, wasn't it? Survival.

Sweat trickled down Jared's back. *Concentrate. Don't think about yesterday. Or tomorrow. There's only now, and the slightest mistake, the barest hesitation, will wipe away any hope of there being any tomorrows.*

Trouble was, he wasn't sure he wanted any more tomorrows. Was sure he did not if they were only going to be like all the yesterdays. . . .

He buried his family that same evening: his father, whose body he'd found sprawled next to the corral; his mother, who had been lying inside the front door, her hand outstretched, even in death, in gentle entreaty; his sister, for whom he'd had to search before he'd found her huddled behind the wood pile. At first, he'd thought she was simply hiding, because her eyes were open, looking at him; then he'd realized those soft brown eyes were frozen forever in a look of lifeless horror.

He buried them all, then said a prayer over the graves. But no amount of praying could erase the sorrow or rage he felt. Or the guilt. He had wanted to be free—free of the farm he didn't want, free to lead his own life. Well, he was free, all right. And it struck him as bitterly ironic that the God he'd been taught to believe was gentle and peace-loving had liberated him in such a hideous, violent fashion.

In the days that followed, he came to see that acts such as his family's murders weren't acts of God but of the devil. He also came to understand that he was by no means free. Thanks to the boy he'd let escape, men started coming after him, Carters by name, relations of the young men he'd caught raiding his home. In order to survive, Tom met the challenges—and won. Reluctantly, and with no planning on his part, he earned a reputation that constantly attracted would-be gunmen whose names weren't Carter. He met those challenges, too, one after another. Somewhere along the line, he became one of those hard-eyed gunmen he'd so foolishly admired. He became a killer, the bearer of the mark of Cain.

For ten years the killing never stopped; he never had a moment's peace or any sanctuary. It seemed that someone was waiting for him in every town. And they seemed to get younger every year. He, on the other hand, grew older and, eventually, weary, too weary to care whether or not he won.

It was inevitable that sooner or later he would make a mistake.

He was in Missouri when it happened. It was late. He'd had a good night at poker, and his pockets were full of money for once. He was walking back to the hotel, thinking about what he would buy with the money. He needed a new saddle, and he'd seen a hat he liked that day in a shop window. He was thinking about Molly, the pretty saloon girl who had caught his eye that night, and whether or not to ask her to have dinner with him the following evening, when a man stepped in front of him, out of a dark alley.

Startled, Tom cursed himself for letting his mind wander. And in that instant, he let his gaze fall from the man's eyes to his hand, hovering over his gun. He didn't think anyone was faster on the draw than he was, but when he saw the man's hand move, he realized with vivid clarity that he was wrong. Though he went for his own gun at the very instant the stranger went for his, Tom pulled the trigger of his Colt a fraction too late—at the same moment he felt a burning fire rip through his chest.

He fell to the boardwalk along with the man he'd still managed to kill, blinding pain wiping all thoughts but one from his mind: he was dying.

He didn't die, though the town doc told him several days later that he had come damn close, as close as any man could and still live. He must have an angel on his shoulder, the doc continued—or the devil, the sheriff retorted. Jared agreed with the sheriff.

He learned a lesson, though, from that night in Missouri. Never—*ever*—take your eyes off your opponent's eyes. Not if you wanted to live. The eyes revealed the soul, and something indefinable always flickered through them just before a man reached for his gun.

In the years that followed, he learned other lessons, too, all of them about survival. He wanted to stop learning them. He wanted to lead a normal life. To settle down, buy a farm, or maybe a ranch, and become a respected member of some nice community. He tried his damnedest to leave his reputation behind, moved constantly in search of a place where no one knew him, accepting any job, no matter how menial. But someone always found him; someone always forced him into a showdown.

Then he would have to move on.

4:03 P.M.

How long had he been standing here, waiting? Three minutes? Maybe four? It seemed like a lifetime. The sun had not moved, nor had his shadow. The door fronts were still closed, the windows still curtained or shuttered.

Regret, deep and heavy, washed over him. He had never felt so alone, even in a life that was, by necessity, a solitary one. He knew the magnitude of his loneliness came from having known what it felt like to belong. Before New Hope, he'd not had that since childhood, so he hadn't realized how lonely he was. But for the past two years, he'd been given a glimpse of heaven. Having it snatched away was more than he could stand.

Still, though he was alone, Jared could feel a hundred pairs of eyes on him: the townsfolk of New Hope, watching the drama taking place on their main street. Were they curious to see the infamous Tom Garrett in action? Were they hoping he'd finally get his just rewards? Was Mary Beth among them?

A sharp crack split the tense silence, but Jared's gaze never left his opponent's face. Carter's gaze darted toward the direction of the sound—a window slamming shut somewhere to the left. Jared knew he could take advantage of Carter's distraction. He could draw. He could kill. Again.

His hand stayed at his side. Carter's gaze darted back to meet his, then dropped for an instant to his Colt, and Jared figured Carter was wondering why he had not taken advantage of his opponent's inattention. The answer was simple: his hand would not be the first to move. It never was. The only time he'd made the first move had been that day in Kansas.

Tom's chance to escape the gunslinger's life forced upon him came almost ten years after his family's death. He was caught in an ambush in Montana, where he had gone searching for peace only to wind up enveloped in a range war.

He was working as a horse wrangler for a big rancher when fighting broke out. An imported gunfighter, hired by his boss's competition, recognized him and jumped to all the wrong conclusions, assuming Tom Garrett was also a hired gun.

The ambush occurred as he was taking horses to an army post. The impact of a rifle bullet hitting his shoulder knocked him from his horse, and when he fell, he hit his head and lost consciousness. He awoke well after dark, alone; his mount was gone, as were the horses the army had purchased. His gun was gone, too, and so were his boots. He reached inside his shirt and felt a small measure of relief upon discovering that his money, a modest but not insignificant sum saved over the years, was still there.

His shoulder hurt like all the furies in hell, but he managed to get to his feet and start walking. Dawn came, then noon. He couldn't go on. It felt like iron had been welded to his feet, and taking even another step seemed an impossible effort. Blood trickled from his shoulder, and he knew he'd lost too much of it. He sank to the ground, his head bowed, his eyes unable to focus.

He remained there, unaware of time passing, fading in and out of consciousness, until the indignant braying of a mule brought him partly out of his stupor. He felt a weathered hand on his face and warm water running down his throat.

The prospector who found him took him to his cabin alongside a stream and, over the course of the next several weeks, nursed him back to health. The old man did him an even greater service, though, inexplicably and for no apparent reason. With a combination of bafflement and wonder, Tom listened to his benefactor relate—with considerable glee—how he'd gone into town and told everyone he had found a dead man on the plain. Buried him, he had, but not before he'd realized the dead man fit the description of that gunfighter, Tom Garrett.

Tom Garrett died that day. And, in that prospector's little shack, Jared Walker was born. With deep gratitude, he gave half of his money to the old prospector; then he headed south, where no one knew him. Where he could start a new life.

Eventually, he wandered into New Hope, a tiny town in southwest Texas. The name alone attracted him. He approached the small bank—the only bank in town—and found William Dale, the owner. Dale answered his questions and asked some of his own. Seemingly satisfied with the answers, Dale gave him a long, searching look, then told him of a property, a neglected ranch, available for the cost of taxes. The owner was dead, and no one had the money or cowhands to take it on.

Money, Dale explained, was tight in New Hope, which was

well off the route of the great cattle drives. Its one saloon was small, and friendly poker games were the only gaming. The hotel was nothing more than a boardinghouse, the blacksmith was idle more often than not, and the bank was barely surviving. There was little to attract strangers.

That suited Jared just fine. He paid the taxes on the property, bought a few head of cattle, and moved into the neglected ranch house. For months, he worked from sunrise often until well after the moon had risen. The leaking cabin was cleaned and expanded, the fences repaired. When neighbors realized he was in New Hope to stay, they held a barn raising for him, and every family within fifty miles attended.

Astounded by the effort everyone made on his behalf, Jared looked for a way to repay his new neighbors. The chance came when he heard three women talking at the general store about how hard it was going to be for the town to hire a schoolteacher because they had no schoolhouse. After all, they said, what teacher worth her salt would want to come live in a town that couldn't be bothered to build a school? That night, he visited Bill Dale and several other men, getting them to agree to the construction. Then he organized the event, and when the time came, he was there with hammer and saw, ready to build.

Jared basked in the glow of having neighbors and of working his own small ranch. He reveled in the hard work and sore muscles and nights he actually slept through until dawn without being awakened by the nightmares that had plagued him for years: haunting images of dead men's faces.

In addition to rebuilding his own ranch, he worked for other ranchers in return for heifers, increasing his herd little by little until he felt legitimate enough to join the cattlemen's association. It wasn't much, the association, but it gave him a sense of belonging he had not felt since a boy.

His dreams had finally come true. All those dreams he'd once thought lost forever. Suddenly, for the first time in years, he had hope. And as time passed, that hope grew. It grew to overshadow the nagging feeling that all was going too well and that it couldn't last. The feeling that, someday, he would have to pay for his bloody past. . . .

4:04 P.M.

Pay day had arrived.

Was it fate, coincidence? Or justice? Jared didn't know.

He had been in the saloon, talking to Bill Dale, the banker, when a stranger stopped in for a drink. Jared hadn't recognized the man, but it seemed the man knew his face—and he was one of Billy Joe Carter's many cousins. He must have gone straight to Billy Joe with the news that his longtime quarry wasn't dead after all but alive and well and living in New Hope.

Not for long, Jared thought. Any minute now, he'd either be heading out to his ranch to pack a saddlebag and leave—or he'd be dead.

The sound of a wagon rumbling down the dusty street behind him broke the silence of the afternoon. Jared heard the creaking wheels, the hoofbeats against dirt, the first sound of movement on the street since the good citizens of New Hope had skittered inside their stores and houses like nervous ants whose hill had been kicked over.

His neighbors. His friends. Bile settled heavily in the pit of his stomach. He should have known that a gunman had no friends, could *never* have them. Nor could he have love.

Carter moved again, still trying to find a place where he wasn't blinded by the sun, probably also trying to gain some kind of mental advantage by dragging it out like this. Jared figured the young gunman knew by now that he was not going to draw first. Hell, Carter knew damned well that he didn't want to draw at all, that he had done his best to avoid this.

Jared took a step . . . two steps . . . to the right, careful to keep the sun at his back. Careful, too, not to look toward the general store. Mary Beth's store. She lived in the rooms above it, and he envisioned her there, huddling behind the curtain of her parlor window with Jonny, her son.

Every word she had said to Jared two days ago still burned his heart, live coals imbedded in his soul. Given a choice, he'd rather take a bullet. But then, he hadn't been given a choice.

Mary Beth, however, didn't see it that way.

He was attracted to Mary Beth the instant he saw her.

He'd been living at his new, if rundown, ranch for three days, scraping by with what food he had packed in his saddlebags, making plans and lists of things he'd need. Lists in hand, he'd ridden into town and gone directly to the general store.

A woman in a blue dress with the most startling blue eyes he had ever seen looked up from a ledger book lying on the counter. A curl fell from her mass of auburn hair that was pulled back and wound into a knot. Her face was both delicate and strong, and she had a dash of flour on her cheek that drew his gaze.

When she smiled at him, her cheeks dimpling and the skin around her vivid blue eyes crinkling, Jared felt as if the skies had opened up and the sun was shining straight into his heart. He realized with a sudden start of amazement that he was smiling, too. God only knew when he'd last smiled.

"You're Jared Walker," she said.

He just stared at her, feeling like a besotted eight-year-old boy.

"News travels fast in New Hope," she said in a husky voice full of warmth. "There's just too little of it."

He had never felt tongue-tied with a woman, but he'd been struck stone silent simply by looking at her. His gaze fell to her fingers, seeking out a ring. To his great disappointment, she was wearing one.

"Do you have any boys?"

The question didn't come from the woman but from a pint-size boy whose face appeared above the edge of the counter, beside her. He, too, had a head full of auburn hair, but it was far less tidy than his mother's. She had to be the boy's mother, Jared reckoned.

"No," he said.

"Girls?" It was obviously second choice.

Jared shook his head.

"A dog?" the boy kept trying.

Jared's smile broadened to a grin. The boy had such a hopeful look on his face.

"I'm afraid not."

"I have some puppies."

The woman laughed. "He's been trying to find homes for those pups for the past three weeks. This is my son, Jonny. Jonny, this is Mr. Walker."

"Hi, Mr. Walker," the boy said. "What about the puppy?"

The idea of a dog suddenly became very appealing. He hadn't had a dog since . . . well, since he was Jonny's age.

He grinned. "You may have a sale," he said.

"They're *free*," Jonny put in breathlessly.

"That's about the right price," Jared replied, his gaze going back to the boy's mother. He wondered where her husband was.

"The only thing that really matters to either Jonny or me is that the puppies get good homes," the woman broke in. "Would your wife want a puppy?"

"No wife," he said shortly. "There's no one but me."

She hesitated for a moment, searching his face, and he understood he was being weighed.

"I like animals," he said, surprised by his self-defense. He never felt the need to defend himself, or to gain anyone's approval. At least, he hadn't felt either need until that moment.

She nodded. "I'm sorry. I didn't introduce myself. I'm Mary Beth Reynolds. I own the store. If you need credit, just say so."

"Your husband?" The question popped out, startling him as much—maybe more—as it clearly startled her.

"My pa died three years ago," the boy said. "Horse threw him."

Jared looked back at Mary Beth, saw a brief shadow cross her face. He stood there awkwardly, not knowing what to say, until Jonny broke the silence.

"Let's go now. You can pick out your puppy."

"I think Mr. Walker needs a few supplies first," his mother

said, her smile back in place. "Then you can show him Queenie's puppies."

"Queenie?"

She winked at him. "Don't let the name intimidate you. Queenie is anything but royalty. She's not very pretty, either, nor are her pups. But she is smart, and I expect her pups are, too."

An hour later, Jared headed toward his new ranch, a homely, yellow puppy—the runt of the litter—in his lap and a sack full of supplies tied to his saddle. He was whistling as he rode.

Harry grew fast—and big—and he accompanied Jared wherever he went. The dog filled one of the empty places in his heart. Mary Beth and Jonny filled another.

Yet, as much as he was attracted to Mary Beth, and as much as he did tend to linger at her store on his trips to town, he refrained from asking permission to court her. Although he sensed she would welcome his overtures, he kept himself firmly in check. He had little to offer a woman. And he knew his past would repel her, would, in fact, repel the entire town.

For nearly eighteen months he lived on dreams of what might be *someday*. Someday, when his cattle herd was strong and profitable. Someday, when the house was fit. Someday, when he felt it was safe, that his past was well and truly buried and wouldn't come back to haunt him. Then . . . maybe then . . . he'd ask Mary Beth if he could court her.

Someday came a little sooner than Jared expected.

He was in town, walking from the bank to the general store, when he saw Jonny running along the side of the street with his dog Queenie chasing after him. The boy was laughing, glancing over his shoulder and calling to the dog, not watching where he was going. When he took a notion to lead the game of tag he was playing with Queenie into the street, he ran straight into the path of a galloping horse.

Jared's years of acting instantly, without hesitation, surfaced in a flash. He made a running dive for Jonny, shoving him out of the way, all the while thanking God he'd been close enough to the boy to do any good. Jonny was unhurt, but the horse's hoof struck Jared's arm, splitting the skin open.

Mary Beth insisted on tending the wound—after all, there was no doctor in town—and as she stitched the cut closed, Jared knew she was having a hard time not noticing the other scars on his upper torso. She said nothing, just raised a questioning brow that disappeared when he offered only a shrug in explanation. He had never known a woman who could resist asking a lot of questions that he couldn't—or wouldn't—answer.

He fell in love with her on the spot. He'd seen it coming, of course, but he'd done his best to keep it from happening. He'd told himself that a man with his past shouldn't get involved with any woman. And yet. . . .

He was a different man, now, wasn't he? A more worthy one. God, he hoped he was, because despite his best intentions, he couldn't resist the gentleness in Mary Beth's hands, the warmth in her voice . . . couldn't resist *her*. She was like water to a man lost in the desert.

What followed that day was a most proper courtship. For five and a half months, Jared made twice-weekly trips to town for the express purpose of visiting Mary Beth. They took walks. He played with Jonny, whom he came to love nearly as much as he did the boy's mother. He even helped New Hope build a church for its new minister when he realized it was Mary Beth's fondest wish that the town have one—though he felt like a hypocrite the entire time and wondered if God would want his blood-stained hands involved in the construction of His house.

The times he liked best, though, were when Mary Beth invited him to supper, and he got to sit at her perfectly set table with her and Jonny—the three of them together, like a family. Jared wanted them to be a *real* family. He wanted to help Mary Beth raise her little boy and a child or two of their own. He wanted to go to bed with her at night and make love to her until they were both too exhausted to do anything but sleep. And he wanted to wake up with her beside him every morning for the rest of his life.

He told himself it was impossible, but the thought that it might not be so impossible wouldn't go away. And, finally, one night five months and sixteen days after the horse's hoof had sliced open his arm, he made up his mind.

Supper was over and Jonny was in bed, asleep, and it was time for him to leave; he always left early so folks wouldn't have anything to gossip about. Instead of leaving, though, he tugged Mary Beth down to sit beside him on the sofa in her parlor. Then he took her hand in his and asked her to marry him.

Her eyes widened, and for a moment, she just looked at him, apparently stunned. He held his breath, heart pounding, waiting for her to say she couldn't marry him because she didn't know anything about him, didn't know who he was or what he'd done before arriving in New Hope two years ago. He'd convinced himself that it was safe, at last, to take a wife, but he wasn't planning to reveal his past to her. If she asked him to explain all his secrets, he didn't know what he'd say.

She didn't ask. She simply looked at him with her heart and soul shining in her blue eyes and said, "I love you, Jared. Yes, I'll marry you."

Then he kissed her. Tenderly at first, then with a hard desperation. He had always been a gentleman with her, had made his caresses gentle, harnessing the fierce desire and the need inside him. But when her arms went around his neck, her breath coming in short gasps, and she melted against him, he was lost.

He rejoiced in her response, in the way their bodies melded together, in the need that swept away convention and caution. Her husband had died five years earlier. He himself had never lingered anywhere long enough to have more than a night's release with a soiled dove. Both of them, for their own separate reasons, had been keeping their needs and desires in check for far too long. That kiss unleashed it all. Their passion rapidly reached the boiling point, then exploded into something else, something neither of them could stop. She gave herself to him completely, and they mated in a fury of love and desire and need.

He stayed in her arms all night long, and they talked of getting married in two weeks, time enough for her to sew herself a fine wedding dress. Then, before dawn, before Jonny—or the town— awakened, he left her.

Jared rode home, smiling the entire way.

* * *

His smile stayed in place for nearly the two whole weeks. Until the day Billy Joe Carter rode into New Hope.

Carter waited for him to ride into town, then confronted him on the street, calling him Tom Garrett and challenging him to a gunfight. It didn't even occur to Jared to deny his identity. He knew then that his dream was over.

He was unarmed, and when Carter told one of his cousins to hand him a gun, he refused it. Then he walked away. In front of the whole town, he just turned and headed for the livery stable, where he'd left his horse. With each step he took, with each glance of mingled anger and revulsion he got from the townsfolk, he died a little inside.

Mary Beth caught up with him at the livery stable door.

"It's not true," she said breathlessly. "All those things that man was saying—they aren't true, are they?"

When he didn't respond, she went on. "Jared, tell me you're not wanted by the law. Tell me you haven't killed twenty men."

Did she really not know him better than that? He couldn't bring himself to answer either question, his or hers. Besides, if he'd killed all the men attributed to him, he would have had to be in ten different places at once.

"Tell me, Jared," she demanded, the blue of her eyes misting, her mouth trembling slightly. "That man was lying. You aren't Tom Garrett . . . are you?"

Even in this remote piece of Texas, she had heard of Tom Garrett.

"He wasn't lying," Jared said, hearing the ache in his voice but unable to hide it.

He left her at the stable door, and she didn't try to follow him.

But Billy Joe Carter did. He rode out to the ranch with his five cousins. Jared met them on his front porch, unarmed. Carter hadn't come to kill him, though. He wanted to do that in full view of the entire town. He wanted to prove himself the best, the man who had killed Tom Garrett in a fair fight. No, he hadn't come to kill. He'd come to threaten.

If Jared didn't face him the following afternoon, Carter said, he and his cousins would burn the town. And he would take particular pleasure in servicing Jared's woman, "the pretty widow."

A few hours after Carter left, Mary Beth appeared at the ranch house door. Jared knew he would have to tell her that he was going to meet Billy Joe Carter in a gunfight, and he also knew he wasn't going to tell her why he was doing it. The men of New Hope were no match for a band of murdering Carters, even if they were willing to fight them. Billy Joe Carter wanted *him,* no one else. And to protect the people he loved—all of them—he would give Carter what he wanted.

But how was he supposed to explain it to Mary Beth?

He should allow her to believe the worst and forget him, but somehow he couldn't bring himself to do it. He could not let her believe he was a hired gun, a cold-blooded killer.

Still, he didn't spare himself. Yes, he admitted, his name was Tom Garrett. Yes, he had killed men—in self-defense. No, he had never been a hired gun. No, he had not killed twenty men.

Then how many, she wanted to know.

He knew, but he could not force himself to say the number. So he stood mute, unable to defend the indefensible. What difference did it really make whether it was five or ten or twenty?

He watched the tears glint in her eyes, the disbelief register. He knew she had hoped he would deny it all. He wanted to take her in his arms, wanted to hold her and kiss away the tears. Instead he turned away so she wouldn't see the wetness in his own eyes.

"I love you," she said in a voice that quavered. "I love you, but Jonny . . ." She paused, then added, "I don't really know you, do I?"

He shrugged, concealing his agony. She knew him better than anyone ever had. He'd thought she understood the need in him, the longing for peace and family and belonging. He had thought that understanding those most important things, she hadn't felt the need to ask questions, to probe and pry into his past. Now he wondered if she simply had not wanted to know the answers, had been afraid to know.

His fingers clenched at his side. God, he wanted—*needed*—to hold her. But he felt unclean. Unworthy.

"Why, Jared?" she said. *"Why* did you do it?"

He stood silent. He could mouth excuses, but none of them would erase the fact that he had killed, not once or twice, but many times.

"Go home," he finally said. "Go home to your son."

"I want to understand," she pleaded.

"What is there to understand?" he said. "I've killed men. It wasn't by choice, but that doesn't change anything, does it? Once a man gets a reputation, they keep coming. They will always keep coming."

She was silent for a long moment, then asked in a quiet voice, "How did you get the reputation?"

His jaw tightened.

"Tell me," she insisted. "Tell me what happened."

"Will you believe me?"

"Yes."

But understand? He doubted it.

His tone was expressionless as he spoke. "I was eighteen and a farmer's son," he said. "One day, some Jayhawkers raided my family's farm and murdered my mother and father, and my little sister. They were getting ready to burn our barn when I rode up. I shot three of them, but one got away. Billy Joe Carter. He was just a kid then. And the men I'd killed were his brothers." Jared drew a deep breath and let it out slowly.

"Their cousins started coming after me, and I killed them, too, in self-defense. Before long I had a name, and men looking to make their own name found me. I tried to find a place where nobody knew who I was, but some gunman always tracked me down."

Jared turned back to face Mary Beth, meeting her gaze as he finished. "I'd be walking down the street and some stranger would step out in front of me and go for his gun. I went for mine faster. It was either that, or die. None of them gave me a choice, Mary Beth."

She shook her head very slowly, and in her soft, husky voice, she said, "You *always* have a choice." Then she left.

He knew then that he'd lost her. No matter what happened with Carter, he had lost Mary Beth forever.

4:05 P.M.

You always have a choice.

Mary Beth's words echoed in Jared's mind as he stood waiting for Billy Joe Carter to make his move.

The wagon had stopped somewhere behind him. He dared not look to see who was in it or if they were in the line of fire. The wagon's occupants, if they had any sense, had darted into the nearest shelter. He wished he could do the same.

Carter's gaze refocused on him once more. Soon, he thought, any second now, Carter would go for his gun. And then he would have to go for his . . .

You always have a choice.

Again, the words taunted him. He didn't believe it, but the very fact that Mary Beth seemed so certain it was true gave him pause. His love and respect for her were great enough that for the first time, it occurred to him that maybe he was wrong. Maybe there was another choice besides kill or be killed.

The sudden barking of a dog drew his attention—though not his gaze. It was Harry's bark. He loved that damned dog, had become attached to him the instant he'd picked him out of the litter. And it seemed the feeling was mutual; Harry followed him everywhere, which was why he'd tied the animal in the back of the general store before walking out to meet Carter. Harry had never been tied, any more than he'd ever been scolded, and only the fear that he might get shot had convinced Jared of the need to tie him now. Harry was voicing his indignation at being left behind, and the loud, forlorn barking ate at what was left of Jared's heart.

Carter's lean body had jerked with the first bark, and the continued barking was obviously distracting him. His gaze darted to the right, then the left; then Jared saw the other man focus briefly on a spot behind him before swinging upward, toward the second story of the saloon.

Out of the corner of his eye, Jared saw one of Carter's cousins step out from behind the corner of the bank and start looking around. Jared heard a shutter slam, several other noises that were quite normal for a town this size. Yet, under the circumstances, they seemed out of place. Only a moment ago, it had been utterly silent.

Jared took a step to the left and tried to block Harry's barking from his consciousness. Tried hopelessly not to think about anything—not Harry, not Mary Beth or Jonny, not his long and sorry list of regrets. Tried, instead, to concentrate on the task at hand. It was far past time to end it.

What was Carter waiting for, anyway? He'd have sworn the younger man had been ready to fire a moment ago.

Heat shimmered in waves coming up off the street, and though there seemed to be no wind at all, dust balls bounced along, heading out of town. The sun burned the exposed skin on his neck, bore into his head, scorched the shirt on his back. A hint of hell.

Harry's barking turned into a howl, a lonely, anguished sound that seeped into his bones.

Carter was still looking around. So was his companion. What did they see? What was making them so nervous?

"Come on, Garrett, draw," Billy Joe yelled.

Why did Billy Joe care who drew first? He had his witnesses. They both knew every eye in town was glued to some window, peering out through the curtains or shutters. Once the gunfire died away, the good residents of New Hope would emerge from their burrows.

Would Mary Beth be among them? Would he ever see her again? Would he ever get to hear her voice or see her smile?

Jared felt a burning behind his eyes, and suddenly, his throat went dry.

"Garrett, did you hear me?" Billy Joe was visibly sweating now. "Draw, dammit! Don't stand there like a coward! Draw!"

Live or die. Kill or be killed.

You always have a choice.

Did he?

Maybe. And maybe now was the time to find out.

One thing Jared knew for sure: he couldn't kill a man in front of all the people he'd come to think of as his friends and neighbors. Or in front of Mary Beth. He *did* have at least one choice, and that was not to kill.

In the moment of decision, relief rolled through him, lifting an immense weight from his shoulders—and from his soul. He felt a kind of freedom he had never known before.

"I won't draw, Carter," he said—loudly, clearly—at the same time he turned away. Not much. Just enough to make his point.

In the next instant, he heard a series of noises behind him. Loud noises. The sound of rifle bolts slamming closed.

He guessed it was Carter's cousins, come into town to see what was taking so long, and he waited for the bullets to hit him. He even mumbled a small prayer, something he hadn't done since the day, all those years ago, that he'd shot the men who killed his family. He'd neither uttered a prayer nor asked a favor, figuring the devil already owned his soul. Yet he prayed now. He prayed Mary Beth and Jonny would be happy—and that they wouldn't see him lying in the dust.

Carter's gaze moved rapidly from side to side. His companion, who had been standing near the bank, began backing away.

Wondering what the devil was going on, Jared risked a glance at the source of the other men's distraction. His body stiffened when he saw Mary Beth standing in the bank's doorway beside Bill Dale, who was holding a rifle.

How long had they been there? His concentration had been so centered on Carter that he'd been unaware of anything but the man and the heat and the dust. For a fraction of a second, his gaze met Mary Beth's, and, incredibly, he saw the flicker of a smile cross her lips.

A movement to his left brought his gaze snapping in that direction. Jared saw Holt Winslow, another rancher, moving up beside him. With Holt was John Curry, the blacksmith, and next to him the gunsmith and the saloon owner. All of them carried rifles.

Spurs jingling to the right drew his gaze. The mayor. The president of the cattlemen's association. Four other men who had ranches in the area. They all carried guns. At the end of the line strode the preacher. No gun in his hand, but he held a Bible.

A window sliding open drew his gaze to the second floor of the hotel. A figure, holding a rifle, sat perched on the windowsill. Another man stood on a nearby roof.

All of a sudden, Carter looked pale. A muscle twitched in his cheek as he, too, took in the force gathering around them. That he was baffled by it was apparent, Jared thought.

But then, so was Jared. He was no longer standing alone. The town was standing with him. And Mary Beth was right there with them. Without moving from the bank doorway, she was reaching out to him, telling him by her presence that she had made *her* choice: she loved him in spite of his past, and she wouldn't abandon him.

Jared felt his battered heart start to pound. It pounded so hard against his ribs he could almost hear it. His throat was so dry he couldn't swallow, and he knew his fingers were trembling as he moved his left hand toward the buckle of the gun belt and began to take it off.

Carter let out a furious shout. "No!" And his hand moved fast—faster than Jared thought possible—toward his gun.

At the same instant his gun belt hit the ground, Jared felt a bullet slam into his left side. The force spun him around, and his right hand—automatically, out of pure instinct—snatched for his gun. But it wasn't there, and at the same moment he reached for it, another bullet hit his hand. With his brain registering little more than the red-hot agony tearing through him, he heard a scream, then the sound of more gunfire. As he slowly sank to the ground, a part of him noted that Billy Joe had fallen.

On his knees and bent double, he put his good hand to his side, felt blood flowing through his fingers, and wondered through the morass of pain if the wound was mortal. In the next instant, Mary Beth was beside him, her hands pressing a cloth to the wound.

"Go," he tried to tell her. "Get out of the street."

"It's over, Jared," she said. "He's dead. His cousin, too."

But it wasn't over, he thought. The shadow of death would always be with him. Perhaps *he* had not killed today, but others had killed for him.

Struggling to sit back, he drew a deep and painful breath. He felt so weak, felt the blood draining from him. He looked down at his mangled right hand. He doubted he would ever be able to use it properly again, much less draw a gun.

"You . . . left . . . ," he began in a rasping whisper.

"I had to have some time," Mary Beth replied. "I felt you had lied to me, at least by silence. And I was so afraid of losing you, of watching Jonny lose yet another father."

He raised his head slowly and met her gaze.

"But then I realized how unfair I was being," she continued, tears streaming down her cheeks. "I realized how hard you've tried since you've been here to start over and make a new life." She took his good hand in hers and squeezed it. "I'm sorry, Jared. I'm so sorry."

Taking his hand from hers to touch her face, he said, "You are so . . . damned . . . pretty." He knew that had nothing to do with her anguished confession, but he felt the need to say it. He knew she understood that it was his way of telling her how much it had meant to him to see her standing there, in the bank doorway, reaching out to him with her smile.

"I love you," she said brokenly.

"The killing never stops," Jared said, his gaze holding hers.

"It stopped today," she said. "You stopped it."

Cal Baker, the minister, kneeled next to him. "Aye, lad. We all saw it. Everyone here saw you unbuckle that gun belt. *"You* made the decision to stop."

"But—"

"They voted, you know," Reverend Baker continued as if he hadn't heard the muttered protest. "Mary Beth visited every man in town, and they voted to back you, every last one of them. They just ran it a little close," he added dryly.

Jared looked back at Mary Beth, and she beamed at him. God, but her eyes were blue. Looking at them, he nearly didn't feel her hands busily wrapping his wounds, trying to stop the bleeding. The other men, about two dozen of them, were standing apart, and he looked at each of them, one by one. Bill Dale, Holt Winslow, John Curry . . . they all gave him a brief nod, telling him that they, too, had made a choice that day and were satisfied with it.

"Some men will do anything to get out of a wedding," Mary Beth said, the tears still rolling steadily down her face.

He nearly chuckled, but it sounded more like a groan. He let his head fall back until he was looking at the sky. A few clouds had appeared and were floating lazily eastward.

"I . . . can't," he said, a harshness in his voice that he hoped covered the anguish in his heart. "There will be others . . . there are . . . always others."

Bill Dale squatted down beside him. "There won't be if we tell anyone who asks that Carter was wrong. That you aren't Tom Garrett and that you, Jared Walker, have been here for years. Carter didn't believe us, and when he threatened the peace, we had to kill him to protect our town."

"No one will ever know any different," John Curry chimed in. "Not from any one of us."

Jared couldn't believe what he was hearing, that an entire town of people was willing to lie to protect him. "What about the others Carter brought with him?" he said. "By now, they're halfway to Kansas, where Carter's got more cousins than this town's got people. They'll spread the word that he's dead, and then—"

"Same story," Bill replied. "If you're not Garrett, then Carter was wrong and we had every right to protect ourselves. If we have to, we'll get the federal marshal to escort any Carter who decides to pay us an unwanted visit back to Kansas. But I don't see it as likely that they'll pursue a grudge against a whole town of people."

Jared shook his head, barely trusting himself to speak. "I can't let you all risk your lives for me."

"You'd do the same for me, wouldn't you?" Bill replied. "Or John or any of the rest of us. In fact, I think you did exactly that."

Jared's silence brought a smile to Bill's face. It said what Jared could not.

"We protect our own, Jared." Bill continued. "The day I met you, when you rode in looking to buy a ranch, I liked what I saw, and I haven't changed my mind."

Before Jared could reply—if he could have replied—Harry and Jonny arrived on the scene. Jared heard Jonny's voice calling the dog, and in the next instant, the big yellow mutt bounded into the circle that had formed around him and began frantically to wash his face with his tongue. Mary Beth gently pushed Harry aside, and Jared looked up to see Jonny, hovering over him, anxiety squinching his youthful features.

"You're hurt."

The pain was receding, or maybe it was only disguised by stronger feelings, feelings like hope and gratitude—and love.

John said, "We have to get you inside."

Bill put a hand under his good arm and started to help him up.

Jared shook his head. "I just need a hand."

The blacksmith offered his, and Jared took it. But Bill and Mary Beth still offered their assistance with hands under his good elbow and an arm around his waist. Pain flooded him as he got to his feet, and weakness; but he looked around, and for the first time in his life he felt tall, and free.

With Bill on one side of him and Mary Beth on the other, he took a step, then another. Then he stopped to look at Billy Joe Carter's body sprawled in the dust.

Live or die. He hadn't lived at all for ten years. He had merely survived. He'd only begun living when he'd come to New Hope.

He stumbled, and Mary Beth put her arm back around his waist.

"We're almost home," she said softly.

Home. His throat tightened, and he felt a wrenching twist of his heart. It had been a very long time since he'd had any home at all, and suddenly it was all around him, everywhere he looked. He saw it in the worried faces of the men who had stood by him, in the boy dashing to open the door, and in the dog dancing at his heels. He saw it in Mary Beth's beautiful blue eyes.

Live or die.

He had finally chosen life.

And love.

Conquest

by

Ruth Glick
(aka Rebecca York)

Author's Note

When Klingons were first introduced in *Star Trek,* they were "the enemy," a violent race of warriors whose alien appearance made them the stuff of nightmares. Then viewers met Worf, the only Klingon member of Star Fleet, and over the course of seven seasons of *Star Trek: The Next Generation,* women around the world learned that "alien" can be sexy and that a Klingon's sense of honor makes him a hero worthy of any woman's heart.

Part I—Climax

Elena slipped the knife under the pillow, then moved quickly away from the bed, clutching the collar of her fur robe tightly around her neck. If she killed her new husband, would the Guardians condemn her for murder? Or would they simply give her to another one of the barbarians? Perhaps it would be wiser to use the knife on herself. Better a quick death than a life of suffering at the hands of a man.

No, not a man, she corrected herself, but a savage. A male animal who bore only a superficial resemblance to a human being.

She shivered, unable to control her reaction to the thought of being possessed by a Jalaran. Since the day a hundred years ago when the colony ship from earth had crashed on Jalar, with no hope of rescue, her people had battled for survival on the harsh planet. It was a world beyond human scope, a world of impossibly high mountains where the air was too thin for humans to breathe, "ironwood" trees so tall they seemed to touch the sky, and oceans full of creatures more fearsome than the nightmares of ancient earth mariners.

The greatest threat, though, had been the Jalarans, the warlike race that dominated the primitive world. Vicious, merciless in battle, they had slaughtered the newcomers, forcing the humans to barricade themselves in stone fortresses on the northern-most continent, where winter was long and dark and summer was nothing more than a brief respite.

Elena, like all of the colonists' descendants, had been raised on stories of the atrocities committed by the natives. The morals of the stories were always the same: it was only due to their superior technology and intelligence that the humans had carved out a tiny foothold on Jalar.

That foothold was precarious, though, and it seemed the cruel, unforgiving planet would win in the end. For, over the years, fewer and fewer children had been born to the colonists, and, in the past twenty years, not a single woman had conceived. The doctors knew the cause of the problem—a type of radiation in the alien atmosphere had rendered the human males sterile—but all efforts to find a cure or means of prevention had failed. If their species was to avoid extinction, the doctors had told the Council of Guardians, they must forge a truce with the enemy; the most fertile human women had to be impregnated by Jalaran males.

Elena counted it as her misfortune to have been named one of those women.

A noise in the hall outside her bedroom door made her body go rigid. Rohan. Her new husband.

He didn't knock but simply opened the door and stepped into the room. She had met him that afternoon at the wedding ceremony, though neither she nor any other of the women had been given the opportunity to speak with the Jalarans to whom they were being wed. He was still very much a stranger, and the sight of him was every bit as shocking as it had been earlier. He was a giant, perhaps six and a half feet tall, with massive shoulders, long muscular arms, and legs like tree trunks. His prominent brow ridges and high forehead, corrugated as it was with bony ridges, seemed more suitable to an animal than a man. Above his forehead, a thick mane of wavy black hair hung to his shoulders, adding to his wild appearance.

His eyes were deep-set and dark, and his fierce gaze pinned her where she stood.

Resisting the urge to fold her arms across her chest, she raised her blond head, her blue eyes flashing defiance as she returned his stare.

He set a heavy leather satchel on the floor. His clothes, she guessed. He had a weapon hanging from his shoulder by a strap—

a long, curved blade mounted on two shorter prongs that connected it to a horizontal handle, both long pieces honed to lethal points at the ends. He removed the weapon, along with the knife tucked into the scabbard tied at his waist, and set them beside the satchel. He broke the silence with a comment that made her flush.

"They told me you are not a virgin. Is that true?"

She nodded tightly.

"Then take off your furs so I can see you." He spoke her language, but with a strong accent, the words sounding like a deep growl.

"It's too cold," she said. She had made sure it would be. "We have to conserve our fuel."

It wasn't exactly a lie. In the season of long nights, when the blood-red sun brought only a few hours of daylight, solar energy was nonexistent. So the large public rooms and corridors of their stone fortresses were as cold, according to legend, as the winter evenings on earth. Each of the small bedchambers had a fireplace, though, and in recent years, radiant heaters had been added.

At the moment, a small fire of solid fossil fuel burned in the grate as if it were the only source of warmth. After staring at the low flames, Rohan strode across the room, pulled aside a tapestry, and found the heater control. Almost at once, the temperature rose several degrees.

He turned back to face her and loosened the fastenings down the front of his gray fur jacket. The jacket was of takkar pelts, she noted, the large and vicious shaggy predators that lived in the eastern mountains. Only the bravest warriors dared to hunt the beasts, and only a warrior who had killed one could wear its pelt. He shrugged off his trophy and tossed it onto the end of the bed, revealing an intricately embroidered shirt that stretched tightly across his massive chest. Her surprised gaze darted over the garment; she would have considered it much too fine for his primitive race.

Elena caught the scent of his body, recognizing it as the unfamiliar aroma that had teased her at the brief wedding ceremony.

Rich and spicy, strangely appealing, it might have drawn her toward him if fear hadn't kept her rooted to the spot.

Casually, he untied a drawstring at his waist and shed his leather pants, tossing them after the jacket. Seeing the form-fitting leggings he wore, which revealed every muscle of his taut body, she gave a small, inaudible whimper. It was impossible not to notice the large bulge at the front of the leggings. Just as impossible to suppress the shiver that raced up her spine. She was trapped in a bedchamber with this creature— this warrior—and he was between her and the knife.

His gaze challenged her. "You have fear of me. Why?"

"I'm not afraid of you," she retorted, although it wasn't true, of course. She *was* afraid of him—and of any man who would touch her.

It hadn't always been so. Before she and Brice were married, she had enjoyed it when he touched her, though they had not made love. Then the doctors had put him on an experimental hormone treatment, hoping it would make him fertile. It hadn't revived his dead sperm, but it had made him rough and rampant in bed. Her wedding night with Brice had been a nightmare, and the nightmare had continued, with agonizing frequency, until he was killed in a skirmish with the Jalarans. She had faced his death with a mixture of sadness and guilty relief.

It was memories of the things Brice had done to her as much as it was fear of this huge and powerful alien that made her shudder when Rohan took a step toward her. Yet she stood her ground as he approached, and she met his gaze when he stopped in front of her.

He took her chin in his hand—not roughly, as she had expected—and lifted her face toward his so that she was forced to look into the depths of his dark eyes.

"Never lie to me," he said. "And I will never lie to you."

"I—" Her mouth was so dry she could barely speak.

"Did you make it cold in here so you could keep on your furs?"

Hesitating briefly, she nodded.

His hand moved from her chin and found the fastening to her

robe, his large fingers seeming to sear the flesh of her throat as he worked the clasp. She dropped her gaze from his as the heavy garment fell away, pooling on the rug about her ankles, leaving her standing before him in a thin white gown cut high under her breasts. She knew it hid very little. She had wanted to wear something less revealing, but the gown had been chosen for her.

He sucked in a sharp breath. "You are too small to bear me sons."

"That's not true!" she retorted. "I—I've had every medical test the doctors could give me, and I'm one of the top candidates for pregnancy. That's why they married me to Brice. And to you."

He chuckled, a deep, startlingly splendid sound that filled the small room. "I'm sorry if I offended you. Are you saying you want to have my sons?"

She felt color flood her face. "I must do my duty."

"Hmm. We will see if we can keep the getting of children from being too unpleasant."

He was teasing her. She saw it in his eyes. Heard it in the rumble of his voice.

Elena frowned, puzzled. She hadn't expected a sense of humor. She had expected him to throw her onto the bed and take her the way Brice had, over and over, until she hurt too much to move.

She didn't know what he saw on her face as the painful memory assaulted her, but she caught a flicker of some unreadable emotion crossing his craggy features. He turned away from her and opened the control panel again, dimming the lights so that the soft pink glow emanating from the lannar stone walls was visible.

She watched as he put another measure of fuel on the fire and stirred the embers with the poker. Then he pulled several cushions off the chairs and arranged them at the end of the rug in front of the fire.

"Come sit with me here," he said.

Glad he wasn't dragging her into bed, she obeyed, kneeling on the rug, her face toward the flames. Still, her whole body was tense as he came down beside her. Instead of touching her, he settled himself comfortably, his back propped against the pillows and the wooden chest at the foot of the bed. Stretching out his long legs, he crossed them at the ankles.

"You're not what I expected," she said in a barely audible voice.

"What did you expect?"

She spoke hesitantly. "I've heard about the way your warriors fight. You kill as many of us as you can. And you fight to the death."

"Honor demands it. Your people came here to steal our world from us."

She shook her head. "That's not true. We came by accident. Our ship was badly off course. We crashed, and then we had no way to send a message home. Do you think we would pick a place like this on purpose?"

"You do not like Jalar?" he asked.

She raised her chin. "Humankind can adapt to anything."

"Your people are proud. It gives you strength."

She stared at him, surprised he understood so well.

Then his eyes narrowed. "But you have no right to steal our planet from us."

She opened her mouth to protest, then closed it again. He was right. If the military force from the ship could have wiped out the Jalarans, they would have.

"And now your race needs us," he growled. "It is fortunate that you did not slay all of our warriors. We will give your women children, and you will teach us your technology. That is the agreement. You have things we need. Like the warmth in this room. Also, your medicines, your machines. They told me that you are a . . . botanist? Someone who adapts your plants to our environment."

"Yes."

"You are studying food productions. And new medicines."

She nodded. Her work was exciting to her. It had become her life, the focus of her energy, throughout her dreadful marriage.

"Still, though I am here, and though we spoke words at a mating ceremony, you have not yet shared your knowledge with us."

"I want to," she answered in a small voice. "The Guardians must approve it."

"Will they allow me to learn to be an engineer? I want to build dams that will harness the power of our rivers."

"Yes," she whispered. They had instructed her to tell him what he wanted to hear, but really, she wasn't sure how much they would let him learn. The Guardians, perhaps of necessity, perhaps out of desperation in their battle to survive, had become secretive and, she suspected, devious. In the first months on Jalar, when it looked as if the natives might wipe them out, the colonists had given up their freedom to the military leaders who made decisions for the good of the colony. Those leaders had become the Council of Guardians, and the Guardians still controlled the colonists' lives. She truly didn't know how far the present regime intended to go in honoring their agreement with the Jalarans.

"It will not be a one-way exchange of information," Rohan said, excitement sparking his voice. "There are things we could teach you about how to live on this world. I have knowledge of plants that I will show you. And I can teach you how to get more light from the lannar stones."

Her eyes widened. "The stones can give more light?"

"Yes. If we cooperate, both of our races will benefit."

"You believe that?"

"I know my people will be better for it."

"And you and me?" she found the courage to whisper.

He gave her a direct look. "I pledged myself to you in a ceremony of your ancestors. I promised to protect you and to stand by you. I would not dishonor that vow."

She had thought of him as a savage, but no savage would speak of honoring vows. He had taken the ceremony seriously. She was the one who had been simply mouthing words.

"I will be your true mate. Your husband, you call it."

She felt a shiver cross her skin as she remembered that he was not in her bedroom for mere conversation.

"When I speak of mating, you are afraid."

She sat with her hands clenched in her lap, her head bowed as she cast him a quick sideways glance. "I won't fight you."

He frowned, and the action accentuated the bony ridges in his high forehead. "Fighting is for the battlefield, not the bedroom," he said in his smooth, deep voice. "Mating should bring pleasure to both a man and his woman. A warrior who cannot satisfy his mate is as scorned as a coward who runs from the enemy."

She raised her head, tried to read his face. "Truly?"

"I told you I would never lie to you. You must learn to trust me."

Could she? It seemed a terrible risk, emotionally as well as physically. He was large and strong, and if he chose, he could hurt her worse than she had ever been hurt. Yet he would possess her body, whether she liked it or not. If she did as he suggested, it would be easier for her.

"I will try to trust you," she whispered, meaning it. Something inside her, some spark of intuition, made her wonder if, perhaps, with this stranger, she had a chance to discover something she had never found in her cold, regimented society.

"Will you tell me what gives you pleasure?" he asked as directly as he had spoken when he first entered the room.

"I don't know," she answered, oddly ashamed at the admission.

"Then we will learn the answer together."

"Maybe I can't . . ."

"Did he hurt you that badly?"

She looked at him, startled, then quickly dropped her gaze. His perception was uncanny—and decidedly not that of an insensitive, uncivilized brute. Unable to lie, she gave him the barest nod.

"What did he do to you?"

"He took his pleasure and gave me none." She had said it. The worst part.

"There is no shame in that for you."

She raised her eyes to his, amazed. He seemed to possess an ancient wisdom that her own people had forgotten. Or perhaps they had never known.

Holding her gaze, he said, "We have a ritual for when a man and a woman come together for first mating. It wipes away the past and allows them to begin life anew, together."

If only it were true, she thought.

"Will you do this with me, Elena?"

She didn't trust herself to speak. All she could do was nod again.

He reached out a muscular arm and pulled his leather case closer. Opening the fastening, he brought out a rectangular bottle and two small glasses of delicate crystal with intricate designs etched into the sides. Again, she was surprised that his culture had produced anything so finely wrought. She watched, cautiously but with fascination, as he solemnly moved his large hand over the containers, chanting words in his own language.

"Hold out your hands," he instructed.

She did, and he carefully set the nearly weightless vessels into her palms. She tried to keep from shaking as he poured a half inch of pale green liquid into each glass, speaking more serious-sounding words as he did so. The unfamiliar syllables seemed to hold a certain power of their own, and the power was enhanced by the strong, confident tone with which he spoke them.

As he took his glass he raised his gaze to her. "Drink."

Carefully, she curved her fingers around the delicate glass and tipped it to her lips, smelling a tangy blend of herbs and spices in a fermented liquid. It tasted the way it smelled, full-bodied and hot in her mouth, hot going down her throat. As she finished hers, she saw that he had taken only a sip of his before setting it on the chest behind him.

The room around her seemed to shimmer as he lifted the glass from her hand. She could feel the warmth from the drink spreading throughout her body, making her limbs feel weak, yet, at the same time, energized. "What did you give me?" she asked.

"Something to make you relax," he replied, "to open your mind—and your body—to possibilities."

A stab of fear shot through her, and she had an urge to run from him—though she wasn't certain she could have.

"Don't turn away from me," he said, his voice tingling against her heated skin. "Don't fight what you feel. Let me touch you—your body and your soul."

The drug had made her mind fuzzy, yet she trusted the sound

of his voice, the look in his eyes. And she suddenly realized that if she denied him what he asked, she would regret it for the rest of her life. When he took her hand and carried her palm to his mouth to stroke the edge of her index finger against his full lips, she closed her eyes. His mouth looked hard, but it felt soft. Sensual. His large, white teeth closed on her flesh, biting, but not painfully. Only hard enough to send darts of sensation along her nerve endings.

Elena made a small sound, deep in her throat, a sound of pleasure that turned to one of surprise when Rohan gathered her into his arms. His mouth moved along the edge of her jaw, his lips and then his teeth. A shiver went across her skin again. This time, though, it was not a shiver of fear.

Tentatively, letting instinct guide her, she touched his forehead, her fingertips tracing the ridges that looked so alien.

"Ah, yes," he growled, his lips blazing a trail down her neck, across her collarbone. Then his fingers twisted in the fabric of her gown, pulling it up and over her head in one quick motion, leaving her naked.

Her breath caught, and as she lay exposed to his intense scrutiny, a little of her fear returned. When his silence became intolerable, she forced a whispered comment. "I don't look like your women."

"Not so different," he murmured, his gaze lingering on her breasts, then dropping to her narrow waist and gently flaring hips. "You are smaller than a Jalaran woman. More delicate. Like a cresteran."

"A what?" she asked.

"In our legends," he replied, "she is a goddess of the forest. Rare. Beautiful. The man who sees her is blessed."

"Oh," she breathed.

He traced his fingertips over her breasts, her belly, then back up again. "So soft. Like the down of sea birds."

She was caught between tears and white heat.

With great care, he bent and rubbed his cheek, then his forehead, against the places where his hands had touched. His tenderness shattered her defenses, and the quivering sensations his touch evoked soon turned to desire. The desire ran, molten, through her veins as he shifted his head and his teeth gently captured one of her hardened nipples.

She looked at his dark skin against her white flesh. He was so different from her. Yet this seemed so right.

He stripped off his clothing, revealing a considerable amount of crisp, black hair and a line of ridges, like those in his forehead, running down his spine. When his arms came back around her, she melted against his large, muscular body. Wantonly, she moved against him, the friction of her smooth flesh against the hair sprinkling his chest and legs lighting a fire along her nerve endings. It was the drug, she reasoned, causing these glorious sensations inside her and making her feel so bold.

For a time, she basked in the fervent attention he paid to her body, his lips and teeth tasting her flesh and bringing it to life. Yet, though she reveled in the new and wonderful feelings he aroused in her, something seemed to be missing. Something important.

"You haven't kissed me," she whispered.

He raised his head from her breast to meet her gaze. "I do not know this word—'kiss.'"

"Your mouth on mine."

She saw instantly that he was unfamiliar with not only the word but the concept. Still, as his gaze focused on her mouth, she also saw that the idea intrigued him.

"Like this," she said, wrapping a hand behind his neck and pulling his head toward hers. Suddenly the aggressor, she pressed her mouth to his, nibbled, opened his lips with a flick of her tongue. His surprise turned to a growl of pleasure, and for a minute he simply let her teach him the basic tactics of the sensual assault. Soon, though, he was kissing her as if he'd been practicing for years.

"Elena." His voice was rough, heavy with passion. "This kiss—it is very . . . stimulating."

"Very," she answered, breathless.

His mouth came back to hers, and they feasted on each other. She had never been like this—wild, abandoned. On fire.

His fingers stroked high up between her thighs, finding the core of her, and she gasped, her hips lifting involuntarily, seeking his touch, which he gladly gave her. She knew she was slick and wet and open to him, and she was astonished. It was the drug, she told herself for the second time. It had to be.

He watched her face as he stroked her, doing what he'd promised, finding what gave her pleasure, until the pleasure became almost too great to endure.

"Rohan. Please—"

"Yes. Now."

He covered her body with his. And then he was inside her, opening her, stretching as she had never been stretched before. Yet there was no pain, only a wonderful sense of fullness, of her body being joined to his.

When he moved inside her, she moved with him, urgently, helpless to do anything but match the strong thrusting of his hips.

"Don't stop. Please don't stop," she called out, the words tumbling from her, over and over, as her fingers dug into his shoulders.

He said something in his own language, something that sounded like an endearment. Then his movements changed, the angle of hips shifting, and, though the difference was slight, the change in pressure was electrifying. Suddenly, all sensation seemed to gather and focus in one small spot. For an instant, every muscle in her body drew taut, and her breath lodged in her lungs. In the next instant, the kernel of tension burst open, and an explosion of intense pleasure rocked her. Taken completely by surprise, she cried out as wave after wave of sensation surged through her. Above her, he gave a loud shout that sounded very much like a warrior's cry of victory, as he found his own satisfaction.

Afterward she buried her face against his chest, unable to stop tears from flowing down her cheeks. Never in her life had she imagined lovemaking being anything like this. And it was not, she knew, induced by any drug. It was him. Rohan. Her husband. Her warrior. She had given him her trust, and he had taken her to a place she never knew existed.

His hands stroked her hair, her shoulders. "I was too rough, and I hurt you. I am sorry."

She couldn't let him think it. Struggling to control her voice, she raised her head so that she could meet his dark eyes. "No. You didn't hurt me. Not at all."

He touched one of the tear tracks on her cheek.

"It was good," she told him. "So good. I never thought . . I didn't know it could be that way."

Relief suffused his fierce countenance. Relief and male pride. "I said your people and mine could teach each other things," he teased.

"Yes. Definitely, yes."

He hugged her to him. "I did not take you to your bed, because I knew you were afraid. But would you be more comfortable there now?" he asked.

"I like it here, by the fire. It's cozy, like the caves where your ancestors lived."

"You have seen them?" he asked, sitting up enough to yank the coverings from the bed, spreading them over her.

"Yes. In the mountains."

"I thought your people stayed in these fortresses, where you think you are protected."

"Not always." She hesitated, then added, "Some of us want things to stay the same. I know we have to change. We have to understand Jalar, learn to survive in this environment."

"I know this, but why do you think it is so?"

"This is our home," she said simply. "The only one we have."

Gathering the covers around her, she stood, took his hand and led him to the small window in the thick rock wall. Through the glass she could see the planet's four moons, three small and one large. Their combined radiance lit the courtyard with an ethereal white light.

"There is great beauty here," she said. "Our home world has only one moon. Our ancestors could never have imagined this."

He stroked her hair, bent to run his lips along her bare shoulder. "I will show you the western caves, where the rocks glow with many colors, and the mountain streams where the slipper fish swim. And the groves where we gather kandali."

"What is kandali?"

"A kind of fruit we use in our cooking."

"I'd like to taste it."

"You will."

She smiled, wondering if she'd get the chance to meet more of his people, wondering if perhaps his mother might teach her to cook the dishes he had liked when he was a child. "They said you come from a village deep in the great forest. Can we go there, too?"

His eyes clouded. "Not yet. Many of the men in my family have died in battle with your race. We will wait until I can tell their widows that we have gotten something good from this alliance."

She nodded tightly, sorry that she had let her enthusiasm carry her too far too fast.

He left her to stir the fire once more, and she returned to sit on the rug. When he came back to her side, he touched his large hand gently to her cheek.

"Sometimes truth is painful. But we will deal with all things together. I want to know you. Not only your body but your mind," he murmured.

"Yes. I want that, too."

"In truth?" The question rumbled low in his chest.

"You said a husband and wife—mates—should never lie to each other." She met his questioning gaze. "I think that's a good policy." She cleared her throat. "When you first came in, you said I was too small to bear your children. Are you still worried about that?"

To her amazement, his expression became slightly embarrassed. "I think I said it because I was nervous."

"You?"

"I knew what you thought of me," he growled. "You expected a beast. An animal. That is what your race thinks all Jalarans are."

"My people are wrong," she said, then added in a rush of

words, "You are a man of honor and courage, a warrior. Yet you aren't afraid to show tenderness to your mate in her bedchamber."

She was amused and touched to see color rise in his dark cheeks. Reaching for his hand, she placed it over the spot where her heart beat in her chest. "You are a man to claim a woman's heart."

"What does that mean?"

She gave him a little smile. "It's an old expression from our home world. Earth. We speak of our romantic emotions as residing in our heart."

He considered the concept for a moment. "I think I understand."

"So I've taught you something of my people," she teased. "And I can teach you more."

He caught the light tone in her voice and arched one very bushy, dark brow. "Things such as?"

Her lips curved in a smile. "Like advanced forms of kissing."

"Ah, yes," he agreed, and he spoke the words with his lips only millimeters from hers.

Part II—The Unknotting

Elena sat in front of the dressing table brushing her hair. It had grown longer in the three months of her marriage, until it caressed the tops of her shoulders. Rohan loved to run his fingers through the golden strands, and it made her happy to give him what he wanted.

She put down the brush and smiled as she took in her vibrant reflection in the mirror. On her wedding night she had wrapped herself in furs to hide her body. Now she wore a translucent white gown that she knew would excite her husband's blood—and add to both their pleasure.

But learning the joy of making love wasn't the only new experience of her marriage. Rohan had expanded her world, literally as well as figuratively. She knew what it was to laugh and talk and share her intimate thoughts and feelings with another person. To argue and discuss and tease and play with a new and exciting freedom. They didn't always agree. Yet they had learned to respect and trust each other.

And three times during her marriage, the Guardians had let her husband take her from the fortress, although always with a military escort. She guessed that the Guardians were using the trips to gather information about the planet, but Rohan didn't seem to mind. He had kept his promises, and more—taking her to glowing caves deep in the mountains and to streams where transparent fish danced in icy water. And he had shown her hidden valleys and windswept plains where she had gathered rare medicinal plants, plants she was even now growing in her laboratories so she could test their properties.

But his latest trip he had made alone. For the past week he had been touring a remote mining installation, and in his absence, the doctors had confirmed what she had only suspected before he left. She was pregnant—with his son. A shiver of anticipation crossed her skin as she thought about telling Rohan the exciting news. His broad chest would puff out, and his ferocious countenance would glow with pride. And her own pride would match his, because although there were other mated pairs, like her friend Sophia who was mated to Karn, she herself was the first woman in the colony to conceive in twenty years.

Elena's smile softened, and a dreamy expression came over her features. Rohan had been right; the getting of this child had not been unpleasant. In fact, each time they had made love, the thrill of joining with him had shaken her to the depth of her soul. He had taught her the true meaning of mating. It wasn't simply a joining of flesh to flesh but a bonding of the souls of a man and a woman committed to each other. Ironic that she should learn from a "savage" what her high-minded race, with all of its supposedly superior knowledge, did not seem to know.

As ironic as the scorn she experienced from her own kind for having lain with one of the enemy. The colonists wanted children, but they were repulsed by the means being used to produce them. Some—those who had opposed the plan for procreation and furtherance of their species—would never accept the human-Jalaran unions as legitimate marriages; indeed, thought they should be terminated. But Elena knew that it had been the luckiest day of her life, the day the Guardians had paired her with Rohan.

The door opened, and her warrior stepped into the room. The smile of welcome froze on her face, though, the moment she saw his expression in the mirror. She was out of her chair so quickly that it toppled over and hit the stone floor. Ignoring the clatter, she crossed the room in a few quick steps.

"What is it? What's happened?" she asked, her fingers closing urgently over his massive forearms. "Is it your family? Tell me what I can do."

It chilled her blood the way he stood stiffly, his hands at his sides, staring at her as if she were a stranger. She searched his dark eyes, and what she saw in their depths made her shiver as if a cold wind had blown into the room.

"Rohan? What is it? Tell me!"

"You have betrayed me," he said, his voice low and grating.

Shocked, she shook her head in quick denial. "No! I would never do that."

He answered with a harsh syllable she'd learned was a curse. Prying her fingers from his arms, he thrust her hands away from him.

She shook her head again, trying to understand this nightmare.

"Can you deny you made a pact with your lying Guardians?" he clarified.

The words hit her like missiles fired from one of his primitive weapons, and she took several shaky steps backward. To give herself something to do, she turned and picked up the fallen chair. Draped across the back was a shawl her grandmother had woven. She had thought she might use it to tease him in their love play; instead, she pulled it protectively around her shoulders and across her breasts.

It was hard to turn toward him again, hard to face the hurt and anger blazing in his eyes. "Explain what you mean," she said.

He gave a harsh laugh. "I'm sure you already know. You signed an agreement. You and the rest of the women who mated with Jalaran men. You were warned to tell us nothing of your technology—nothing of use. The men sent to work with us were instructed to show us only things a child would learn in his first years at one of your schools. Do you deny that?"

She wanted to look away from his accusing gaze, but she kept her head high. "I—I was told by the Guardians that we should not discuss our technology, that the men you worked with would decide what to teach you." She swallowed hard. "They said it was because . . . because we couldn't judge what might be of strategic importance. That we might make a mistake. But it was innocent. We—"

He cut her off again. "You expect me to believe that?"

Her mouth was dry, and she had to swallow hard before she could speak. "You taught me never to lie to you."

He snorted. "It would seem, however, that I did not teach you honor. I saw your name, Elena, on the piece of paper you signed."

Her hands squeezed so tightly that she felt her fingernails digging into her flesh.

"Yes, I signed the paper thrust in front of me. But it's not the way you're making it sound. We were told it was important to go slowly with the project."

When he only continued to give her that cold, hard stare, she went on urgently. "Rohan, the Council of Guardians is made up of old, suspicious men and women who have been frightened by years of war with the Jalarans. They have not lived with and come to know you as I have. The Guardians were afraid your leaders might have agreed to the matings to further some hidden agenda of their own—that you might have come here with ulterior motives. But I—that is, some of us have been working to change their opinion."

"No." Rohan spoke the single syllable without hesitation. "You wanted us for breeding stock, to give you children, but you never intended to give us anything in return."

"Rohan, let me explain how it was," she pleaded.

He shook his proud head. "Do not waste your breath. It is

over. We are going home. I will find a true mate among my own kind."

The terrible words fell on her like physical blows. She felt dizzy, and she reached behind her, her hand searching for—and finding—the edge of the dressing table to steady herself. Her breath was coming in little gasps, and her skin felt clammy.

Perhaps he didn't want to listen, but she had to tell him, "I signed that paper before I ever met you, when I was frightened of what you might do to me." She sucked in a ragged breath. "But really, I didn't have any choice. We are not a free people. We do what the military dictates, or we suffer the consequences."

"Then I am sorry for you," he said. "But that does not excuse your actions."

Her vision swam, but she was determined not to collapse in front of him. Jalarans respected strength and courage, and she did so want her warrior's respect. "What about the vows we took?" she asked. "You said they bound us together."

"You are the one who dishonored those vows."

"No. I've been true and faithful to you."

"In your fashion."

She reached out, her hand stretching toward him, the news of the baby on her lips. In the next instant, though, she let her hand fall to her side, and the words went unspoken. If she told him of the baby, it might make him stop and think, but she couldn't use the child to hold him to her. If he did not want her for herself, then she did not want him.

"It makes no difference that I love you?" she asked. "That I have been doing everything in my power to change the Guardians' edict?"

She saw something flicker in his eyes. Something that gave her a tiny spark of hope. But before the spark could grow, he turned on his heel and left.

For a full minute, Elena stared at the closed door, listening to the silence Rohan had left in his wake. Then, with a strangled cry, she sank into the chair and burst into tears.

Part III—Resolution

It was bitterly cold, so cold that the north wind swooping into the courtyard cut through Elena's heavy furs and chilled her to the bone. Still, she came here often, because the air inside the stone corridors and living chambers of the fortress seemed stifling. As did the walls themselves. From here she could see the red sun hanging like a glowing coal in the sky and the craggy peaks of the distant mountains.

Rohan had taken her to the mountains. She cherished the memory of that trip. Yet she had never seen his home in the great forest. Nor would their son see it. Not ever.

Sorrow threatened to overwhelm her. Trying to outrun it, she moved rapidly along the stone walkway. She didn't glance back, yet she knew that the guards, who kept her in view at all times, were following. Maybe they would freeze their worthless balls off out here, she thought with silent and bitter humor. What did they think she was going to do, climb over the wall and disappear with the precious baby whom the Guardians considered state property?

It had been three months since she'd seen her warrior or heard any word of him. Three months of dragging herself through each day as if it were an endless sentence. Damn the Guardians, she thought. Damn the timid, fearful society that had bred her. She didn't belong here anymore. Not since Rohan had taught her to think differently. In truth, sometimes she did dream of running away, of going somewhere she could raise her son to be a warrior like his father.

But she had no place to go. It was only a dream, a refuge.

She knew that many called her a traitor, though never to her face. Maybe she was. Certainly she was changed, and she feared the changes in her behavior would make the Guardians decide it was best to take her baby away from her as soon as he was weaned. Her hands squeezed into fists. They didn't know her strength. She'd fight to keep him, fight to keep what was hers, because he was all she had left.

Behind her she heard a startled gasp. Whirling, she strained to see through the dim light. One of her guards had fallen to the ground. The other was drawing his weapon, but he was too late. A hooded figure stepped out from behind a stone pillar and grabbed him around the neck. He grunted and went down, his weapon flying from his hand. Before it landed on the ground, the assailant grabbed it and began running toward her.

She might have screamed for help. Instead, she kept silent, nor did she struggle as he scooped her into his arms and slung her over his shoulder. Dashing along the walkway, he darted into a depression between the stone walls, where a low doorway had appeared, though she knew there had been no sign of one. At least, no apparent sign.

Her kidnapper bent double, clearing the arch without bumping her against the stone. Then he shoved the thick stone door shut behind them, throwing them into complete darkness, for the rocks here did not glow. Never slackening his pace, he pounded down a narrow passage, half crouched, carrying her weight as if she were no more than a sack of feathers. She could see nothing, hear nothing but his harsh breathing and the drumming of his booted footsteps. Yet the spicy scent of his body filled her nostrils and made her giddy.

"Rohan! I can run on my own feet, you know."

"Quiet," he commanded. "We are still in danger."

Her heart pounded wildly in her chest. What if he knew? What if he had only come to claim his child? The idea tore at her. But then, she wondered, would he be bouncing her along on his rock-hard shoulder if he had known of the pregnancy?

He didn't stop until they emerged from the mouth of a hillside cave. When he set her down, she looked to see that they were on the other side of the shimmering silver river that ran past the fortress, separating it from the forest of ironwood trees. The trees rose, arrow straight, toward the sky, and they stood at the edge of them, far enough back to be hidden by their graceful, overlapping branches from view of the guards walking the parapets of the fortress.

While Rohan struggled to shove the large rock across the entrance to the tunnel, muscles straining as he inched it into place,

Elena looked with wonder at her surroundings. The deep, dark forest was absolutely forbidden territory to her people, and she doubted any had dared venture into it. Truly, it was a fairyland. Through the fernlike leaves of the great ironwood trees, red light filtered downward, giving everything a warm glow, and beneath her feet, a carpet of tiny, star-shaped white flowers spread across the forest floor. Defying the cold, they shimmered in the muted light like snow and filled the air with a sweet perfume.

For the first time in months, Elena breathed deeply, breathed the scent of freedom.

Rohan, too, was breathing hard from his labors when he turned to her. Having obliterated all signs of their escape route, he lifted a large hand to touch her cheek, to brush back the blond hair that had fallen across her eyes.

"Did I hurt you?" he asked urgently.

She shook her head, staring up at him.

"I thank you for not calling out to the soldiers," he said in a rough voice.

Her chest tightened as she realized he wasn't sure he could trust her. "I would never do that. But, Rohan, if they catch you, they'll kill you."

"They will not catch me," he said with all the arrogance she remembered.

"But they'll be looking for me. They won't let the—" She stopped abruptly, feeling her stomach clench, waiting for some sign that he knew about the child.

He merely went on as if she hadn't interrupted. "Your Council of Guardians does not know about this tunnel. Now I have given away the secret to you." His face was tense, strained. His arms were stiff at his sides, the way he had looked the last time she had seen him.

She held herself stiffly, too. After all the long, lonely months, she had given up hope of ever seeing him again. She surely never would have imagined that he'd kidnap her. But *why* had he done it?

"What are you doing here?" she asked, her eyes searching his. "Why did you come back?"

To her astonishment, he dropped to one knee in front of her, crushing some of the flowers, releasing more of their heady scent. She had never viewed her warrior from precisely that angle, and it was a strange experience.

"For you," he growled. "I came back for you, if you will still have me."

She looked down at him, and although hope was beginning to grow within her, she chose her words carefully. "You said I betrayed you, that you would find another—" She broke off, unable to repeat the terrible thing he had spoken to her, although it had been much on her mind through the lonely months.

His answer was a shuddering groan. "I was wrong to hurt you with those words, Elena. I would not seek another mate. Yet I have tried to live without you, and I cannot."

She couldn't hold back a little sob. "Oh, Rohan!"

Falling to her knees, she clasped him to her. Then his arms came around her, and they held each other, rocking together on the carpet of flowers, murmuring broken words and phrases.

"I missed you so much . . . so much."

"I need you."

"I need you, too."

She lifted her head, and his lips found hers in a long, greedy kiss that made her blood sing.

"I dreamed of doing that," he growled. "Dreamed of it every night. Your lips on mine, the way you taught me that first time."

"Oh, yes. Yes."

"It was wrong to leave you," he ground out. "I was blinded by my pride and by what I have been taught to call honor. I could not accept that you had acted according to your own honor, in the only way left open to you. So I followed the orders of my commander to break off the marriage and return home." He shook his head. "Our leaders are as irrational as your Council of Guardians, Elena. They have decided any commingling of the blood of our species would only lessen the Jalarans' strength. A decree has been passed and sent to every city and village. No Jalaran may ever again mate with a human, and we are to keep apart from you in all ways." He took a deep breath, his gaze raking her features. "But I had to disobey. And now I cannot go back."

She clung to him more tightly. Moisture clouded her eyes and spilled down her cheeks as she stroked her fingers over the ridges of his forehead—once so foreign, now so dear to her. "If you can't go back, what will you do?"

Tenderly he wiped away her tears. "Do not cry, my cresteran," he murmured. "Everything is going to be all right now that we're together again."

She raised her gaze to his. "But where will we go?"

"Somewhere safe. You and I, along with some of the other mated pairs who were forced to part as we were—we will all be safe, together."

Her eyes widened. "That's what happened to Sophia! Karn came to take her, as you did me!"

Rohan nodded.

"We all thought she had wandered too far on a plant-gathering expedition and been captured—or killed."

"She is not dead. She is with Karn." With a smile, he added, "And it is plain that she is happy to be there."

"But *where* is she?"

"Far from here. Across an inlet of the southern ocean.

She thought of the vast sea with its deep purple waves, dangerous currents, and huge predators. "How did you get there?"

"In air cars we captured in battle from your soldiers, then repaired," he answered. "My people have been using them for years. Our night vision is much better than yours. We fly in the darkness when you would not think to look for us. Karn and I, along with three of the other Jalarans mated to human women, searched for weeks, and we have found a place where we can make a home. No one will find us."

His expression took on a certain familiar smugness as he continued. "We've discovered a cave—an enormous cave with walls of rock that glows brighter than any I have seen. My friends and I found it with the mining equipment that I liberated from your engineers."

"Liberated?"

He dismissed her challenge over his choice of words with a wave of his hand. "Our cave is big enough for a whole city. I have already started to build a house for us near one of the hot springs."

Her eyebrows shot upward. "Hot springs?"

His lips stretched into a grin. "Yes, you will be able to take a hot bath whenever you wish."

It sounded lovely, but still she had doubts. "Rohan, how will we live in a cave?"

Again, that smug look crossed his features. "We have taken the tools we need and enough stores from your people and mine to feed us for a full cycle of seasons. There are fish in the cool streams that flow near the entrance, and I have trapped pelds from the plains for breeding, so that we will have meat. The animals appear to be doing well, living in the cave."

She nodded. Pelds were docile grazing animals that lived in herds. She had thought herself of raising them for milk and cheese, but the Guardians had vetoed the suggestion.

Rohan continued. "You are going to use the lights we have installed to grow food for us and the animals."

She tipped her head to one side. "You counted on me being there to do that?"

Any trace of arrogance left his gaze, and his tone was utterly sincere as he spoke. "I hoped. I prayed to the gods that you would come with me."

She gave him a fierce look. "I will follow you anywhere you choose to take me, if you promise never to leave me again."

His eyes burned with an intensity that robbed her of breath.

"You have my word, Elena. My solemn oath as a warrior."

That was enough for her: his solemn oath. "Rohan, I love you. I never stopped loving you," she told him.

They embraced once more, and Elena felt the joy flowing back and forth between them.

Slowly, with clear reluctance, Rohan loosened his hold on her. "We must go," he told her, helping her to her feet. His fingers clasped hers tightly, and his gaze smoldered as he looked down at her. "I want to kiss you again, but if I do, I will lose all reason and drag you down to the ground with me."

The words and the desire in his eyes made her body turn to hot liquid. "Are you sure there isn't time for that?" she whispered, yearning to join with him in this magical place of their reunion.

He growled something rough and urgent deep in his throat. "Do not tempt me past endurance, woman. I dream every night of mating . . . no, as you say, of making love with you. It has been too long since our bodies were joined. I need you, Elena, but I will wait until we are far from here, in a place where your soldiers will not search for you. And then I will make love with you—and give you the child I promised you."

Her heart filled to bursting. He didn't know about the baby. He truly had come back for her, and her alone.

She gave him a slow smile. "You already have given me what you promised," she replied softly, taking his hand and slipping it beneath her fur so that he could feel the gently rounded curve of her abdomen.

He sucked in a sharp breath, and his dark eyes blazed with an emotion too intense to name. "My child is already growing inside you," he said. Then his expression became grave. "Did you know of this when I left?"

"Yes." Her hand pressed more tightly over his. "I had just learned for certain the day before you came back from that trip with the engineers."

"And you did not tell me," he growled. "You let me walk away from you. From our child."

"That day—" She gulped. "I was waiting for you, planning to tell you that I was carrying your son."

He made a low, strangled sound. "A son."

She nodded, then swallowed hard. "It felt as if the world had crashed down around me when you said you were going away. Yet I didn't want to use the baby to hold you. I wanted our bond to be strong enough."

He took her gently in his arms. "It was enough, my cresteran. But I did not know it then. I was not wise enough to understand the feeling that I have for you—this fullness in my heart you call love. Will you ever forgive me for leaving you?" He swallowed hard. "For saying I would seek another mate when I knew in my soul that the two of us were joined for all time?"

She clasped her arms tightly around him. "I forgave you the instant you scooped me up and carried me out of that wretched prison. My people lock themselves inside of it, believing they can create their own world. Their own reality. But the real world is out here"—she glanced at the forest surrounding them—"and this is the world I want to live in, with you."

Leaning back in his arms, she met his gaze, and with the certainty of a woman who knows she has found her one true mate, she said, "Please, Rohan. Take me home."

Little Beast

by

Corey McFadden

Author's Note

I sat down to watch the latest screen version of Jane Austen's *Pride and Prejudice* with one eyebrow cocked and a lip ready to curl. When Colin Firth made his first appearance on screen, the eyebrow came down and my lip set in a smile. Handsome and arrogant, Colin brings life to the magnificent Mr. Darcy, who has always epitomized for me the perfect romantic hero: proud, remote, brought at last to realize that love transcends artificial societal restraints. And when Colin's gloved hand touches that of Elizabeth Bennett, as he leads her forth to dance, the sparks are visible!

"Hiding among the palm fronds will not avail you this time, Little Beast."

"Shhh! Go away!"

"As flowery as your fetching frock may be, Lysbeth, it simply does not pass for natural flora. Give it up."

"Go away, or you'll be sorry!"

"I am always sorry when I tangle with you, brat. Nevertheless, I am sent to fetch you, and fetch you I shall." Suiting the action to the words, Gavin Broward reached in among the lush vegetation, his hand closing gently but firmly around the slender arm of Miss Lysbeth Anne Katherine Digby, soon-to-be affianced to Sir Cyril Cardwell, late of Italian residence, now proud master of the enviable Cardwell estate, his unfortunate papa having recently sought his Eternal Rest via one ill-trained jumper.

"Gavin, I declare, if you don't let me go, you'll be wearing your dinner home this evening!" Lysbeth sputtered, as he hauled her unceremoniously from the jungle setting.

"And won't that make a splendid impression on your intended." Gavin stood her in front of him and cast a critical eye on the disheveled baggage.

"He is not my intended! I'll simply refuse him. I do not wish to be engaged. I want my Season!" Lysbeth stomped her foot imperiously, and several bits of plant life tumbled from her skirts.

"It's more likely he'll refuse you, Lysbeth. You have the manners of a mule."

"Good. Sit next to me at dinner, and I'll be happy to demonstrate the extent of my manners."

"Now that is a frightening thought," Gavin said absently, soothing the folds in her pretty dress, plucking loose several wayward sprigs that had thus far refused to be dislodged. He turned her about, approving of the fine, flower-embroidered satin. Lysbeth's usual attire ran to shapeless bleached muslin, fit more for the kitchen than the drawing room, although suitable, to be sure, to the hoyden's favorite pursuit of galloping on any wild beast that would stand still long enough to be saddled.

And that was the problem, of course. Lysbeth had been allowed to run wild since birth, the strain of which event had done in her delicate, well-bred mother. The newly widowed, somewhat befuddled Sir Harry Digby, an amiable soul, given more to country pursuits than the proper rearing of an infant daughter, had simply returned his attentions to his hounds and horses, placing the matter in the hands of a long string of matronly nurses and governesses, many of whom could curdle milk at a glance, and none of whom could long tolerate the exploits of Miss Lysbeth Anne Katherine Digby.

Ten years her senior, Gavin, heir presumptive to the neighboring estate, had always found the brat to be amusing, if occasionally outrageous. He had indulged her unladylike behavior, all the more so in these last few years, since his age and standing had taken him to London, where he had seen how drearily predictable real ladies could be. Now, however, he began to perceive that the taming of Miss Lysbeth Anne Katherine Digby was long overdue. And quite likely impossible.

"Stand still, Little Beast," he said impatiently. "How have you done this to your hair?" He did not consider himself much of a lady's maid—indeed, his talents lay more with the undoing of chignons, rather than the repair. Nevertheless, he made a game effort to fiddle the stuff up where it belonged, not, come to think of it, that he had any idea what Lysbeth's hair ought to look like when done up properly. He had never seen such a thing.

"It will do you no good, you know," she muttered darkly. "My hair laughs at pins, and, anyway, that's how I like it." Indeed, as if to prove her point, the unruly red curls sprang away from his awkward touch. Her hair was soft, however, and smelled fresh-washed, thank heaven. Her new stepmama was having some effect, if only by dint of threats and a display of sour temper.

Only upon Sir Harry's recent, and most surprising remarriage, had Lysbeth experienced any parental notice whatsoever, and Gavin was not at all certain the child was any the better for it. The new Lady Sarah Digby would not have been his selection for doting stepmama. Long on lineage but short on wherewithal, the fading beauty, herself widowed by her rake of a husband, had set about in short order finding a comfortable berth for herself. Sir Harry, hapless as always, had been quite smitten by the not-quite-young widow, and had found himself married in no time. It was all the same to him, of course, as long as his lady did not think to interfere with his hounds or his horses.

She did not. Lady Sarah did, however, seem to wish to interfere with the raising of Sir Harry's daughter, wasting no time in preparing the seventeen-year-old girl for a precipitous launch into society. Indeed, it seemed to be Lady Sarah's plan that Lysbeth should be wooed, won, wed and away, all in the time it usually took a demoiselle to select her wardrobe for the coming Season.

Lady Sarah was nothing if not tenacious, and so this afternoon found her balky stepdaughter hiding in the conservatory, the bemused neighbor sent to fetch her for the long-awaited introduction to the sacrificial victim . . . er, intended.

"There. I believe that is as presentable as you are able to be," Gavin said, standing back with approval, but keeping her hand held tightly, since her rather overlarge feet fairly danced with the urge to flee. He tucked her hand firmly under his arm and marched her in the direction of the drawing room, where he had left Lady Sarah tapping her foot, and Sir Harry and Sir Cyril deep in a fascinating discussion on dog breeding.

"What's he like?" came a small, surly voice at his elbow.

"Oh, monstrous, really. He's ghastly-looking, fat as a duchess, all spotty, with very bad teeth, and the most amazing knock-knees I've ever seen. You should suit admirably. He won't be marrying beneath himse— Ow! That hurt!"

"Serves you right," she whispered through gritted teeth.

They made their way into the hallway that led to the drawing room, Gavin limping. Thank God for the thickness of his Hessians, although he could be sure there would be a bruise tonight on his shin bone.

"I'll not agree to marry him, you know," she said, sounding a bit forlorn.

"My dear Lysbeth, I'm afraid you must face the fact that young ladies have small choice in these matters." He patted her arm gently. It was rather a shame, he thought. Lysbeth had real spirit, the makings of a truly interesting character. It would be a loss to him when she finally metamorphosed into the vacuous butterfly he knew she'd become, once under the seductive London influence.

They stepped into the drawing room, and he felt her shrink against him. Quickly, he stepped away. It was time the girl learned that casual physical affection was best reserved for private moments. Not that Lysbeth was much of a one for the hugs and kisses demanded by the ladies of London as tokens of undying affection. He supposed it had something to do with her having been motherless since birth, but anyone rash enough to look for a kiss from Lysbeth was more likely to find a nipped nose instead.

"Er, ah, Cyril, I say, here's my daughter, what?" Sir Harry fumbled about, looking as if he weren't really quite sure who she was. "Lysbeth, come here. Here's Sir Cyril. Say how d'ye do, gel."

Out of the corner of his eye, Gavin saw Lady Sarah cringe at what passed for a proper introduction in the Digby household. Beside him, Lysbeth stood ramrod stiff and mutinous, making not the slightest move toward executing the obligatory maidenly curtsey. Without stopping to think, Gavin delivered a swift elbow to her ribs, earning him a dark look but having the desired effect. With a nervous glance at her stepmama, Lysbeth dropped a perfect curtsey. Surprising, really, that the chit actually knew how.

"How d'ye do, Miss Digby?" came the proper response from Sir Cyril Cardwell.

But when the man straightened, he smiled at the girl. And Gavin did not at all care for the expression in his eyes.

* * *

"You don't waste much time, do you, Cyril?" Gavin asked, trying to keep the irritation out of his voice. They had arrived in London late this morning, Gavin having been kind enough to offer the gentleman a seat in his brougham. He hadn't really wanted to come to London, this being the off-season, but Cyril had been all afire to get to the city, ostensibly so that he could alter his overly continental appearance. The man had been raised in Italy by his mama, who loathed all things British except the money that poured into her accounts from his father's estates. Cyril had made quick work in Bond Street, and Gavin had the grace to admit, if only to himself, that the young man at least seemed to have plenty of scratch, something Lysbeth would need if she ever developed a taste for city living.

He could not suppress the smile that curved his lips at the thought of how he had left her, smack on her backside, perilously close to an unfortunate pile of horse manure, sputtering and cursing. She broke her horses herself, and it was a wonder they hadn't broken her. She could beat him occasionally, not always, and it depended on which horse she rode. She had never beaten him when he rode Sultan, and the day she did he'd stop racing for good.

"I've a few lady friends I wish to call on, Broward. Care to join me? Most entertaining they are, I assure you."

"Surely you jest, Cyril? Any lady who *is* a lady is in the country at this time of year. And if she is not, her butler will say she is, to save face."

"Ah, but I don't mean real ladies, my dear chap. Naturally, I refer to the *demimonde*. Don't much care for real ladies. Bore me half to death."

"Well, indeed, they can be tedious," Gavin answered, even more annoyed. While he was never loath to have a tumble, he preferred not to pay for it. Didn't find it necessary, really. There were always willing lovelies, and he preferred to have exclusive rights, at least for the duration of a discreet affair. "Still, Cyril, if you've been abroad these past fifteen years, how would you know where to find the *demimonde* on such short notice?"

"My dear mama prides herself, on a wealth of useful knowledge, sir," Cyril said, with a broad wink. "And she is not stingy with details. She did so wish her boy to feel at home in a strange land."

There it was again, that look in his eye. The way he'd looked at Lysbeth. Gavin felt the hair stand up on the back of his neck. And he made up his mind in that moment to tag along, although he had planned to beg off. There was something about this Sir Cyril Cardwell that seemed . . . off, somehow. And if the man planned to marry his little beast, Gavin damn well intended to get to the bottom of it.

Gavin felt sick. Sick and stupid. The girl wouldn't leave him alone, but for the life of him, he couldn't find the urge to bed her. This was the lowest rung of the *demimonde* ladder. Indeed, it was a whorehouse, plain and simple, and if this girl was an example of the finest the establishment had to offer, then it was not one of the better whorehouses. She had a certain coarse attractiveness, though it was more a matter of powder and paint than nature's inclination. And her gown, a magenta-colored satin, none too clean, spilled her prodigious bosom from a neckline that was downright stingy on material. A recent bath would have been nice, but what she lacked in soap and water, she made up for with a dreadful, cloying perfume, too much and too cheap.

He could feel his stomach trying to rebel, and he took a deep breath. He cursed himself for having drunk the foul brandy she had offered, sure now it had been drugged. No doubt he was supposed to feel relaxed and amorous. And generous.

"Daisy, I fear I am somewhat indisposed," he said, moving her hand firmly from where it should not have been.

"I can make you feel better, sir." She giggled, reaching again for the fastenings of his breeches.

"I think not, please," he said, pushing her hand away again. "Where is my friend?"

"Ooh, you want us all together, luv? I like that," she said with a smile that showed bad teeth. "Only, Madame said as 'ow 'e was goin' wi' Bessie. An' Bessie . . . well, Bessie goes in for the special trade, if you know what I mean. Still, if you like, we could join any of th'others. There's several gennlemen 'ere tonight. You like it wi' men, too, then? That do cost a bit more."

"I do *not* like it with men!" Gavin fairly shouted, sitting up. He regretted the movement instantly, his head throbbing. Whatever the stuff was in the brandy, he hoped it didn't kill him. "And what do you mean by 'special trade?' Where is my friend?"

She pouted. No doubt her evening's pay pucket depended upon his satisfaction. Right now he'd pay her just to stop pawing him and point him in Cyril's direction. And if this evening's escapade reflected the man's taste in ladies, Gavin would have a serious talk with Sir Harry about the suitability of the proposed match.

" 'E likes it rough. 'E likes to 'urt the girl, you know. You don't like that, do you? I don't do that sort of thing meself, but I'm sure there's someone else available." She looked hopeful. Perhaps she might be taken off the hook by the peculiarity of his predilections. At least she had moved her hands away from his breeches. He shook his head trying to clear it. It seemed he was getting stupider by the minute. She couldn't have said. . . .

He grabbed her arm and spoke through clenched teeth. "Where is my friend?"

" 'Ere now, didn't I just say I didn't do that sort of thing?" she said, trying to twist out of his grip.

"Tell me where he is. Now, please, Daisy. If you do not, I shall tell Madame you are entirely unsuitable." He didn't much like threatening the girl; but it had been she who had served the brandy, so he supposed she had this one coming to her.

"Third floor," she spat out. He let go of her arm, and she scrambled away, rubbing it where he had held her too tightly. He'd regret that, too, if he could think straight.

"Take me there," he said. Holding the back of the elaborately upholstered settee, he hauled himself to his feet. The room spun.

"I'll get in trouble," the girl said, and all four of her eyes looked anxious.

He shook his head again and then there was only one of her. "You'll get in trouble if you don't, my girl," he said, holding on to the arm of the settee. "What the devil does she put in that foul brandy, anyway?"

"Oh, maybe you got too much. She measures out double for big men like you. It's just to make you relax, like. Be friendly and 'appy." Daisy smiled tentatively, perhaps hoping he'd go along with the plan.

"Well, I don't feel too friendly at the moment, and happy is out of the question. I might be persuaded to tell Madame how pleased I've been with you this evening, if you will be so kind as to escort me to my friend. We can take a back stairs if that will be safer for you."

She brightened considerably. "You'll act pleased, then? Because I don't fancy gettin' put out of 'ere. I'm on trial, like, and there's worse places, you know."

"I'm sure," he said darkly. "Here," he said, reaching into his waistcoat pocket. "In case my friend and I leave in rather a hurry, I want you to have this. Just for you, mind." The girl's eyes widened. No doubt the coin was considerably more than she was used to receiving for an hour's work. She pocketed it with a surreptitious glance at the door. Then she offered him her arm, and he took it. Walking was not going to be easy. They took a few steps forward, and he found he was leaning on her.

They made a rather slow progress through the back halls of the surprisingly large establishment. Doors in the long, dark hallways were shut, and from more than one he heard unmistakable sounds. But a cool breeze blew through the halls from an open window somewhere, and his head cleared a bit. Up a long flight of stairs, away from everything else, they paused at last.

" 'Ere's Bessie's room," the girl whispered. Now there was obvious fear in her eyes, and it was she clutching at his arm, rather than the other way around. "We should go back down, please. I don't dare get caught up 'ere."

"Go back down, then," he said gently. It was not fair to get her in trouble only because he was livid with Sir Cyril Cardwell and his vile tastes. "I'll stop in and see Madame on the way out, and tell her how charming you've been."

She gave him one dubious glance, then fled down the hallway, her violently colored satin gown reflecting a hellish light from the candles in the wall sconces.

Gavin had raised his knuckles to rap on the door, when his movement was arrested by a blood-curdling scream from within. Wasting no time, he turned the door handle, only to find it locked. The woman screamed again, then whimpered piteously. Gavin took one step back and threw all his weight into a booted kick. The door crashed inward and slammed against the wall.

"What the bloody 'ell!"

The sight that met his eyes was shocking. Sir Cyril Cardwell was naked. That, of course, was not a shock, given the circumstances, nor was the woman's state of nudity. What appalled Gavin were the leather strips that bound the woman's wrists and ankles to the bedposts and the blood running down her chin from a cut on her lip. Sir Cyril held, high above his head, as if he had been interrupted in mid-stroke, a cat-o'-nine-tails, its evil knots glistening in the candlelight. The woman had stripes across her chest and arms. Her eyes, turned now on the interloper, blazed with rage, and something else, perhaps a mockery of the sweet passion Gavin had seen in the eyes of his lady loves.

"What the devil do you mean bursting in here like this, Broward? This is a private appointment, and, as you can see, we're busy."

Gavin stood frozen. His head wouldn't clear, and he felt suddenly, viciously sick. He stumbled backward, into the dim light of the hallway. Behind him, he heard the door slam shut.

Taking in air in great gulps, Gavin swallowed the gorge rising in his throat. As the nausea receded, he fought for a clearing in his head. Holding his hand against the wall, he made his slow way down the hallway, to the back stairs. He saw no one in the dim halls, but the moans and grunts coming from behind the closed doors had an eerie, vile sound. As much as he craved a deep breath of fresh air, he made himself stop in the little front office to compliment Madame on the lovely Daisy. And pay her.

* * *

"Sir Harry, you must try to understand. The man is . . . unnatural in his tastes. He is simply not a suitable match for Lysbeth." In the four hours it had taken Gavin to reach the Digby estate from London this morning, he had tried out every possible explanation in his still-throbbing head. There was simply no way to discuss the matter at all. And yet, for Little Beast's sake, he must.

"Confound it, Gavin, I can't break off the engagement now. 'Twould cause the most dreadful scandal. Lady Sarah simply wouldn't hear of it."

"Sir Harry, have you understood a word I've said?" Gavin had long been aware that his neighbor was not the sharpest of men, but he had rarely minded until now.

"Well, Gavin, my boy, you're young yet. You don't p'raps understand that gentlemen need the occasional, er, different sort of stimulation to, er, ah . . ."

"Dammit, man. He was *beating* the woman. She was running blood! That's not stimulation, it's criminal assault. I'll not have Lysbeth married to a monster like that!"

"Don't know that it's any of your business, really, sir," Sir Harry muttered, beginning to look annoyed. He cast a longing glance out of the window, anxious, no doubt, to be among his hounds and horses, who might possibly function on the same intellectual level, except that horses and dogs frequently understood what was being said to them.

Feeling trapped by the man's stupidity, Gavin asked, "What do you know of this man, Sir Harry?"

"Oh, splendid family!" Sir Harry beamed. "His father and I were the greatest of shooting companions. Excellent shot, he was. The boy comes of good stock. He's all right, just had a bit of unfortunate influence from that woman George married. Never could see it m'self. Entirely too Italian to suit me. So terribly foreign, and all that. She took the boy off to school in Italy when he was but a pup. Only came back for holidays, y'see. He just needs to be reminded of English ways."

Gavin gaped. "Sir Harry," he began, speaking slowly, "I don't think this has anything to do with a foreign upbringing.

It's something that's set inside him, like the workings inside your pocket watch."

"Look here, boy. I'll give it some thought. Discuss it with Lady Sarah, that sort of thing. Don't trouble y'self further. P'raps I'll have a chat with young Cyril about delicacy in these matters. Er . . ." He looked discomfited. "You should know that gentlemen behave this way with whores but not with their wives. Indeed, few men want anything to do with their wives in that regard."

He snorted with uneasy laughter, but Gavin could not force a companionable smile to his face. Talk it over with Lady Sarah, indeed. As if the woman gave a damn for Little Beast's happiness. No one cared about the child. No one but himself.

"Well, that's all settled, then," Sir Harry said heartily. "Care for a little shooting? The weather's capital!"

Gavin shook his head, not trusting himself to speak. With a happy nod, Sir Harry took himself off.

Poor Little Beast. Gavin slammed his fist hard against the marble mantelpiece, then winced as the pain shot through his hand.

"Well, that was certainly worth walking downstairs to see."

Lysbeth's voice unexpectedly at his back made him feel even more foolish.

"Bet it really smarts," she went on relentlessly. "And it wasn't smart. Is that a play on words? Cyril says I have to learn to be dreadfully clever in my wordplay if I'm to be the toast of London."

"What?" Gavin turned incredulous eyes on the girl, then thought he must be seeing things. She was all tricked out in lace and silk, little sniggles of embroidered stuff fluffing around on her dress. And her hair was pinned up. Truly pinned up. No red bits flying about her head like something terrifying out of Greek myth. She had a long neck. And high cheekbones. He'd never noticed before, but then, her face was uncharacteristically clean this afternoon.

"What on earth are you all got up for?" he asked, dropping heavily into the nearest wing chair. Was that a flash of hurt in her eyes? No, couldn't be. Little Beast wouldn't care what he thought of her dress. Indeed, she must be chafing under the horror of it all. Lady Sarah's orders, no doubt.

"Cyril says he likes to see me look like a lady."

"Cyril likes you to look like a lady?" Gavin repeated stupidly. No doubt the drug was still affecting his senses.

"He said I'm quite pretty, really. No one's ever said I was pretty before."

"Well, of course you're pretty!" he snapped. "You don't need to be told that." Odd, the way she was holding her head, chin up, a little smile on her lips. Rather sophisticated for Little Beast. She was quite pretty, at that. All the more of a tidbit for that monster to attack.

"When did he tell you this? What sort of a conversation is that for you to be having with your parents in the room?"

"Oh, they were nowhere around," she said with a giggle. "Cyril and I went for a walk."

"You did *what?*" he asked, sitting bolt upright. His blood was thundering in his temples. "Are you telling me you went out unchaperoned with that—with Sir Cyril?"

"Papa didn't care. I don't see why you should!"

"Well, I do! Do you want to be ruined before you even set foot in London? Do you wish to be known as an easy country slut before your first ball? Oh, I can hear the whispers now that will accompany the introduction."

"How dare you?" she cried, stamping her foot. "I'll have you know he was the perfect gentleman!"

"Was he? Can you promise me he did not lay a hand on you?"

"Well . . ."

"Well, *what?*" he thundered. "Did he or did he not lay his hands on you?"

"Well, not much really . . . ," she floundered, looking anywhere but at him.

Gavin's heart was pounding so loudly she should be able to hear it. If the churl had harmed her in any way. . . . "I'm waiting," he said, his voice low and threatening.

"He just—well, he rather kissed me," she said all in a rush.

"You let that strange man *kiss* you?" he growled. "Are you mad? Have you no upbringing at all? If you were my daughter, I would turn you over my knee. You are *never* to let him touch you again, do you hear me? Why the devil did you let him kiss you, anyway? You loathe him, remember?" Gavin rubbed his temples, but it didn't help.

"I have no idea what you could possibly mean by that, sir. Certainly my feelings toward my betrothed are none of your business."

The girl tossed her head. Actually tossed her head, as he'd seen a hundred demoiselles do at a hundred balls. How the devil had she learned that trick, stuck out here in the country with only Sir Harry to emulate? Next she'd be snapping fans around her face, and him supposed to interpret every snap.

"I thought you were going to refuse the man."

A flash of anger in her green eyes told him that the real Lysbeth lurked in there somewhere. " 'Tisn't any of your business, indeed. But if you must know, I've decided to accept the situation. Just as you told me I must."

"I told you?" he said, gaping.

"Indeed, you did, just night before last. Remember, you said I didn't really have any choice."

"Well, yes, but I didn't mean—I didn't mean for you to go and marry the cad!"

"He isn't a cad. He's a real gentleman. Not that you'd know such a thing if it jumped up and bit you in the arse!"

"A real gentleman wouldn't jump up and bite me in the arse, and, by the way, a real lady wouldn't say 'arse'!"

"She wouldn't?" Lysbeth asked uncertainly.

"No!"

"What would she say, then?"

He took a deep breath and studied the ceiling carefully, fighting a sudden urge to scream or laugh or both. "As I reflect upon it, Little Beast, I do not believe a lady would refer to that particular portion of the anatomy at all."

"Really." She flounced herself down on the wing chair opposite him, looking thoughtful. "No," she finally said, shaking her head, "that cannot be right. Sometimes, one simply must refer to the arse. It's bound to come up in the course of conversation once in a while."

"Rarely, Little Beast. Please trust my judgment on this matter. Rarely, indeed."

"I thought you were bringing Cyril back with you," she said.

"He made other plans at the last minute."

"When will he come back?"

"How the devil should I know?"

"What on earth is the matter with you, Gavin? You've done nothing but bite my head off since I came in."

She was so vulnerable. He'd never thought of her as vulnerable before. But that was because he hadn't thought of her at all, not really. Playmate, child, desecrator of perfectly good boots, perhaps. But now she seemed different.

All grown up. Kissable. Vulnerable.

Odd that the woman was vulnerable where the child was not.

"I'm sorry, Little Beast. I've got a pounding headache. Too many ruts in the road," he added quickly, as if the mere reference could bring last night's scene before her eyes.

"Oh, well," she said, bolting to her feet. "That explains it." She crossed to stand behind him, placing her fingers against his temples. Her hands were cool and soft to the touch. She rubbed gently, and he sat back against the cushion, closing his eyes.

When he awoke, he was all alone.

Lysbeth studied her reflection in the glass Lady Sarah had moved into her room with peremptory orders that she make use of it often and to good purpose. She turned her head to one side, then the other. It wasn't much use. It was the same face, no matter how she pouted or smiled. And not a dimple to be seen. Cyril had said she was pretty, but she was smart enough to realize that he had been trying to steal a kiss at the time.

Perhaps she should have been more coy. Gavin had certainly seemed upset enough about it. Although she doubted that a single kiss would brand her the slut of the Season, as he had shouted at her. Of course, he knew London and she did not. To be on the safe side, she would be more coy tonight. She would keep her distance from Cyril, be something of a mystery woman. . . . Yes, men liked a bit of mystery in a woman, didn't they?

She lowered her eyelids and her chin, and, cocking her head to the side, peered up with a deep, unfathomable expression at her reflection. Well, that couldn't be right. Made her look like a half-wit with a bad neck.

Cyril had returned not an hour ago. She had watched from an upstairs window as the hired London coach had delivered him to the door. He certainly had acquired a great many things in his two days in London. Bandboxes and trunks were handed down by a weary-looking coachman to the Digby retainers who had dutifully trudged up the stairs with one load after another.

Her door opened a crack. "Lysbeth!" her stepmother's voice hissed. "Come along, girl. You're keeping everyone waiting!"

Her heart pounding, Lysbeth made her way down the stairs after her stepmother. And as she entered the drawing room, she raised her chin and tossed her head.

"Look where you're going, Little Beast! Now I've got sherry splashed on my cravat. Takes hours to tie the dratted things."

"Hush, Gavin, you'll make him think I'm clumsy!" she whispered, looking around hurriedly for Cyril. There he was, over by the window with Papa. They were looking out and Papa was gesturing broadly. She stood uncertainly, waiting to be noticed. Her stepmama had hurried away, probably to the kitchen to browbeat Cook.

"And our property extends several thousand acres, Sir Cyril." Sir Harry's words drifted over to her. "Quite a profitable estate, really. Excellent hunting, of course. And it will all come down to the gel someday. No entailments, delighted to say."

"Quite the fine gentleman, I must say. Discusses her property and ignores her," came Gavin's dark voice in her ear.

"He doesn't know I'm here yet," she said, *sotto voce.* "What are you doing here, anyway?"

"Oh, such manners. You will be the talk of London. Mind, I

said 'talk,' not 'toast.' Don't do it," he said, sidestepping an incipient kick. "Ladies don't kick gentlemen in the shins."

"I begin to see that being a lady has its drawbacks," she muttered, still keeping an eye on Sir Cyril, who had not, as yet, turned to acknowledge her presence. Perhaps he was near-sighted. Or hard of hearing. Yes, it must be one of those, of course, because he had been most attentive at their last meeting.

"Being a lady is a dreadful bore, Little Beast. You won't like it one bit, you'll see."

"Don't call me 'Little Beast.' It's not dignified."

"How about brat, or poppet, or . . . yes, I've got it—Carrot Top."

She turned a fierce glare on him. He smiled, which was all the more infuriating. She was not a child, no matter how he teased her. "I should like a bit of sherry, please, Mr. Broward," she said, with, she hoped, just the right touch of elegant disinterest.

"Ha, sherry for you, indeed! More like a cup of warm milk I should say. Shall I ring for Nursie?"

She took one menacing step forward, and he grabbed her arm, smiling all the more broadly.

"Behave yourself, now. Ladies do not strike gentlemen in the drawing room. 'Tisn't done."

"Where do ladies strike gentlemen?" she asked, as he led her over to a settee in the corner, the one that faced away from the window where Cyril still stood with Papa.

"Oh, in the face usually. Sometimes in the gut, if they're quite annoyed. And, of course, a kick in the arse is most effective."

She giggled and tried to pull away, but he held tight. She wanted to sit somewhere where Cyril would have a nice view of her, when he finally turned around. This dress was rather fetch-ing, she thought, smoothing its folds. And the neckline was sur-prisingly low. Made her feel quite daring.

"What have you done to your hair?" Gavin queried, seating her firmly on the out-of-the-way settee. He stood in front of her, eyeing her with a frown. "It's too done up. Makes you look too old. And that neckline is most inappropriate for you. You're not even out yet."

It took just a heartbeat, and then the *double entendre* dawned on them both at the same time. "Oh, Gavin, how could you?" she sputtered.

"Sorry, Little Beast," he replied, eyes twinkling. "Perhaps I should get you that sherry after all, and wave it under your nose. Delicate sensibilities and all that."

Out of the corner of her eye she caught a movement, and she turned quickly, a smile on her face. But Cyril was not looking at her. He stared, instead, at Gavin. A long look passed between them, one she couldn't quite understand. Antagonistic, private. Chilling. And the expression on Gavin's face was . . . well, unless she was badly mistaken, he appeared to be *jealous*.

Now that was an intriguing thought. . . .

Gavin lay atop the bed covers, fully clothed, balancing the nearly empty brandy snifter on his chest and cursing himself for a fool. He was a neighbor, nothing more. Half Sir Harry's age. He had no rights whatsoever in the matter. And yet he could not bear to see his Lysbeth marry this vile, perverted man. The very way he looked at her, as if she were the prey and he the hunter, smug, sure of himself, hungry. . . .

Gavin cursed again, thinking that he should have gone home hours ago rather than allow himself to be stuck here, where he surely would get no sleep. Not that it was unusual for him to have accepted the obligatory offer to stay overnight; he frequently did so when the evening ran late with cards and brandy, preferring a warm feather bed to a chilly half-hour ride in the dark. Tonight, however, the thought of leaving had been unbearable, knowing that Cyril would be sleeping in this house, only a few doors down from where Lysbeth lay, asleep, innocent dreaming, no doubt of her beloved. Her demon lover.

And so he had lingered and watched all evening as the dastardly Cyril had schemed to get Lysbeth alone. Gavin knew he had made an idiot of himself, dogging the man's footsteps. Would Miss Digby show him the conservatory? Yes, Miss Digby would, but Mr. Broward invited himself along as well. Would

Miss Digby care for a stroll in the night air? Indeed, Miss Digby would be delighted, but Mr. Broward trotted along beside her like a well-trained dog.

By the end of the tiresome evening, Cyril was no longer hiding his contempt, Sir Harry looked confused, and Lady Sarah, vexed. Lysbeth, however . . . now that was another matter. Gavin fancied she had been somehow relieved at his presence. He had tried this afternoon to scare some sense into her as far as being alone with the brute went. Perhaps she actually had listened.

Not that the chit wasn't smitten with the man. She behaved with the greatest of precision, tight, delicate, rigid in her every response, glancing frequently at himself, as if to say, "See how ladylike I am?" But it was obviously a strain for her. Had to be. She certainly was new at it.

What did she see in the brute, anyway? Cyril was handsome enough, in a well-tailored sort of way, but then, so were many of their set. Of course, she hadn't seen many of their set, tucked away here in the country. And as far as wit was concerned, Cyril was no better, or worse, than any other toff, occasionally vacuous, strained, and cavalier.

Supper had been excruciating, Sir Harry nattering on about his hounds, Lady Sarah looking bored, Little Beast doing an excellent impression of a wax dummy, and Cyril staring holes in the girl's bosom.

And there it was again, the problem Gavin kept revisiting. No matter where his mind went, it always came back to this: how could he let his Little Beast marry this depraved lecher? Dear God, suppose he carried the French Pox?

Gavin sat up abruptly, swinging his feet over the side of the bed, an image rising, unbidden in his mind: Lysbeth, naked, crying, bleeding, Cyril standing over her with a whip in his hand. . . .

The stem of the brandy glass snapped. With a bitter oath Gavin hurled the pieces across the room.

Fool, he called himself again. *He* should be the one—not Cyril, not any other man—marrying Little Beast. Blast it all, *he* was the man who loved her, wasn't he?

Yes. Yes, he was. And, he suddenly realized, he had loved her as far back as he could remember, had he bothered himself to notice. Lysbeth should be his to cherish all of their days, to nurture, to keep safe. To love. But, because he was a bloody fool, because he had not bestirred himself to see what had been, all the while, right at the end of his nose, that monster would have her instead.

Muttering more foul oaths, Gavin stood. He needed more brandy. Enough to drink himself insensible, like Sir Harry, so that he could bear the emptiness. Lord knew, it was the only way he'd get any sleep. Last night he had dreamed of Little Beast's soft lips kissing his own, of her arms tightening around him, of her sweet laughter. Tonight the demons would howl in his dreams.

Lysbeth couldn't sleep. She was confused and unhappy. The feathers in her mattress were all lumped up the wrong way from her tossing and turning, and if she hit her pillow one more time, the room would look like a snowstorm in January.

She had awakened, blushing, after a most unmaidenly dream in which she was being kissed. It had been quite . . . well, breathtaking. Though not so surprising, she reassured herself, for a young lady about to embark on her matrimonial journey.

Only in the dream, it had been Gavin kissing her, not her betrothed.

It was hot in the room, much too stuffy for this time of year. She threw the bed covers off, letting the cool air circulate on her warm skin. The feel of the dream kiss lingered. How Gavin would laugh at her if she told him about it. He had such beauties hanging on his arm in London. That much she knew from Molly, the downstairs maid, whose brother was Gavin's valet. Molly would say little, fearing no doubt to corrupt the master's daughter, but she had let slip that there wasn't a lady in London—and some, she added with a broad wink, who weren't quite ladies—who wouldn't swoon over Gavin Broward's notice.

It was quite disgusting, really, that he should be such an absolute pig where women were concerned. She had asked him about it once, careful not to reveal that she had a secret source of information, but he had laughed at her and told her such talk was not proper for a child's ears.

And that, Lysbeth acknowledged, was probably the reason she had accepted Sir Cyril's proposal: to show Gavin Broward that she was no child, and that if he couldn't appreciate her, well, then, there were others who could.

But she was having regrets about the haste of her decision. Sir Cyril was nice-looking, she supposed—not so handsome as Gavin, of course—and certainly a fastidious man, overly so, perhaps. He had fussed the house down at supper when she had jostled the table, spilling the red wine on his breeches, sending the butler running for the salt. Gavin, of course, had sat there smiling wickedly at her, oblivious to the dried sherry stain on his cravat, that, too, of her making.

But Lysbeth knew enough about the *ton* from the city papers, which eventually made their way into the Digby household, to know that no toff ever suffered from being called too fastidious. Nor could she say she found anything offensive in Sir Cyril's manner. Oh, to be sure, he was precious and arrogant and flippant. And supercilious and superficial, and something of an ass, really. But these traits, too, she knew must be mere social affectations, shed within the privacy of a marriage to reveal the quite sensible fellow underneath.

No, it was something else entirely, a look in his eye that she couldn't quite put into words, a look that made her feel exposed and frightened, that made her feet itch to run like the very devil in whatever direction he could not follow. He had maneuvered close to her several times this evening, managing a surreptitious squeeze here and there. Nothing about his touch made her crave more of it, which was entirely the opposite of the way she'd felt in the dream tonight, when Gavin had kissed her and she hadn't wanted to wake up. Gavin had stuck to her side all evening, effectively thwarting all of Sir Cyril's efforts to cut her out of the herd, and she had been extremely grateful, although Gavin certainly would never know it.

It all came down to that, really. Gavin didn't like Sir Cyril. And if Gavin didn't like him, well, then how could she?

Lysbeth sighed and turned over yet again, but it was no use. The bedclothes were in shambles and the feather mattress more like a trough than a bed.

And now she was hearing things. What? Creaks, a little squeak. Like the one her bedroom door made when she tried to open it stealthily.

She sat bolt upright. Only the knowledge that she was in her own home, where no one meant her any harm, stopped the scream that rose in her throat as she saw that, indeed, the door was swinging open, the hallway black beyond it. She fumbled for her bedside candle, annoyed to see that her hands shook as she struck a light. As the flame grew, she held the candlestick high.

This time she did not suppress a gasp as Sir Cyril slipped into the room, closing the door behind him. He turned to her, a smile on his face, eyes glittering in the light of the candle.

"You're awake. Good. I had to see you. You consume my every thought, my beauty."

He moved toward the bed, and Lysbeth could see that he was none too steady on his feet. "Sir Cyril, please stop there. You must go. This is most improper." She set the candle back on the nightstand. Awkwardly, she shifted the bed covers, trying to cover herself. She slept in a long nightgown, but she was under no illusions as to what could be glimpsed at beneath the thin lawn.

"Are you frightened of me, my dear?" He seemed to linger on the word "frightened," as if he enjoyed the sound of it.

He smiled again, slowly, and this time the look in his eyes did frighten her. Badly.

"Certainly not, sir. I know that you mean me no harm or disrespect. Nevertheless, I do believe you have been drinking and, so, are perhaps unaware that your being alone with me under these circumstances would certainly cause injury to my reputation."

"Of course, my dear. But only if anyone found out. And any number of ladies would tell you that I am most discreet in these matters."

"Sir Cyril, there are no 'matters' between us to speak of. Please leave at once."

Instead, he walked toward the bed, not taking his eyes off of her.

"Stop this minute, or I'll scream. I swear I will!" she said, scrambling to pull the covers higher over her chest.

"Oh, I wouldn't bother, my dear," he said, sitting on the edge of the bed. "I left your father snoring like a sow in the drawing room. And your stepmama, I understand, sleeps with earstoppers so as not to be disturbed. And the servants are all in the attic, aren't they?"

"Isn't Mr. Broward here? He usually stays the night," she offered, her heart pounding. She had retired early, leaving the men to their cards and brandy. But surely Gavin was here . . .

"He left. In something of a snit, I must say. I won a pile off of him. The man is a dreadful card player."

Lysbeth felt her heart sink. If Gavin had gone home, indeed no one would hear her scream.

"Why don't you relax, my dear? I can make you feel wonderful. Truly wonderful." He moved his hand slowly to her face. In the candlelight, his fingernails gleamed, a little too long, a little too perfect. A man should have hands that looked like a man—

"Don't touch me!" she snapped, striking his hand away.

His eyes widened, and he looked at her quizzically. He was close enough that she could smell the brandy on his breath.

"You struck me," he said softly. "That means I get to hit you, doesn't it?" Like the strike of a snake, his hand flew to slap her—hard, across the cheek.

"I'm sorry!" she cried. "But you must leave, sir. Immediately! Please! I beg of you!"

"You beg me?" he murmured. "Now, that sounds quite pleasant. Perhaps you'd beg me more successfully on your knees, my dear."

"I-I don't know what you're talking about, sir, but you must go!" She scrambled away from him, her legs catching in the covers.

"But we're not through talking, Lysbeth," he said, grabbing

her arm too tightly. "I will tell you when we're through with our little chat."

He pulled her to him, and she gasped as his other arm went round her.

"Please stop! Please! You must!" she cried, but relentlessly, his face came nearer and nearer. His lips hung suspended over hers. The sour brandy smell of his breath nearly gagged her. Oh, how could she have ever thought she wanted to kiss this man? And then he swooped, catching her lips hard against his.

He forced her lips open with his own, wet and demanding. And then, shockingly, he stuck his disgusting tongue into her mouth. It was too much! She bit down hard, and he jerked away, crying out. He sat for an instant, his eyes angry, staring at her, his mouth open. She could see blood on his tongue.

Then he smiled slowly. "I'll make you pay for that, my dear," he said, his voice low, his breath coming in pants. "Perhaps you enjoy hurting me? I will certainly enjoy hurting you." He reached out and grasped her nipple through the nightgown.

"Stop it! Stop it!" she cried, trying ineffectively to slap his hand away.

His fingers squeezed without mercy, giving her a vicious pinch, and with his other hand he grabbed the back of her head, pulling her hair hard, so that her head snapped back. Then he fell on top of her, pressing himself against the length of her trapped body.

Even as the shriek tore from her throat, she knew it was hopeless, that no one knew or cared, and that this evil man would ruin her forever. Then Sir Cyril's hand came down over her mouth, choking the very sound out of her.

Gavin came back upstairs on stockinged feet, a snifter of brandy in his hand. Sir Harry had been sprawled across one of the larger divans snoring like a bear, oblivious to all. Gavin had shaken him, planning to help him up the stairs to his bed, but had given up, seeing that Sir Harry was most likely to remain unconscious for many hours yet. He was disinclined to haul the man's carcass up two flights.

The hallway was dark and Gavin had to stop to remind himself to which room the butler had shown him at the end of the long, painful evening. Well, Lysbeth's room was first, that he knew, and his was quite at the other end of the hallway. Cyril was in one of the rooms between his own and Lysbeth's. Pity the bastard wasn't in the barn with the other pigs.

He froze at what sounded like a man's cry of pain, wondering if Sir Harry was in distress and needed help. No, surely that sound would not carry up this far, and indeed, he had firmly closed the drawing room door on his way out. He listened for the space of a few heartbeats, but hearing nothing further, padded softly on.

The shriek, coming from Lysbeth's room, cut through his heart like a knife. Hurling the snifter away from him, he lunged for the door handle and shoved the door wide.

Before him, he saw his worst nightmare come to life: Cyril on top of Lysbeth, his hand pawing roughly at the nightgown caught between her legs, his other hand clapped tightly against her mouth, and she whimpering and thrashing wildly, futilely, against his weight.

Rage rose like blood in Gavin's eyes, and he moved like lightning, without stopping to think. While Cyril continued to rut against Lysbeth, oblivious to all else, Gavin crossed the room, seizing a large brass candlestick as he passed the reading table and raising it high above Cyril's head. There, he paused to look at Lysbeth. Her eyes were open wide, the terror of the damned reflected in their depths. As she caught sight of him, she stopped moving utterly, her gaze desperate in mute appeal. He gave her a smile and, with great deliberation and not inconsiderable strength, brought the candlestick down on Cyril's head.

The dull thud against Cyril's skull would have been sickening had it not sounded so pleasant. The man collapsed suddenly, like a bladder with the air let out. Gavin stood, staring, the sound of blood rushing in his ears.

"Get him off me, please," came a small voice.

"Happy to oblige, Little Beast," he replied, seizing the man by his shoulders and rolling him away from Lysbeth and onto the floor.

The bastard landed with another satisfying thud. His eyes were closed, but his chest still moved evenly up and down, more the pity. A great gash had opened from temple to chin, running blood, and Gavin picked up a towel that hung from the washstand near the bed and pressed it to the cut, not to stanch the bleeding, but to save the fine carpet.

Then he turned to look at Lysbeth. She was a mess, hair wild, lips swollen. Great tears rolled down her cheeks. She never cried. She had always made quite a point of it.

Stepping over the inert form of Sir Cyril Cardwell, Gavin sat down on the bed, reaching with his thumb to wipe away the traces of her tears. She breathed in great hiccoughing gasps. He gathered her into his arms and held her tight, careful not to hurt her.

"Shh," he whispered into her hair. "It's all right now." He stroked her red curls. She smelled of lilacs.

It took some time for her sobs to subside, and all the while Gavin kept one eye on Cyril's unconscious form.

At last she seemed over the worst, and Gavin pulled away, holding her at arm's length, looking her up and down. Her gown was ripped down the front, and her beautiful, perfectly shaped breasts gleamed pale in the candlelight. Very gently he pulled the two halves of the gown together, scowling as he saw the nasty purpling bruise on her nipple. She reached up and held the gown together, her face reddening.

"Where else has he hurt you, sweetheart?" he said softly. He could see no other injury, and he felt sure he had come in time to stop the worst of it.

"Nowhere, really. I'm all right, I suppose," she said, but two more large tears spilled out from her eyes.

He reached for another towel and wet it with water from the pitcher. "Here," he said, dabbing gently at her face.

A moan from Cyril brought Gavin instantly to his feet. "Are you waking up, you sorry sod?" he growled, giving Cyril a sharp kick in the ribs with his foot.

"Get away from me, Broward," Cyril coughed, trying to sit up. He raised his hand to the side of his face, his eyes narrowing as he felt the gash.

"I'll have you brought up on charges for this," he hissed. Struggling to his knees, he leaned back heavily against the washstand, closing his eyes. "When I leave here, I am going straight to the local magistrate to swear out a warrant for your arrest on charges of attempted murder." He opened his eyes, and the malevolence in his expression was like a physical blow. "I think I'll include Miss Digby as well, as accessory after the fact. It is perfectly obvious that you both set me up. Why, the little slut invited me in here tonight and made advances. Quite a coincidence, your being right outside her door when she gave her well-planned scream, wasn't it?"

"Gavin, that's not true!" cried Lysbeth. "I would never do such a thing!"

"Of course you would not, sweetheart," Gavin replied smoothly. Still, having heard the fear in her voice, he reached out behind him, and as he had hoped, he felt her clasp his hand tightly. He would have turned to take her in his arms, but he dared not leave them both vulnerable to this monster. "And you needn't worry," he added for her benefit. "Sir Cyril is bluffing, and we can easily prove it."

"Naturally, I shall hire a coach for London this morning," Cyril went on, as if no one else had spoken, "White's, Almack's, the usual haunts. I think I can guarantee that by nightfall you'll be in Newgate, and the little slut will be ruined."

Not by so much as a flicker did Gavin show how deadly a threat this really was. Instead, he smiled slowly, and, behind him, gave Lysbeth's hand a squeeze. "I cannot find anything to concern me in what you say, Sir Cyril. The magistrate will, of course, come here, and then he will see for himself the extent of the injuries you inflicted on Miss Digby. And, naturally, my testimony will be quite different from yours."

"It will be your word against mine, Broward," Cyril snarled. "I remind you that my family have been stalwart members of society far longer than yours. Your grandfather was, as I recall, a merchant?" This was delivered with a sneer, but if it was meant as a deadly thrust, it fell far short of the mark.

"Indeed, he was, Sir Cyril," Gavin replied, "and a fine man, I might add. Made quite a family fortune, using his brains. Which commodity, I am sorry to say, you seem to lack."

"The vicious little bitch attacked me! A man is allowed to defend himself, even against a woman."

"You're a follower of this Marquis de Sade I've been hearing about, are you not?" This was a shot in the dark, but Cyril's silence on the point told Gavin all he needed to know. "You do remember Bessie, I trust?" he pressed on.

Uncertainty shadowed the man's eyes. "I don't know anyone named Bessie," he said darkly.

"Allow me to refresh your recollection, sir. Bessie is the harlot who, two days ago, in London, you were beating with a cat-o'-nine-tails." Behind him, he heard a gasp from Lysbeth.

"No one will take the word of a whore over mine," Cyril spat out.

"Perhaps not standing alone, sir. But it wouldn't be only her word. It will be my word, and that of Miss Digby, as well as the mute testimony of both Bessie's and Miss Digby's injuries. I'm quite certain we could call, as well, upon the Madame and young Daisy. And who, I wonder, would we turn up if I sent inquiry to Milan? That's where you and your mother lived, is it not?"

For a blind shot there was no question that it sank deep into the target. Cyril's face drained of what little color it had. "My life in Italy is without blemish, sir, as is that of my mother!" he sputtered indignantly.

"We'll be happy to confirm that with a thorough investigation, sir." Gavin let it sink in. He did, indeed, intend to investigate Cyril's past. It should prove quite fruitful.

For a moment they stared at each other, Cyril's swollen and purple face ghastly in the flickering light. If Cyril could be bluffed, Lysbeth would be saved. But one wrong move now and the stain would follow her forever. Even a duel of satisfactory outcome would not clear the crippling taint from her name, should Cyril decide to air his charges. And even if they could convince society that she was victim rather than perpetrator, everyone knew that an assault of this nature spelled ruin for the girl, titters and whispers following her wherever she went. Utter silence was the only hope.

"Here is the alternative, Sir Cyril," Gavin said, deliberately keeping his voice cool. "You may do as you wish, go to the magistrate, spread your excrement throughout London society. If you do this, we, of course, will ruin you. The *ton,* as you may not yet be aware, is a most unforgiving lot. Perhaps you are used to a certain license in Italian society, even a certain privacy. Here, we are a small island, quite rigid in our ways, and we do not have such luxury. You may cause Miss Digby some mild distress, but in the long run, the matrons will flock to her defense." This was not in the least true, of course, but Gavin was counting on Cyril's lack of familiarity with the inner workings of London society.

"You, on the other hand, sir, will be anathema," Gavin continued, leaning down, pushing his face closer to the other man's until their noses fairly touched. "Wait until you see how the invitations dwindle to the point where you'll be happy if Bessie invites you over for a nice beating on the house."

"How dare you, sir?" Cyril sputtered, pulling back. Then, stumbling to his feet, he pushed away from the washstand. "I'll ruin the pack of you!" he snarled.

Gavin noticed that he could barely keep his balance. "It's your choice, Sir Cyril," he said simply.

For a long time neither man spoke.

"No one will ever marry the little fool now, you know," Cyril sneered. He moved slowly away, holding on to the furniture, hobbling to the door.

"Ah, but there you are quite mistaken, sir," Gavin said calmly, watching his retreat. "I am quite determined to marry Lysbeth myself." The remark earned him only a malevolent glare before the man disappeared into the black of the hallway.

There was not a sound in the room. Gavin waited until he heard Cyril's labored footsteps receding down the hall; then he moved to shut the door.

He turned and caught sight of Lysbeth. She was kneeling on

the bed, clutching the bed covers against her chest, green eyes
wide and swimming with tears. He felt as if he could drown in
their luminous depths. Her red curls tumbled around her gamine
face, catching the light of the candle. She looked so beautiful.
And so vulnerable. How had he not known how much he loved
her?

"What do we do now?" she whispered.

"Nothing, sweetheart. You are safe. He will do as I have said.
He'll dare not do otherwise."

"No, I do not care about him. I mean what . . . what do
we . . . Did you really mean what you said about marrying me?"
she finished awkwardly.

"I did," he said, smiling, waiting for her to rush forward and
throw herself into his arms.

She did not. After a long pause, she said, "I-I don't think I
want to get married."

He stared. Surely she couldn't mean. . . .

Ah, of course. He smiled indulgently. "Little Beast, in spite
of what you may have gleaned about proper proposal etiquette,
I assure you this is no time to be coy." Poor girl must be feeling
terribly confused. He strode forward and sat himself on the bed,
reaching for her hand.

She pulled away.

"What is it?" he asked, beginning to feel a vague alarm.

"I said, I don't want to get married," she repeated, a little
defiantly.

He stared at her, and it slowly dawned on him. "You don't
love me," he said, stupidly, feeling a sinking dread in the pit of
his stomach.

"Of course I love you!" she declared, with a great indignant
bounce on the bed. "I don't suppose I've ever loved anyone so
much in my life as I love you."

"Then why . . ." She *did* love him! Amazing how quickly
that sinking feeling vanished.

"I just don't want to be married," she muttered, looking away.

"Why not?" he asked, determined to be patient.

She did not answer. When he reached for her hand, she pulled away again, looking dark and mutinous.

"What's wrong, sweetheart?" he asked, exasperated despite his resolve.

"I don't like it," she finally said, so low he was not sure he had heard her correctly.

"Don't like what?" he asked, utterly at a loss.

A long pause. Then, finally . . .

"You know." Her voice was barely a whisper.

He stared at her. She was blushing. Most uncharacteristic.

"Perhaps you had better tell me plainly, so that I don't misunderstand," he said slowly, but he rather thought he did know what was bothering her.

"I don't want any man to touch me, ever again. Not ever! It's just disgusting!" She finished with another flounce that nearly bounced him off the bed.

"I see." He took a deep breath. "Lysbeth . . ." He took her hand again, and she did not flinch. But she would not look at him. "Has anyone told you that the things that pass between a man and his wife are quite pleasurable? For both?"

She stole a glance at him. "For the woman, too?" she asked, but she sounded as though she didn't believe him.

"Yes, indeed, for the woman, too. How else do you suppose the planet got so well-populated?"

He was rewarded with a little smile and took the opportunity to close the space between them, sliding closer on the bed. She did not pull away, but then, if she moved any farther back, she'd bump her head on the headboard.

"Would you like to try a kiss?" he asked tentatively. He did not want to frighten her, but in the space of the past few minutes, it had come to matter a great deal to him that she like what would pass between them.

She turned to him, eyes wide and frightened. "I suppose we could try," she said softly, but he could hear the tremble in her voice.

Very gently he reached for her, pulling her to him, burying his face in her red curls. "I want very much to kiss you, my

Little Beast," he whispered. "And I do so want you to like it."
He traced his lips through her hair and nipped at her ear.

She gave a shudder, but pressed closer to him. Down, down,
past her ear, along her jaw, he moved, and then she turned her
head slightly, and their lips met. It was hard to be gentle, hard
to hold himself in check. She was so sweet, with soft, innocent,
trusting lips, pursed like a child's. He moved his hands to the
back of her head, burying them in her soft hair. Very gently, he
pulled her closer. She did not resist. He felt her hands reach
around his waist. It felt good to be wrapped in her arms.

He deepened the kiss, moving his lips against hers, and gently
ran his tongue across her soft mouth, pushing, just slightly. Her
lips parted, and he felt her sigh against him. His tongue sought
hers, and a thrill ran through him as he felt her respond, deep
within herself, with a passion soon to be born—born, he hoped,
of love.

Gently, he disengaged his lips from hers, pulling back to gaze
earnestly into the beautiful green eyes of his beloved.

The little beast giggled.

"What is it?" he asked, a bit startled. Possibly a bit hurt. No
one had ever laughed at his kisses.

She sat up, her eyes dancing merrily in the candlelight.

"What?" he repeated, perhaps testily.

"Oh, Gavin, don't you see?" she cried, throwing her arms
around him. "I thought . . . well, when that man touched me it
was all so foul. I hated the very thought of it. His touch, the smell
of him, everything about it was nauseating! I thought, perhaps,
that this was the way of it, that ladies didn't enjoy that sort of
thing at all, that they went through the marriage just disgusted
and sick all the time, loathing the very thought of going to bed.
But now I find—" She broke off to beam at him. "Well, it isn't
that way at all, is it? I love it when you touch me. I love your
kisses. I want you to make love to me every day. I love you,
Gavin. I think I've loved you since the day I was born."

For a moment he couldn't speak for the lump in his throat.
He buried his face in her hair, taking in the scent of her. "I love

you so much, Lysbeth," he finally whispered. "Does this mean you'll marry me?"

She pulled back and eyed him quizzically. "Well, I'm not quite sure, yet, Gavin," she said thoughtfully, but mischief danced in her green eyes. "Kiss me again, and let me see."

With a low growl he gathered her in his arms, feeling her gasp as he crushed her to him, pressing his lips against hers. With an instinct born of the ages, she opened her lips, her tongue finding his, and he groaned, pulling her even tighter to his chest. Her arms inched around him, her hands pressing against his back, as if she, too, were trying to bring them closer. It was hard to remember that he must not frighten her, hard to hold himself back. She sighed against him, and he could feel his resolve thinning.

With a gasp, he pulled his lips away from hers, holding her face, drinking in the sight of her in the candlelight.

"Well?" he rasped, hands twined in her hair.

She traced a gentle finger down his face, and he seized it between his teeth, gratified to hear the moan that escaped her.

"I believe I might be prevailed upon to accept your proposal after all, Mr. Broward," she whispered, breathless, her eyes glowing. "Perhaps, however, you might just kiss me one more time, so that I can be quite certain."

And so he did.

Legend

by

Mary Kirk

Author's Note

When I was five, I asked my mother why everyone had to die. Because they just do, she said. Everyone dies. But someday, *some*body might not die, I insisted. She gave up the argument—but I never really changed my mind.

When I first met Duncan MacLeod (played by Adrian Paul on *Highlander: The Series),* a part of me wanted to say, "See, I *knew* it could be true." And although my adult mind knows that Duncan MacLeod is a work of fiction, some child-part of me believes he's quite real and that he and I and a few lucky others share a great secret.

" 'Tis true," the bearded man said. "Long ago, on this isle, lived a race of people who were immortal."

The little girl frowned. "What do you mean 'immortal'?"

"Exactly that," her teacher replied. "They did not die."

"But how could that be?" she argued. "You have taught me that all life has a beginning and an end."

"Aye," he agreed. "And I have also taught you that every rule has exceptions. The people called Gwynhils were such an exception. From the moment of a Gwynhil's birth, he was free from all sickness, and as long as no misfortune befell him, he continued to grow and to age. Of course, life is dangerous. Gwynhils were not immune to mishap and, so, eventually would come to cynadd, which, in their language, meant first death. Like mortals, they died, yet they then awakened. And from that moment on, they ceased to age, and though they might die again, many times over, they continued to reawaken, whole and unharmed."

The little girl's blue eyes were wide with wonder. "They must have been children of the gods."

The teacher smiled. " 'Tis as good an explanation as any as to their origins. In truth, no one knows from whence they came, for they were here long before anyone can remember. Before the Christians brought their one god to Prydain that is now called Britain, before the Romans set out to rule the world. Before the Phoenicians or the Greeks. 'Tis said they were here at the dawn of time. And on this mist-shrouded isle, to which no ship had ventured, they prospered."

"No one knew about them?" the girl asked.

"For a very long time, no," her teacher said. "The Gwynhils, however, knew much about the rest of the world, for they were great travelers. And what they learned on foreign soil, they brought home with them. Metal working, shipbuilding, music, languages, the healing arts—their knowledge was extensive, mayhap more so than any other civilization, although they lived without pretense."

"If they never became ill," the girl said, "to what end did they learn the ways of a healer?"

"They sought knowledge for its own sake. And, perhaps because they themselves never fell prey to illness, they were intrigued by its power. In any case, they were a benevolent people. For brief spans of years, a Gwynhil might live among mortals, serving as a healer or a bard. They were wise men and women whose skill and counsel were valued."

Silently, the little girl contemplated her teacher's words. Then her puzzled frown appeared once more. "If they prospered here, and if they truly could not die, then where are they now?"

The teacher sighed. "That, I fear, is a sad tale, for the Gwynhils were slain."

"Slain? But how? And for what cause?"

"The 'how' of it was a simple task. A stroke of the sword through the heart—'twas one of the very few ways an immortal could be brought to final death, which they called tyradd. The 'why' of it is a story of treachery and greed. Those who learned of them came to steal the source of their immortality, the black rock, ducarreg, for which the island was then named."

The girl's look became wary. "A *rock* made these people immortal? I believe you are inventing this tale."

He chuckled. "I assure you, 'twould require more imagination than I possess. No, the Gwynhils were quite real, as was ducarreg. 'Twas a magical rock that burned and gave off heat. The Gwynhils considered it a gift from Donn, god of the underworld and son of the Mother Goddess. They believed ducarreg was Donn himself, manifest to them, and that by their companions burning a small piece of it when they died, life was restored to them through Donn."

Still skeptical, the girl said, "Why have I never seen this ducarreg, nor heard of it?"

" 'Tis gone," the teacher replied. "Those who came to steal it destroyed that which they had come seeking."

"And with it, all of the Gwynhils," the little girl concluded.

"Well . . . perhaps not."

"You said they were all slain."

"I said they were slain. I did not say 'all.' Indeed, a tale is told of two immortals, a man and a woman, who survived the slaughter. 'Tis a tragic tale, for it tells of the end of a civilization. Yet 'tis also a story of hope and courage—and, most of all, a story about love."

Eagerly, the girl asked, "Will you tell me?"

"Aye," her teacher replied. "Listen, now. This is how it was. . . ."

They were dead. All of them. His family, his friends. His people. Everyone he had ever known and loved. Their bodies lay strewn upon the ground, their clothing soaked in blood that spread from identical wounds: a stroke of a sword through the heart. Nay, they never would rise again.

Rowan staggered through the field of corpses, mute with horror, sickened by the smells of death and acrid smoke, the latter of which rose in wisps from the charred remains of his village. As he made his way into the midst of the ruins, his gaze was drawn by a sight nearly as shocking, and as inexplicable, as the carnage surrounding him: the sacred outcropping of ducarreg around which the village had been built was gone, and in its place was a wide and gaping hole.

At least four twelves of the massacre's victims lay around the pit in a tangled ring, their bodies left to rot at what had been the foot of their holy shrine. There lay Liath, his mother's sister, and Ness, Liath's daughter. Here were his companions Maol and Brannoc. Tor, the head of the council of elders. Ciara, with whom, in the distant past, he had oftentimes shared a bed.

He found his mother's body beneath the peach tree in front of the smoldering ashes of her small dwelling. Halting beside her, he sank to his knees. His body trembled; his breath came in short, labored gasps. As he looked at the lifeless form of the woman who had borne him, a roaring began in his head, and it grew until, finally, it burst forth in a howl of anguish. Once he had begun, once the sound had broken from him, he could not stop it. He howled until his throat was raw and the only sound he could make was a hoarse groan.

Still, he crouched there in the blood and the ashes, rocking back and forth, his hands covering his face. Time passed, but he was unaware of it. A breeze stirred, and the stench of decaying flesh filled the air. The summer sun reached its zenith. Yet he did not move.

He was still kneeling beneath the peach tree, bent double, when a soft and trembling voice spoke behind him.

"Rowan?"

He jerked upright and turned. "Ailia?" Leaping to his feet, he rushed toward the russet-haired young woman, catching her as she stumbled into his arms.

"I thought I was the only one left," she cried.

"As did I. Ailia, what—"

" 'Tis wrong, I know, to feel any happiness when they are all . . ." Her voice broke. "I cannot help it. I have never been so glad to see anyone as I am to see you."

"If 'tis wrong, then we are both accursed," he said. "For I am equally glad to see you."

She dissolved against him, sobbing, and though questions pounded at him, he did not ask them. She was not capable of further speech, nor, in truth, was he. Holding her, he let them sink to kneel upon the ground, and there, surrounded by the dead, they shared their grief. It mattered not that they knew little of each other or had seldom had reason to speak. As they clung together in mutual anguish, he felt a bond forge between them as strong as any he, in all of his twelve-twelves and ten winters, had ever felt with anyone.

When her crying had subsided to whimpers, he held her away to take in her bedraggled appearance—her hip-length hair a mass of tangles, her clothing dirty and torn, smudges of dirt on her face and hands.

His voice was ragged as he spoke. "Ailia, who did this?"

" 'Twas the Romans," she whispered.

His breath hissed out between his teeth. "You are certain?"

She gave a jerky nod. "I knew from the descriptions in the Chronicles—the armor and shields and weapons. They came in three ships, a horde of them . . . heavily armed, and. . . . Oh, Rowan, they were . . ."

Words failed her, but he understood. Although there were men among the Gwynhils, like himself, who had learned the ways of the warrior, they could not have withstood an attack mounted in earnest; isolated by the sea and protected by ages of secrecy on their island far to the west of Eire and Prydain, his people never had seen need to prepare a defense. The Romans, who, twice twelve winters ago, had spilled over the channel from Gaul to take Prydain, would have found them easy prey.

"But why would they come only to slaughter and burn?" he asked. " 'Tis not like them to—"

"They came for our ducarreg," she said.

He sucked in a sharp breath. "They *knew?*"

"Aye." Ailia's lips twisted in bitterness. "Still, they saw need to prove its power. They broke Conal's neck, then built a fire and threw ducarreg into it."

"And he reawakened," Rowan muttered.

" 'Twas all the proof they needed. They stripped Donn's shrine to the ground and began digging a tunnel."

" 'Tis called a mine."

"Nay, 'tis a sacrilege," she insisted. "Arias told them that Donn would wreak vengeance upon anyone who desecrated his holy ground, but they would not listen. They . . . they laughed at him. Then they"—she broke off, shuddering—"they gave him tyradd. A sword to the heart. 'Twas clear, then, that we had been betrayed. Someone must have told them not only about ducarreg but of how our people reach final death. Oh, Rowan, who could have done such a thing?"

He sat back on his heels, shaking his head. "No Gwynhil would violate his traveler's vow of silence, not with knowledge. Mayhap a Roman witnessed a reawakening and followed our traveler." Thinking aloud, he continued, "One thing is certain. We have believed our island safe and our existence unknown for so long that we overlooked the obvious. 'Twas inevitable that the Romans would learn of us. Their quest for power is insatiable, like nothing this part of the world has ever faced."

"They are godless butchers," Ailia whispered, her dark blue eyes reflecting the horror she had witnessed. "The leader put his men to work hauling ducarreg to their ships. Crate after crate was brought out of the mine and tossed about with no more concern than if it had been grain. For three moons it went on. And while our men were tied and guarded, the women were made to serve the Romans food and drink."

Casting him a quick glance, she continued in a voice that trembled with fury. "They plundered our land, they slept in our homes and ate our food, and whenever the thought struck them, they took whichever woman happened to be nearby—in full view of any other vermin who cared to watch. And many did." She paused, then muttered, "Mightily happy with themselves, they were, and I believe they might simply have gone away when they had finished with their thievery if their accursed mine had not erupted."

Shaking with rage, Rowan did not immediately grasp the import of her words. When he did, he frowned. "Erupted?"

Ailia waved a hand toward the chasm, mayhap four-twelves paces away, where Donn's shrine had stood. "It happened three days ago, at midday. There was a terrible rumbling beneath the earth. Then the ground burst open with a sound so loud that it shook the trees. When the dust settled . . . well, you see what happened. Their mine had but a small opening, large enough for several men to pass through, with timbers to prop up the earth around it. Now, 'tis only . . ."

A grave.

Neither of them said the words, but Rowan was certain they were both thinking them. He had little knowledge of mines yet had never heard of one erupting. Still, he believed that he knew what had caused this mine to erupt, and Ailia's next statement echoed his thoughts.

" 'Twas Donn's vengeance," she said. "The Romans were warned that our god would show his fury at being stolen from his home, and he did."

"Were any of our people in it?" Rowan asked.

She gave her head a quick shake. "Nay, we were not permitted near."

He was grateful, if bitterly so. For if any Gwynhils had been buried by the eruption, he would have been compelled to unearth them and bring them to reawakening, and he doubted that he could have accomplished the task. Nor would Ailia have been of any help, he thought, noting how thin she appeared—thin to the point of being frail, her once-pretty, blue linen peplos hanging from her slender shoulders as if it had been intended for a much larger woman.

Ailia continued. "The eruption made the Romans afraid. Mayhap, they saw, finally, that Donn would not allow them to go unpunished. Yet their fear soon turned to a terrible fury. Their leader ordered all of our people put to the sword, as if the eruption had been our fault, and his soldiers carried out the deed. They packed every piece of ducarreg they could find into crates and took them to their ships. Then, yesterday, they set fire to the village and left."

"They took *all* of the ducarreg?" Rowan said, the sickness and rage in his gut turning suddenly to cold dread.

She nodded. "They crept upon the ground, picking up every tiny piece. Even the dust made by the eruption was swept into bags and taken. I watched them. I have been staying in the cave near the cliffs." Dropping her gaze, she murmured, "I was picking mushrooms, and on my way home I saw their ships anchored off shore. I—I was frightened, so I sought refuge in the woods. I have watched every day, waiting for a chance to help, believing that, surely, such a chance would come. It did not, and when the eruption happened, and . . . the deaths were ordered, I . . . I watched that, too. And I did not scream nor make any sound at all, because I did not want them to find me. Still, I should have tried to do something!"

"Nay, you should not," Rowan said, nonetheless knowing he

would have felt the same—indeed, did feel the same, as if returning earlier from his hunting trip on Bachynys, the tiny island off the southern coast, would have accomplished anything but to bring about his own death. He, who often had ignored the law against traveling alone, was to have been gone no more than a moon but had stayed nearly four, only because he had been enjoying the solitude; had he returned when he had been expected, he, too, would be lying here, skewered through the heart.

"There was nothing you could have done without being killed for your efforts," he said. Then, gesturing to the small leather pouch she wore on a cord around her neck, he said, "Your dairn—you have it, do you not?"

His fear grew as she shook her head, removing the pouch and showing it to him. Every Gwynhil wore one, and in them they carried tiny pieces of ducarreg—dairns; if they met death by mischance, their companions burned the ducarreg and reawakened them. No Gwynhil would leave even the village, much less the island, without his dairn. No Gwynhil, that is, save himself.

Rowan knew that his people considered him incautious, among other things, yet he had always discounted the charges as the naggings of ancient men and women who had long-since forgotten what it meant to be truly alive. He realized—now, 'twas too late—that they had been right, at least in one respect; he had taken his immortality for granted. Having reached cynadd at twotwelves and one, he had possessed the strength and vigor of a man in the prime of life throughout all the winters since. Little threatened him, and so, he had lived without fear. Until now. Staring at the empty pouch Ailia held, Rowan experienced terror for the first time in his long life.

"I burned the dairn," she said. "I thought that some Roman blade might have missed the heart for which it had been aiming, and I hoped I might reawaken at least one person. 'Twas but a very tiny piece, and I am not certain—"

"The size does not matter," Rowan interrupted her. "They are all at tyradd, or they would have reawakened. Still, I would have done as you did—I would have tried, despite that the dairn was the last piece."

"But you have *your* dairn . . . do you not?"

He brought his gaze up to meet hers and, slowly, shook his head. "I burned it for Maol. We were hunting hawk on the cliffs, and he fell. The next day, I was halfway across the channel to Bachynys when I realized I had not replaced the dairn. I did not wish to row back and did not think 'twould matter." And 'twould *not* have mattered, since he had been alone, with no one to burn the ducarreg should he have met with misfortune.

He expected Ailia to give him, at the least, a reproachful look or some other sign of disapproval for the risk he had taken, but she did not.

Rather, she whispered, "Rowan, what are we to do?"

The lost, frightened look in her tear-reddened eyes reminded him of how young and innocent she was and forced him to rein in his own inner turmoil. She had not yet reached cynadd, had never left their island, and so, had never met a mortal. About them and their world, she knew only what she had heard or read in the Chronicles. Until now, she had never met evil. 'Twas bad enough for him to return home to this horror; he could not imagine how devastating it surely had been for Ailia to sit by, helpless, and witness it.

Moreover, she appeared to be starving, indeed, must be, after three moons of living in a cave, having only that which she could forage to eat.

As gently as he could manage, he told her, "We must honor our dead. We will give them back to Donn and to the Mother by burying them in the place where they worshipped."

She tore her gaze from his and looked toward the gaping hole. "How can we make a proper grave, when the stream will soon fill it with water?"

'Twas true, what she said; the stream that had passed close to Donn's shrine in its course through the large and sprawling village had been cut off by the eruption and now ended at the crater's west wall, its waters spilling down the side in a gentle falls.

" 'Twill not be like other graves," he agreed. "Yet it seems right that they should lie in that place, the gateway to Donn's underworld, despite that it means lying beneath the water."

She stared at the pit for another long moment, then gave him a single nod. The effort she was making to gather her courage was almost tangible, and he greatly admired her for it. 'Twas an intolerable duty they had to perform.

They performed it together, using a system of ropes and pulleys. With Ailia tying ropes onto bodies they had collected at the crater's edge, Rowan climbed into the pit, lowering and weighting each body before climbing out to begin the collection process again. 'Twas back-breaking, as well as gruesome, labor, and 'twas made worse by the constant flow of water into the pit; although the water level had not yet begun to rise, the saturated soil was a quagmire.

It soon became apparent to him that Ailia was exhausting herself, attempting to drag and carry bodies, and he bade her stop. She continued to make herself useful in other ways, though. Seeming to know when he needed food and drink, she provided it, using vegetables from ruined gardens and the deer he had brought home from his hunting trip. Then, each day at sunset, when he was covered in mud and tired beyond thinking and wanted only to bathe and to sleep, she had soap and hot water waiting for him. And at dawn, he awakened to find that his tunic and bracae had been washed of the previous day's mud.

Until the last body was buried, Rowan held out hope that someone might be missing from among the dead, someone who was traveling on foreign soil. He knew, though, 'twas in vain. This year marked the Mawr Dathliad, a dwysin times a gros—twelve times twelve-twelves—winters that the Gwynhils had kept Chronicles, the ongoing account of their lives on Tirducarreg, their journeys, and their cumulative knowledge; those who had been away had come home for the celebration that was to have taken place at harvest time.

Rowan kept track of how many he buried, tying a knot in a rope for each body: two gros and one, which accounted for every Gwynhil known to exist. Excluding Ailia and himself.

At the end of the fourth day, when he had weighted the last

body, Rowan climbed out of the pit to sit at its edge, exhausted, caked with mud, and sick at heart. Ailia came to stand beside him, and together they surveyed the mass grave. He judged it to be twelve and eight paces wide; he knew, having climbed the rope so many times, 'twas two-twelves and ten deep. Although that morning the water level finally had begun to rise, 'twould be many days before it reached ground level and, thereby, rejoined the stream with its former path, which lay on the opposite side of the pit.

" 'Tis finished, then?" Ailia asked.

"Nay," he replied. "With all of the ducarreg gone, this place is no longer glanelle, and Donn will not have reason to abide here. Mayhap he has already abandoned us, and if he has, our people will not be taken to the other side, with him." The thought had been one among many plaguing him. To his people, many things that came from the earth were glanelle—sacred. Trees, rivers, springs: all were born of Madron, the Mother Goddess, who was the earth itself. Of Her children, Donn was the most powerful, and Rowan shuddered every time he considered what further acts of vengeance Donn might commit if he and Ailia could not appease him. "We must make it glanelle once again," he said.

"How?" she asked. "We could not return the ducarreg to the ground, even if we had it back from the Romans."

"We will make a grove," he replied, praying silently 'twould suffice.

He could see in Ailia's wide-eyed look that she did not believe they could accomplish the deed. He was determined, though, and mayhap noting his resolve, she offered no argument.

They set about the task the following morning, and he soon realized that his plan would have been doomed to failure without her. He had navigated ships safely through storms and hunted cats bigger than men in the mountains of Gaul, but he knew almost nothing of things that grew in the earth. Ailia, however, knew a great deal and offered her counsel with a gentleness that made the work less daunting.

Together, they prepared the ground surrounding the grave,

clearing debris broadcast by the eruption and turning the earth. They then scoured the surrounding countryside for the appropriate saplings. Gathering only a few at a time and only the most healthy, they carefully dug the young trees from the ground and carried them to the village.

By mutual agreement, they planted a triple ring of yew, the death tree, around the perimeter of the grave. Then came a ring of the sacred oak, twelve of them in all. Finally—and with somewhat less reverence—they planted a circle many trees deep of fast-growing fir; these, they placed close together in order that the branches would quickly tangle and, thus, hide the inner grove from view.

The moon passed through a full cycle, and summer began to wane. Rowan came to take for granted that Ailia and he would spend each day together, parting rarely and only for brief periods. For, although neither of them had said as much, 'twas understood between them that neither wished to be alone. They worked together, ate their meals together, and passed the night on pallets made on opposite sides of the same fire.

They did not discuss what they would do when the grove was complete. Rowan saw the questions in Ailia's eyes, though, and Madron knew, he himself thought of little else.

In truth, he was being driven by two equally powerful urges. First, he needed ducarreg; Ailia's and his lives depended upon it, and find it, he would. He *must.* Second, he wanted revenge. His people were not warriors. Moreover, to them more than any mortal race he had ever encountered, life was sacred; they did not believe in killing. He had killed, though, fighting beside mortal men whose causes he had believed were just. And, when he found the mortal who had destroyed his world, he would not hesitate to kill again.

He could not satisfy either of the urges driving him, however, without first securing Ailia's agreement. When the grove was finished, he would broach the subject. Now was not the time. This, as he and Ailia worked to give their people a fitting burial, was a time for grieving, a time for silent reflection. A time to think not of the world but of the spirit.

For the first half of the moon, he thought of very little but the companions with whom he never again would hunt, his mother whose voice he never again would hear, even the ancient men and women who had comprised the council of elders, with whom he had often disagreed but whom he had respected and revered. Then, however, raw grief began to ease. As the newly formed pond filled to the brim and the stream once more picked up its course, life again began to seem possible, if not attractive, and Rowan's thoughts turned more often not to the spirit but to the flesh.

Although they spoke little and only of the matter at hand, he was deeply aware of Ailia's presence. She was, after all, the only other living person on Tirducarreg and the only other one of his kind who remained on earth. Yet 'twas more than her uniqueness that drew his attention.

He remembered her as a comely child. She had grown to be a beautiful woman, with eyes the color of twilight and a slender but shapely body—a body that became ever more shapely beneath the light folds of her sleeveless peplos as the effect of near starvation disappeared. Moreover, she was fryth, fertile, a condition that lasted only from the time a Gwynhil female reached womanhood until her cynadd. During that time, a woman was exceptionally alluring, mayhap more so because, in all but a few cases, she was marked as gwarhardd, forbidden to any man. As was Ailia.

Gwynhil laws were ancient and strict, and none more so than those that governed mating. 'Twas so for good reason, Rowan believed, for once agreeing with the elders, for Gwynhil women met death in childbirth with uncommon frequency; indeed, only a very few survived the experience without reaching cynadd. What was far worse, for many women, first death met in childbirth was tyradd; they did not reawaken, no matter how much ducarreg was burned.

'Twas a matter of great mystery why this was so, but then, as the elders were quick to say, many things about their immortality could be understood only as the workings of Donn. For his part, Rowan had always thought that causing women to risk final death in order to bear a child was Donn's way of preventing the people whom he had blessed with immortality from increasing their numbers beyond what he deemed proper.

Regardless, the elders were unwilling to leave the lives of their women—and, hence, the continuance of their race—entirely in the hands of the gods. Together with the midwives, whose judgment as to which women might survive childbirth had been honed throughout the ages, they sought to protect fryth women by dictating which ones would be permitted to conceive. Any woman who was not granted such leave was made gwarhardd.

No man could touch a woman who was gwarhardd. Nor could the woman leave Tirducarreg; for, while their history had proven that a Gwynhil man could not get a child on a mortal woman, the fryth Gwynhil woman might conceive by a mortal man. This was an event known to have happened only once, and beyond the danger to the woman's life that was involved, 'twas considered a calamity by the elders, to be avoided at all costs.

Rowan had long-since learned to ignore a woman who was gwarhardd, nor had it ever been difficult to do so. There were other women—and far more of them—who, having passed cynadd, were not forbidden. Moreover, the mortal world was full of women whose lives would not be at risk should they lie with him—and he had lain with more than a few.

'Twas different now, though. It seemed to him worse than ironic that his choices had been reduced, suddenly and with brutal finality, to one woman. And she was not a choice at all.

The day came when the grove was complete. With the last tree planted, Rowan stood, with Ailia beside him, inside the inner ring of yew, at the edge of the grave, and together they prayed. They prayed to Donn that he would forgive the sacrilege committed by the Romans and not abandoned their kin. They prayed, too, to Madron, who was both the Giver and Taker, from whom all life flowed and to whom all life returned. She was the earth, the very land upon which they walked, and the trees and flowers, the mountains and springs and lakes that sprang from Her, were evidence of Her powers. They prayed that She would take their people back into Her womb and harbor their spirits.

The sun was setting behind the western hills when their prayers were finished. Its long rays, shooting toward them from the horizon, turned the surface of the water, pooled at their feet, into a bronze mirror. For several long minutes, they stood in silence. Then, Rowan spoke.

" 'Tis done," he said.

"Aye," Ailia agreed. "And now we must decide what we will do. Although I suspect you have made your choice."

Startled, Rowan looked at her. She was staring at the water, and the setting sun, behind her, haloed her profiled features and turned her long mane of dark russet hair into a red-gold cloud.

"Why does it surprise you," she asked, "that I know your intention to search for ducarreg?"

When he did not answer—indeed, could not—she glanced at him briefly. " 'Tis true, I have not reached cynadd, but I have lived for two-twelves and three years among many who have long-since passed into immortality. I know what importance ducarreg holds for you, and were I in your place, my single goal would be to find what I had lost."

Rowan did not know which made him more uncomfortable: that she knew his thoughts so easily or that his long-held notions about the innocence—nay, ignorance—of someone not old enough to have reached cynadd were being challenged.

"So," she continued, "although that which was taken was known to be the only ducarreg on our island, you must find another source."

"Aye," he said. And because she had a right to know, he added, "And if I do not find it, I will go after what the Romans took."

That, apparently, had not occurred to her.

"You cannot!" she said. "Rowan, they will kill you, as they did the others."

"How would it matter?" he returned. "Without ducarreg, I will reach tyradd, in any event."

"But to seek the Romans! 'Twould be a senseless death."

"Nay, 'twould be an honorable one."

She shook her head. " 'Tis not honor but vengeance you seek to satisfy in finding—and, I suspect, killing—these Romans."

"Killing one will do—the one who ordered the slaughter."

She was silent for a moment, and he could feel the distress emanating from her.

"And what of me?" she said. "Where will I go when you are dead and I am truly the only one of our kind?"

"I have thought of that." Turning toward her, he continued in what he hoped was a persuasive tone. "A small isle lies off the western coast of Eire where seven druid priestesses dwell. The high priestess is a friend. You would be welcome in her home, I am certain. When I find the Romans who stole our ducarreg and recover it from them, I will come back for you. We will decide then what is best to do."

Without looking at him, Ailia asked, "And if you do not return? What am I to do if this Roman whom you want to kill, instead, kills you?"

"As I said, you will be safe with Enya and her priestesses."

"Safe from what? Death? Or life?" She gestured toward the grave at their feet. "Why not give me tyradd now and be done with it?"

Rowan frowned, bewildered by her reaction and surprised at the uncommon anger in her tone. "I do not understand. Why would you not live among those good women?"

She did not answer immediately. Crossing her arms, she shifted slightly on her feet, appearing suddenly uncomfortable. "Did it not occur to you," she said, "that I might wish to take a husband and live as other people do?"

Nay, not in his wildest imaginings. "Ailia, you cannot," he said.

"Because I am gwarhardd?" she returned, a measure of bitterness coloring her tone. "Those who named me such are no longer, and I would choose another path for myself."

"You would dishonor our laws?"

"It does not seem to me dishonorable to want to continue our race. Quite the opposite."

He studied her carefully, reassessing. He had found her to be kind and unselfish and skilled in practical ways that made life more pleasant—a comfortable, if somewhat dull, companion. He realized that he had not done her justice. She was not dull; she had been numb with grief—a thought that made him wonder how she must view him, for, Madron knew, he himself had felt this past moon as if he were walking in the underworld. They had both poured their grief into the physical labor of burying their dead and planting the grove, but now, although the anguish of the shocking loss would always remain with them, the worst was past. And it seemed that behind the veil of grief, Ailia had more spirit, and more wit, than he had imagined.

With new respect, he told her, "I would not hold you to laws that I myself do not countenance. I have never believed that the mixing of Gwynhil and mortal blood would be the tragedy that the elders have declared it."

She turned her head quickly to look up at him, clearly surprised.

"If that were the only reason for you not to take a mortal mate," he continued, "I would gladly aid your cause to do exactly that. But, Ailia, you know as well as I how often our women meet death in childbirth. Your own mother reached cynadd giving birth to you, as did mine. Mine reawakened. Yours did not. And without ducarreg, any death would be tyradd. You must wait until I recover it before you risk death in *any* fashion."

She pressed her lips together, and he could see that she was suppressing the urge to say she did not believe he would recover it.

Instead, she said, "Then, if you insist upon this quest," I will go with you, for I would as soon die a quick death with you as age interminably, alone among women devoted to some god whom I do not know."

" 'Tis unthinkable," he said. "I will not take you into what will surely be a battle."

"I will not join your priestess."

"She is not *my* priestess."

"No matter. I will not join her. And if you will not take me with you, then I will remain here."

"I cannot leave you on Tirducarreg, alone."

"Then do not go."

He opened his mouth to argue, then closed it. The look in her eyes—the sparkling light of determination—told him that she would not change her mind. And, too, 'twas unseemly that they should argue over the grave of their dead.

Sighing, he said, "We will not settle this now. At sunrise, I will begin the search of the island. Mayhap 'twill not be necessary to go after the Romans."

"You believe that there may be more ducarreg here?"

"Nay, I believe the Chronicles are true that say Donn's shrine was the only source on our island. Still, I must look."

"Then, I will help you."

He accepted her offer with a smile. "I would welcome your help, as well as your company." And he would, for the truth was, he, who nearly always chose solitude over companionship, still did not want to be alone. Solitude that was not chosen but forced upon him held no appeal at all.

They began their quest at dawn.

Setting out on horseback, they planned to stop at the hunting shelters scattered about the island to collect the blankets and other stores kept in the small huts for those who had provided the village with game. Rowan thanked Madron that the Romans had left undisturbed the ponies pastured north of the village; their ancestors had been brought to the island in ages past, along with deer, boar, sheep, and goats, as well as wolves to keep the others from overrunning the island. Although the bands of sturdy ponies roamed at will, a few animals were caught from time to time to be used for work, as well as travel to the far reaches of the island. He and Ailia set out with three, two that they rode and one that would carry the stores from the hunting shelters.

From the village in the southeastern corner of the island, they traveled north through the hills along the coast. Putting to use what little knowledge he had of mining, Rowan considered that copper and iron often came from such hills and so, he reasoned, might ducarreg—never mind that Donn's shrine had sprung from nearly flat earth.

He was relieved when they passed the harbor his people had used time out of mind and saw their two seagoing vessels resting calmly at anchor; if the Romans had found them, they would have recognized them as superior to their own and taken them. Then he would have had to build another, and in yet another bitter irony, he did not have the time. He wanted to be gone from the island in spring.

When they reached the rocky northern coast, where the first wisps of autumn nipped at the air, blowing off the sea, he led them south, into the deep forests of the island's interior. Although he knew the land, had been over all of it many times, Ailia was seeing most of it for the first time. It seemed that she found reason for excitement in each new thing, whether 'twas a tree with which she was unfamiliar or a bird song she had never heard. Healing plants, in particular, interested her, and she gathered many, roots and all, hoping to grow them at home.

Rowan did nothing to quell her efforts, though he saw little point in them. He saw no point in anything but finding ducarreg. Without it, he reasoned, all else was for naught. And so, while Ailia gathered and tended her plants, he studied the earth, searching for signs that might lead him to his goal.

At the end of the first half cycle of the moon, he had found nothing to light even a small spark of hope, and his mood was becoming progressively worse. Yet he knew the futility of his search was not the entire cause of his irritable state; an ever-increasing portion was Ailia.

Watching her shift uncomfortably on the back of the gentle gray she rode, Rowan knew she had yet to adjust to the pony's motion and, consequently, suffered.

He wished she would complain. 'Twould have given him some cause to dislike her, and his need for such cause was growing with frightening speed. She did not complain, though. Rather, she was cheerful and obliging, performing her share of tasks, even when he could see she was stiff and sore from riding. She also listened well, he discovered, as he complied with her many requests to tell her about his journeys; her intelligent questions and her extensive knowledge of the Chronicles made him aware that she had been well-tutored and that what she lacked in experience was made up for by her quick reasoning.

'Twas her kindness, though, the generosity of her spirit, that he found the most pleasing thing about her. That and her beauty.

By the gods, she was beautiful, and she seemed to grow more so each day. He thought his eyes must be deceiving him, yet it seemed as if, with each rising of the moon, her body grew more lush, her skin more luminous—as if the Mother Goddess had found, in Ailia, the perfect place to display Her best work. He found the results increasingly difficult to resist.

Indeed, the more desirable she became to him, the more obsessed he became with the obvious but dangerous truth: in Ailia's body—and in her body *only*—his seed would find fertile ground.

He never had expected to beget a child and, for the most part, never had cared. Yet he could not help but think of times he had traveled among mortals—who, it seemed, had children as often and as easily as they breathed—and been envious of their way of life. Aye, he had envied mortals their children. And when he looked at Ailia's tempting but forbidden body, the desire to create a child arose within him with breath-stealing force.

Nor did she discourage his imaginings. Indeed, he was all too aware that the attraction he felt was shared. He saw it in her eyes, in every shy, maidenly glance she gave him. And he felt it in the slight but unmistakable trembling of her body every time, by chance or design, they had occasion to touch. There were far too many such occasions.

By mid-moon of the second moon's cycle of their journey, he felt like a stag in rut. Or rather, he thought, like the wolf upon whose pelt he slept across the fire from her each night. He knew wolves, had hunted them often, and in all his winters of tracking the clever beasts, he had observed that the packs in which they lived were not unlike mortal families. Each pack had its lead male and female, and these were the only pair allowed to mate. The others lived in abstinence.

He and Ailia had not been the lead male and female of their pack, nor would they ever have been. He was considered too reckless, too unsettled, too defiant of the laws. She had been declared unfit to bear young. Yet she and he were all that re-

mained of their pack. The only two who could see to the continuance of their line.

And had not Ailia herself said as much? Had she not told
him that she considered the perpetuation of their race an honorable cause? And did he not owe his people the same duty?
Was he not, after all, the *only* man with whom she could mate
to keep their bloodline true?

The notion grew stronger with each passing night. Yet Rowan
knew that with these thoughts of duty and honor, he was merely
seeking to justify his desire.

Their journey was brought to an end two moons after it had
begun by the first snowfall. 'Twas but an early snow, only a
light dusting that quickly melted, yet Rowan knew it heralded
the coming of winter. Soon, they would be unable to travel, nor
would they be able to find ducarreg when the ground was covered in snow and ice.

It had been, as he had expected, a futile search. They had ridden
the entire coast of the island and over much of the interior. Either
ducarreg was not to be found or he did not know where to find
it.

He made his decision, as always, alone. He was loath to tell
Ailia, though, for he was certain she would disagree.

'Twas mid-morning, and they were standing on a high cliff,
in a field of tall grass and wildflowers. While the ponies grazed
a short distance away, they directed their gazes to the place far
below them, where the great river that flowed from the north met
the southern sea. 'Twas a stunning sight, the towering, incoming
waves crashing upon the river's out-flowing waters, the sunlight
sparkling off of the churning foam that was a result of the endless
battle. For a long while, the raw splendor of the scene held them
in silent thrall.

Finally, Ailia spoke softly. "I am sorry, Rowan. I know that
you had hoped to prove the Chronicles wrong. Mayhap in spring
we can—"

"In spring, we will leave Tirducarreg," he said. " 'Tis too
late to leave before winter sets in. I will not risk a crossing on

rough seas, but when the season turns and the sea is calm, we will take our leave."

"To find the Romans who have our ducarreg?"

"Aye." 'Twas a lie. Gradually, over the past days, he had come to accept that he, alone, never could find, much less recapture, the stolen ducarreg. Nor was he any longer being driven by revenge; 'twas a fool's quest, a motive for the very young and for mortals whose brief lives often were guided by extremes of passion. Far better to let the gods have their vengeance in their own time and in their own way.

"I will not take you to Prydain with me," he said, "so do not bother to suggest it. I will take you to Eire, where I do not believe the Romans ever will gain a hold."

A long silence ensued before Ailia spoke again.

"Rowan, you know that in this quest 'tis not ducarreg you seek but death."

He hesitated briefly, then said, "If I cannot have one, I would as soon have the other. I have no desire to live as the only one of my kind."

Another moment passed in silence.

"Am I not of your kind?" she asked.

He gave her a look of mild reproach. "You know as well as I that though we are both Gwynhil, we are not the same. You could live as a mortal, with a home among them, growing old with those whom you would come to know. Although you may live many winters before death finds you, you will, in any event, appear to age. I will not. I will appear exactly as you see me, no matter the number of winters that pass, and so, I cannot have mortal companions whom I keep so long that they notice I never change."

Staring at the sea, he continued in a tone that only hinted at the sadness and pain inside him. " 'Tis more, though, than the worry that someone might learn I am immortal. I cannot live among people toward whom I would come to feel affection, only to have to bury them, one after the other, until I am the only one remaining who knew them. Would I then begin again—and yet again—to make another home? How many mortal lifetimes would I be forced to live before I reached tyradd? If I reached it at all." He shook his head. "I do not want to know the answers to those questions."

Drawing a deep breath, he let it out slowly. "I have lived already through what the mortal world has experienced as many different times. I have memories that no living mortal shares. And 'twill only grow worse." The people with whom he had expected to share the memories of an immortal lifetime lay dead at the bottom of a pool of dark water, and the only course he could see for himself was to join them. In death, as in life, he belonged on Tirducarreg and nowhere else.

Turning toward Ailia, resisting the urge to take her hands in his, he spoke urgently. "For you, 'tis different. You live now, in *this* time, and this is the only time that need concern you. Ailia, allow me to take you to Eire, where the mortals are not unlike us in their ways and their beliefs. We will find a village where you might settle, mayhap as a healer, for you are skilled in that way and healers are most welcome, always, in mortal communities. However you choose to present yourself to them, you will belong in their world in a way that I never could."

Shifting his gaze to stare once more at the sea, he added, "As you said, you might take a mate and bear him children. I would as soon you did not risk it, yet 'tis your choice to make." And he would allow her to make it, though the notion of her lying with another man—any man, mortal or otherwise—had become intolerable. He had no right to feel possessive of her; she was not his, nor could she be, no matter how much he might wish it.

He felt her gaze upon him, felt her studying him, and he shifted a little under the scrutiny.

With what he had come to recognize as uncanny perception, she said, "You do not intend to go after the Romans. You intend to take me to Eire, then return to Tirducarreg to seek tyradd. Tell me truly, Rowan, 'tis your plan, is it not?"

He glanced at her briefly. "And if it is?"

"Then I will stay here, with you. And if you are determined to join the others in the underworld, I will join them, as well."

Chilled to the marrow at the very notion of Ailia seeking

death, he let out a sound of frustration and flung himself away from her. Taking several strides, he pivoted back to face her and spoke in harsh tones. "I will not countenance any talk of your death at my hands or your own. If you do not wish to live on Eire, I will take you anywhere you choose to go. But you cannot remain here. There is simply no purpose in it."

"There is," she argued. "This is my home." Taking a step toward him, she continued. "Rowan, I have not lived in all the times that you have lived, but I know of them through the Chronicles. And I cannot forget that I know them. A child—a very *young* child—might be taken from his home and put in another and, eventually, come to forget the first. But I am not a child, and I cannot wipe the memories of the life I have led on Tirducarreg from my mind, as if they never happened."

She moved another step closer, one hand held palm-upward in a gesture of pleading. "If I do not share your memories, we, at the least, share the knowledge of our race and all that our civilization was. Can we not allow that knowledge to give us comfort and to bind us? Can we not live in peace here, together, on the land that has been our people's only home?"

Caught between the conflicting urges to embrace her and to walk away from her, Rowan did neither. Instead, he remained rooted, his gaze locked with hers as he said, "We cannot stay on Tirducarreg, Ailia—only the two of us."

"And why should we not?"

"Do not force me to speak of it. We both know why 'tis not right for us to live here, alone."

She neither flinched nor looked away from him as she replied, "I believe 'tis the only choice that *is* right." Then, however, her gaze fell from his, and her voice dropped to a murmur. "Mayhap, though, I am mistaken. Mayhap you find me . . . ill-favored."

Was she mad? Could she truly not know how he felt, standing here, looking at her—seeing the sunlight captured in the long strands of her hair, noting the color that crept into her cheeks, watching the soft rise and fall of her breasts as she took those tense, shallow breaths?

Nay, she was not mad; she was simply young and uncertain.

And he wanted her more than he could remember wanting any woman he had ever known.

"You are not mistaken," he said, his voice rough with both emotion and restrained passion. "You know, as a woman always knows when a man desires her, what is in my mind when I look upon you. But, Ailia, you are gwarhardd."

When her gaze shot upward to clash with his, and she started to speak—he was certain to argue—he stopped her with a quick shake of his head. "Nay, I am not bound to follow the elders' declaration for its own sake. Why would I, now that they are with Donn, when I did so only as it suited me while they were alive? 'Tis not respect for them that guides me but the certain knowledge that nearly all of our women who bear children meet death in the act."

The color in her cheeks deepened, yet her discomfort over the intimate turn of the conversation did not prevent her from pursuing the matter. "How do mortal men go on when their mates die in childbirth?"

" 'Tis different," he countered.

"How is it different?"

"In numbers alone, if nothing else. Mortal women do not die as often. And even if they did, mortals risk death every day from all manner of causes. They expect it."

"As do I."

He did not. Rowan clamped his jaw closed against speaking the words. It did not surprise him when Ailia spoke them for him.

"Rowan, I know it must be difficult for you," she said, her voice warm and soft like autumn sunshine. "To have lived as long as you have, believing that you would go on living, most likely, forever, then suddenly to face tyradd, mayhap tomorrow— or today. I can only imagine how terrifying it must seem to you."

What terrified him even more was hearing his private fears put into words. "Aye," he said, unwilling—unable—to elaborate.

She seemed, nonetheless, encouraged by his simple response. Moving through the tall grass, she came to stand directly in front of him, hesitating, then placing a hand on his arm, below the sleeve of his tunic. "I am not immortal as you are," she said. "And, now, I never will be. I have only one life, and I will not live it in fear of dying. If I am to die, I would like the chance to bear new life."

His skin burned where she touched him. It required enormous effort for him to speak, much less to tell her, " 'Tis a chance you could have with a mortal man."

She shook her head slowly. "I do not want a mortal man. I want you."

"I am the only man here. On Eire you might—"

"I do not need to know any more men. I have lived all my life among more than a gros of them, and I tell you that if those men were not dead, and if I were given leave to choose a mate, I would choose you."

Heart pounding, he looked down into her lovely, upturned face and tried to find within himself the strength to turn away from her. He managed—just—not to sweep her into his arms, but the sight of the tears gathering in her blue eyes made it impossible to withhold himself from her entirely.

"Ailia . . ." His fingertip brushed a tear from her cheek. "If you had passed cynadd, I would not be standing here like an untested lad, shaking with need for you. Rather, I would be showing you how beautiful you are to me and how much I have come to care for you. But you have not passed cynadd. And I will not." He heaved a ragged breath. "I tell you, I could not bear to see you die giving birth to my babe, when I would have no means even to attempt to reawaken you. I could not bear to be the cause of your death."

"Oh, Rowan . . ." Another tear rolled down her cheek. " 'Tis true, I cannot swear I will not die. But do you not see? Death is part of life, indeed, the very beginning of it. You know, as do I, that without the darkness of night, there would be no dawn. All life that flows from the Mother has a beginning—and an end. What comes between the two is a gift, and I would not reject that gift because I fear the end may come too soon." Lifting her hand from his arm and placing it on his chest, where he knew she could feel his heart's rapid pounding, she continued. "Please, do not let your fear deprive you—or me—of whatever gifts the Mother sees fit to bestow. Please, do not let me come to my end never having known you."

Her plea breached his last defense. For a long moment, his gaze remained locked with hers. Then, with an anguished sound—and a certainty that the gods would condemn him for what he was about to do—he ploughed his fingers through her hair, bent his head, and covered her mouth with his.

She uttered a small sound of surprise. Then her breath rushed out in a quiet moan, and she surrendered herself to his passion. Her body melted against his; her mouth opened to allow him entry, and the moment he tasted her, he was lost. She was sunshine and honey, innocence and purity; she was all good things that flowed from the Mother. Truly, she was the Goddess's own daughter, and he, with every deep, ravenous kiss and every touch of her soft, inviting flesh, paid homage to She who had made her. Made her for him. For he came to believe 'twas true, that she was his and only his and that Madron had designed their mating. Surely, some god had, for he had no control in this, none at all; he was but a poor creature, consumed by need and the single-minded purpose to join his flesh with that of the woman in his arms.

He took her down to lie amidst the flowers and the tall, sweet grass, and there, with the waves crashing on the rocks below and their bodies bared to the gentle sunshine, he gave her what she had said she wanted. For 'twas what he wanted, too, more than he ever had wanted anything in his long life. Driven to satisfy both their desires, he drank from her mouth and suckled at her breasts and let himself drown in the nectar that flowed from her like sweet wine to drug his senses. All the while, he reveled in the sounds she made and in the delicate strokes of her hands over his skin—strokes that became less delicate and more urgent as the need for completion overwhelmed all else.

He sank his body into hers with a groan of regret for her momentary pain and a sense that he had joined with the Goddess Herself. The wet, welcoming passage that tightened around his hardened flesh compelled him beyond the realm of physical sensation, called to him to give her what she required. And he did. Aroused past thought or reason, he gave himself up to the rhythm of creation, letting it carry them both on its rising tide to fulfillment. And when they arrived at the crest, he exulted in her cry of pleasure, thrilled to the feel of her arms clutching him to her. And he poured his seed into her fertile womb with a sense of joy and of gratification beyond anything he, in all the many winters of his life, had ever found or even dreamed existed.

The feelings he discovered that morning on that flower-adorned cliff overlooking the sea lingered throughout the last days of autumn as they worked together to prepare for the deep cold of winter.

While Ailia picked apples and scavenged root vegetables from the village gardens, Rowan hunted deer and boar, which he then dressed and smoked. When they added their provisions to the grains and flour they had collected from the hunting shelters, they both agreed they would not starve.

Nor would they freeze. Having chosen a site in the forest to the west of the village ruins, they built a small dwelling of log, stone, and mud. As Ailia made garments for them from the furs and hides of the animals Rowan hunted, he furnished their home with a table, two stools, and a rope bed wide enough for two.

When the deep cold came, they were ready. At night, as Rowan lay with Ailia in his arms, both of them snug and warm beneath piles of furs, he was happier than he had ever been, which was saying a great deal. And if, sometimes, most often in the deep hollow of night, the thought that she might be taken from him intruded to mar his happiness, he fought to ignore it.

Still, the thought was there, and it became more persistent when, as the snow enveloped them in winter's folds, her belly began to swell with his child. Outwardly, he rejoiced with her; inwardly, he clung to the belief 'twas what she had wanted, what *he* had wanted—indeed, what the Mother had planned all along.

Yet he could not stop the voices, voices he had heard so many times: the stern, censuring tones of the elders, denouncing him for having broken yet another law and issuing exhortations that the punishment of the gods would surely follow. In truth, he lived in dread that because of his actions, Ailia would die and that soon . . . all too soon . . . he would be the only one. The last immortal on earth.

The irony was inescapable: that it should be he, who had always craved solitude, who had defied the laws to walk the soil of foreign lands alone . . . that *he* might be the last survivor of his race. More ironic still, the notion terrified him. For although he had traveled the world over, he had carried his people in his heart wherever he had gone. 'Twas the knowledge of his home on Tirducarreg and the certainty that he would be welcomed back into the fold no matter how long he had been gone—or what law he had broken—that had given him the strength and confidence to face the ages. The world around him surely would change, still his home and his people would remain constant.

Yet it had not been so. The Romans had slaughtered his people, all save one. And she had become everything to him. She was his heart, his home, his purpose in living. She was, in truth, all he had. If he should lose her, as well. . . . Surely, the gods would not be so cruel.

Spring came, releasing the earth from winter's frozen hold and offering Rowan brief respites from anxiety. Pouring himself into physical labor, he worked to replace the saplings in the grove that had died, tending both old and new in the way Ailia had taught him. He also made improvements to their hastily built dwelling, replacing the hides on the windows with shutters and covering the earthen floor with planks, as well as adding a baking oven, a spinning wheel, and a weaving loom.

As Ailia's time drew closer, she begged him to perform another task, and upon it she was most insistent. If she should die giving birth to their child, she told him, he would need to be prepared to care for the babe, which meant, among other things, having a ready supply of milk. Rowan loathed any reminder that Ailia could be taken from him. 'Twas unnecessary, he told her; she would nurse the babe herself. Yet the worry that clouded her blue eyes finally made him agree to do as she asked.

Thus committed, he tracked the herd of sheep that the Gwynhils had kept in the meadow between the village and the wood where he and Ailia now lived; with no one to tend them, the animals had scattered in all directions. They were relied upon for their wool and their meat—and, quite often, their milk. For when a woman met death in childbirth, upon reawakening, she was not only infertile but unable to produce milk; thus, only a very few women nursed their own babes.

Gathering the flock, he herded them back to the meadow, where he kept occasional watch on them. And when Ailia's time drew nigh, he brought two of the ewes and their young to live in an enclosure by their forest home, feeding and watering them daily to ensure that they would remain hearty, should he need them. All the while, he prayed to the Mother that he would not.

Ailia was brought to bed with child a full twelve moons after he had returned from Bachynys to find her living among the dead. 'Twas the height of summer and hot, and she labored long—too long—at the grueling task of giving birth.

Watching her, hearing the cries she tried to suppress, Rowan felt the fear that had been building for many moons inside him come to a head. She needed a midwife; she had only him, and he knew only the barest essentials about the process. Raging inwardly against his helplessness, he did his best to reassure her and to ease her suffering. Mostly, he prayed.

The moon rose and set twice, Ailia's cries were reduced to whimpers, and still the babe would not be born. Watching Ailia fade in and out of awareness, Rowan's fear turned to panic, and his panic drove him to desperate measures. He was about to reach inside her body and try to pull the babe from her when, suddenly, her eyes opened wide, her body tensed and, with a growl of extreme effort, she pushed the babe from her.

The infant slid into his hands in a wash of blood.

"Rowan . . . ?"

" 'Tis a girl," he said in answer to Ailia's whispered inquiry. Quickly, his hands shaking, he cut and tied the cord and swaddled the babe, who made small but healthy sounds of protest at being thrust from her former home.

"Is she . . . ?"

"She is perfect." Gently, he laid the infant in the crook of her arm.

"Oh, she is beautiful," Ailia said, her voice barely audible. "She has your black hair."

"Aye," he replied, fingers trembling as he brushed a damp lock from his mate's forehead. "And your blue eyes."

It should have been a time of joy, as they marveled together over the life they had created. For Rowan, however, joy was a distant memory. When Ailia's face contorted with another pain, he helped her to deliver the afterbirth, and as he attempted to bathe away the blood, he felt the cold fingers of dread claw at him. There was so much blood. And it kept coming. He could not stop it. All he could do was sit beside Ailia, hold her hand, talk to her, and watch her life slip away.

He told her how much he cherished her. He told her all the things they would teach their child and how, when she was old enough, they might sail to Eire and meet friends he had made there not long ago. As Ailia lay with her eyes closed and her face growing ever more pale, as the babe slept peacefully beside her, he went on talking.

Outside the window near the bed, the stars faded, and the night sky gave way to the blush of dawn. At the same instant the sun shot its first rays from the eastern horizon to sparkle in the mist clinging to the trees of their forest, Ailia opened her eyes and looked at him.

"I would name her Mai," she said.

" 'Tis a good name," he replied.

"Take care of her for me."

"Ailia . . ."

"Swear it."

"Aye, I swear. But Ailia—"

"I love you, Rowan," she said.

And she was gone. Her eyes drifted closed, she let out a sighing breath—and she did not draw another.

For several long moments, Rowan sat motionless on the stool beside the bed, gripping her limp hand and staring at her chest, willing it to rise and fall. But it did not.

His heart pounded; his throat began to ache, his eyes to burn, and it became nearly impossible to breathe. A sound escaped him—a wrenching groan—and, suddenly, tears were pouring down his face, and he could not stop them. Burying his face in his hands, he let grief take him, and for a long while it consumed him, wracked his body with great, choking sobs and flooded his mind with remorse.

He had killed her, 'twas certain. He had succumbed to temptation and, in doing so, had traded what could have been many winters of intimate companionship—winters of love—for a few moons of happiness and physical satisfaction. He was a fool, an arrogant, reckless fool who had proven himself unworthy of his people's regard and, worse, of his woman's love.

He did not deserve to live. And he would not. He would seek tyradd. 'Twould not prove difficult. He would throw himself off the cliffs and let the sea take him. Better still, he would tie a boulder to his ankles and roll it into the pool in the grove and, thus, rejoin his people. He would do it before the moon rose, the sooner to be done with this vast well of pain that was the sum and total of what life had become.

Aye, he would seek death, indeed, would welcome it, for besides being arrogant and reckless and unworthy, he was a coward. He was not prepared to go on for winters, mayhap many gros of them, belonging nowhere and to no one. He could not face life—could not face the ages—alone. He could not.

'Twas then, as he wallowed in this pit of grief and despair, that there came a reminder that he was not, after all, entirely alone: the small, whimpering cry of his daughter.

The sound intruded, sliced through his misery and made his breath catch in his throat. He raised his head and looked at the tiny bundle, lying beside her mother. Hesitating for an instant or two, he reached over and lifted the babe into his hands. She stopped crying, looked at him briefly, then, with a tiny sigh, went back to sleep.

His daughter. Mai. He had sworn to Ailia that he would care for her, which he surely could not do if he were dead. Nor would it satisfy his vow to take the babe to Eire and leave her with some kind mortal. Nay, he was sworn to discharge the duty himself.

And so, he could not seek tyradd. Not as yet.

Rowan heaved a ragged breath and forcibly hauled himself back from the brink of that deep, silent pool that awaited him in the grove. Aye, he must live long enough to raise Mai, and he would do so not out of duty but out of love. For he had loved Ailia as he had loved no one else, and he would love and care for their daughter. Not here, on Tirducarreg, but on Eire, among the people with whom she would have to live her life. For a time, he would make those good people his people, as he had done at other times and in other places. Then, when Mai was grown and settled, before anyone wondered why her father appeared to be the same age as she, he would plan to meet with some mishap. Some fatal mishap. And then . . .

Then, if the gods were kind and forgiving, he would be rejoined with Ailia.

Sighing deeply, Rowan rose and placed his daughter in the small bed he had made for her, which sat beside the larger one on the new plank floor. Looking down at her, he thought that he had best go milk one of the ewes before she awakened, hungry. First, though, he must take care of Ailia; he would bury her after seeing to the babe's needs, yet he could not leave her now, lying in a pool of blood.

The tears that occasionally ran down his cheeks were a sharp contradiction to his stoic countenance as he went about cleansing his mate's lifeless body. He bathed her gently from head to toe, even doing his best to arrange her hair in a single braid, as she liked to wear it, draped over her shoulder. The blood-soaked blankets beneath her had been replaced, and he was spreading a lightly woven one of flax over her when he was brought to a sudden halt, his heart leaping to his throat, by the sound of a soft and trembling voice.

"Rowan?"

His head turned sharply, and he looked to find Ailia watching him. "Sweet Mother!" He dropped to his knees beside the bed, grabbing the hand she held out to him and clutching it to him.

"I was certain—" He broke off, barely able to manage a hoarse whisper. "Ailia, I believed you dead."

She blinked a few times, frowning slightly. "I was."

His hand caressed her cheek. "My cariad, it could not be so. If you had been at tyradd—"

"I met death," she interrupted him, her voice growing stronger. "I am certain."

"It does not matter. You are here, and you are alive, and I— By the Goddess, I do not care how—"

"No." She laid a finger against his lips. "Listen to me. It *does* matter." Rolling to her side, she propped herself on one elbow, bringing her face no more than a hand from his. "I swear to you, Rowan, I have not been lying here asleep or in a stupor. I have reached cynadd, and I am now reawakened."

He did not believe it. But, by the gods, he was not going to argue the point. With a low, choking sound, he engulfed her in a tight embrace. And then, somehow, he was sitting on the bed, and she was half lying across his lap, the blanket fallen away from her body and her breasts pressed to his chest. With his face buried against her neck, he rocked her, saying her name and telling her over and over how much he loved her. All the while, she clung to him as fiercely as he did to her.

When the urgent need to hold her had lessened somewhat, he pulled back far enough to look at her.

She searched his features and, raising a hand, drew a slow line with her fingertip from his cheek to his jaw. "I am so sorry," she said, "for the time you spent believing I had left you. But I will not leave you again, I swear it."

Her eyes were clear and bright, her skin warm. And he did not understand at all how it could be so. He was about to speak, to say again that he did not care how or why she was alive, but she shook her head.

"Look at me, Rowan. Let your eyes tell you what your mind and heart cannot yet believe."

For an instant, he remained frozen, swamped by a mixture of joy and bafflement and worry that she could yet die. Then, as she drew the blanket away, baring all of her lovely, naked form, he let his gaze travel downward, over her. The signs were all there, undeniable: the rosy hue of her skin, the notable lack of discomfort of any kind. Her breasts were perfect, round and full—but not so full as they had been. And her belly, the skin of which had been slightly flaccid only a short time ago as he had bathed her, was nearly flat, with but a hint of a womanly curve. In truth, she looked exactly as she had before she conceived, her body's inborn ability to restore itself having done its work.

He shook his head slowly. "Ailia, I see 'tis true, you have reawakened, which can only mean that you, indeed, met death. But 'tis not possible—"

"Aye, 'tis possible," she said.

He began another protest. "Without ducarreg—"

"We do not need ducarreg. We have never needed it. And do not scowl at me so. 'Tis truth I am speaking, and you have the proof of it before you."

That, he could not deny. And so, he listened as she spoke words that contradicted everything he, and every other Gwynhil who had ever lived, had believed throughout their chronicled ages.

"Our people thought that Donn's power to restore life resided in ducarreg, that he gave it to us, and hence, that we were gwynhil—his blessed race." She shook her head. "But 'twas not so. Aye, we were blessed, but not by Donn. 'Tis the power of the Mother that reawakens us, Rowan, and that power does not reside in any rock, but in ourselves. She who made us lives within us."

Rowan thought of all the arguments he might offer, not the least of which was that he had never heard of anyone—not a single Gwynhil in all of their recorded history—who had reawakened without the burning of ducarreg. But then, he reasoned, no Gwynhil ever would have considered *not* burning ducarreg only to discover if 'twere possible, and their laws, their lives, their entire world, had been designed expressly to ensure that no one ever would think to try.

In any event, all arguments, large and small, paled in the face of Ailia, vibrant and very much alive, in his arms.

Drawing a deep breath, he let it out slowly. "Tell me how you know this."

"The Goddess told me," Ailia said simply. Then, with a little frown, she added, "I cannot explain it. Somehow, She was with me. I did not see or hear Her, yet I felt Her presence and Her love. And I felt Her sadness." Her frown deepened. "She mourns the deaths of our people, Rowan. And I believe that in making Herself known to me, She hoped, somehow, to atone for the loss. That by reassuring me of Her presence and allowing me to know the truth about Her part in our lives, She was . . . I do not know how to say it . . . showing me . . . no, giving me—giving *us*— something from which to draw strength." With a frustrated sigh, she muttered, "I only wish She had given me the right words to tell you, for you must believe me or 'twill all be for naught."

"I do believe you," he said, and at her look of surprise, he smiled. "How could I not? I have no other justification for why you are here, with me, appearing as beautiful as you were the first time we lay together. Or why, when I never thought to hold you again, I am able to do this . . ." Pulling her close, he lowered his head and gave her a long and tender kiss.

As the kiss ended, she sighed his name against his lips. He kissed her again, briefly; then smiling, he set her away to lean down and lift Mai from her bed.

Placing the babe in her mother's arms, he said, "Mayhap you would like to hold her, now that you are able to take more pleasure in it."

"Aye, I would," Ailia said, instantly enthralled by her sleeping daughter, whom she cradled to her.

Rowan tucked them both close to his side with an arm around Ailia's shoulders, and with his head resting lightly against hers, he let the peace and happiness of the moment settle over him. Through the window, he could see that the morning's shroud of mist had lifted from the trees, leaving the forest awash with amber sunshine.

His whole world was awash with sunshine.

Burying his lips in Ailia's hair, he murmured, "I have be-lieved all along that Madron was guiding me. Even when I feared that I would pay dearly for having lain with you, a part of me held fast to the conviction that the Mother had kept you safe from the Romans—and mayhap She did the same for me by having me linger on Bachynys—so that we should have one another. Mayhap, She could not save our people, yet She saved us. And I believe She meant for us to mate, and for Mai to be born. And, so, we are still gwynhil in Her eyes."

"Oh, Rowan . . ." Ailia raised her gaze to meet his. "You truly do believe me, then."

"Aye," he said. "I am certain 'tis the Goddess's own truth you have spoken. As I am certain that we will live happy lives on this island, which, as I think of it, must bear a new name."

She did not hesitate to suggest one. "Tirgwynfyd."

The blessed land. He gave a single nod. "Aye, 'tis fitting."

"But do you not still wish to go to Eire?" she asked.

"Mayhap, when Mai is grown," he replied. "In time, we will—all of us—have need of others. Yet I believe 'tis possible that we may not need leave our isle in order to find such community. The Romans have come, and so, I warrant, will others."

"You believe the Romans will return?" Ailia whispered.

Rowan smoothed the worried frown from her brow with a quick kiss. "Nay, cariad, do not fret. Their purpose in coming is already served—and by now, surely, they have learned 'twas a futile purpose at that." And he prayed the Goddess would forgive him for hoping that the captain who had ordered his people's deaths himself had tested death's clutches—with the ducarreg burning uselessly beside him. "Still, there are those on Prydain and in Gaul who would not live by Roman law, nor with Roman gods. Given the opportunity, they may find their way here."

Ailia considered his words for several moments, then turned her attention back to Mai. "How long will it be, do you think, before they come?" she asked.

Rowan sighed. "Mayhap tomorrow. Mayhap many winters. Regardless, I will not live in fear of their arrival. Rather, I will put my trust in Madron, who today has given me more than any man could hope to have." Planting a kiss in her hair, he said, "She has given my beloved mate back to me, and She has given me a daughter. I would have been more than grateful for those gifts, alone, as any man would be, but She has seen fit to increase my happiness and, thereby, my gratitude. For She has said that we will live forever. And forever will I be in Her debt."

And as he watched Ailia with the babe in her arms, the thought passed through his mind that he had everything he desired, and that he knew everything he needed to know. Whatever else came, when it came, they would face it together.

"Aye," Ailia said softly. "Together."

Rowan smiled.

"And did others come?" the girl asked.

Her teacher chuckled. "We are here, are we not? Aye, others came, from Britain and Eire."

"And did those who came learn that Rowan and Ailia and Mai were immortal?"

He shook his head. "No, the Gwynhils were able to move from settlement to village to town, as the need arose. And in this way, throughout the ages, they have watched over the civilization that grew to replace the one they had lost, tending and nurturing it, as they did the young trees of the grove they planted. And, all the while, they have kept the secret of their immortality from all but those few to whom they have entrusted it."

The girl's eyes widened. "But they do not live here *still*, do they?"

" 'Tis said that they do, along with their descendants, for Mai took a mortal husband to whom she bore a son and a daughter."

Clearly stunned by the possibility, the girl asked, "And are their descendants immortal, too?"

"Alas, not," the teacher replied, "although those of Gwynhil issue tend to lead exceptionally long and healthy lives."

The girl sighed. "Oh, I wish that I were like them. I wish that I could *know* them. Do you think I ever will—that I ever *could?* "

"Who can say?" He studied her thoughtfully. "Perhaps, when you are grown. But to be the sort of person to whom Rowan and Ailia might reveal themselves, you must live by the same principles that led him to her, and that have guided them both through all the centuries since."

"What principles are those?" the girl asked.

Her teacher arched an eyebrow. "I would have you tell me."

She thought for a long while, her forehead creased in concentration, before offering a hesitant reply. "Is it that the truth is to be found not from without but from within one's self?"

The teacher nodded. "Aye, and what else?"

With a bit more confidence, she said, "That love is the most important thing of all. Even if everything else we have is lost, as long as we are able to love, we can survive."

"Which means . . ."

She took a deep breath and finished. "That 'tis not greed nor revenge, not anger nor fear, that should guide us, but love. For only when we are guided by love do we find true happiness and peace." Looking for approval, she said, "That is right, is it not? 'Tis about love that the tale of Rowan and Ailia teaches us."

Well pleased, the teacher smiled.

The Growing Season

by

Patricia Gardner Evans

Author's Note

From Dr. Kildare in the 1960s to Dr. Doug Ross *(ER's* George Clooney) in the 1990s, big- and small-screen docs have caused an epidemic of "female troubles"—irregular heartbeats, heart flutters, terminal sighing. So it's only fair when a doctor contracts an incurable case of love.

"The patient presents . . ."

The greenhouse door slammed, but Annie Reeves didn't bother to turn around. She knew who it was. Which was good, she thought as she stretched toward the black tubing overhead, since ladders were not her strong suit. She muttered under her breath as the ladder taunted her with a subtle wobble. She wouldn't be in this fix if the person who had just come in had been on time for work this morning. Actually, he probably had been on time—on time to hang around the love of his seventeen-year-old life while she watered the bedding plants before opening. "Darn it, Charlie, if you don't stop mooning around Jeanne Rae and put us all out of your misery by asking her out, I'm going to hire Chad Mitchell to show you how to do it."

"How old is Jeanne Rae?"

Charlie's voice was changing, but that deep? And he knew how old. . . . Without thinking, Annie whipped around, catching a glimpse of tall and dark before the ladder took advantage of her imprudence. It dithered between falling right or falling left before making up its mind on backward.

After a minute or two Annie could breathe well enough to remember that he'd been by the door. How had he moved fast enough to catch her—if being squashed flat qualified as a catch? "You're not Charlie," she gasped, overstating the obvious.

"Nope. John," he struggled to croak. Fortunately his brain was functioning better than his voice, John Haney thought. He'd been directed to "the tomato lady's," and from the name, he'd expected a great-grandmother in rubber boots, coveralls and a floppy hat, wearing *eau de manure*. Before her attempt at flight, he had observed no boots, no coveralls, no hat and—especially—no great-grandmother. Not even a grandmother. His nose wrinkled. Manure would have been an improvement, though. She made a feeble attempt to raise her head off his chest, making him aware of his hands. Used to making lightning-fast assessments, he noted denim covering the greatest as— Bottom, he reminded himself sternly. After the past six years, his language needed sterilization. "Are you hurt?"

"No, I'm okay." She managed to get her head up this time, which increased the pressure of her lower body interestingly, and blinked big, beautiful eyes at him. Yes, indeed, the tomato lady was some tomato. His hands flexed their agreement.

"I'm sorry." Annie groaned silently as the smell finally registered. She must have pulled loose the fertilizing line when she fell. "I'm so sorry. Are you hurt?"

Oh, no, he was feeling no pain. Well, actually he was; she was heavier than she looked, but the pain was negligible. "I'm fine," he said, but she began trying to push herself off him anyway. Fortunately, he was used to making lightning-fast decisions, too. "Since neither of us is fatally wounded, how about dinner tonight to celebrate?"

Annie stared at him, finally finding words in her mouth. "I never have dinner with men whose hair is longer than mine." Reeking of well-aged fish oil and mortification, she scrambled up and ran.

"Physician, heel thyself . . ."

Annie pawed through the magazines, looking for one younger than the three-year-old sitting across from her. Why did doctors only stock old magazines? Maybe the new one would pitch all these out and bring in fresh ones, from last year. She sat back in her chair empty-handed and tried to catch at least one of Nan Pickering's eyes. As receptionist, office manager and benevolent dictator of the only doctor's office in town, Nan could—*should*—have given everyone the complete story on the new doctor, but she'd refused to give out even the stingiest detail. Most people said it was because Nan was enjoying the power of having a secret in a town that hardly knew the meaning of the word, but Annie suspected the real reason was she didn't know any more than the rest of them. Nan had taken her vacation early so she could be on hand to help Dr. Fitz's replacement "settle in"—i.e. learn who was boss right away—and so had missed the replacement's unannounced and unobserved visit to look over the practice and the town. Dr. Fitz wasn't to have retired until June, but his daughter's twins had not only come early but turned into triplets besides. Dr. and Mrs. Fitz had rushed off to Oregon before Nan returned, so all anyone knew was that the new doctor was single and late of the U.S. Navy, the assumption being that he was retired and "older."

Giving up on Nan, Annie glanced around the full waiting room. She doubted there were many real ailments here this morning. The "patients" just wanted to be the first to get the scoop on the new doctor. *Her* reason for being here was medical, not gossip mongering, she thought with a morally superior sniff.

Some bony part of Tall and Dark had made a lasting impression on her side in the form of a spectacular bruise with matching ache. The ladder had gotten in a lick or two as well, and her right calf had a permanent charley horse. At the busiest time of year when she needed to be racing like a jack rabbit, she was inching along like a snail—with a limp, no less.

She smiled at the baby in a carrier on the chair beside her. This appointment was a good opportunity to ask about another medical matter, too. Unconsciously her smile turned a little wistful. Tall and Dark's knee or elbow wasn't all that had made an impression on her. She refused to add the third part of the old standby; it was just too trite . . . however true. Doubtless he had come down from the city; people often drove out on the weekends to buy bedding plants from her and trees from a grower up the road. There was even less doubt that she'd never see him again. She dismissed the stranger with a brisk mental shrug—the one that had been getting a lot of exercise the last few days.

Marcella Skeats, the nurse, appeared around the corner and

called her name. All of the office staff had agreed to stay on, at least temporarily. Annie followed her and recited her inventory of bruises and aches. Since she didn't have an excuse full of danger and drama for her pitiful condition, she opted for humor, which made, Annie could admit in hindsight, almost as good a story—especially since she would never sight Tall and Dark again. The shrug got another workout.

Still laughing, Marcella left, closing the exam room door behind her. Seconds later, Annie heard her chart sliding back out of the rack on the other side of the door. The knob turned, and she started a smile of welcome as a man with a white coat, stethoscope and fresh haircut walked in.

"You!" At least she hadn't said "Tall and Dark," although it was small comfort.

"Me," he said agreeably. "Also known as John Haney." He'd worried that fall had done some damage. Before leaving for a shower and a change of clothes, he'd given his beeper number to one of her staff with instructions to call if her employer didn't seem to be feeling well. He'd just walked into his apartment when his beeper went off, but it was the real estate agent telling him the owners of the house he'd bought wanted to move the closing to that afternoon. He'd been tied up with paperwork and moving until last night, but he'd managed to swing by the nursery where the sight of her rearranging sacks of peat moss assured him that she was mobile at least.

He was smiling at her expectantly, and Annie finally thought to put her hand out. He had manners, at least, waiting until a woman offered her hand instead of sticking his out first. "How do you do, Dr. Haney," she said, certainly sounding unwell enough to need a doctor. His hand was big and warm and apparently electrically charged. When he released her hand, she resisted the urge to shake away the lingering tingle.

"I'm doing fine, Miss Reeves, but you aren't." Using a glance at her chart as cover, he disciplined a grin into a frown of doctorly concern. If it were possible to crawl into an exam table and disappear, she would have done it. Setting down the chart, he moved in front of her. "Let's take a look at your side."

Since it didn't look like her wish to fall through the floor was going to be granted anytime soon, Annie decided her only choice was to be as brisk and businesslike as possible. "Of course." She pulled her shirt out of her slacks, grateful for at least one small favor: the bruise was just above waist-level.

He whistled softly. "That's a beaut of a bruise; makes mine look like a measle."

Mentally, Annie rolled her eyes. Only a man would admire a bruise, yet another "guy thing." He probed around the bruised area, and Annie couldn't help a flinch.

His hand stilling, he glanced up immediately. "Does that hurt?"

"No." She lowered her voice an octave to normal. "No, it doesn't hurt." She only wished it was that simple. His hands were amazingly gentle and, unfortunately, very conscientious. She clamped her teeth together. He had already seen her slapstick routine; she was not going to humiliate herself further. "I hope your 'measle' doesn't hurt too much." He had to have some aches and pains, too, which she did feel guilty about, however late in coming.

"Not at all," he murmured.

That distraction exhausted, she looked around for another. He smelled wonderful. Of course, the last time he'd smelled like a carp that had been sunbathing for a week but—she sucked in her breath and held it as one long, blunt finger tested a rib—he really did smell great, kind of spicy-citrusy. He shifted a little, thoughtfully giving her a new distraction. His hair was great, too, dark brown but silvering gorgeously. It was straight and lying close to his head now that it was short, but she remembered it had been a little wavy when it was longer. Why she'd made that idiotic comment about his hair she didn't know; it had only been fractionally longer than hers, and hair length didn't matter to her anyway. She'd just had a sudden and inexplicable attack of blind panic and said the first thing her lame brain came up with.

"Nothing cracked," he muttered, making one last probe, "or bro—"

Twisting out of his hands, Annie wrapped her arms around

her ribs and laughed like a maniac. While she gasped and gulped and struggled to get herself under even a facsimile of control, she wondered if she could walk across the exam room, find the door and escape, all with her eyes closed, so she wouldn't have to see his reaction to her latest attempt to be the fourth Stooge.

"Well, that confirms it. You wouldn't be ticklish if you had a bum rib."

Annie forced her eyes open to see him standing in front of her, his expression bland. "That's good to know," she said weakly.

Clearing his throat to hide a laugh, John consulted the chart he already had memorized. "You mentioned general aches and pains. Any of them as bad as your ribs?"

She grimaced. "Not even close."

He set down her chart and patted the end of the exam table. "Swing your legs up here so I can take a look at that charley horse."

Annie complied, discovering his hands had fully recharged when he picked up her left calf. His fingers found the nasty knot and began kneading. After an initial painful jolt, the knotted muscles began to untie and relax. Melt, actually. He had magic fingers, like those goofy beds that used to be in motels when she was a kid. The bill would be more than a quarter, but cheap at twice the price, she thought dreamily.

"What are you taking for the pain?"

What pain, she almost said. "Aspirin, but it's not helping much."

"I'll give you samples of something stronger that'll reduce the inflammation better, too. You can buy it over the counter, but buy the generic; it's cheaper." For all he knew, whatever he'd just said was monkey babble. She had the softest skin . . . baby skin.

It was all Annie could do to nod. In another minute, she was just going to flop back on the table, every muscle in her body mush.

"Good muscle tone," he observed, professionally, of course.

"Must be all those ladders I climb up," Annie said wryly.

"And fall down." Her smile and laugh were endearingly sheepish. He forced his reluctant fingers from her calf and stuffed them into his pockets. Much more "massage" and she was going to think he was some kind of pervert. "If it kinks up again, press down on the knot with your thumb and rotate." That bit of medical advice brought something else to mind—same action, different result—and he was very glad he had opted for more formal slacks and lab coat his first day rather than the tighter scrubs he preferred.

Annie waited for him to demonstrate the proper technique again—not that she needed it, of course, but he might need the practice—but he was more interested in making notes on her chart.

Done scribbling, he looked back at her. "Anything else I can do for you this morning?" There were several things she could do for him, but not this morning, unfortunately.

Annie took a moment. Nan and the rest of the office staff took the vow of maintaining confidentiality as seriously as any priest in a confessional, but she'd still rather keep this between just herself and the doctor until the results made it obvious. She took a deep breath. This would have been so much easier with Dr. Fitz . . . unsexy . . . older . . . unsexy . . . homely . . . unsexy Dr. Fitz. However, she had given the matter a great deal of thought, made her decision, and now that she had, she didn't want to waste any more time. "I want to have a baby."

John sat down abruptly; fortunately, the exam stool was under him, more or less. Holy sh— Automatically he searched for a socially acceptable substitute, then realized his vocabulary redevelopment hadn't progressed enough to cover this particular situation. Mentally he wiped a hand down his face. He was farther gone than he'd thought. For a second there he'd thought she said "your" instead of "a." And the fact that it had only startled him, not panicked him, proved just how far gone he really was.

"Do you have a father in mind?" He'd had the office staff brief him on his first day's patients, especially this one, and they had happily given him the Cliff Notes version of her life.

Her parents had relocated to Arizona, and Annie had graciously ceded the family home to her brother, because he had a family and she didn't. She'd used her teaching degree—with honors— for several years before taking over a run-down greenhouse operation, raising tomatoes and other fresh produce year-round for the town and better restaurants in the city. During the outdoor growing season she added bedding plants to her inventory. Most interesting, and important, nobody mentioned a boyfriend, fiancé or lover—no man at all.

"No. I'll use artificial insemination," she said.

"You want to be able to order exactly the father you want?" he asked mildly.

"Some women might, but that's not my reason. I'm thirty-seven and don't want to wait any longer to have a family." Though if she were placing an order, Annie thought abstractedly, the ideal donor was sitting right in front of her.

"You're only thirty-seven; it's possible you might marry again, soon." Very possible.

"I'm immune."

"Natural immunity or acquired?" he asked straight-faced.

"Acquired. My first and only marriage vaccinated me," she said dryly.

Like most of the general public, she thought any vaccination provided lifetime immunity. "You could adopt."

"I could, but that can take years, and, besides, I want to experience the whole process, pregnancy, birth, everything."

"I'll remind you that you said that in the delivery room." He laughed, then added conversationally, "You don't have to use artificial insemination to become pregnant, of course. Some women choose someone they know, to make the process less . . . clinical."

That earned him a large frown. "It would hardly be fair to use a man like that. Not asking him and tricking him into being an involuntary father is reprehensible, not to mention dishonest, and any man who would voluntarily father a child he knew beforehand he wanted absolutely nothing to do with would be a rotten candidate. Donors for artificial insemination have no knowledge of the recipient, much less a personal relationship." Suddenly "the process" did seem disturbingly cold and clinical in a way it hadn't before.

"Maybe the chosen man would want to be involved in his child's life," he tested her further.

She gave him an appalled look. "That could cause a whole other set of problems. No," she declared flatly, "artificial insemination is much more sensible, far less nuisance."

John nodded solemnly while suppressing a wince at that word "nuisance." The nuisance she was dismissing so blithely was men, of course, but he could understand her diagnosis. His staff had shared their opinions of her ex-husband, whose name seemed to be Jerkbastardsonofabitch. "I'll check with a couple of my colleagues to see what's available in the city." He figured that was why she'd brought it up, because if she already knew, she wouldn't have—and it suited his purposes as well. "Naturally, you want to be sure the clinic is reputable and has a good rate of success. You do realize it's a pretty expensive proposition."

"I have money saved."

He pretended to be struck by a sudden thought. "You know, a year or so ago I read about a method that could save you significant expense. I'll do some research on that, too. Maybe you read about it, too—the turkey baster method?"

"I think I read something about it." She wasn't, Annie discovered, prepared to discuss the finer details of this, or any other method, with him. "I don't think a child would be too thrilled to learn his or her father was a turkey baster," she joked to dismiss the entire subject.

"Sounds better than a syringe, which kids associate with getting a shot," he pointed out. "Turkey basters bring to mind Thanksgiving, and kids usually love Thanksgiving. I know I did." His expression turned wistful. "All that great food . . . pumpkin pie, mashed potatoes and gravy, cranberry sauce, sausage stuffing—"

Some damaged brain cell made an X-rated association on its own, and Annie cleared her throat abruptly. "Yes, well, I don't really need to decide on the, ah, method today." She gave him a narrow look, not sure if he was as innocent as he sounded or putting her on.

Seeing he'd laid it on a bit thick, John shut up. Slow down, he counseled himself. She needed time to catch up, especially since she hadn't even started yet. "I'll do some reading and checking around, then report back to you," he said busily, standing. "It may take some time, but"—he used the charmingly avuncular smile one of his med school professors had recommended perfecting because it would be more useful than a stethoscope—"we want to do this right."

A minute later, he ushered her out of the exam room, then pretended to scribble again on her chart so he could watch her walk down the hall. She really did have a great . . . bottom.

She turned the corner, and he turned toward the closed door. So she was determined to have her own personal "growing season" and had chosen a "sensible" conception alternative. It was a sensible alternative, but it was most unsensible for her. She'd have her baby—and maybe one or two more—but she was going to do it the old-fashioned way, with him.

When he'd first seen the town two weeks ago he'd known, in no rational way, that it would provide him with everything he wanted. He just hadn't expected the woman he wanted to literally fall into his arms the first day. He pulled his next patient's chart out of the door rack and rapidly scanned the update on Mr. Blasi's kidney stone. Oh, yes, they would do this right. And, besides, for the honor of his gender, he had to correct that "nuisance" misdiagnosis.

"Condition: Guarded"

Taking her first swallow of coffee, Annie closed her eyes to better savor its jolt. Hank's high octane, fully leaded coffee was guaranteed to rev up any engine, and this morning hers needed revving. With the extra hours she put in during the growing season, she was a regular at the diner, with her own booth even because Hank and the waitresses knew she didn't have time to wait if it was crowded. With no time for lunch even on the run most days, she needed one of Hank's "manhandler" breakfasts to sustain her.

Hank had worked her way from waitress to cook, then proprietor when the original owner of the O.K. Diner retired. She'd promptly put up a new sign that said "Hank's Diner," but, in the way of small towns, it was still "The O.K." It wouldn't become "Hank's" until she retired and the next owner put up a new sign.

John saw her before the door closed behind him, sitting at "her" table, a mug of coffee in her hands, a little smile on her face. He'd like to think the smile was because she was thinking of him, but he suspected the real reason was the dose of caffeine charging through her system.

He started through the smog that clouded the big, round front table where the smokers were exiled. The diner was a classic, happily stuck in the fifties, featuring feisty service with a smile and a slam of the water glass, red vinyl booths with gold buttons, counter stools, plenty of chrome and mom-style, fill-you-up food.

Annie snapped wide awake as if someone had yelled her name. She was actually looking around to see if someone had when she saw the reason. She hid a scowl behind another swig from her mug. It was no wonder she was oversensitized to his mere presence—well, perhaps it was, but she wouldn't wonder about it. He had been the main topic of conversation the past three weeks. Covertly she watched his progress through the diner. He was stopped repeatedly by those wanting to shake his hand, offer him a place to sit. Not playing favorites, he sat with someone different every morning, although not her, luckily. Everyone in town was infatuated with him—with one notable exception. Those who had made an appointment with him came away with the same praise: he was slow to prescribe drugs and tests, quick to reassure and—probably most important—treated every question as if it were worth asking.

She couldn't disagree since her experience was the same. He left chatty little updates on her answering machine detailing his progress in researching artificial insemination clinics in the city, and she appreciated the information even if what had seemed so urgent didn't seem so pressing now. Probably because business was taking so much of her time at the moment, she assured herself.

Her breakfast arrived, and she started to eat. Now he was talking to Joe Frank, the local building contractor. As Joe stood up, Hank came out of her kitchen and joined them in the aisle. Hank was a good advertisement for her own cooking; customers could lie to themselves that it couldn't be fattening because look how skinny Hank still was after all these years of eating it. Joe gestured with his coffee mug toward the ceiling over the smokers' table, and both Hank and John Haney nodded. Hank went back to her kitchen, but not before giving the doctor a sappy smile, and Annie stopped in mid-chew. She didn't believe it. Dr. Fitz had tried for years to convince Hank that putting the smokers near the front door wasn't enough to lessen the second-hand smoke risk for everyone else, that she needed an exhaust fan over the table, but Hank had insisted the door sucked out smoke every time it opened just as well as any fan could. In three weeks, John Haney had changed her mind, and not because Hank was that worried about public health, Annie thought sourly as she resumed chewing. Oh, no, the argument that had finally convinced her was a long, lean body, sooty eyes and a partly shy, mostly cocky smile.

"Mind if I sit down?"

There was the smile again, but she was immune, Annie reminded herself as she glanced up. However, she wasn't rude. "Of course not," she said with a smile that was cool, aloof, impersonal . . . most definitely not sappy.

Before he could say anything else, Pauline Wilder, the waitress, set a mug of coffee in front of him. "I've put in cream and two sugars, just like you like, Dr. Haney," she simpered.

Annie wondered how much more of her Denver omelet she would be able to gag down. Pauline had gotten her AARP card three years ago, for heaven's sake. "Pauline, could I have some more coffee?" She hadn't had to ask for a refill before John Haney came to town, she reflected.

"Sure, hon. You need more cream?"

"No, thank you," Annie said sweetly. All the waitresses remembered, normally, that she drank her coffee black.

Pauline left, and he took a healthy drink of his coffee before smiling at her again. "Have you had a chance to read the article I sent?"

Besides the phone messages, he'd sent a copy of an article from a medical journal on the "turkey baster" method. The article had included an interview with the woman who had pioneered the process, and her earnest testimonial to its practical advantages had been hilarious. "It was very informative," she said primly. "And thank you for keeping me apprised of your research on clinics in the city."

He nodded soberly as Pauline returned with his food, and Annie realized that Hank must have taken his order for it to arrive so fast. Pauline sped back with the coffeepot, topping off his cup and refilling hers, then stopped several booths down to gossip. Suppressing a sigh, Annie spread marmalade on half of her English muffin. She knew the subject, of course. As if to make up for their lack of advance information on the new doctor, Nan Pickering and the rest of the office staff passed on whatever trivial detail of his personal history they learned, with others contributing whatever tidbits they gleaned. Consequently everyone knew the highlights of his childhood; number, whereabouts, marital and parental, status of his siblings; condition and location of his parents and other major relatives; where he'd gone to school . . . and that he'd never been married. He'd interned in a big city ER, then gone into the navy to do his residency, becoming a MASH-type doctor, the military equivalent of an ER physician, she guessed. His life was an open book, no secrets, Nan boasted—thanks mostly to her, of course—but Nan was wrong. He did have a secret, a big one, one he clearly didn't want anyone to find out, and she had, Annie thought smugly.

"The flowers I got from you are doing great."

"Good." Technically he hadn't gotten them from her, but from Connie, the assistant manager. She would never do anything so juvenile as avoid him, but those sacks of steer manure and compost out back hadn't been inventoried for at least three hours. Connie later reported that he'd wanted the flowers for the window boxes outside his office; all the businesses on Main Street had window boxes, and he wanted his to "fit in."

As if he really needed to worry about fitting in, Annie thought dryly as Pauline dropped off unnecessary extra strawberry jam for his toast. It did, though, explain what he'd been doing in the greenhouse the day she'd flattened him; she had wondered, a little. And the flowers he'd picked out did look terrific, the petunias a riot of color and spicy scent shown off by nicely weird sea holly. He had a good eye, she admitted grudgingly, and he hadn't hurt her business any, either. There had been a run on petunias, sea holly and window boxes, and she'd sold out of all three in less than two days.

"Aches and pains and charley horse better?"

"All gone. The samples and . . . massage worked."

John hid a grin behind a slug of milk. She could try all the terse answers she wanted, but that one little pause gave her away. That and her suddenly flushed cheeks. She knew her immunity was weakening, and he could almost feel sorry for her. Almost.

Annie gulped half her glass of ice water; she had better use her ammunition before it melted. "I was cleaning out some old magazines last night and found something interesting," she said casually as she spread his strawberry jam on the last half of her English muffin. Sneaking a glance across the table, she caught the flicker of alarm before he put on an expression of polite interest.

"Really?"

"Mm." She took her time taking a bite of her muffin, chewing and swallowing, savoring the moment. "I didn't know you were 'The Doctor.' "

John considered trying to brazen it out, but the ornery gleam in her eyes promised that wouldn't work. "Have you told anyone else?" he asked quietly.

"No, and I won't," she said, as quietly. Suddenly she was thoroughly disgusted with herself for being so sophomoric and petty. "But I have to admit I am curious; why are you keeping it a secret?" Many men would have made sure everyone knew the second they hit town.

A year and a half ago his picture had been on the front page of virtually every major news publication in the world. The photo had said it all, no caption or names necessary; he was simply "The Doctor." The photo had been taken following a terrorist attack at the Athens airport seconds after John Haney had arrived to catch a flight to Turkey for a seminar he was supposed to give on the latest advances in combat triage. He gave a hands-on demonstration at the airport instead.

Even as bullets were still flying, a tourist had the presence of mind—or loss of it—to grab his camcorder and record the attack and one man's frantic efforts to save the wounded. The footage was bought by CNN and broadcast repeatedly, but it was a single frame taken from the tape that became famous worldwide. It showed John Haney, stethoscope around his neck, the brilliant white of his naval uniform splattered and streaked with bright red blood, cradling the head of the man who had just died in his arms. The photo caught perfectly the look of despairing failure and furious grief on his face. What made the impact of the photo even greater was that the dead man in his arms was clearly a boy, and just as clearly one of the terrorists. The anguished doctor holding the body of an enemy he had tried so hard to save captured the obscenity of unreasoning hate and violence that had made the boy just as much a victim as any of the other casualties. The photo translated that message into a universal language that apparently even the terrorists who had staged the attack must have understood because no one had ever claimed responsibility for it.

The amateur photographer won a Pulitzer; and John Haney, far more than fifteen minutes of fame. He was interviewed by Ted Koppel, was the ABC evening news "Person of the Week," and it seemed she couldn't turn on the television or open a newspaper or magazine without seeing him. Then, without explanation, he vanished. "You were everywhere; then, overnight, you just disappeared. What happened?"

"I got laryngitis."

She understood immediately, which, when she thought about it later, worried her no small amount. "Laryngitis, huh?"

He nodded gravely. "Terminal."

She played along. "And no more interviews and personal appearances effected a miraculous recovery?"

"Yep."

It was her turn to nod. "It must have gotten to be like that old actor's joke for you—'I'm not a doctor, but I play one on T.V.' "

"Yeah, like that." Exactly like that—and she'd instinctively understood. The pleasure that surged through him wasn't sexual but just as satisfying.

He was grinning, which explained, Annie thought bemused and bedazzled, why she hadn't recognized him until she saw the old magazine. He had been in uniform, filthy, out of the context she knew him in, and, most of all, he'd looked like he would never find anything to smile about ever again. The fact that he had didn't mean he'd been unaffected; one proof was that in all of the pictures taken eighteen months ago, there hadn't been a trace of silver in his hair. Another was his refusal to continue the interviews and appearances. She could understand why the navy brass had been so anxious to put him on public display. With all the bad press the military had gotten the past few years, they must have been ecstatic to have a genuine hero who was intelligent, articulate, and better looking than most movie stars to boot—the ideal recruiting poster. But because he was a genuine hero, he had probably been embarrassed and definitely irritated by all the attention because he didn't consider he had done anything but his duty.

She had a sudden, inexplicable urge to cry. Fortunately, Pauline came by to refill their cups yet again, making a conversational pause necessary. She took a sip of hot coffee to melt the lump in her throat. "I seem to remember talk of a movie," she said guilelessly.

Wincing, he shook his head. "A couple Hollywood types called with big plans, and I told them that was fine, but my story was only going to take about fifteen minutes, so what were they going to do with the other hour and forty-five minutes."

"A lot of movies have been made with less."

"True." He glanced around, then leaned across the table, lowering his voice. "The real reason I said no was that I wanted Tom Cruise to play me and they were talking Pauly Shore."

Her giggle was such a delight that John decided it was worth having his secret found out. The force and joy of life was so strong in her . . . and balm to his wearied soul. While her guard was down, he decided to press his advantage. "I hear there's a big town picnic on Memorial Day. Are you going?"

"Everybody goes." Suddenly Annie realized she was leaning across the table toward him, too. Alarmed, she sat back. He must be magnetically as well as electrically charged.

"Good. Since we're both going, we can go together." He gave her a smile designed to proclaim harmlessness.

For some reason the image of a killer whale, as dangerous as it was beautiful, flashed into her mind. "I'm not sure when I'm going, but maybe we can get together over hot dogs." Despite all the practice it had been getting lately, her shrug didn't come off as dismissively as she hoped.

Patience, John reminded himself, again, was frequently the most important part of a cure.

". . . and call me in the morning."

They got together over hot dogs. Cradling the toddler in her arms, Annie wriggled back on a blanket spread in the shade of a sycamore to lean against the trunk. How they had gotten together, she wasn't quite sure. One minute she was talking to her brother, and the next she was sitting at a picnic table with a paper plate holding a hot dog, cole slaw and beans in front of her and John Haney beside her. And a lick of heat inside her when his thigh bumped hers.

"Getting in some practice?"

Annie jumped a little. She'd been looking for him—just out

of idle curiosity, to be sure—and here he was sneaking up on her from behind. "Giving my brother and sister-in-law a break," she said, as her nephew Daniel started to fuss again. "He's teething."

He dropped down beside her on the blanket, in a single smooth, undoctorly motion. There was a marked increase in the number of women getting up at the crack of dawn to jog around town lately, although she suspected it was due less to a sudden interest in fitness than the new doctor's skimpy running shorts and his legs.

"Here. I'll give you a break."

He reached out arms that suffered nothing in comparison to his legs, although she was annoyed with herself for noticing. She had some kind of weird spring fever, Annie decided, handing Daniel over. He settled the little boy against his chest, one big hand patting Daniel's little bottom gently while he rocked slightly, very slowly back and forth. Daniel laid his head on the strange man's shoulder and relaxed completely. It was an utterly masculine and sweet picture. He should be a father, Annie thought, and felt a sudden peculiar sadness she couldn't explain. "Marcella said you're getting your house furnished."

"Yeah, I found a couple of chairs and a couch and a bed at the Sit 'n' Sleep," he said, mentioning a local store that had better stock than its name would imply. "I still need a dresser and something for the dining room."

He shifted his hand to Daniel's back, rubbing with a slow gentle rhythm, and the toddler's eyes closed on a blissful sigh. Those magic fingers. . . . To her disgust, Annie caught herself sighing, too. As if mutant spring fever weren't bad enough, she had a life-long susceptibility to T.V. doctor shows, and he bore some resemblance to a T.V. doc she'd die before admitting she'd had a secret crush on. "You might try the antique store by the Git 'n' Go."

"I will. I've got to do some landscaping, too. Maybe you can give me some advice?"

"Certainly. Come by the greenhouse; any of the staff is qualified to help you."

He'd have preferred a less impersonal offer, but that sigh and the look on her face—for all of two seconds—was personal enough. "Good. We'll meet for bedding plants soon, then," he deadpanned, then changed the subject. "Going to the dance next week?" He'd learned there was a town dance the first Saturday of every month, and that she usually went.

"I haven't decided yet." He was going to ask her to go, and of course she'd say no.

"Well, maybe we'll hook up there."

He didn't sound as if it mattered to him particularly one way or the other, making her disgusted with herself again for caring. Someone called his name, and he glanced toward the ball diamond where teams were forming. He handed the sleeping Daniel back to her; then he leaned across and kissed her.

Seconds or possibly hours later, he stopped. "You're going too fast for me," she whispered, not because she didn't want to wake Daniel, but because that was all she had the strength for.

"You can keep up if you try," he suggested. He planted a quick kiss on her forehead, then stood up and went off to play ball.

Annie gave the greasy white paper bag in front of her a baleful look. Missing breakfast because she'd overslept, she'd given in to starvation mid-afternoon and gone to the nearest drive-in. "If you are what you eat, I must be fast and cheap," she muttered.

"A man can hope."

She looked up at the man leaning in the doorway, not with surprise but fatalism. "No, he can't," she said firmly.

He only laughed, shoving away from the doorjamb and coming toward her. Annie concentrated on removing her lunch from the sack. Leaning against the counter between them, he appropriated a couple of her fries. Munching contentedly, he glanced around. "You really have a great place here, Annie."

"More like a hobby that got out of control," she muttered. Feeling a glow just because he said her name was worse than pathetic, she thought disgustedly, as bad as feeling a thrill because she shared a secret with him. Annie glowered at him. Filching her fries, stealing kisses . . . although the latter, strictly speaking, hadn't been stolen, exactly. The first time, at the picnic, she had considered protesting, but as he kissed her, slow and deep, decided against it. Then at the dance. . . . Ah, the dance, where he'd held her in his arms, and they had kissed each other, drowning each other in more slow, deep kisses. She sighed deeply. It was past time she stopped blaming electric-magnetic nonsense and spring fever and admit the truth: her affliction was serious, life-threatening even. "Why are you here?" she asked grumpily.

He took a drag on her Coke before answering. "Well, we've gotten together over hot dogs, hooked up at the dance and met over marigolds. I think it's time we had a real date, don't you?" he asked reasonably.

No, she didn't, not if she had a single working brain cell left, but, by the time she landed in the Reeves family gene pool, the one for self-preservation must have evaporated. "When?"

"Tonight."

"All right," she agreed, almost belligerently.

John barely hid his surprise. He knew he was noted for the speed with which he operated under less than ideal conditions and for his high rate of success, but he had expected her to put up more of a fight before surrendering. His eyes narrowed on her. Unless she was planning to back out. . . . "I'll pick you up at seven-thirty for dinner." He pointed to the burrito she'd unwrapped. "And I can promise you something better than that."

Five hours later he was sure she was trying to back out; the upset stomach she claimed as the excuse for breaking their date was just a little too convenient. John rapped firmly on the metal door of the trailer parked behind the greenhouses. It was well-maintained but old and definitely a trailer, not a "mobile home." Nan Pickering said Annie had moved into it after her divorce to save money for the house she wanted. The one she'd wanted most was the one he'd just bought.

He was getting ready to knock again, harder, when the door opened, and instantly he saw that her excuse was more than valid. The short pink zip robe she wore did nothing for her green face.

"The burrito," he said.

Nodding, she managed a wan smile. "Gone, but not forgotten." He stepped forward, and she stepped back before it occurred to her that he was coming in.

As he passed her, she noticed his double-take at what looked like a four-foot, greenish club with white hair and thorns standing beside the door. "That's Albert, my guard cactus."

He did a third take, squinting thoughtfully at the white tufts sprouting wildly from Albert's "head." "I see the resemblance," he said slowly. "It does look like Albert Einstein."

Annie gave him a horrified look. She had never told anyone why she'd named the old-man cactus Albert because it sounded too weird. That he saw the same bizarre resemblance she did could only mean they shared some basic, primal part of themselves.

He stopped in the middle of the living room. "Do you have any decaffeinated green tea?"

Annie shook her head dumbly.

"That's okay. I brought some." He raised the black satchel in his hand. "It's good for intestinal upsets. I'll make you some while you go lie down."

He went into the tiny kitchen, and she heard him fill the tea kettle. Thinking she'd get rid of him in a minute, she slumped down on the sofa. She didn't even realize she'd closed her eyes, much less dozed off, until they opened much more than a minute later to see him squatting in front of her, holding out her blue mug. He even squatted great, Annie thought absently.

"I thought I told you to lie down," he chided her gently while she dutifully sipped the tea. It wasn't too hot or too sweet, but she was still surprised to find it gone.

"Now bed." Taking the mug out of her hand, he slipped an arm around her and stood them both up.

"I don't want to go to bed," she whined in a credible imitation of an over-tired four-year-old. Somehow "bed" sounded much more alarming than "lie down." She tried pulling away like a four-year-old, too, with no more success.

Keeping a firm hold on her, he pulled back the spread, sat her down on the edge, then pushed her back gently. Too washed out to fight him, Annie fell back against the pillows. Maybe, she hoped, if she kept her eyes closed, he'd go away. They flew open when he shifted her to make room to sit himself beside her, but paradoxically fluttered closed as soon as his big hand landed on her stomach and began to rub. She almost smiled when the crampy soreness proved no match for his magic fingers as they finished the job begun by the soothing warmth of the tea.

"What are all the magazines for?" Several had slid off the bed and hit the floor.

"Girl pornography," she murmured, eyes still closed.

Pages began turning, and he laughed softly. "I see what you mean. This is really hard-core interior decorating and gardening." He paused, all humor gone from his voice when he spoke again. "I'm sorry I bought your house."

"I just took too long to make up my mind." She tried to shrug, but her bones had melted. The bed dipped as he stood up, and she groaned unconsciously, already missing him.

The bedside lamp went out, and she decided she should at least open her eyes long enough to thank him and say goodbye, but before she could, she heard two thumps on the thin floor followed by the rattle of change. She reared up on her elbows, although her blissfully lethargic body was very slow to cooperate. "What are you doing?"

"Getting ready for bed," he said matter-of-factly. In the dim light from the living room, she could see he was wearing only a T-shirt and boxers.

"You cannot spend the night," she said, as firmly as melted bone could.

"The burrito may come back, and I don't like making house calls in the middle of the night." He climbed into bed next to her, pulled her firmly against him spoon-fashion, and began massaging her stomach again.

A small part of her was watching all this aghast, but the majority part snuggled against him. A sudden thought did manage to jolt her. "Your car!"

"It'll be all right. This is a good neighborhood." There was a thread of humor in his voice.

"No, no, it's not all right." She struggled to sit up, but his arms were lead ropes around her. "Someone will see it, and it'll be all over town by noon tomorrow that you spent the night here."

John smiled to himself. She was overestimating the time by at least two hours. "It's dark. Nobody'll see it." If he hadn't parked under the bright nightwatchman light.

She sighed in resignation and relaxed again, her bottom tucking firmly against him, and she jolted again. "Is that what I think—"

"Autonomous response," he said with a yawn. "Nothing to worry about." Not for her, anyway, John thought wryly, manufacturing another yawn.

Even Annie couldn't believe she bought that, but she settled back. She wriggled closer, stealing a little of his warmth. "Why did you decide on a small town instead of a big city ER?" she murmured.

Despite the self-torture, he snugged her tighter. "I 'saw the world,' " he said softly, parroting navy recruiting posters, "and decided what I really wanted was to have a family and patients I'd know for a lifetime instead of a few desperate minutes, to go home every night at a decent hour, drink lemonade out on the back porch and maybe read a book until the sun goes down."

She heard the smile in his voice and smiled, too. "That house has a great back porch." She felt herself drifting and turned her cheek on his arm so she could smell his skin as she fell asleep. "I can't get married again," she said drowsily. "I can't risk a relapse and have to have another divorce vaccination."

"Don't worry," he whispered. "Everything will work out fine."

"Prognosis: Terminal"

Nothing was working out fine, Annie thought as she pushed through the diner door. He'd been gone when she woke up, leaving no note, not even about taking two aspirins or calling him in the morning, nothing. And he hadn't called her, either. She faltered momentarily as she started toward the back of the diner. And now he was sitting, if you please, at her table!

"Good morning," he said cheerfully as she sat down across from him.

Before she could say anything, Pauline slammed a mug of coffee down in front of her, slopping it over the rim. Wiping it off pointedly, Annie raised the mug and took a big sip that she barely managed not to spit across the table. At least half a shaker of salt had been dumped in it! Glaring at Pauline, she drained the glass of water in front of John.

Pauline glared back. "Anne Agatha Reeves, I'm ashamed of you. You didn't even have the decency to make the poor man breakfast. Your mother raised you better than that."

Annie forbore pointing out that her mother hadn't raised her unmarried daughter to have men spending the night so they would need breakfast. "He didn't have the decency to stay long enough to have breakfast," she muttered. She heard a strangled sound, and turned her glare on the man across the table. He raised his eyebrows in innocence.

"Seduced and abandoned. I expected better of you, missy." Hank had come out of the kitchen to throw in her opinion. "Wham, bam, not even thank you, man."

Keeping a wary eye on the big spatula in Hank's hand, Annie stared at the other woman in disbelief. "Nothing happened! He just sat up with me because I had an upset stomach."

"Well, lie down is more accurate."

Annie stared at him in greater disbelief, and the dedicated healer gave her an apologetic shrug for his insistence on honesty. "We just slept together!" she snapped, more loudly than she intended. Finally aware of the dead—and rapt—silence in the rest of the diner, Annie looked around. The other diners had pursed-mouth condemnation for her and sympathy for him. Why had she ever thought living in a small town was so wonderful?

Pauline and Hank left with parting humphs and dirty looks.

"We didn't do anything!" Annie leaned across the table to whisper furiously.

"Well, we could," he said helpfully.

She gave him her version of prune-mouthed condemnation. "I know what you're trying to do. You spent the night figuring everybody in town would know and expect me to marry you."

He sipped his coffee calmly. "You will."

"You're two years younger than me," she hissed, but despite conscientious effort, she couldn't make that into the major side effect she wanted it to be. So she tried forlornness. "I can't afford the time to be sure a marriage is taking before I have a baby."

"It will take," he said hard-heartedly.

Sitting back, she thought hard. It was time for drastic measures; the doctor needed to learn that persistence wasn't always the best medicine. "All right," she said, slapping her hand on the table. "I'll make an honest man of you." The startled look on his face gave her a perverse thrill.

She stood up. It wasn't necessary to get everyone's attention first, she thought sardonically. "I'd like to invite you all to a wedding, today, at noon, at the courthouse. We sincerely hope that as many of you as can will attend." She smiled sweetly at him when she finished. He'd stand her up, of course, and town favor and sympathy would shift back to her.

He didn't stand her up. Annie looked around with the odd sense of being out of her body. Instead of the judge's chambers, the wedding was taking place in the courtroom, and there still wasn't room for half of the people who wanted to attend. The judge took his position, and Connie shoved a bouquet into her hand, then gave her a little shove to get her moving.

She began walking down the aisle toward the front of the courtroom, not quite sure if her feet were working or not. Immediately after their wedding announcement, Hank had thrown everybody out of the diner, then dragged her off to her house where it seemed like half the women in town showed up. As a result she was wearing the traditional "something old, something new, something borrowed and something blue." Hank had brought out her grandmother's lace veil, and the dress Nan's daughter was supposed to wear before she eloped was both something borrowed and new. Jeanne Rae and Connie had scalped every blue larkspur, delphinium, giant pansy and love-in-a-mist, combining them with baby's breath for a bouquet of something blue. They had also cut the biggest giant white carnation for John's suit.

He was standing straight and tall and so handsome, watching her approach, waiting for her. When he'd actually shown up, she'd known she couldn't embarrass him in front of the whole town by backing out. They could get the clerk to tear up the paperwork after the ceremony. The marriage wasn't valid, she told herself again, if it was never officially recorded.

John wasn't sure his conscience was going to let him go through with this. The look on her face wasn't panic, exactly. The judge caught his eye and winked at him. The whole town had abetted his course of "treatment" for Annie Reeves, and a cynic would say that their motivation was to keep a doctor by marrying off one of their women to him. He was cynic enough to know that was part of it, but he also knew how fond they all were of Annie and that they wanted only the best for her. It was more than a little humbling that they thought he was good enough for her.

Just as he had decided to put an end to her misery, she slipped her hand into his and smiled tremulously up at him, and his heart turned over. "I love you, Annie," he vowed softly. Her smile strengthened, and they turned to face the judge.

Leaning against the porch railing, Annie watched the first firefly wink over the lawn. The wedding had lasted ten minutes, the impromptu potluck party afterward almost until dusk. Feeling an arm slip around her waist, she leaned her head back against his solid shoulder to look up at him. His head bent, and they shared a hungry kiss. Finally their mouths eased apart, and Annie settled back against him with a long sigh. "I just married you for the house, you know."

Wrapping both arms around her, he rested his chin on top of her head. "Well, one reason is as good as another, I suppose," he said philosophically.

"And because I'm terminally, incurably in love with you," she added.

He spun her in his arms. "Although some reasons are better than others."

This kiss lasted even longer than the one before, and they found themselves halfway to the bedroom when it ended. "It occurs to me that I was negligent in my medical responsibilities; I forgot the premarital exam, but better late than never, I guess."

She gave him a suspicious look. "It doesn't involve any turkey basters, does it?"

"No," he promised solemnly. "No turkey basters."

"Good. I wasn't married to that idea, you know."

"No," he said, looking down at her, suddenly completely sober. "You're married to me."

Her smile was pure joy and happiness. "Yes, I know."

Nobody's Angel

by

Barbara Cummings

Author's Note

Whatever role Jimmy Smits plays (Bobby Simone on *NYPD Blue,* or the favored son in *Mi Familia*) there is a core of honor that permeates his character. Yes, he's strong, sexy as sin, respectful of women, and all the good things a hero should be. But it is his integrity in the face of overwhelming temptation that has endeared him to me. What, I wondered, would an ancestor of his be like? The answer, for me, is Fernando de la Hoya, a hero worthy of any woman's dreams.

The four-wheel bounced in and out of the rutted drive leading to the dilapidated ranch house. Sedona Skye gritted her teeth and held on to the wheel. She'd been planning "one last look" at her deceased father's Arizona spread for a long while, and the foreclosure notice in yesterday's mail had served as a wake-up call. It was now or never. So it had to be now.

Something about this beautiful, red-rocked land—the land for which her father had named her—always made her feel close to him. Parking her land rover, she toured it all: the empty stalls; the crumbling hundred-year-old well; the neglected ranch house, where she found a family of squirrels had taken up residence. Then, getting back into the rover, she made the drive to the place her father had most loved: his silver mine.

Trudging up the hill toward the open shaft, she picked up a weather-beaten sign. *Dream Maiden.* Her father's name for the mine. She flung the board onto a heap of rusted equipment and shielded her eyes against the mid-morning sun—always bright, always hot.

One last ride, that was all she wanted. One last rush into the bowels of beauty, to carom down the tunnels in an ore trolley, pull up at the end of the longest run, get out, pick away at the once-prosperous veining, do what her father had spent his last years doing. Who knew? She just might strike it rich.

Picking up an old battery-powered miner's lantern, she went into the cobwebbed entrance. Four rusted-out ore trolleys stood waiting, one braked at the top of the long tunnel. She knew it was crazy. She had a noon lunch date with Veronica, and three interviews, beginning at two, with sous-chefs interested in working for her Denver Tex-Mex restaurant. To say nothing of the danger.

But then, like her father, she'd never been afraid of taking risks. Kept life interesting.

Grinning at the silliness of it all, she claimed a small pick ax, shook the dust out of a dented hard hat, and slapped the hat onto her head. The batteries in the hat's light still worked, though their glow didn't penetrate far. No matter. She knew every inch of the tunnels.

Choosing the most twisted one—the one in which the de la Hoyas had found the big silver vein that made their fortune—she cajoled the trolley into position at the top of a small rise. Without taking time to prime the relay systems, she climbed into the sleigh-like contraption and eased off the brakes. Gravity did the rest.

As usual, the trolley picked up speed as it rounded the first turn. She applied a little pressure on the brake so it didn't jump the track. The metal squealed, sparks flying into the darkness. She squealed, gripping the trolley's sides. She loved the roller-coaster feeling and the gloom and doom atmosphere. The faster she went, the more excited she became. The big turn was right ahead, and she braced herself to give enough pressure to the brakes so she wouldn't jump the tracks. But when she pushed forward on the old handle, the darned thing snapped like peanut brittle.

And she took off like a demented rocket.

She had news for the world. With death certain, she did *not* see light at the end of the tunnel. Only black space showed up ahead, and she hurtled through it, walls whizzing by in a flash of unholy sparks that too closely resembled a welcoming barrage at the entrance to hell.

Screaming did no good, but she screamed anyway. "God, please, don't let me die! Please! Let there be an angel down there to catch me!"

The words were hardly out of her mouth when, just ahead, a great wall appeared. She knew these tunnels, every shaft, curve, and straight-away. There was no wall there. She crashed into it anyway. And went right through it, into the blinding sunshine. The tracks vanished. The trolley slammed into a mound of dirt, went nose down. Her hard hat flew off. And she tumbled over and over until, suddenly, she met a solid object.

She shook her head, flexed her bruised and battered muscles and began to rise. With her head still spinning, she wondered vaguely how she'd managed to get back out of the mine. Then she caught sight of what had stopped her tumble, and she froze.

Old scuffed boots, hand-tooled with intricately carved tips, topped by soft suede pants. Long, hard male legs. Sexy, sinuous legs. Muscular thighs, slim hips. A gun holstered low around those hips and tied around one of those thighs.

Sedona gulped, her gaze sweeping upward. He filled out his old shirt, too. Big shoulders—wide, hard. Nice chin. Better mouth—agape for one second, then slammed shut in a fierce scowl. She ignored that and took in his chiseled cheekbones, slight shadow of a beard, hooded eyes. Brown? No, black, like his hair and the low-riding hat. She searched the shadows near his eyes and could have sworn she saw sparks flickering there.

She didn't know who he was, but she did know that this was nobody's angel. In fact, she wouldn't have been surprised to see horns sticking out of his Stetson.

She reached out to make sure he was real, and he backed off at her touch, wary. Judging from that hot glare he gave her, he was also furious. Why? Because . . .

Because she had been trespassing. Good grief. The gun. He was the sheriff.

More than a little bewildered, Sedona began to uncoil, feeling every muscle scream in protest. Yet she gave a half-hearted grin. "Hi. I'm Sedona, Thomas Skye's daughter? I was just taking a last stroll. Couldn't resist exploring. Thought I might find the silver Dad always thought—"

Spanish curses were beautiful, but just as mean-spirited as English ones, flying out of that finely chiseled mouth. They ended in a strangled growl so feral that she knew this was not the sheriff. And she also knew that she was in a whole lot of trouble.

When Fernando de la Hoya saw what came tearing through the wall of his mine, the shock froze him in place. The trolley, he recognized. There were three on order from his suppliers. The female, he did not. At first he wasn't sure she could be real; thought, perhaps, she was a ghost. Now, though, he knew what she was.

Thief! She wanted to plunder his mine. His fury surged upward, and he hauled her up by her collar, glaring into her golden-flecked green eyes. "So, you would take away *my* silver from *my* mine? I, Fernando de la Hoya, tell you that anyone, woman or man, who tries to steal from me will be arrested." With the palm of his hand, he nudged her forward. "For now, I will guard you while one of my men rides into town for the sheriff."

Sedona shook off his hand and turned to squint up at him. "You're Fernando de la Hoya?"

With no effort, he picked her up, turned her around, and gave another gentle shove. "Of course. This is my land. My mine. Who else did you think to find here?"

Anyone else.

But wait. Maybe this was a relative of the original de la Hoyas. That was possible, wasn't it? Sedona started to turn to him once more, determined to find out how he was related to the de la Hoyas. But then, as she caught a better glimpse of her surroundings, she jerked to a halt.

Where were the four rusted ore trolleys? Where was her land rover? And that big shed—it hadn't been there a half hour ago. Nor had the hitching post, or the four horses that were tied to it. Nor the three men at the bottom of the hill, who were hunkered around a fire with a cast-iron pot suspended above it. One of the men was pouring coffee into what looked like a tin cup.

Sedona's head whirled, fear gradually building. She tried to convince herself that someone was playing a trick on her. But who? Nobody even knew where she was. Besides, common sense told her that in the short time she had taken her ill-fated ride, no one could have accomplished the changes she saw before her. Changes that amounted to the complete transformation of her father's land.

Her gaze swept the scene. No road led up to the ridge, only a well-worn horse path. Not a single pole, with or without electric wires, was in sight. And the tracks her trolley had ridden a few minutes ago were gone.

On the other hand, Fernando de la Hoya was present and accounted for—a man who had died before her grandmother was born. He had a hand on her back and kept nudging her onward, toward the big shed, where he'd said he would hold her while he sent for the sheriff. Sent for. Not called.

Okay, Sedona, girl, you're not in Kansas anymore . . . or Denver . . . or 1998. Maybe you're in a coma. Or maybe you died and this really is hell. Or maybe Einstein was right and there is no beginning or end to time. . . .

She didn't like comas, dying, or hell, so Einstein sounded pretty good. She remembered the old paranormal soap opera, *Dark Shadows,* and how characters always fell into time warps. Yeah, right. But unless she was still in the mine, unconscious, perhaps dying—and it sure didn't feel like it—she had no other explanation for what was happening to her.

No beginning or end to time. That comforting thought would do for now.

Fernando de la Hoya disliked forcing women to do anything. But he had to get this woman—this thief—inside, where he could contain her. As he walked behind her, his hand felt every undulation of her body, and he had to clamp his teeth against the erotic stirring in his loins. *Jesu Cristo!* The infernal woman wore pants, and they emphasized a deliciously rounded backside that moved like an oiled pendulum.

Dios! Never had he seen a woman in pants. Light-weight denim pants, braided leather belt like the Indians wore, but a soft shirt that— in the quick glimpse he had gotten before he pushed her away from him—hugged her breasts like silk. And what was that thing he felt under her shirt? Not a modest chemise but some harness that pushed up her breasts, rounded them in a way that made his pulses race.

He shoved her through the shed doorway, out of the roaring heat of the sun, and closed the door behind them. He nodded toward one of the carved wooden chairs. When she plopped into it with a loud sigh, then leaned back and crossed her legs, he shook his head and frowned.

"Do you not understand the proper conduct of a woman?"

"Proper conduct?"

"You sit and dress like a man. You are forward and brazen and—"

"Now just one minute!"

"—you are a thief."

"I'm *not* a thief."

"You yourself have said that you are here to find the silver in *my* mine."

Sedona assessed Fernando de la Hoya's aristocratic hauteur. It seemed rehearsed, as if he had taken a role and put it on. There was a troubled intensity in his brown eyes, a haunted need or drive. She had the most amazingly clear sense that he was in terrible pain, as if someone had hurt him to the marrow of his bones and was wringing the life out of him.

Suddenly, inexplicably and without warning, some deeply buried part of herself welled up inside her. He wanted to turn her over to the sheriff, but all she wanted to do was wrap him in her arms, cradle him against her breast, soothe him, wipe out that pain.

No more of that. She had to get a hold of herself and take charge of this situation. Although, she thought, she did *not* want to get him riled.

"I'm sorry," she said. "I was joking. I'd never steal. That's not the kind of woman my father raised."

One eyebrow peaked. "Did he name you Sedona?"

She glared at him. "As a matter of fact, he did."

A slight smile. "You love him, no?"

"Yes. Loved. Still love." Her voice cracked. "He died two weeks ago." Then she added in a whisper, *"Two weeks and a hundred years from now."*

Fernando must have super-human hearing. "What do you mean, a hundred years from now?"

Well, he had a right to know. "I don't belong here."

This time, his smile was broad and full and tiny crinkles appeared at the corners of his very dark, truly beautiful, eyes. "I think I already knew that," he said with a chuckle.

"No, you don't understand."

Before she could explain, a knock sounded at the door and one of the men poked his head in. "Señor Nando . . . the creek. It is two inches lower today. And the sun, it is drying the bed fast. There is no more run-off from the mountains."

Fernando swore. "How many days do we have left?"

"No more than a week."

"Then pray for rain."

"All are praying, Señor. But God, He does not hear us."

When the door closed, Fernando pulled a chair out and sat down slowly, as if a weight pressed on his shoulders. He looked up at the ceiling and shook his fist. "I have enough troubles, and You sent this woman to me? Dante is right. You do not hear us."

When he turned back to her, he didn't blush, fiddle, apologize, or evade her gaze. Sedona liked that. He seemed a straightforward, honest man who believed in his God and didn't hesitate to converse with Him, even with a stranger sitting right there. How many men did she know who would feel that comfortable with themselves? Hah! None.

"To get back to our problem," he said. "What hundred years?"

She tried to explain her world and what had happened—as if the time warp explanation, which she was desperately clinging to, were the only reason for her being in his world. She told him that he would strike silver, the ranch would prosper, and he would be a force to be reckoned with. She described the changes that were coming, explained that she didn't belong here, but here she was, and . . .

He inched his chair farther and farther from her, his eyes dulled with disbelief. "You are insane. These things do not happen."

"They will happen. They did happen."

"No! Ay, no!" Once more he addressed the ceiling. "I do not need a crazy woman. A woman, yes, to bring order and cook for us." He sighed. "Jesu, You must have a twisted sense of humor, to send me this woman. If she says these things in front of other people, they will lock her up in the new insane asylum!"

"You need a cook?"

Nando reluctantly admitted his inability to keep his hacienda running smoothly. "I need someone to feed my men, who have not had a decent meal in two weeks. The hacienda has deteriorated since my housekeeper married and moved away. I cannot supervise it. I and my men are too busy keeping cattle alive. Seven weeks we have been without rain. Yesterday the well ran dry. You heard what Dante said. Another week of this, and the cattle will die. The water, it is important, for the cattle and the mine. Without it, I will lose everything."

As he talked, she heard the underlying anguish and pain, echoes of what she'd seen in his eyes. But forget wrapping him in her arms to comfort him. She had a better idea. She was a chef and could feed five hundred people a day. A dozen men or so was nothing. And she was a good housekeeper, too. She'd been keeping house for her father and herself since the age of twelve, when her mother had died.

"I'm a very good cook," she said. "And I can take care of your hacienda." Stubbornly, she set her chin and squared her shoulders. "I'll help *you* if you'll help *me* go home."

For one moment her bravado made him wonder if God *had* sent the answer to his prayers. Then his common sense asserted itself.

"No, no." He gave his head an adamant shake. "A woman who wears pants and shows off her breasts and talks loco—she will end up in the woman's ward, behind bars and bolted doors. What good will you do me then?" He shook his head again. "No. You cannot help me. The sheriff will see to you."

She could not let that happen—tied to a chair in some Dickensian horror show. "I know where you can find water."

He pivoted back to stare at her, and his expression spoke of desperation. Otherwise, she was certain he wouldn't have listened.

She pulled out all the stops. "I promise you, if you dig where I show you, you'll have all the water you will ever need."

"You can promise such a thing?"

She nodded. "And I promise another thing. If you do not strike water, then you can send for the sheriff and I will go with him without a struggle."

Over the rocky expanse of foothills, treacherous in many places, she rode astride. His mother would not have done such a thing; but reluctantly he admitted it was more sensible. And—may all the devils be damned—more alluring. Certainly, she was beautiful. The wind whipped that red-gold hair so that it looked like a horse's mane, and it plastered her shirt against the fullness of her breasts. They didn't sag, and she didn't seem uncomfortable—so perhaps that harness she wore was good for more than attracting men's attentions and arousing them past the point of no return.

Damnation! He had no time for the calls of his flesh.

Nando gritted his teeth and paid more heed to where Sedona rode, on a direct course to the hacienda. Yet, she turned her head often, searching for something, her look seeming both frightened and sad. It surprised him to see her shoulders slump and a few tears course down her lovely cheeks. Before he could react, she stiffened and shook her head hard, and the tears stopped. Kneeing the horse, she pulled away from him and galloped full out, leading the way to the back entrance of the hacienda, rounding the barn, and drawing up to the hitching post in front of the main house.

She did not immediately alight from the horse, but sat staring at the two-story white-washed log house and the covered porches he had insisted be added to each floor to cool the interior.

As he rode up beside her, she turned to him. "It's what I always imagined it should be. Strong. Sturdy. Yet as beautiful as a wedding cake."

She smiled with the brilliance of the sun, and Nando froze. He could not tear his eyes from her. She was telling him something, asking him to trust her. But how could he? She talked of impossible things. Yes, she had proven her knowledge of the land and the way the ranch was laid out, but she could have been spying on him for weeks.

Forcing his gaze away from the truth he saw in her eyes, he reminded himself of what his father had taught him: men did not succumb to women, their charms or their logic.

"Show me the water," he said.

A few minutes later, Nando shook his head, muttered a dozen imprecations, and jabbed his boot into the sandy soil—the place where Sedona insisted there was fresh water. His men—who had by now heard of the woman who had fallen at his feet in the mine—laughed behind their hands at him as he paced wildly back and forth. Never had they laughed at him. Never had they dared. Until this . . . this . . . this *woman* had invaded his life. He had to put a stop to the laughter. He had to gain control. If his father should see this, hear about it—

Nando shuddered with anger, swallowed hard, and whirled on the woman. "What is this devilment? Do you take me for a complete fool? Do you think I have not already had all these sites surveyed? Three dowsers went over this land. Found nothing. A geologist from Denver took samples of the soil and rocks, and made many strange maps. No water, he said. Not here. Not anywhere near here."

Sedona mashed her hands on her hips and leaned toward him. "Here. Right here. Where I am standing. Dig. You'll have gallons of water. And the underground spring runs all the way to the mine, where the silver is thirstier than your cattle."

"Impossible!" He turned and ordered, "Get into the kitchen where you belong. My men are hungry. Do what a woman does. I will do what a man does and trust in the experts."

"Who have not found water," she muttered. Determined, she stood her ground, the only ground in the area where water could be found. "Stubborn macho jerk!"

He spun around and glared, biting his words through a jaw tense with fury. "Don't mock me in front of my men. Don't make me drag you into the house. Or do you prefer the sheriff?"

Sedona's body went numb. That threat was a low blow, and judging by the calculating look in Señor de la Hoya's eye, he knew it. But she could see that her thoughtless outburst might have caused him to lose face with his workmen. "I'm sorry I shouted at you. I'll try not to do it again. However, don't think you've won the water war. This is where you will find it, and I will prove it." She headed directly for the house and her first chore—making supper.

Inside, Sedona's steps faltered. The main room—where the squirrels had been nesting that morning—was beautiful. Rough-hewn beams, wide plank floors, carved Spanish-style furniture, rugs woven of every color in the rainbow. And silver everywhere: plates, candlesticks, a large crucifix over the mantel. "Who did this? Surely not the high and mighty Señor de la Hoya."

A sudden shift in air current made her nostrils flare as she caught his scent, and she realized he was right behind her. Calvin Klein, eat your heart out. *This* was what a man should smell like. Sandalwood soap, polished leather, pheromones strong enough to make the hair on her arms stand on end.

"So, you think the high and mighty Señor de la Hoya a boor as well as a macho jerk. Someone who would not appreciate beauty and elegance and not want to surround himself with things which soothe a man's soul."

She turned to face him, and her breasts brushed against his chest. Gulping for air, which suddenly seemed to be in short supply, she backed away a little and managed somehow to offer a compliment. "It is truly magnificent. A tribute to your culture and your impeccable taste."

Nando swore silently. Now how was he ever going to tell her that his mother and two sisters had helped him choose everything. This woman made him say things he did not intend, do things he never would think to do. He should tell her the truth. But he liked the way she looked at him, the way the golden sparks in her eyes danced with pleasure and delight. He liked her body, and he liked . . . her. Even if she was loco.

He swallowed a quick rush of longing and nodded toward a rounded arch on the left. "The kitchen is that way. If you need help, call for Carlos. I have cattle to bury."

Twenty minutes later Sedona knew she was in even bigger

trouble than she'd thought. Okay, she could mix tortillas from scratch and cook them on an open fire. But she had never had to grind the damned corn in a mortar and pestle. Whoever had developed the food processor was touched by God. Every arm muscle ached, and her shoulders felt like boulders—immovable. But Carlos had said there were seventeen men to feed that night, sometimes twenty-six. If she didn't hurry, they would be eating boiled corn mush.

Cooking with lard and bacon grease made her shudder, but two hours later she had reasonable facsimiles of chicken burritos, Spanish rice, and refried beans. While the men ate around a table in a large lean-to, she headed for the barn to find a pick and shovel.

Nando wouldn't dig for water? Okay, then she would. At night. All night, every night, if necessary. She'd find his water, and then he'd have to help her to go home.

Five days later, with cattle dying and horses near collapse and the entire spread on the verge of complete disaster, she'd dug a hole the size of a fledgling volcano. Nando hadn't tried to stop her. Every time he walked past, he simply shook his head and muttered something about loco females who were more stubborn than mules. She ignored him and kept digging. Her hands were blistered, and her muscles had developed so much that by the time she got back to Denver, she'd be eligible for the Broncos' front line.

Damn. The sand had been easy. But tonight she'd hit rock, and she couldn't chip it or pick it. It just wouldn't budge.

Carlos' hissed whisper came to her from the gloom near the fence.

"The dynamite, it is in the storage shed, señorita."

She hadn't heard him approach, so intent had she been on digging. "Dynamite?"

"How else, señorita?"

"I hadn't counted on that."

He laughed, a soft rumble that was not unpleasant, perhaps

even friendly. Her spirits buoyed. Could she make him her ally? "I know nothing about dynamite. Do you?"

"Si, señorita. It makes a great noise. Boom! And everyone comes running."

"Are you teasing me? Or do you think me insane for digging here?"

Carlos moved closer to her, but not too close. He shrugged. *"Quien sabe?* Who knows? If you are loco, you are also a good cook, a good worker, and a very stubborn woman. Like the señor."

"Nonsense! I'm nothing like the señor."

"Si, señorita, you are. For almost a week, now, we have watched you, my *compañeros* and I, and we wonder who will win this contest of wills. Myself, I think you are stronger than any woman he has ever known, as well as more determined. Why else would you dig where he tells you not to dig?" Carlos came closer to inspect the monstrous—and dry—hole. "You are certain there is water there?"

"Absolutely."

"An angel told you, perhaps? In a dream, hmm?"

"No angel. My father—may he rest in peace. He was a rancher and a miner. He knew everything about this land."

"He is dead, *su padre?"*

"Si. I mean, yes. He died only three weeks ago."

"Ah, I see. His spirit—the spirit of a man who knew this land—he came to you and told you where to look. That is different, señorita. Perhaps we can find your water after all."

Sedona stifled the impulse to contradict him, instead latching on to one key word he'd spoken. "We?"

He motioned into the darkness, and several men warily approached.

"Dante," Carlos said, "we will need the dynamite."

The older man sighed. "Señor Nando will not be pleased."

Señor Nando was furious when the first blast sent him flying outside, half-dressed, with rifle and handguns primed, ready to take on an army of invaders. When he saw the lantern-lit scene, he thundered, "Have you all lost your wits? Following this woman's orders is madness!"

Dante shrugged. "What is madness is not to try. We have no more than a day before the ranch dies. If we do not find water, we have lost only a little dynamite. If we do, everything lives. But you are the patrón. If you wish us to stop, we will stop."

Nando could not argue with that logic. He stole a look at Sedona, who stood as quietly as the others, waiting for his decision. But her body was tense, hopeful. When he kicked at the dirt and sighed, "Keep digging," she smiled. Not in triumph, but in joy.

He wanted to see that smile every day of his life. In the morning when he woke up. At night, before closing his eyes. *Jesu Cristo!* In only a few days, this stubborn woman had invaded his land, his home, and his heart. *Dios!* What was he going to do about her?

Dante stayed very close to Sedona, keeping up a running conversation with looks and grins and chuckles that made her more nervous than she'd been in years. They watched together as Carlos set another charge of dynamite.

"He is not happy, the señor," Dante said. "No one has ever made him swear so often. No woman has ever gotten him so angry as you. And never has he allowed a woman to sleep in his house while he sleeps in the guest quarters."

"Guest quarters? I thought it was his office and bedroom."

"Ay! For a smart woman, you are sometimes not so smart." He waggled his eyebrows suggestively. "The señor stays away from you for reasons of his own, eh?"

The next blast sent a rumbling through the ground that shook the earth, and a gigantic geyser burst through the final layer of rock, wetting them all to their skins. The men danced and shouted.

Nando stood stupefied, staring not at the water but at the woman who had saved his land and his dream. As water rushed over her, she laughed, her hands outstretched to catch the precious liquid. And every drop found feminine hills and valleys to rush over, around, and down—here, in the open, in front of his men. His men who were looking at her, too.

With a growl, Nando crossed the yard and swept Sedona into his arms, hugging her close. He told himself he was doing it so that his men, who had been too long without women, would not be tempted beyond reason. But the truth was, he did it for himself, for he wanted no other man to look at her, no other man to feel as he did. Hungry for her—only for her.

Laughing, Sedona threw her arms around his shoulders, and when he felt her lips brush the artery in his neck, he almost dropped her. Instead, he clasped her even more tightly to him and strode quickly toward the house, through the open door, and up the central stairs.

When he arrived at the room she had been using, he stopped, for the first time uncertain. Because of the water, it was as if they had no clothes between them. He could feel every inch of her breasts, harness or no harness. And he could feel her soft, round bottom. With all his strength, he held his need in check, until she snuggled closer and breathed deeply, and his control—maintained by sheer will ever since she had dropped into his life—shattered.

His lips brushed her forehead, her cheek, her closed eyelid, which fluttered under his kiss. He smiled and found her lips, trembling, half open, expectant. He nibbled first, and his tongue tasted a delectable sweetness. It beckoned, and something primal rose within him. He wanted to touch her everywhere, possess her, show her what love was, as if she were knowing it for the first time. It bothered him slightly that he was probably not her first—couldn't be, given the forward way she had about her around men. But perhaps this was better. . . .

When his right hand found the underside of her breast and his fingers brushed across her nipple, Sedona hardly heard Nando's unsteady whispers, so lost was she in the wild, needy sensations he drew from her. He was a fire that ignited tiny sparks in her veins, and she reached up to bring him closer.

He laughed, and his hand found the hottest part of her. "Wanton. But from now on, only for me."

Clarity was not welcome but insistent. This was not 1998. That was not an endearment. He actually thought her wanton. Easy pickings. So there was no real emotion behind what they were doing, only sexual release. She had always known that for her, with any man, mere sexual release was not, could never be, enough.

She pushed his hand away. "No."

He laughed. "You wish to play? *Si,* we will play. And do so much more."

She shook her head. "I am not playing. I said *no.*"

A throbbing physical pain filled him, but he struggled to get it under control and to try to understand what had happened. He set her on her feet and took two backward steps. "What kind of woman are you? You wanted me, did you not?"

"Yes."

"Then why do you now resist?"

She wished she could take her pride and wear it like a mantle, making her invulnerable and stern. But he had touched a place so deeply buried that she couldn't control it or shut it off. Because she had chosen a different path than her friends, those words, so easily said by him, had hurt. And they had hurt because *he* had said them. Foolish, but there it was.

Suddenly tears swam in her eyes, and one trickled down her cheek. She could barely get out the words, "I'm not wanton."

Nando felt his heart stop. He held his breath until it slammed back into an irregular beat. He thought he had been in pain before. It was nothing compared to watching Sedona struggle to maintain her dignity. *Dios!* In his haste to lose himself in her body, he had forgotten those parts of her spirit that made her infuriating, but that he also admired: her self-assurance and pride.

He sighed, straightened, and ran his hand through his hair to steady himself. His eyes sought hers. "Forgive me. What just happened will not happen again. This, I promise you."

The next day, he moved Dante's elderly aunt, Esmeralda, into the main house so there would be no gossip—and no more opportunity to respond to the hunger that had consumed him the previous night. Still, the promise was not easy to keep. He saw Sedona every day—chatting to the men, working in the kitchen garden, serving meals, cleaning the house. She had taken to wearing clothes Esmeralda provided. Colorful skirts, embroidered blouses, wide belts. They were full and unstructured, hiding more than they revealed, as they should, of course. But they also made her look less like a woman than her pants and silk shirt.

He wished he had that night to live over, those words to take back. He did not, could not. But he did have other nights, many of them, when he and Sedona sat in front of the fire together, reading, talking, never acknowledging the tension that was building between them—nor that he had a promise to keep. It was there, however, at every turn.

Moby Dick brought an animated recital from Sedona about things called movies, and he could see a faraway look in her eyes, a yearning to be back where images of people moved on a screen. Even the mundane triggered her. A discussion about cleaning the chicken coops turned into a lesson on composting and "miracle grow"—whatever that was. He could only count it a miracle that she confined such conversations to him alone. Thus far he had managed to keep others from hearing her wild tales.

Everywhere, at every turn, he ached. First, from the awful effort it took to keep her craziness hidden. Second, from the awful knowledge that her world was real to her and that it continually beckoned her away from him.

Finally, the night arrived when she came to him, and he knew even before she spoke what she was going to say.

"The well's full," she began, "and there's enough water for the mine."

His heart lurched. "You want to go back." When she nodded, a great sadness possessed him. If he acknowledged her desire, he would lose her. She would dream herself into the insane asylum. He could not watch her squander her sanity. He could not let her go like that—or any other way. "Why do you persist in these fantasies? Do you not know the consequences?"

"Yes. But I must try."

"You will fail or go mad."

"But don't you understand how important it is to try?"

More than anyone else, he did. He nodded. "I can still hear my father's words when I told him that I was leaving the family and his rule. *'You will fail miserably and come crawling back, like a dog, with your tail between your legs.'* That is what he said."

So that was the thing she had seen that first day, Sedona realized. Those words were the demon that haunted him. How awful, to be rejected and ridiculed by your father! She took a step toward him, then stopped, her hand outstretched, trembling slightly. "Nando, he was wrong. You won't fail. You have strength, courage, and just enough pride to make it all work."

That she had more faith in him than his father was not surprising. With a crooked smile, he admitted, "Your pig-headedness at digging the well helped me recover that courage, and once more I have faith in myself."

"But not yet in me."

"What you expect me to believe is unbelievable."

"Yes. Your father must have thought that, too."

Because their bodies could not love, their eyes dueled and their spirits clashed. There were so many reasons why he should not give in to her mad fancies. But only one that he should. He must swallow his fear for her and believe in her, as she did him.

"We will be laying the tracks for the next several weeks. As soon as they are finished, we can search for your world."

She crossed to him in a heartbeat. "Thank you."

The joy on her face only accentuated the beauty that was there. His fingers caressed her cheek, and he felt and saw her body tense, then soften. She smiled.

He leaned closer to her and whispered, "I want to kiss you. Say *no,* and I will not do it."

Sedona stared up at him. It would be so easy, that no. But her heart was too full. He had shown limitless patience, and, when she knew that everything he believed told him not to, he had still agreed to help her, keeping his promise. She wouldn't find a man like him in a million years.

But then, she didn't have to find one. She had him, and he was here with her now. She was falling in love with him—she'd known that for days. And she also knew she would have to leave him. There simply was no other way. All of which meant, she had no time to waste. Here and now were all they had.

Sedona took Nando's hand in hers and turned it to place a kiss in his palm. "Yes," she whispered.

Two large, gentle hands caressed her cheeks, tilted her head upward. He looked down at her, and she saw an infinite sadness in his dark eyes. She touched his cheek, and he lowered his head, blotting out the sorrow, bringing indescribable pleasure with his kiss.

When he finally drew away from her, she whispered, "Please. Again."

He gulped in air and effortlessly picked her up, settling her on his lap. She could feel his arousal, hard, pulsing, and as he took her mouth again in another drugging kiss, she savored the sensation, reveling in the fact that she could do this to him. The kiss went on and on, until waves of pleasure made her gasp for breath.

He drew back a few inches and touched his forehead to hers. "I want you to stay."

"I know." She brushed her lips against his and kissed the corners of his mouth. "But it's too complicated with me here." She nestled her head onto his shoulder and sighed. "You can't relax. You can't be yourself."

"I could be anything with you."

She smiled, wishing that were true. "Then, why haven't you celebrated finding the water?" When he didn't answer, she wound her arms around his chest and hugged him. "You can't even invite your neighbors to the ranch for a fiesta to rejoice in your good fortune."

"I have little fear for myself, but when I think what could happen if others found out about your fantasies, I am afraid for you."

"You don't have to be afraid."

"Yes, I do. I could not bear to have you shut up for the rest of your life. I could not bear losing you that way. Alive, yet dead to me." He kissed her gently. "Please. Forget everything else and stay with me."

She lifted her head and looked deeply into his eyes. "As what? Your housekeeper?"

"That, yes."

"Your cook?"

He grinned. "You are a very good cook."

"Your mistress?"

The grin vanished, and he stared at her, inviting her with his heated gaze to accept that role.

"I can't do that, Nando. I know that you would give the most wonderful pleasure in the world to my body, but my soul would be in torture." She shook her head. "It's best, for both of us, that I go back home."

"I don't believe there is a back home."

"You don't have to. I *know* there is. Now, we just have to find a way to get there."

Though he did not believe her, Nando had his men lay track as Sedona mapped out. The first tunnel went deep into the mine, through the wall where she had appeared. It twisted and turned— just as she instructed—and the mound of rock outside got bigger and bigger. The men grumbled—digging and laying track, without trying to find silver, was hardly what they expected—but they carried out their duties. Soon there was a long, winding, deeply pitched tunnel, which his new ore trolleys easily navigated.

He and Sedona would not have been able to explain to the men why Sedona was taking rides in the ore trolley, so their "experiments," as she called them, had to be conducted at night. Every night, when his men had gone to bed, they went to the mine. He would light a few lanterns, loosen the rope from the pulley, help her into the ore trolley, then push her over the first rise.

He could hear her as the trolley picked up speed. He knew she wouldn't use the brake. Speed, she said, was the most important thing she needed in order to reach her world. But each night she failed, and he would haul her back up the long tunnel with the rope and pulley, dreading her sadness, not wanting to hear her say again, *"Maybe tomorrow night. . . ."*

On the ninth night, while Nando waited at the mine entrance for her usual shout to pull her back up, Sedona held to the sides of the ore trolley and peered, wide-eyed, into the pitch blackness of the deep shaft. As usual, the trolley picked up speed as it rounded the first turn. She applied a little pressure on the brake, and metal squealed and sparks flew into the darkness. She squealed and gripped the sides, hurtling through black space, walls whizzing by in a flash of sparks.

Déjà vu. It was happening. She knew it as surely as she knew her name. If she reached out, she would be able to touch the difference—the time warp, welcoming her back to her own world, her own time.

If she reached out . . .

If she reached out, she would be there. In 1998. Which meant, she would *not* be here, with Nando. She would be there, and he would be here. And everything they had shared, were sharing, would be . . . *por nada,* as Carlos would say. For nothing.

Suddenly, Sedona's heart leaped to overpower her head, and she gave the new, solid oak brake handle a steady pull, slowing the trolley. She didn't question why she no longer wanted the very thing that had been driving her every waking moment for weeks. Heck, if she could get back tonight, she could get back any night. So why did she have to leave right this minute?

As the wheels squealed in protest to the brakes' pressure, a shower of sparks lit the shimmering time-gate in front of her. It undulated, as if calling a greeting or offering an invitation. So when the trolley slowed to a stop, she did what she was quite sure any reasonable person would do—she reached into the void and for a moment felt the tug to go home. Quickly, she pulled her hand back, surprised it was still the hand she knew. Then, for a long while, she simply sat and stared at the magical portal.

* * *

Restless, Nando paced the mine entrance and squinted into the darkness of the tunnel down which Sedona had disappeared. The light from one of the dozen glowing lanterns reflected off something shiny. It was half buried in a pile of muck in a corner, but a few tugs were all he needed to unearth a battered miner's hat. It had some kind of round protuberance on the front. As he was shaking the dirt off, he heard Sedona call to him, and he tossed the hat to one side so he could turn the handle on the pulley.

When she came into view, he was stunned to see her laughing and crying at the same time. She swiped at her tears as she climbed out of the trolley. Looking up at him out of the corner of her eye, she took a deep breath, then shook her head.

"I think it's going to take a hundred years to make this thing deep enough and long enough," she said.

She smiled what seemed to him a very brave smile, but when he tried to take her into his arms, she shook him off and backed away.

"Did you hear me?" she asked. "I said it would take at least a hundred years."

"I heard you."

"Don't you care?"

It was hard to tamp down the joy he felt, but he was a de la Hoya, and as such, had been schooled to hide his deepest feelings. So he merely stared at Sedona and said, "I care, Sedona. Deeply."

He took three steps toward her. She took three steps backward. And promptly tripped over the miner's hat he'd found.

She pulled it out from under her, examined it, gasped, and tossed it aside. It bounced against the trolley, rolled several feet, and came to rest front up.

Nando stared at it, then at her, then at it. Although its glass was dirty, it gave off a yellow light. He picked the hat up and held it out to her. "Is this yours?"

She nodded. "Good batteries."

He ignored her indecipherable words and pointed to the light. "What is this?"

"A lamp." She took it out of his hands and got to her feet. "See this switch?"

"Switch?"

"This button on the side?"

He saw it. A black thing with ridges. "A switch—"

"If you push it in . . ." She pushed it, and the light went out—then pushed it again, and the light came back.

"Witchcraft!"

"Now who's talking crazy? It's not witchcraft. It's electricity, powered by batteries."

"I have heard of electricity. But they need roaring rivers to produce the energy to make it. This is not electricity."

"Yes, it is. I don't understand the science of it." She unscrewed the light and shook the hat, dislodging two small but very fat cylindrical objects. "But these are what make it work. They're called batteries. See this plus sign? It's the positive side and goes here. And this minus sign is the negative side and goes in the opposite direction. Once they're in the right place and the light is screwed back on . . ." She did it as she was talking, once again pushing in the switch to make the light come back.

Nando ran his fingers over the glass. "This is real."

"Yes."

"And you brought it with you when you . . . came here."

"Yes."

"So there *is* a back home."

"Yes."

"With miraculous things such as this."

"Oh, many, many things, things far more wonderful than this. Things you have never dreamed of."

Staring at the lamp, Nando murmured, "I understand now why you want to return." Then, turning away, he walked toward the horses, tied at the bottom of the slope.

A full moon lit the trail back to the hacienda. Nando was silent, giving no indication of what he was thinking or feeling. Sedona wanted to draw him out, soothe his fears, if he had any, or answer his questions—because he must have millions of them.

But she, too, kept silent. How could she speak when her mind whirled? In that mine shaft she had acted. Now, she needed to think about the consequences of her actions—not to mention her motives.

At first, she had been nearly desperate to return home, because she didn't think she belonged in Nando's world. But she had adjusted, and now she felt at home here. She looked forward to her daily chores, to the excitement of being part of Nando's grand experiment, the satisfaction of seeing the ranch blossoming into all it was destined to be.

But being part of what she knew as history was not, she realized, what had stopped her tonight from going home.

She stole a glance at Nando, and instantly, her heart gave a little leap, and some unruly butterflies took to fluttering in her mid-region. No one had ever—not ever—made her feel this way. What did she have in Denver? A Tex-Mex restaurant and a few friends. Here, she had Fernando de la Hoya. If she had to give up something—and it sure looked as if she did have to—she didn't know how it could ever be him.

She slowed down a little so she could feast on him without him noticing. He sat tall in the saddle, his broad shoulders bouncing only slightly with the gait of his stallion. His strong, muscular thighs gripped the horse's flanks, turning him with gentle pressure rather than a dig in the ribs.

Except for that first day, she thought, that was how he had treated her. With gentle pressure, kind words, praise, and respect. And even though he wanted her in his bed, he bowed to her decisive no.

Where would she ever find a man like that in Denver? Did she even want to look for one? Why would she, when she had the prototype right here? And in her dreams. And in her heart.

Love. Four simple letters. A simple word, more complicated than nuclear fission. Nuclear fission. That's what his presence created inside her. The nucleus of every cell exploded when he was near. She smiled. He didn't even have to be near. It was enough merely to think about him. Boom! Her core melted, her heart ached. She loved him. Wanted him. Needed him. So why was she trying to leave him?

Because she wouldn't be his mistress, only his wife. And that was impossible. Wasn't it?

Fernando de la Hoya—patrón of one of the largest ranches in the valley, feared by some, respected by all—was helpless to give the woman he loved what she needed. The full moon mocked him. It was as if the shadow of the man up there were laughing at him, at his impotence. *Si,* that was the word. Though his body throbbed with desire when he was near Sedona, it was a useless thing. She would not take what he could give. And he could not give what she would have taken. Batteries. Switches. Lamps. And other indescribable wonders.

Though she said it would be a hundred years before the tunnel was long enough, he was a more practical man, one used to giving orders, having them obeyed, and reaching his goals. He merely had to work harder, push his men farther, find the right angle, the right incline, the right way back. For her. If she would not take him, what other gift did he have to offer?

After they bedded down the horses, he stopped her on the front porch and laid his hand on her shoulder. "Do not worry, Sedona. We will find a way. Even if we must work all day and all night."

She shook her head. "No. It's enough, Nando. You've tried harder than anyone could have, even when you didn't believe it was true. Let's face it. I'm stuck here."

She smiled—bravely, Nando thought—but he saw the trembling of her lower lip, and his heart went out to her. "Is that so terrible?"

"No. It's not terrible. In fact, it's been mostly wonderful. But . . . well, it's lonely. I have no one and nothing here."

"You have me. Us. We all love you. If we had been successful tonight, you would have left a terrible emptiness in this place."

"Only this place?"

When she raised her gaze to meet his, he saw immediately
what it was she was asking him. Her eyes were filled to the brim
and over flowing with something he could only identify as love.

"Ah, God, Sedona . . ." He pulled her into his arms and nuz-
zled the top of her head. Her hair was soft and smelled of the
wildflower water she used to rinse it. Wildflowers. Wild. Like
her. Like the wildness in his heart when she was near, the wildness that longed to be tamed by her, with her, in her.

Smiling down at her, he said, "You are the wrong woman for
me, you know. And yet you are exactly the right woman. You are
loving and kind. And you are brave and fearless, even of me. You
are the woman I need at my side." He kissed her, deeply and with
a passion that quickly left them both breathless. "Always at my
side. As my wife," he whispered.

"What did you say?" she breathed raggedly, her lips against
his.

"I said, I need you to be my wife."

"Not your mistress?"

His lips curved against hers. "Only in our bedroom." Pulling
back a little, he framed her face with his hands and locked his
gaze with hers in the moonlight. "Sedona Skye, I know I am a
poor substitute for your batteries and switches, but will you
marry me?"

She threw back her head and laughed joyously. "Batteries
and switches? I would give up more than that for you."

"You are."

"No. I'm giving up nothing. I have everything I want, everything I need, and everything I love, right here. With you. In your
arms, and, very soon, I hope, in your bed."

"How soon?"

"How about now?"

Passion crackled in the air all around them as he picked her
up and strode quickly through the house and into his room. He
closed the door and locked it, then carried her to the bed, where
he laid her gently onto the colorful embroidered throw. His hands
combed through her hair and spread the strands around her head
like a lion's mane. "Ah, *mi cariña,* you are so beautiful."

Taking his hand in hers, Sedona pressed a kiss into his palm. "You make me feel beautiful."

"Soon you will feel all the beauty God gave to us."

He made the awkward part of undressing into a symphony. He shed his clothes quickly, but took an eternity with hers. Each small tug was followed by a caress, then a kiss, until her entire body was tingling with pure desire. He drove that desire ever higher when his hands, mouth, and tongue paid homage to her breasts. His suckling was gentle but insistent, and waves of pleasure ran from the laving of his tongue to her hot, melting center where his fingers teased and aroused. Loving him, certain that it was right to share that love with him, she opened herself to his touch and his passion.

When his body covered hers, he looked down into her eyes and smiled. *"Te amo,* Sedona. I love you. Always."

"And I love you." She gripped the sheets as he slid into her, fully prepared for the pain. She was totally unprepared, though, for his reaction.

"Ah, God . . ."

He tried to pull away, but her legs gripped him and urged him back inside her. "Please. It's all right."

"But—" He shook his head and muttered a curse. "I thought—"

She pulled his head down and kissed him. "Some day I'll tell you about the other things in my world, things not so wonderful as batteries and switches. Long ago I decided that my body would only be given to the man I loved. That's you."

Nando's heart soared, not because she was—had been—a virgin, but because he was the man to whom she had given her unconditional trust and love. "Ah, *mi cariña,* thank you."

"You're welcome," she murmured. "Now show me all the beauty God gave to us."

He did more than that. He opened the gates to heaven and brought her safely home.

* * *

"I, Fernando Octavio Renaldo de la Hoya, take thee, Sedona Alice Skye, to be my lawfully wedded wife . . ."

In the sight of God and all Nando's family and friends, Sedona gave her heart, her soul, and her dreams into the hands of the man she loved. And although Renaldo de la Hoya strutted and could not quite bring himself to say "well done" to his son, Francesca de la Hoya was warm and kind to her new daughter-in-law.

While Nando saw to the comfort of his guests, who were scattered over the flower-bedecked yard in front of the ranch house, Francesca drew Sedona over to stand beside her and her husband.

"My youngest son is his own man now," she said. "Your influence, I am certain."

Sedona smiled at the older woman. "He was always his own man, Doña Francesca."

"But," Renaldo said, "there is yet no shine of silver from this so-called mine of his."

Inside, Sedona's temper snapped, crackled, and popped, but she bit back a quick retort, raised her hand to Dante and Carlos, and smiled serenely. "Don't worry, Don Renaldo, it won't be long."

Before she had finished speaking, a loud rumbling silenced the fifty guests.

Nando made his way to Carlos and Dante as they rolled an ore trolley into the center of the wedding feast. Nando took one look at the contents of the trolley and spun to find his wife. She beamed at him as she walked to stand by his side.

"You have given me so much," she said. "A new life, a new world, a perfect love. This is all I could give you. And I must share the credit for this gift with your men, who worked tirelessly for hours each day and night."

"In secret," Dante said. "She insisted." He reached inside and extracted a small piece of ore which he raised for all to see. "The first silver from the mine." He bowed and held it out to Nando. "From all of us, Don Fernando. But most of all from your wife."

Nando took the ore and touched the unmistakable tracing of silver that winked in the sunlight. He looked at Sedona and did not try to hide the gratitude, pride, and love he felt. "You did this for me."

She shook her head. "I'm more selfish than that. I did it for both of us."

"Ah, Sedona, how much I love you."

To the cheers of their guests, he kissed her, trying to express that love in another way. When he came up for air, he smiled. "I'd like to present this to someone . . ."

She nodded, and he scooped up two chunks of the silver-streaked ore.

She followed as he slowly crossed the yard, coming to a halt in front of his parents. Renaldo put out his cupped hands, and Nando smiled at him. "Our heritage gave me the will to succeed. That, you taught me. Perhaps not the way you think you did; but I learned it nonetheless." He dropped the first chunk into Renaldo's hands. "To our heritage." Then he turned to his mother and placed the other piece of silver in her hand. "For your love and understanding."

Later, while they were saying farewell to their neighbors, Nando put his arm around his wife and drew her close to his heart. "My father thinks we are mismatched."

Sedona giggled. "For once, he's right. And star-crossed. And so headstrong that we're certain to clash at every turn."

"What an interesting life we are going to have, Sedona."

"It will be like no other, Nando. A journey into the future. There are so many wonderful things waiting for us. I'll tell you about them, and they'll come true."

"But there will be many things you cannot tell me about, which will also come true."

"Like what?"

"How it feels to have our child growing inside you."

"Oh, Nando . . ."

"Watching our family increase and our lives prosper. Growing old together, always loving each other."

"Promise?"

Nando swept his hand in the air. "Look around, wife. This

land is filled with promises and dreams. Only tell me what you dream and I will work to make it come true."

"You already have, my love. You already have."

AVALON

by

Mary Jo Putney

Author's Note

I loved the beauty and romanticism of the movie *First Knight*. In particular, Sean Connery's marvelous portrayal of King Arthur inspired me to create a new twist to the legend, giving Arthur the happy ending that he deserves.

Firelights shimmered along the lethally sharp blade as Arthur Pendragon, High King of Britain, raised Excalibur in one hand. He studied the sword, musing. When the Lady of the Lake had given him the weapon, it had been a promise of glory and a pledge of victory. But that had been many years ago, when he had been young, passionately in love, and equal to anything. His faith that he would have the courage and wisdom to lead Britain to victory had been absolute.

Life had been so much simpler then. He hadn't realized that the barbarians would attack in endless waves, drowning yesterday's victory in today's blood. The bards sang endlessly of his courage and leadership, calling him an immortal king whose deeds would never be forgotten, but songs would not save his people from Saxon blades.

"A cup of wine, sire?" It was young Sir Galeron, the king's personal aide, who made the offer. Arthur accepted the cup and drank a little, more to please Galeron than because he wanted it. The boy had an earnest, honest nature that reminded Arthur of the young Lancelot.

In fact, the Saxon maidservant who had died giving birth to Galeron had claimed that Lancelot was the father when she commended her babe to the king's care. Arthur had made inquiries and discovered that the girl had been very free with her favors. It was quite possible that one of the knights of the Round Table had fathered her child, but Arthur privately considered Lancelot an unlikely prospect. Lancelot was too self-contained, too disciplined, for casual affairs with maidservants. Nor was there an obvious resemblance to Lancelot as the boy grew. If anything, Galeron resembled Arthur, who had certainly not bedded the unfortunate wench.

Yet even though the boy's father was a mystery, Arthur had never regretted fostering him. Galeron was a good lad, loyal and wise beyond his years, and already a fine knight. He would be a great leader of men, if he survived long enough.

Thinking of the battle that would be fought on the morrow, Arthur rose from his seat by the camp fire and sheathed his sword again. His bones protested the motion, because he was old, old. Oh, a warrior still; he doubted that any man in the enemy camp on the far side of the valley could defeat him in single combat. But his forces were vastly outnumbered and his spirit frayed beyond repair by the knowledge that his own son, Mordred, had invited King Hengist's Saxon horde to Britain.

How could Mordred not see that he'd invited the wolf into the fold? Because of his bitterness. For that, Arthur must bear much of the blame, though his crime against his son had been an unwitting one.

Arthur had been a lusty youth when Morgause had come to him after his first battle. She'd not needed her sorceress' wiles to entice him into her bed. He'd been afire with exhilaration at his great victory, eager to celebrate with his first taste of a woman's intoxicating flesh. She'd given him a full measure of passion, her eyes glittering with secret knowledge. Then, in the cool light of dawn, she revealed that he was her own half brother, and that in the heated madness of the night they had conceived Arthur's doom.

If he had been king long enough to have developed the ruthlessness of command, perhaps he would have slain her then and saved Britain this fatal day. But probably not. He'd been unable to harm a woman, even a malicious enchantress like Morgause.

Certainly he'd had no wish to harm Guinevere, his lovely child bride. Aware of the affair between her and Lancelot, he had remained silent, knowing that he was not the husband she would have chosen for herself. It was Lancelot of the Lake, young and strong and idealistic, who had won Guinevere's heart.

Caring for them both, Arthur had looked the other way, tacitly allowing the pair to find what happiness they could. But when the affair became public he'd been forced to act, for a king could not allow his queen's adultery to go unpunished. With tears in her eyes, she had admitted her guilt and begged forgiveness for her betrayal.

But she had refused to forswear her love for Lancelot, so Arthur had had no choice but to condemn her to the stake. Privately he had been glad when Lancelot had rescued her. He could not have borne the sound of Guinevere's death cries if the flames had consumed her.

His marriage to Guinevere had been a political one, and he'd never been able to give her the devotion she craved. He had told her once, when she wept on his shoulder, that his heart belonged to Britain. It had been a partial truth, and easier, he thought, than telling her that his love had been given to another long before Guinevere had been born.

The image of the woman who possessed his heart appeared to his mind's eye. Though more than mortal, the Lady of the Lake had been pure female, and the most enchanting creature he had ever known. He'd loved her then, and he loved her still, though he had not seen her in many years.

Too restless to sleep, he began to walk among the camp fires that surrounded his own tent, Galeron quietly following behind. Knights and men at arms and pages ate and drank and laughed a little too loudly to show that they did not fear the battle that would come on the morrow. Arthur stopped here and there, exchanging words at every camp fire. It mattered not what he said, only that he showed himself calm and unafraid.

At the back of his mind was the knowledge that the Lake of Avalon, home to the Lady, was only a few miles away. When he reached the edge of the camp, he paused to look through the night, imagining that he could see the glint of moonlight on the water. Avalon, the magical heart of Britain.

He started to turn away, then hesitated. If this was to be the last night of his life, he must make his farewells. "Galeron, saddle my horse."

His attendant bowed, then went to obey. A few minutes later,

Galeron returned with two horses. Arthur swung into his mount's saddle. "I will go alone."

Galeron frowned. "Sire, you should not. What if you meet a patrol of Saxons?"

Arthur arched his heavy brows. "I'm a canny old lion, boy," he said dryly. "It will take more than wandering Saxons to bring me down. Leave me."

Galeron accepted the order with visible reluctance. Arthur briefly touched the young man on the shoulder, then rode across the moon-touched plains to the lake.

Alone, he was free to indulge his memories. He had been no more than a lad when first he came to Avalon. He had already drawn the sword from the stone and won his first battle against the Saxons. Many of the great lords had acclaimed him as the rightful king. But there were others less willing to accept a boy of mysterious parentage, even one backed by the power of Merlin's magic.

It was Merlin, Arthur's teacher, friend, and trusted advisor, who had said, "To be a king for all Britons, you must win the blessing of all the powers of the land, Arthur. Not just the Christian Church, but those who follow the old ways."

Arthur had frowned. "How can I win the support of the ancient ones?"

"Go to the lake that lies beside the plains of Camlann."

Arthur drew in his breath. "The lake that is said to contain the magical island of Avalon?"

"There you can find what you seek," Merlin replied. "But first you will be tested. There will be danger and mystery. To overcome that, you must listen to your heart."

Arthur nodded, not fully understanding. He'd learned early that the meaning of Merlin's advice could usually be known only after the event had passed.

He sought Avalon alone, riding out at dawn from the hill fort that later became Camelot. The quest made him uneasy in a way that he had not felt when confronting death in battle. The old gods still had power, it was said. A dark, mysterious power that the Church said came of the devil. . . .

The ride was long, and it was dusk when he reached his destination. Vast and still as a mirror, the lake was a place of otherworldly beauty. Drifting in the center was a mist that glowed with pearlescent splendor as it caught the rays of the setting sun. He found it curiously difficult to determine the size and shape of the mist, or of the lake itself.

Now that he'd arrived, he hadn't the faintest idea how to go about achieving his goal. Merlin was always cursedly vague about such things.

When in doubt, start with what must be done. Arthur dismounted and rubbed down his horse, tethering the beast so it could graze. By the time he finished, it was almost full dark. He looked to the lake and saw that the uncanny mist had expanded until it almost touched the shore. It shone soft and ethereal in the pale moonlight.

He took a deep breath, then silently raised his arms, holding his empty palms toward the lake as a sign that he came in peace. In his mind he called, *"I am Arthur of Britain. Will you grant me an audience?"*

Slowly a tendril uncurled from the main mist and arched toward the shore until it disappeared in the cattails a dozen feet from where he stood. The shape was that of a bridge. He was being invited to Avalon.

Or perhaps he was mad. Reminding himself that if he was wrong the worst that would happen was a ducking, he stepped forward and set his right foot on the arch of mist. It supported his weight in a wordless proof that he was about to leave the world he knew for a place of uncertain magic.

Heart hammering, he walked into the mist. The path was resilient beneath his feet, not unlike soft turf. The normal sounds of frogs and wind-rustling cattails were swallowed up, and he could see nothing but gray fog.

With neither sight nor sound to guide him, he tested each step warily. The blade-straight path was less than a yard wide. A misstep would send him plunging into the mist, and he knew with cold certainty that what lay below was nothing so benign as water.

He walked for what seemed like a long time, surely long

enough to have crossed the lake and reached the other side. Yet the path continued. The edge of his caution wore away, replaced by boredom.

Then an unholy shriek pierced the night, and a fiery object hurtled out of the fog directly at him. Instinctively he dropped to one knee to avoid the assault, at the same time whipping out his sword. He almost slashed out blindly at his attacker. Barely in time he remembered that Merlin had once warned him not to strike at the unknown, for he might heedlessly slay a friend.

The fiery object scorched just over his head, then snapped around swift as a snake. As the creature stopped a dozen feet away, hovering with slow beats of gossamer wings, Arthur saw to his amazement that it was a dragon smaller than a man. Sleek and covered with shimmering gold scales, the creature was as beautiful as it was alien. No longer breathing flame, it regarded Arthur with enigmatic eyes of emerald green.

The dragon was the emblem of the house of Pendragon, and to injure or kill one would surely invite disaster. Intensely relieved that he had restrained himself from striking, Arthur got to his feet and sheathed his sword. Then, as if the creature were a strange horse or dog, he reached out slowly, praying that it wouldn't suddenly decide to incinerate his sword hand.

The dragon drifted forward through the mist until it was within touching distance. Arthur flinched when the creature opened its mouth, but what emerged was a slender red tongue, not flames. Delicately it lapped at Arthur's hand and wrist, the tongue warm and startlingly sensual.

Gently, he caressed the dragon's narrow head, and found that the golden scales had the cool, silky feel of polished agate. The dragon shivered with pleasure at his touch. Arthur was chilled to think how close he had come to killing the creature.

Amusement touched his mind. Did the emotion come from the dragon? Arthur murmured, "Are you saying you would not be so easily killed by a mere mortal?"

The emotion changed from humor to satisfaction. Then the dragon rolled like a diving otter and disappeared into the mist. If dragons were made like mortal creatures, this one was female.

He had never thought of dragons in terms of gender. Were there dragon babies? Dragon sweethearts? Now that he thought about it, the golden dragon had showed a feminine grace and delicacy.

Bemused, he resumed his passage. After a weary, unmeasurable time, he began to feel vibrations in his feet. Something large and heavy was coming toward him with the steady beat of a war-horse.

Even so, it was a shock when a coal black destrier suddenly loomed out of the mist directly in front of him. The path was barely wide enough for the horse.

The rider pulled his mount to a halt. A massive knight armored in black, he wore a helmet that totally covered his head except for a narrow slit over his eyes. Ominously silent, he swung from his mount and edged around his horse, stepping carefully so that he would not fall from the path. Then, radiating malevolence, he drew his sword.

Arthur drew a deep breath. Merlin had said he would be tested. But surely no knight would attack an unarmored man? Raising his voice to counter the sound-killing mist, he said, "I am Arthur of Britain. What are you called, Sir Knight?"

The black knight responded by lunging forward, his great sword stabbing. Barely in time, Arthur whipped out his blade and warded off the attack. Then he struck a swift counterblow. His sword skidded harmlessly from the black chain mail. What should have been clamorous was eerily quiet as the mist swallowed the normal sounds of clashing weapons.

The knight attacked again. Weighed down by his armor, his movements were slow but lethally powerful. Arthur blocked the blow and retreated.

He had forgotten the narrowness of the path. One heel landed on air, and he lost his balance, almost falling into the mist. For a moment, panic nearly overwhelmed him. He had fought knights such as this one, and fought well, but always he had been equally armed. This unasked-for combat wasn't fair!

In his head, he heard Merlin say dryly, "Do not expect life to be fair. Accept what is, and do what must be done."

Icy calm settled over Arthur as he grimly fought back with

his wits as well as his sword, using his advantages of lightness and speed to dart in, strike a blow, and retreat. Yet though he fought better and struck harder, he was unable to damage his opponent. In contrast, even glancing blows from the black knight were dangerous to Arthur. One slash laid open his ribs and thigh, another cut deeply into his sword arm. If he did not end this fight quickly, he was doomed.

He charged forward and struck a mighty blow to the black knight's helmet. God willing, he'd knock his opponent's head to one side and open up an armor joint at the throat for a killing blow. But though the knight swayed, he recovered quickly and countered hard, his heavy sword crashing into Arthur's with brutal force.

Arthur's blade splintered, leaving him with the hilt and a ragged stub of blade. He cried out, horror-struck at losing the sword that had proved his kingship. Not only was it a dreadful omen, but now he was at the mercy of a murderous, fully armed knight.

Do what must be done. If he couldn't fight as a knight, he must try another way. But what?

The bridge, narrow and treacherous. As soon as the thought struck, Arthur hurled himself low and hard against the black knight's legs, using the weight of his body to knock his enemy off balance. With a strange, rusty squeal, the knight slowly toppled from the bridge into the mist. There was no splash. He was simply—gone. At the same instant, his horse vanished.

Half over the edge himself, Arthur barely managed to drag his body back onto the path. For long minutes he lay shaking, dragging air into his lungs with great hoarse gasps. Merlin had spoken truly that he would be tested!

When he had recovered a little, he got painfully to his feet and examined the shattered remains of his weapon. The blade was broken beyond any hope of mending. His mouth tightened as he remembered the wonder and elation of pulling the gleaming sword from the stone, then brandishing it above his head as the surrounding lords and knights acclaimed him as the true king.

On impulse, he drew back his arm, then hurled the ruined

hilt into the mist. The sword had been born in magic, and it was fitting to return it to a place of magic.

Now he was unarmed save for the dagger on his belt. In the heat of battle, he'd scarcely been aware of his injuries, but now pain stabbed through his arm and ribs and thigh, and blood saturated his garments. Clumsily he tore strips of fabric from his cloak and bound the wounds as best he could. He must turn back and seek aid, or risk bleeding to death. He was in no fit shape to face another opponent.

No. The instinctive response was followed by insight. He'd thought he had proved his right to the throne by leading his small army against a vastly larger Saxon host and winning. After that, all men had acknowledged his courage and generalship. But now he saw how much more there was to being high king than courage.

In a way, fighting the Saxons had not been difficult. Oh, he'd been afraid beforehand, mostly that he would disgrace himself and fail his people, but once the battle fever rose he'd felt no fear or fatigue or pain. Even the specter of death held no power over him. He'd fought like a berserker, and afterward learned that victory was a draft headier than the strongest wine.

Far harder was the task before him now—to continue into the unknown when he was injured and drained and hope was dim. But a true king should be willing to face hell itself for the good of his people. If Arthur turned back from Avalon, he was not fit to rule. And if the tests ahead were beyond his strength— well, he would die as a king should.

He resumed his trek, limping heavily on his injured leg. As the path unfurled endlessly beneath his feet, he became increasingly light-headed from loss of blood.

Then he saw a glow ahead. The dragon again? He'd welcome her company.

The unmistakable outlines of land slowly took shape in the mist. Invigorated by the sight, he began to move faster.

Then he discovered the source of the glow and stopped dead. A wall of fire lay across the path, blocking the way to Avalon.

To reach the enchanted island, he must go through the flames. The fierce, consuming flames. . . .

He had not come so far to turn back now. After filling his lungs with air, he raced forward with all his remaining speed and strength. Head down and arms crossed over his face, he plunged into the inferno.

The heat was annihilating, razing every fiber of body and mind and casting a blinding light on all his flaws. He was weak, unworthy. What arrogance had made him think himself fit to rule? His failings would bring his people to despair and death. For the sake of Britain, he should stop running and surrender to the fire. . . .

He would never surrender. Blindly he ran on, until he abruptly emerged from the flames into cool, apple-scented air. Chest heaving, he stumbled to a halt on grassy turf, not even surprised to see no marks of burning on his body or clothing. Only his mind and spirit had been seared, tempered like a blade in another test of his worthiness.

Behind him the waters of the lake lapped gently, while before him was a garden drenched in sunlight. Had he been in the mist all night and this was a new day, or was Avalon not of the world he knew? He suspected the latter, but was too tired to ponder it.

A small brook ran beside a flowering apple tree to his right. The sight made him aware of his desperate thirst. He lurched toward the water, but his legs gave out and he collapsed to the soft turf.

As he fell into darkness, he had a mad, hazy vision that a gilded dragon was spiraling down from the azure sky.

Arthur awoke slowly, the fragrance of apple blossoms sweet in his nostrils. He felt kitten weak and his wounds still throbbed, but the pain was a mere shadow of what it had been. He opened his eyes. Above his head, branches of flowering apple blossoms wove a lacy pattern across the sky.

He shifted his gaze. A coarse wool blanket covered his naked body, and he felt a straw pallet beneath him. But how?

A voice like singing bells said, "You must be thirsty."

Startled, he turned his head. The most beautiful woman in the world was sitting next to him, simply garbed in a gown the light, clear green of young apples. Or perhaps he should call her a girl, for she was no older than he. Her features were delicately perfect, yet there was strength in her firm chin and humor in the curve of her generous mouth. A thick braid of lustrous gold hair fell over her shoulder to her waist. The mere sight of her made him feel stronger and more alive. He wanted to reach out. To touch, to taste. . . .

Ignoring his fascinated gaze, she offered him a goblet filled with water. "Drink."

Obediently, he swallowed when she held the wooden vessel to his lips. The water was cool and delicious. Only when he'd emptied the goblet did he realize that he might have taken a fatal misstep. It was said that to eat or drink in the land of Faerie would doom a mortal to stay forever. Not that he really believed in Faerie, but still. . . .

His voice a hoarse croak, he asked, "Where am I?"

"In Avalon." She grinned, dimples appearing in her smooth cheeks. "And no, you haven't just lost your soul to Faerie by drinking that water."

He was beyond being surprised that apparently she could read his mind. Her deep, mesmerizing green eyes seemed capable of seeing anything. He frowned, thinking there was something hauntingly familiar about those eyes. "Who are you?"

She scooped another cup of water from the brook. "The Lady of the Lake."

He became very still. "I have heard you called many things. Sorceress, witch, the Queen of Faerie. Some say you are good; others damn you as wicked, an eater of souls."

She sighed. "I cannot control what others call me. I do not think of myself as wicked, but then, who does? I'm sure that even Lucifer sees himself as a hero."

Curious, he asked, "How do you see yourself, my lady?"

She looked startled, then pleased. "Do you know, I've never been asked that. I suppose I see myself as many things. As a gardener." She extended her hand to a small bush with tight pink buds. The buds instantly began unfurling into lavish bloom. She bent forward to inhale the fragrance, becoming utterly absorbed in that simple act.

Then she turned her attention to him again. "I am also a healer, fortunately for you. Your wounds were grave, and you had lost much blood." She leaned forward and efficiently examined the light, clean dressing on his injured arm. A shock like the crackle of wool on a cold day went through him at her touch.

She gave a nod of satisfaction. "Very good. In Avalon, healing is much swifter than in the outside world."

Then she drew down the blanket and checked the bandage that ran around his ribs. He shivered at the intimacy. Though she might think of him as a patient, in his eyes she was the most desirable of women. He prayed to the Blessed Mother that she would not examine the wound on his thigh, for then he would surely humiliate himself.

She tucked the end of the torso bandage more securely, then hesitated, her expression changing from a physician's detachment to more personal awareness. Her fingers skimmed delicately over his chest, spanning the breadth of his shoulders. With the same absorption she'd shown when sniffing the flower, she murmured, "You have a warrior's body. Tall. Powerfully muscled."

Her hand moved lower, fingertips trailing through the dark hair that arrowed downward. "But also lithe and swift. The body of a hero."

Heat flared through him, not the blaze of pain but the scarlet burn of desire. He sucked in his breath, hoping she would think his response was from pain.

As she touched the edge of his blanket, he caught her wrist. "Best not, Lady," he said huskily. "For truly you are an enchantress."

She snatched her hand back, color rising in her cheeks. "I'm sorry," she stammered, looking very young.

To cover up the awkward moment, he said, "You know who I am, I think."

Her eyes darkened. "Oh, yes, Arthur of Britain. I know well who you are. Your coming has been long foretold."

Her appearance did not change, but he became aware of how much more she was than she seemed. Yet never evil, he believed that in his bones. "Why was I sent here?" he asked quietly. "Merlin said I must prove myself to the followers of the old ways, yet now that I am in Avalon, I think the answer is more complex."

"You are perceptive." Her brows drew together reflectively. "You come of mixed blood, born of a Roman father and a Celtic mother. The knight who fostered you taught you the Roman virtues—courage, discipline, duty, reason. Now the time has come to embrace the virtues of your Celtic heritage. Faith. Magic. Spirit. If you can master those, you will become a king such as Britain will never forget."

Her words made sense in a way he would not have understood when he'd begun this quest. "The mere existence of Avalon does much to teach me about magic. And surely the obstacles I encountered while crossing the water were magical."

"They were tests of temperance, pragmatism, persistence. To be a king requires much more than warrior courage." Her expression became grave. "Your life will not be an easy one, Artos," she said, using the Celtic form of his name. "You will need the best of Celt and Roman to accomplish your mission."

He arched his brows. "What is my mission?"

She hesitated, searching for words. "Your mission is the sum of your life. Only at the end can you truly understand if you have succeeded or failed."

He was unsurprised by her reply. Being obscure seemed to be a requirement for sorcerers. Realizing how fatigued he was, he covered a yawn. "Sorry. I've never fallen asleep while talking to a beautiful lady, but I'm about to do so now."

"No need to apologize. Healing takes energy. After another sleep you will be well again." She made a gesture with her hand, and an exquisitely carved harp appeared beside her. She ran her fingers lovingly along the strings, creating a golden shower of notes. "Rest, Arthur of Britain. Rest and be well."

She began to play a gentle lullaby, the delicate notes ringing with otherworldly loveliness. He relaxed and closed his eyes. What more could a man ask than to fall asleep to the entrancing music of the most beautiful girl in any world?

Arthur woke again at dawn feeling entirely well. The air was filled with bird song and rich scents and serenity. He savored it all, feeling wholly at peace for the first time in his life. Silently he offered a prayer of thanks. In the future, when life sent pain and sorrow, he would always be able to return to this garden in his mind.

Gradually he realized that a warm weight was resting against his right side. He turned his head and discovered the Lady curled up against him, fully dressed and lying on top of the blanket. Apple blossoms had fallen in the night, scattering scented petals over her slim form. She looked very young and utterly enchanting.

Desire surged through him with stunning force. He wanted to kiss the soft curve of her throat, lick the hidden valley between her breasts, bury himself in entrancing female mysteries. His body trembled with wanting.

But she was a sorceress and a healer who had saved his life. Though he was called king, he was a mere mortal of only eighteen summers. The thought of making an advance was presumptuous beyond bearing. Yet he could think of nothing else.

Tartly he reminded himself that if she became angered by his boldness, she might turn him into a toad. He slid away, taking care not to disturb her.

But it was impossible to leave without at least one touch. He brushed his lips against her temple in a feather kiss. Her eyes opened, and she regarded him with a clarity that surely must have seen right through to his imperfect soul.

"I'm sorry," he said awkwardly. "I didn't mean to wake you."

"You asked what I am," she whispered, her stark gaze holding his. "I am a woman." She raised her hand and cupped his cheek. "And lonely. So very lonely."

He caught his breath, scarcely daring to hope, but the message in her eyes was unmistakable. "I, too, am lonely," he said unevenly. "If it is your will, it would be my honor and my delight to join with you to banish loneliness, if only for an hour."

With a vulnerability that touched his heart, she said, "The honor and delight are equal, Artos, just as you and I are equal, though our gifts are different." Her cool fingers curved around his nape. "Let us not waste a moment of the little time we have."

The desire he had tried to suppress flared into hot, demanding life. He bent and kissed her richly welcoming mouth. She was more luscious than a ripe peach, more intoxicating than wine. He wanted to devour her, make her a part of himself, yet he held his hunger tightly in check so that he would not spend himself in a blaze of passion that was too soon over.

He bared her exquisite body, then explored every silken inch of her, trying with passionate intensity to return the pleasure he was discovering in her arms. Jesu, but she was magnificent, a blend of sweetness and fire and magic that seared his very soul.

After driving each other to fever pitch, they came together in the ultimate intimacy. In union he found not only bewitching pleasure, but more, so much more, for their joining was of the spirit as well as the body. He *knew* her, experienced the shape of her soul, her compassion and wisdom, her awesome power and her sorrowful loneliness.

He should have been frightened by the awareness that he was as open to her as she was to him, but he wasn't. For the first and, he sensed, the last time in his life, he had found someone who could accept everything he was. Not just Arthur, the High King of Britain, but Arthur the boy who had wept at night for the mother and father he had never known. Arthur the young man who had been handed the crushing weight of a kingdom, and was torn by doubts he dared not reveal. Arthur the lover, who longed for a true mate but knew that kings did not marry for love. And Artos, who in the arms of the Lady of the Lake discovered the Celtic magic of his mother's blood.

In the final rapture, their souls met and briefly twined as one. Then, as ecstasy ebbed and he was alone once more in the solitary cell of his skull, he held her in his arms, stinging tears in his eyes because he had discovered love.

They dozed, still twined together. He awoke feeling the beat of her heart where her breasts pressed against his chest. Guessing that she was also awake, he murmured, "Do you have a name, my Lady of the Lake?"

She tilted her head back to gaze at him. "Some call me Morgaine, and others name me Morgan Le Fay, but I prefer Morgana."

He stroked back her shining hair. "Did you bespell me, Morgana? For that was more than mortal pleasure."

She shook her head. "I would not cheapen our joining with magic, my lord. Whatever you felt was real."

He had guessed as much, but was glad for her confirmation. "I love you, Morgana." He kissed her temple. "I . . . I feel that you are the other half of my soul."

He feared she might laugh at his declaring love when they had known each other so briefly. Instead, she said softly, "As you are the other half of mine. I foresaw that Arthur of Britain would come to Avalon, and that he would be a great hero. But I could not guess what you would mean to me."

She kissed him with desperate tenderness, eyes shining with unshed tears. "I love you, Artos. Goddess! I wish that you could stay with me, but that cannot be. You must return to your people."

Her words were like a splash of ice water. Unable to bear the thought of losing her, he said urgently, "Then come with me, Morgana. I shall make you my queen. We will rule Britain together."

She shook her head, the tears bright in her eyes. "That is impossible. My work and my life bind me to Avalon, as yours bind you to the outer world."

He buried his face in her tumbled golden hair, inhaling the ravishing scent of apple blossoms and woman. "May I visit? I would gladly brave dragons and black knights and fire to be with you."

She shook her head again. "The heart and soul of a king must be with his people, not forever turning to his mistress.

You are not free to indulge in a consuming love, and there can be nothing less between us, Artos."

He knew she was right, and the knowledge was like a stone on his heart. Aching, he released her and got to his feet. "I don't know whether to give thanks, or to curse that I have found you only to lose you so soon."

"Give thanks, beloved." She also rose, her slim body heart-breakingly beautiful in the morning light. "I, who have been alone so long, swear to you that it is better to have loved briefly than not at all."

Someday he would agree with her. But now the anticipation of loss was too raw, too painful. He turned to the pile of his garments neatly folded by the pallet. Like his body, they had been perfectly mended and showed no mark of the black knight's sword.

After he dressed and had girded his belt around him, he turned back to her. She had donned the apple green gown again, but instead of braiding her hair she'd left it loose around her shoulders.

Before he could say farewell, she raised one hand to forestall him. "You must be gone by sunset, but we have a little time yet, for the hours run differently here than in your land. Dine with me. Then I shall show you something of Avalon."

He broke off a sprig of apple blossom and tucked it behind her ear. "I will go with you gladly anywhere you choose to lead, Morgana."

First she took him to a bower where a feast of fresh cheese and warm bread, fine wine, and clover honey, awaited. As they ate, he committed every image to memory. The tilt of her head when she thought. The slow, teasing caress of her hand when she handed him a goblet or slid a sweet, luscious grape between his lips. Her sparkling delight when he teased her in return.

After their meal, she took him on a tour of the orchards and fields of Avalon. The island seemed far larger than could fit in the middle of the lake, but he supposed that was part of its magic. She explained that others lived on Avalon, but at her request they were allowing Morgana and her guest privacy.

As they entered a small wood, Morgana said, "I have three gifts for you. One is the gift of self-healing. Though my magic cannot preserve you from mortal injury, your lesser wounds will always heal swift and clean."

"I thank you," he said sincerely. "But you have already given me so much. How can I accept more when I have so little to offer in return?"

She shook her head with a little smile. "You have given me more than you know, Artos. I am in your debt."

He drew her into a kiss, his hand sliding down her shapely back. She was so small, the top of her head barely reaching his chin.

Before the kiss could intensify, she slipped from his embrace. Then she pushed aside a branch to reveal a small glade where a brook widened into a shallow pool before trickling away again. Gesturing to the pool, she said, "The next gift is there."

He knelt by the water, then caught his breath. Beneath the still surface lay a sword of shimmering splendor. Reverently he reached into the pool and grasped the hilt. It came to his hand as swift and true as Morgana herself.

He stood and cut the air with the superbly crafted blade, bright droplets of water spraying as he tested the balance. The weapon felt as if it had been forged for his hand alone. Exultant power surged through him. The sword from the stone had been a fine weapon, but this one was nothing short of miraculous.

"The sword is called Excalibur, and none but you may wield it," Morgana said in a voice that rang with prophecy. "I swear that it will never fail you in battle."

He turned to her, eyes shining. "Words cannot do justice to my thanks. Not only is this the sword of a king, but whenever I touch it, I shall think of you, Morgana."

He sheathed the blade in his empty scabbard, which—magically?—was a perfect fit. Then he reached out to caress her cheek, his heart overflowing with love. "Morgana." Gently, he stroked his thumb over her soft lips, wondering if there would be time to make love once more before sunset. "Beloved."

Her lips separated, and her tongue came out, catlike, to lick his thumb. The touch crystallized the vague sense of familiarity that he felt whenever he looked into her green eyes. "Jesu!" he breathed. "You were the dragon I met on the lake, weren't you? The green of your eyes, the gold of your hair—they are the colors of the dragon."

"I wondered if you would recognize that. You should, for you are Artos Pendragon, and you also bear the dragon's blood." She held out her hand, something fierce and untamed deep in her eyes. "Come fly with me."

"I can't fly," he protested, though he took her hand for the simple pleasure of touching her.

She pulled him to her, but instead of giving a kiss, she bit him on the neck hard enough to draw blood. A shock like lightning blazed through him, melting bone and sinew into new forms that were shocking, yet profoundly right.

Morgana jerked away, transforming in the space of a heartbeat into the golden dragon. As she hurled herself into the air on gilded wings, Arthur launched himself after her. The tempest that raged through his veins was so turbulent that he did not question his own metamorphosis. He knew only that the golden dragon was his love and his mate, and he must claim her as his own.

As his great wings bore him upward, Morgana gamboled across the sky with mad abandon, her scales shining red-gold in the long rays of the descending sun. He followed with single-minded fervor. He was the crimson dragon, born of blood and fire. In the manner of all wild creatures, he must master her, for she would never yield to a weakling.

Higher and higher they spiraled, the golden dragon flaunting her speed and elusive grace as he studied her like prey. When he was ready, he soared above her, then suddenly swooped like a falcon, slashing through the sky and seizing her lithe form in his talons. She struggled frantically until he bit her on the back of the neck. Her sleek scales were diamond smooth against his long, rough tongue.

As she stilled in submission to his greater strength, he mounted her in an act of flagrant male possession. She tossed her head back with a dragon shriek of feral joy. Shattering passion raged through him. She was free and wild and his, his, *his*.

They plummeted toward the earth like stones, their supple bodies writhing together in reckless ecstasy. As they neared the stony ground, she convulsed with a rapture that triggered his own release. He trumpeted his triumph to the skies as harrowing joy consumed him.

He returned to his senses just before they smashed into the earth. Instinctively he spread his wings to break their fall, pulling her protectively against him and twisting so that his larger body would absorb the worst of the impact.

Then they were safe on the ground, tumbling together in human form through a bed of clover. Once more she was a slender girl, her breathing as harsh as his own.

Dazed and panting, he cradled her in his arms, beyond speech. Their first lovemaking had been passionate but also laced with tenderness. This astonishing union had been as primal as earth, wind, and fire. He believed in magic now, aye, believed in it soul and sinew. This brief time on Avalon had changed him forever, and he would be a better king for what he had learned.

When her breathing steadied, she pushed herself up on one elbow and gave him a crooked smile. "You make a fine fierce dragon, Artos."

"And you, queen of my heart, make a fine fierce teacher." His palm shaped her damp face as he tried to memorize the form and texture of her features.

She glanced at the sun, which was low in the sky. The light died from her eyes. "It's time, Artos."

They rose and walked hand in hand to the pebble-strewn beach, arriving just as the lower edge of the sun touched the horizon. As they approached the water, a tendril of mist began to unfurl lazily from nothingness to the shore.

Arthur stopped and turned to her. "The third gift is your love, isn't it? And that is the greatest gift of all." He bent and kissed her with all the yearning of his soul. "I will love you forever, Morgana."

She blinked back tears. "And I you, Artos."

He forced himself to break away and walk to the misty bridge. But as he set one foot on the yielding surface, he made the mistake of looking back. She was standing very still, her golden hair ablaze in the setting sun and silent tears running down her face.

He spun about and raced back toward her. With a choked cry, she ran straight into his arms. Desperately he caught her up, sweeping her from her feet. "Jesu, Morgana, tell me there is a chance we will meet again!"

She buried her face in his neck, her slim frame shaking. "There is a chance," she whispered. "Since the future isn't written yet . . . Goddess willing, there is a chance."

Wordlessly they remained locked in each other's arms as the sun swiftly slid below the horizon. When only a sliver of crimson showed, he gave her one last, despairing kiss.

Then, shoulders rigid, he turned and stepped into the mist.

Arthur gazed sightless at the dark lake, his mind turbulent with memory. Even after almost four decades, the image of Morgana was as vivid as if they had parted but an hour before. He whispered into the night, "Will I see you tonight, my love?"

Over the years, he had made many pilgrimages to the lake when chance brought him near, always hoping to see her. Perhaps, if he were blessed, even touch her hand once more. It had never happened, and now he supposed it never would.

"You and Merlin taught me to listen to my heart, like a good Celt, and my heart does not think I will survive tomorrow's battle, beloved. This must be goodbye." He started to turn his horse, then said haltingly, "My love for you has been the brightest, truest joy of my life. The one thing that belonged to me alone. May my God and your Goddess watch over you forever."

Then he kicked his patient horse into a canter and headed back to the camp, High King of Britain once more.

* * *

The sky was lightening in the prelude to dawn. With regal deliberation Arthur rode his destrier along the line of his assembled troops. He had not built a kingdom by waiting tamely for the enemy to strike, so he'd marched his men through the darkness to this spot just below the brow of a hill overlooking the enemy camp. Careless in his confidence, the Saxon king, Hengist, had chosen the site rashly. Now he was vulnerable. Arthur doubted that a dawn attack would be enough in itself to defeat the Saxons, but it would certainly improve the odds for the British.

Even in the gray light, he could easily identify the silhouettes of the knights of the Round Table with whom he had shared so much. There were his nephews, brawny Gawain and his three younger brothers. Loyal Kay, Arthur's foster brother. Handsome Odbricht of Norway who had crossed the sea to come to Arthur's aid. Young Galeron, who carried the dragon banner of Camelot and stayed protectively close to his king. So many brave men, both noble and commoner.

Arthur loved them all, but none could replace Lancelot of the Lake. Not only had Lancelot been the finest knight of the Round Table, the equal of Arthur himself, but he had become Arthur's closest friend after Merlin withdrew from Camelot and went to live in his beloved Welsh hills. How many nights had Arthur and Lancelot stayed up late sharing wine and talk and laughter as the barriers of rulership fell away? More than once Arthur had found himself wishing guiltily that Lancelot had been his son rather than tormented, resentful Mordred. But fate had decreed otherwise.

In a resonant voice pitched to carry to every man, Arthur called out, "You know for what we fight—for Britain, our homes, our lands, our families. There is no better cause." He paused, letting the silence gather weight and texture. "I will not lie and say that victory is assured. We face great odds. But I tell you true—never has a king been more proud of the men who fought by his side."

A shout went up, then another and another, the voices gathering until every man in the army was roaring his allegiance.

When the tide of courage was at its height, Arthur turned and raised his arm. "For God and Camelot, follow me!"

He chopped his arm down and spurred his horse forward, leading his bellowing men down the hill. The cavalry slashed through Hengist's camp, followed by the foot soldiers who cut a lethal swath through the unprepared Saxons.

It was a powerful first strike, but the enemy regrouped quickly and the battle was joined. Though Arthur's forces were vastly more disciplined, the Saxons did not lack for courage or numbers. The fighting settled into ruthless hand-to-hand combat, vicious and deadly. With the instincts of a lifetime of war, Arthur was always in the thick of it, rallying his men and hammering the enemy with his great sword.

But for every Saxon who fell, there were three more to take his place. As the sun rose to its zenith, Arthur's troops were beaten back and slowly encircled. His nephews Gawain and Gaheris had fallen, along with Odbricht of Norway and nearly half of the British army. Arthur fought on grimly. Though victory might be impossible, every Saxon killed was one less to wreak havoc on Britain.

Then, during one of the odd battle lulls when the action swirled away in other directions, Galeron called out, "Sire, more troops are coming!"

Arthur shaded his eyes with one hand and looked to the east. A large band of cavalry was charging to the battle, pennons snapping in the wind. It took him a moment to identify the device on the leader's banner. Then his mouth twisted. "It's Lancelot, come to ensure our defeat." He glanced at Galeron. "You are too young to die in a hopeless fight. Go now, by your king's orders."

"No!" Galeron retorted. "I live or die at your side." He glared defiantly at Arthur, his face filthy with dust and sweat.

Arthur smiled wryly, thinking that the boy's eyes were almost as green as Morgana's. "You're too insubordinate to be a knight. You have the stubbornness of a king." Accepting Galeron's decision, he cantered forward to strengthen his line where the combined forces of the Saxons and Lancelot would hit.

But stunningly, the newcomers attacked the Saxons instead of joining them. Lancelot's loyalty to his king and Camelot had overcome the terrible breach caused by the affair with Guinevere.

A fierce, unholy joy renewed Arthur's strength. Rallying his exhausted men, he led them into a charge that smashed the Saxons between two armies. Across the seething mass of soldiers, he could see Lancelot and his knights ferociously carving a path toward the surviving British troops.

The enemy force began to crumble, some soldiers throwing down their shields and running while others clumped together and fought with desperate fury. Then Hengist himself charged out of the melee, heading straight toward Arthur. "It's you who must die, old man!" he bellowed. "You are the heart of this rabble, and when you are gone Britain will be mine. Face me, old man, or be named coward!"

If Hengist fell, his army would disintegrate. But before Arthur could take up the challenge, a knight broke from the mass of Saxons and galloped after Hengist, shouting, "No! You promised that the king would be taken captive, not killed!"

Amazed, Arthur saw that the knight was Mordred. Did his bastard son care for Arthur's life, or did he recognize and relish the knowledge that captivity would be crueler than death? Impossible to say—they had never understood each other.

Mordred caught at the bridle of Hengist's horse. With a furious roar, the Saxon swung his great ax at the man who had invited him to Britain. It landed true, and Mordred pitched from his saddle in a gush of blood.

Piercing sorrow stabbed through Arthur. Though Mordred had betrayed Camelot, he had still been Arthur's only son, and he must be avenged. Face like thunder, Arthur spurred his weary horse toward Hengist.

Then Galeron galloped between the two kings, dragging his mount to a halt as he brandished his sword at Hengist. Arthur swore. His aide did not lack courage and one day would be a great knight. But now he was too young, not yet come into his full strength, to face a mighty warrior like Hengist.

Arthur kicked his destrier into one last burst of speed. The heavy horse shouldered Galeron's mount aside. Then, Excalibur blazing in the noon sun, Arthur attacked his enemy. In the clashing of kings, Arthur sliced Hengist's throat even as the Saxon's ax smashed through Arthur's chain mail and deep, deep into his vital organs.

Hengist fell first, dead before he hit the muddy ground. Arthur managed to remain astride for a few moments longer. He saw the wave of shock that passed through the Saxon troops when they saw the death of their king. It was followed by swift terror and loss of will. Victory belonged to the British.

Only then, slowly, did Arthur slide from his horse to the bloody turf. He felt surprisingly little pain. As if from a great distance, he heard cries of horror, then other shouts that meant the surviving Saxons were fleeing the field, pursued by the combined British forces. Few of the enemy would return to their homeland and raise new armies.

Content, Arthur allowed the blackness to take him.

He emerged from a scarlet daze to find himself lying on a pallet. His armor had been removed and wide, crude bandages wrapped around his torso in a futile attempt to halt the bleeding. All around him were grief-stricken faces. The nearest was Lancelot, his fair hair matted from sweat and the pressure of his helmet. He'd aged a decade in the months since he'd left Camelot. Tears were running unheeded down his cheeks.

"Lancelot," Arthur breathed, his voice scarcely more than a whisper. "I'm glad . . . you came."

"I could not stay away when you needed me." Lancelot's expression tightened. "Can . . . can you forgive my betrayal, sire?"

Arthur tried to lift his hand to touch Lancelot's arm, but his limbs were numb, incapable of movement. "Your actions today have absolved the past. Give . . . give my blessing to Guinevere." He paused to gather his strength. "Mordred?"

"Dead." It was Galeron who answered, his drawn face that of a man, not a boy. "We've sent to a monastery for a skilled surgeon, sire. He will heal your wound."

Voice a harsh rasp, Arthur said impatiently, "The injury is

mortal. It is time to think of the future." He drew in a pain-racked breath as he wondered who to name as heir now that Gawain, his oldest nephew, was dead, along with his brother Gaheris. Neither of Arthur's surviving nephews had the will or temperament to rule.

Arthur closed his eyes, letting his Celtic intuition range free. The answer came swiftly, surprising but right. "I name . . . Sir Galeron as my heir."

The young knight gasped, "Sire!"

Shock showed on other faces. Someone growled, "The boy is half-Saxon!"

"Britain needs a young, vigorous king." Arthur's gaze met Galeron's as he conveyed his steely conviction. "Will you accept this charge?"

Galeron's face paled at first. Then, slowly, acceptance and determination settled over him. "I will, my lord king."

Gathering his strength for one more effort, Arthur glanced around the circle of faces. "Lancelot. Kay. Gareth. Will you swear to support him?"

"With my life's blood," Lancelot replied, voice shaking.

His face twisted with grief, Kay said, "Your wish is my command, brother."

Gareth, Arthur's oldest surviving nephew, said gravely, "I swear it, sire."

Arthur relaxed, his eyes closing. Pain was coming in great, crippling waves. The end was near. Only one more thing remained to be done. He whispered, "Take me to the Lake of Avalon and put me in a small boat. Then . . . send me into the mist." Perhaps there, God willing, he might see Morgana once more before he died.

"It isn't fitting," Kay protested.

Before he could say more, Galeron snapped, "It is the king's will! Bring a litter."

As someone went to obey, a gruff voice said, "Surely the king's sword should go to his successor. 'Tis too fine a weapon to waste."

"No!" Galeron and Lancelot spoke together. Galeron added,

"Excalibur is Arthur's. No lesser man shall ever wield it."
Hands took hold of Arthur then, moving him to the litter, and
he mercifully lost consciousness.

He awoke to find himself beside the lake. It was full dark,
and flaring torches illuminated a throng of silent watchers, not
only the exhausted survivors of the battle, but commoners who
had been drawn by the news of Arthur's imminent death.

"Does the king yet live?" It was Galeron's voice, parched
with sorrow but already becoming accustomed to authority.

Warm fingers touched the pulse at Arthur's throat. "Aye, he
lives," Lancelot said bleakly. "But only just. We must find a
boat."

Then Sir Kay gasped, "May the Blessed Mother preserve us!
Look!"

Another voice said with awe, "Perhaps she *is* the Blessed
Mother."

Painfully Arthur turned his head. Emerging from the mists
was a magnificent, shining barge. Gracefully it slid across the
still waters toward the stunned watchers. In each corner stood a
slim female figure holding a torch, and in the center . . . in the
center. . . .

He caught his breath with a joy so sharp that it drowned the
physical pain. The Lady of the Lake was coming to take him
to his final rest.

Silently the barge touched the shore. Garbed in queenly
splendor, Morgana rose from her gilded throne and moved to
the front of the vessel. In the rich voice he had never forgotten,
she said, "We have come to take Arthur to Avalon. There I shall
heal his wounds, and he will dwell until Britain needs him once
more." Her serene gaze went from man to man, lingering on
Lancelot and Galeron.

In awed silence, the knights raised Arthur's litter and trans-
ferred it to the barge. Arthur was beyond speech now. Pain and
Morgana were the only realities.

Lancelot placed Excalibur by Arthur's sword hand. Arthur

managed to brush his fingers against Lancelot's in a wordless farewell. The man who had been his closest friend made a choked sound. Then, head bowed, he stepped from the barge.

Unaided by human hands, the vessel slid away from the shore. As the barge glided into the mist, one by one the weeping men and women of Britain dropped to their knees in an anguished farewell to their king.

Arthur's vision was blurred, but not so much that he could not see her beloved face, subtly different after so many years, yet instantly recognizable. The impact of her beauty pierced him to the soul. "Morgana." He exhaled roughly. "My prayers have been answered. I wanted so much . . . to see you one last time."

"Artos." She bent and kissed his forehead with gossamer tenderness. "I had feared this day would never come." When he tried to speak again, she touched his lips with one slim finger. "Hush, love. Do not waste your remaining strength."

Then she laid her hand on the terrible wound in his side. Miraculously, the pain eased. When she saw that he was comfortable, she cradled his head in her lap, her gentle hand smoothing his silvered hair. "Now sleep, beloved. Sleep."

He exhaled, content. A man could ask nothing more than to live with honor, then die in the arms of his one true love.

Slowly Arthur emerged from the mists in a place beyond pain. He opened his eyes, and saw that above him a lattice of apple blossoms swayed against the sky. How appropriate that heaven should look like Avalon. At least, he assumed that he was in heaven; this certainly didn't look like hell.

"Would you like some water?"

He turned his head. A vision of beauty knelt beside him, a goblet in her hands. "This is paradise indeed if an angel might look like my Lady of the Lake," he murmured.

Morgana smiled with a familiar sparkle of mischief. "This is Avalon, my love, not paradise. And I am most assuredly no angel." She raised his head and held the goblet to his lips so he could drink the crystal spring water.

When he was finished, she gently lowered his head to the pillow. "I have a perfectly good palace, but I thought you might like to wake here, as you did once before."

Then she drew down the blanket and checked the dressing on his side. It was very much like the first time they had met, except that a lifetime had passed.

Weak but blessedly free of pain, he raised a hand and touched her hair. Silver strands glinted among the gold, and lines around her eyes showed the passage of time. How tactful of Morgana to show herself as a mature woman rather than as a girl young enough to be his granddaughter. "You are even more lovely now than when we met."

"And you, Artos, have fulfilled all the promise of your youth." Her fingers laced between his as she studied him. "In your face is strength and wisdom and honor. The face of a man among men. A hero among heroes."

Their gazes locked as the years melted away. He drew an unsteady breath, once more giving thanks that they had been granted this time to say goodbye.

Morgana gave her head a little shake. "I could drown in your eyes, Artos. But I shall save that for later." She tucked the blanket around him again. "You should be walking tomorrow, and entirely well within a week."

He frowned, disoriented. "That's impossible. Hengist cut me in half, or near enough. You said that your healing could not preserve me from a mortal wound."

"I could not save you when you were in the outer world, but Avalon is a different matter." Eyes sparkling, she tickled his cheek with a sprig of fragrant apple blossom. "What I told your attendants was the truth—that on Avalon you will heal and return to the strength of your prime as you await the time when Britain needs you again."

Her gaze drifted out of focus. "I see you, stern and brave and just, in the far, far future. You will be called Well . . . Wellington. And beyond that, too, as a man named . . . Winstone, I think. No, Winston. You will save Britain from a hellish fate."

Stunned by her announcement, he scarcely heard her predictions. "So I will live." His mouth twisted. "But my survival matters little compared to the fact that I failed in my mission. The Saxons will come again. With so many of the knights of the Round Table fallen, Britain will be unable to withstand them."

She shook her head vehemently. "You did not fail. No man could hold off the Saxons forever, but your courage has bought enough time to save the best of Britain. The blood of Celt, Roman, and Saxon are blending together, as they are joined in Galeron. Someday the people of this land will rule the world, I think." Her expression softened. "It was so good to see Lancelot again. What a man he has become! And Galeron. He'll make a worthy king. You and I can be proud of our descendants, my love."

"Lancelot is our son?" Arthur gasped, even more shocked than when she had announced that he would live. Yet he believed her without question, for there had been such affinity between him and Lancelot from the first.

Her smile was radiant. "As I said then, you had given me more than you knew. I kept him with me until he was old enough for fostering. Then I sent him to France. He doesn't really remember those early years, of course, but they are why he was called Lancelot of the Lake." She sighed ruefully. "Avalon seemed very quiet after he left."

"So he is the son of my body as well as the son of my heart," Arthur said, awed. "And Galeron is our grandson?"

"Conceived one night when Lancelot took the Saxon maidservant to his bed as he pined for Guinevere," she explained. "Then he left Camelot on a quest and never knew that she had borne him a son. Galeron looks like you, I think, while Lancelot favors me."

She was right, he realized. Now that he knew, the resemblance in coloring and features between Morgana and Lancelot was clear, just as Galeron had a look of Arthur. "My intuition guided me more truly than I knew. Britain will be in good hands."

"Aye." Morgana smiled at him with the warmth that had first captured his heart. "And now it is time for us, and for the love that had to be put aside."

He pulled her down into his arms. She settled against his uninjured side with a happy sigh, her head resting on his shoulder. The never-forgotten feel of her body transformed his disbelief into joy. This was no dream—they truly were together.

"The greatest gift I could imagine was to die in your arms," he said musingly. "But now, my Lady of the Lake, I have found the highest bliss of all." He turned her face up for a kiss. Their lips clung, and from the response of his body he realized that he was indeed healing, and very quickly.

The kiss ended, and he gazed into the magical depths of her green, green eyes. "The greatest joy of all, Morgana, is to spend eternity in your arms."

Author's Note:

The Arthurian legends have provided inspiration and magic to readers and writers alike for well over a thousand years. Often Arthur is pushed to the side as attention is focused on the tragic love affair of Lancelot and Guinevere. This time, I wanted Arthur to be at the center of the story, and to find the reward due a great and noble king.

There are so many versions of the Arthurian legends that it wasn't hard to put together the pieces into a pattern that I liked. For example, sometimes Excalibur was the sword Arthur pulled from the stone to prove that he was the true heir to the throne. Other versions say that Excalibur was given to him by the Lady of the Lake.

Generally, the stories end with the Lady of the Lake and her attendants coming to take the mortally injured Arthur to Avalon after the battle of Camlann. The Lady is often associated with Morgan Le Fay, who in the later versions was Arthur's half sister and enemy. However, my research revealed that in the earliest stories Morgan was not Arthur's sister, nor was there hostility between them. It has even been suggested that she was his lover, an interpretation that fits perfectly with the story I had already conceived. Not only that, Lancelot of the Lake was fostered by the Lady. Irresistible!

Arthur may or may not be an historical figure, but it doesn't matter. The legends about the man T. H. White called "the once and future king" are still a vital, living tradition. It's a rare pleasure to spin my own version of the story.